I0770712

KENNETH BROWN

QUEST
FOR THE
CRYSTAL

The Mountain King Series - Book 4

Adgitize Press

THE MOUNTAIN KING SERIES

By Kenneth Brown

Haskell – Orphan to King (Prequel)

Eclipse of the Triple Moons

Zita's Revenge

Rescue of the Stone Warriors

Quest for the Crystal

COPYRIGHT PAGE

Quest for the Crystal

Published by Adgitize Press

Copyright 2023 by Kenneth Brown

All rights reserved, including the right to reproduce this book, or portions thereof, in any form.

An Adgitize Press Book

Streamwood, IL

First Edition: January 2024

ISBN - 979-8-9890372-2-3

Library of Congress Control Number: 2024902115

ADGITIZE PRESS

Cover Art by

Book Brush

Cover Design

Kenneth Brown

Developmental Editor

Mary-Megan Kalvig

Copy Editor

Joan Young

Thank you for purchasing this Adgitize Press Book.

- Get the latest information on New Releases
- Insider Looks at Outlines, Plots, Characters, Deleted Scenes and Exclusive behind the Scenes looks at Kenneth Brown's Writing
- Sneak Peeks at Chapters of Upcoming Books
- Ask the Author Questions
- Exclusive Offers
- And MORE

Find out more about the exciting prequel to The Mountain King Series. The eBook version is exclusive to members of the Kenneth Brown Readers Group.

Find out how Haskell lost his parents, and rose from orphan thief to become King Haskell, the Mountain King. An exciting tale of intrigue, fear and magic.

Go to https://kenbrownauthor.com/ for more information.

CHAPTER 1

Zita rested her forehead on the brick walls of her castle bedroom to cool her head. Prince Krunal had returned to Velidred castle with enough support to make himself king. She couldn't allow him to take control of the castle after those teenagers from Earth defeated her father. The prince wasn't even from this area but had grown up as a prince in the Kallurian province. Since her father's defeat at the volcano, the prince had taken up residence in the black castle, and now he wanted to make himself king.

No! She wouldn't condone his rise to power in *her* castle.

Zita had grown up as a princess in this castle, and now her status had dropped lower than a servant. She hadn't had time to make the necessary connections with the wealthy and powerful people to stop this travesty. With Prince Krunal's return, she had run out of time to take control of *her* kingdom. There must be some way she could foil Prince Krunal's plans and ensure her own rise to power at the castle. If only her father or mother were here to help.

She laughed. Her father, formerly King Haskell, couldn't help. She had stripped him of most of his magic, and he languished in the Ice Castle many hundreds of miles from Velidred. And her father had killed her mother, Queen Noreen, many years earlier.

Zita stared in frustration at the rough black volcanic brick that separated her room from the others in the Velidred castle. Prince Krunal had given her a room next to the servant's quarters. She had to take action. She wondered if her mother could help. Two years ago, she had tried to contact her from the dead but had failed. Maybe her conjuring skills had improved, and she could get the advice she needed.

She opened the small box she kept under the bed. Inside were items that would help her with her magic this evening. She pulled out a small leather pouch that contained a small quantity of the cremated remains of a former wizard. The former wizard's powerful skills had been reduced to ashes and bones. She grabbed her stegox coat off the wall hook and pulled up the hood. She needed advice and hoped she'd have success with her return-from-the-dead spell. The others didn't need to know where she was going. Coming out of her room, she hurried down the hallway that led to a door into the stables area.

Darkness encased the Velidred Castle courtyard, and she hurried to the gates. Wisps of fog encircled her as she reached the gate. The guards knew her and would allow her to leave the castle and return. It's not like she planned any harm.

The guard said, "A little late for a former princess to wander the meadows."

Zita shook her head. "I need to see someone."

He said, "This fog is coming in fast, and I heard the howl of a stegox in the meadow. You might wish to speak with that person tomorrow."

She scowled at the guard who stood a head taller than Zita. She didn't care. "You might wish to get out of my way. Right now."

He hunched his shoulders. "Okay, but I warned you." The guard un-locked the gate door, and held it open for Zita.

She huffed, rushed through the door, and took the path that led to the castle cemetery. Her mother's crypt stood in the gray graveyard. A stegox roared in the distance. The fog outside the castle thickened within twenty yards, and she heard the guard laugh.

The main road out of the castle led to the junction to Crossroads and the mountains, but Zita found the path that would take her to the cemetery. Before leaving the road, she looked back at the castle and could barely make out its black walls and the torches that burned at night.

She thought she heard steps behind her in the distance but didn't see anyone in the deepening fog. The hair lifted on the nape of her neck as she felt her heart begin to race. *Maybe I should wait until tomorrow. My attempts to talk with Mom have failed in the past, and there are people in the village that may find this a good opportunity to get back at my father by making sport of me.*

Zita steeled her resolve and continued in the direction of the crypt. The fog quickly enveloped her, and she hoped it helped hide her. Few people visited the cemetery during the day, and she suspected no one visited it at night. After walking for a while, she felt she should be close but hadn't yet reached her destination. *The path only leads in one direction,* she reminded herself. *It's just the fog.*

She stopped and listened. Were those footsteps on the path following her?

A few more steps and she reached the old royal cemetery where her mother had been laid to rest. Many former kings and queens of Velidred were interred here. Zita had no other ancestors in this graveyard as her father was a blacksmith's son and her mother a daughter of a royal family whose castle stood many miles away.

Zita listened once more for the sound of animals or footsteps and heard nothing. She opened the old gate, and it squealed loudly in the quiet night fog. With a quick step through the doorway, she closed the iron door, which squealed once more. *Well, I'll know if anyone else is following me with all the noise this gate makes.*

It seemed colder and quieter in the graveyard. The fog thickened and after a few steps she couldn't see the two-foot-high brick walls that encircled the burial ground. An owl hooted in the distance, and a cold chill ran down Zita's back. Using her magic, she produced a soft blue glow lamp as she hurried to her mother's crypt.

What had seemed like a good idea when she left her tiny room now seemed dangerous and unwise. Night animals scurried between the gravestones which made her look left and right for danger. *Come on, get a grip, girl. There's no danger here; squirrels won't hurt you.* She wasn't sure she believed that statement.

Her mom's crypt stood in the southwest corner, and Zita passed statues, gravestones and large monuments as she walked among former royal families. The shadows seemed to take on life and move as she passed trees with bare branches and stone statues that had lost their original shapes from years in the rain and weather. She felt her heart speed up, and she increased her pace. She'd been in the graveyard at night before, but the thick fog spooked her.

After long moments of trepidation, she stood before her mother's stone crypt. It looked hard and cold. A little stone and wood entryway held oil lamps and she quickly lit them. *There. That makes it a little less ... scary.*

Ten-foot-high figures of the god and goddess of the Velidred moon stood on either side of the entryway. Moss and lichen grew on the pedestals. Her mother didn't believe in the moon gods, but her father, who had been born under the sign of the Velidred moon, was a staunch believer.

Zita wavered on the subject. Sometimes she believed and other times she suspected it was a joke by the wizards and priests to get money out of the populace. Tonight, she wasn't worried about the Velidred gods. She needed to speak with her dead mother.

Zita took out the key that opened the crypt door and checked behind her once more to verify no one followed her. The door opened smoothly, and Zita entered the interior chamber. She descended three steps and found two candelabras with seven candles each. With a wave of her fingers, magic emanated from her, lighting the candle wicks.

The smells of dirt, stone, and a light mineral scent wafted in the room. She hated that smell, for it reminded her once more of her mother's fate.

Once the candles were lit, she felt her body relax. Her mother's burial vault stood to her right, her father's vault waited on the back wall for when he died, and Zita had a space on the left wall. She shook her shoulders as a creepy feeling spasmed down her back.

Zita took out a small slip of paper that contained the incantation to bring back a spirit from the dead. She had spent a fortune in coins to get this spell, and she had been disappointed when it failed the first time. Older now, and with stronger magic, she expected it to work.

She calmed her mind and took a deep breath.

Mother, mother, in the grave

From behind death's veil, peel forth the stave.

Your spirit is not lost to death's delight

Rise forth from eternal sleep, rise tonight.

By the power of moon and bone,

By the power of water and stone,

By the ancient powers of yore,

Come forth, dear mother, and bore

Through the chains that hold you tight

To death's door; appear to the light.

The ties that bind us from our birth

To love that lasts despite dearth.

Rise forth from life's last gasp.

Escape death's grip and come at last.

Zita opened the leather pouch, extracted a tiny amount of the former wizard and pitched a pinch of bone and ash into the air. With a flip of her wrist, she sent a burst of fire at the falling material which flashed red and blue. The candles extinguished on their own, throwing the room into darkness.

She waited, not concerned when nothing happened immediately. The wizard who had sold her the incantation said it might take a couple of minutes before the ghost materialized. She was instructed to stay calm and think of her loved one that she wanted to communicate with, and soon the person would appear. A mouse chirped in the corner and then scampered off with a soft padding of feet.

She rubbed absently at her arms as the winter chill seemed to grow icy in the stone chamber. Zita waited. Had it been two minutes? She searched the dark room for a sign of her mom, maybe a thin luminescent outline of her mother's body. Nothing appeared, and she heard the mouse dart again across the stone floor.

Zita felt her chest tighten and tears well in her eyes. She swallowed hard. The incantation had failed again. Her mom wouldn't be talking with her tonight or ever. She closed her eyes and let her body sag against the door, as she slowly slid down to sit on the floor.

Her heart thudded dully in her chest. Aloud she begged, "Why did you have to leave me so soon Mom? You didn't have to leave with Cugbert that night. Sure, Dad had been a bully, but we were happy. Well, I was happy."

Heat built behind her eyelids as tears began to flow. She had come and talked with Mom throughout the years after her mother's death, and that always comforted her even if she didn't get any answers. "I don't know if you heard, but it looks like Prince Krunal is making himself king. I want to fight him, kill him or something to prevent him from being king. What can I do?"

Zita waited for an answer that she knew would never come. A sour taste formed in her mouth as she realized that once again the people who said they loved her had let her down. It had happened so many times in her life, she should be used to it now.

She lowered her chin to her chest and closed her eyes. Zita didn't know how long she sat in the crypt's interior chamber. Time seemed to stand still, and a dull ache formed in her head. Cold had seeped into her body from the stone floor, and she decided the time had come to head back to the castle. With a wave of her fingers, she lit the candelabras and looked at her mom's burial chamber once more. She placed her hand on the coffin. "I'll come back and talk with you again, Mom. I miss you." She kissed her fingers and touched the coffin once more.

After a moment of reflection, Zita extinguished the candles and opened the crypt door. Fog crept down the stairs as she hurried out of the chamber. She locked the door and doused the exterior lights. Two steps away from the crypt, a hand grabbed her arm.

CHAPTER 2

Zita yanked her arm from the attacker and prepared a spell, only to find a lock on her magic. Her attacker had left her defenseless. Blood pounded in her ears, and she sucked in her cheeks, ready to scream.

The attacker placed a hand over her mouth. "Quiet, don't scream. It's me."

She looked into dark brown eyes, recognizing Taka, the desert wizard, a member of the Council of Nine, and a very powerful man in the Velidred Castle.

Zita struggled to pull away as she mumbled into the hand across her mouth, "What are you doing? Let me go."

"I'll let you go when you promise to be quiet."

Zita relaxed her arms and posture.

"That's better," Taka whispered, but he didn't release his grip on her arm. "Now listen. I stood outside the crypt, and I heard you inside."

Oh, no. She felt a weakness in her legs and worried she'd faint as the blood drained from her head. *If Taka heard me, then he's going to take me to the prince, I'll be imprisoned, and hanged for treason.* She struggled to get away.

"Be still." Taka held firm.

Taka had always been a loyalist, and Zita knew he'd give her up to the prince, without mercy. The larger man had stripped her of her magic and held her tight. She had to think of some way to get away him.

The fog had thickened again, and she couldn't even see gravestones and statues that should be only a few feet away. Maybe she should go along with him, get him to relax his grip, and then she could run. She relaxed once more.

Taka followed her behavior, loosened his grip on her arm, and removed his hand from Zita's mouth. "I'm not going to harm you."

She shook his arm away and stared up at him.

"Where did you get that incantation?" Taka asked.

"It's none of your business."

"I'm trying to protect you. The incantation is an old desert-people curse to bring enemies and troublemakers back from the dead. When it works, it leaves them walking Aloheno for the rest of eternity. You won't do your mother any favors by resurrecting her using that method."

She placed her hands on her hips. "Well, she doesn't have to worry because it didn't work."

Taka whispered, "Keep your voice down. It didn't work because they didn't give you the whole chant. They left out something very important. They always do because they can be killed if the desert-people find out who sold it."

She folded her arms over her chest. "Why should I believe you? You tell me what they left out." Zita looked off into the fog, searching for a place to run.

"I will never tell you. I knew your mom, and I wouldn't bring her to the netherworld, where she would forever feel the pain of her injuries."

The man had to be lying. The person who sold Zita the spell had promised that anyone she resurrected would be whole and never die again. She needed her mom's advice, and if the desert wizards weren't so tight lipped about spells like this, then instead of talking with Taka, she'd be enjoying her mother's conversation.

Taka droned on about how dangerous the spell was, but Zita searched for an escape route. She knew this part of the cemetery well and planned out in her mind a path that might work. Her heart beat so hard that she worried Taka heard and knew what she planned. Taka wasn't a young man, and Zita figured she had the ability to out-run him.

"If you've ever seen the resurrected by this method, you'd have nightmares every time you closed your eyes."

Zita decided on the path to escape, and she hardened her stomach. As Taka continued talking, she looked left, feinted in that direction, and then sprinted right. With a couple of quick movements around the stone monuments, she found herself breathing heavily, standing behind a statue of the god of Pantaleon. In the fog, it would be hard for Taka to track her. Was he serious? Could she really leave her mom walking the netherworlds in pain?

Taka walked in her direction and whispered, "Listen to me. I tell you, I'm here to help."

She searched for her magic, but he still had her blocked. She needed to learn that spell. As he got closer, she ran to the crypt of King Leathern the Second, rumored to lay in the crypt without a head, because he had attempted to kill his own father.

"Stop running."

Zita listened in the darkness and fog. Her actions had scared animals from their nighttime activities, and they darted off through the winter snow. She tried to control her heavy breathing, but fear and exertion caused her to make more noise than the animals.

A person stood a few feet from her. Or was it a statue? She couldn't tell. After she left the safety of King Leathern the Second's crypt, she wasn't quite sure where to go next. Zita stared at the statue. It had to be stone because it hadn't moved since she arrived here. That meant Taka stalked from behind. She sprinted toward the statue.

Taka tackled her to the ground.

She struggled and tried to scream, but he cut off her air with magic.

He leaned in close to her ear and whispered, "I want you to meet some friends of mine. We have a task for you that you will find enlightening."

CHAPTER 3

Zita struggled under Taka's grip as he brought her back to the Velidred village that stood outside the castle gates. She had expected him to take her to the castle guards after he overheard her talking about killing the soon to be king. Instead, they were heading to the less desirable section of the village, an area that even Zita didn't like to travel at night.

The fog weakened when they reached the village. Not many houses had candles burning, leaving Zita wondering how much time she had spent at her mother's crypt.

They reached the Squeaky Wheel Tavern, and Taka pushed her toward the door. Taka still had her magic blocked, leaving her with no methods to protect herself. She worried people in this part of the village might recognize her and pulled her hood tight around her face to keep hidden. *What game was he playing at?*

Taka opened the tavern door and led the way into the crowded room. Noise filled the room as a man played a wooden flute while a woman sang bawdy songs on a raised platform in the far corner. All the tables were crowded, mostly with men drinking ale and playing cards or a dice game. The heavy smell of spilled ale, and pipe and cigar smoke filled the room.

Zita removed her hood in the warm, smoky room, and a few of the men gave her a glance, a smile, a wink or a snarl as Taka led her to a table in a corner of the tavern. Three old men sat at the table. They were playing a dice game, but stopped when Taka and Zita arrived.

She recognized one of them, Dakarai, a low-level wizard that used to work for the business man Gadiel. Ha! He didn't just work for Gadiel, he acted more like the head henchman for Gadiel's organization. Dakarai didn't come with Gadiel and Zita when they had traveled to the Ice Castle, but seeing Dakarai made Zita wonder what Taka's plans were for her.

She remembered the brown eyed Dakarai when he had coal black hair. Tonight, the gray hair outpaced any remaining black hair he once had.

One of the men at the table pulled Taka off to the side and whispered. Probably because the old man couldn't hear very well, he was loud enough for Zita to hear. "Why did you bring her? She's too noticeable to be in this group and will just cause problems. I thought you were done with Haskell and wanted to become the Velidred king yourself."

And there it is. Taka's true colors were showing through. Zita grabbed the coat she had just taken off, pulled it over her shoulders, and said, "I'm heading back to the castle."

Taka pushed the old man back toward his chair. "Shut-up!" Then he turned to Zita. "No. We need you."

"I have no desire to hang from the gallows because you want to become king."

"Can you shut your trap?" Dakarai asked. "Are you trying to get us all killed? There are prince's spies in the tavern. Whisper or just leave."

"No, she's not leaving." Taka pushed her toward the bench next to the third man.

She recognized him now. Lenny, another of Gadiel's men. The old man hadn't aged well, and smelled of unwashed clothing. She noticed him leaning to his right, and his left-hand shaking. *Are these men the masterminds to help Taka become king? We're all going to hang.*

Taka pushed in next to Zita, and she scooted closer to Lenny. Taka said, "Zita is going to acquire some missing items for us."

"I'm not acquiring anything for you." She reached out for her magic, but the desert wizard still had her blocked.

Dakarai leaned in toward Zita from across the table. "If you ever want to use magic again, you'll join our group."

Zita couldn't believe it. A low-level thug like Dakarai knew how to prevent wizards from reaching their magic? Gadiel must have taught this trick to these guys. She needed to learn how to cut off wizards from their magic source. She remembered her dad had used something similar when he went to the volcano during the eclipse to force the castle wizards not to interfere with the rushing magic that came from the moons.

Zita asked, "Taka, did you study under Gadiel?"

A serving woman walked by with a tray of food, leaving behind the smell of cooked meats and fresh cut cheese. Zita recalled she hadn't eaten supper, and the food beckoned.

"We're not here to talk about my relationship with Gadiel. I need you and two of the boys here to go to Lord Haskell's manor. There's something there you need to acquire for me."

"Why can't the boys pick it up themselves? Three outstanding men like the ones seated at this table shouldn't have any problems getting anything you want."

It happened so fast; she didn't see it coming. Lenny lashed his shaking arm in her direction and slapped her hard on the cheek; a ring the man wore sliced her face. Her head whipped around spraying spittle and blood across the floor.

The third man laughed loudly. "The little princess is finding out who's running this show."

Pain poured across her cheek, her throat tightened, and her lungs constricted, making it difficult to breathe. These men were serious about whatever they wanted. Her thoughts were spinning and she had difficulty listening to the conversation.

Taka took Zita's chin in his hand and pulled her head toward his. "I need you to get something for me. It has your dad's mark on it, and the boys," he nodded in the direction of Dakarai and the third guy, "don't have the power to retrieve the item I seek."

Zita tried to pull back, but Taka held firm. She saw the problem now. There must be a magical item Taka wanted, and he thought as King Haskell's daughter, she had the ability to touch it, where the old men at this table were unable to due to a magical lock her father had placed on the artifact.

Taka gripped her chin tighter and nodded Zita's head. "Tell me you will travel with the boys and help us out of this little predicament."

He had her. She knew the brutality of Gadiel's henchmen, and she wouldn't be allowed to live unless she did what they said. She knew of servants in the castle who were missing fingers or arms, or who were forever disabled because of Gadiel and his motivation techniques. She never should have allowed Taka to capture her like this.

She took a deep breath and nodded.

Taka released her chin. "Okay, I thought I could count on you to work with us."

Zita hoped Taka couldn't read her mind, because she planned to kill everyone at this table after she got the artifact. She couldn't risk being bullied by this group. She knew they would never stop asking for favors and were willing to do anything to force her to their demands.

"This is where we believe the item is hidden." Taka pulled a folded document from his pocket and opened it on the table. The document showed a floor plan of her dad's old house, a house given to him by the king when Haskell was a teenager, near Zita's current age. This is when Haskell had first become a lord, which would later help him to become king and wreak havoc throughout the other kingdoms.

Taka traced his finger across the rooms. "In the upper master bedroom, people believe that Haskell had a hidden safe. Lenny and Sims have been all over that room and have never found the safe. It must be magic that we hope will be visible to family members. Like you." Taka smiled as he nodded in Zita's direction.

Sims! Of course, the third man at the table. Her dad had spoken of him and of how her father had outsmarted him when they were young. Dad talked about Gadiel and his team, and Sims' name produced disdain and anger in her dad.

"Do you really think my dad would set a spell that his daughter could break through? That would have put me in danger from every ne'er do well in the kingdom." She looked at the thugs at the table and smirked. "I don't think he would even allow me to touch the magic safe."

Dakarai said, "It's a hunch we had, that maybe now that you're over sixteen, you might inherit certain magic."

Zita looked at Dakarai and shook her head. "I don't think so. Dad wouldn't risk his valuables to his precious daughter. I'll go with the guys and see, but I doubt I'll be able to help."

Sims quickly pulled a knife and brandished it at Zita. "Bringing her here is putting us all in danger. She told us herself that she can't help us. Let's slit her throat and find another way to get it."

Zita stared into Sims eyes, a cold, brutal, and sometimes out-of-control crazy man. With Sims traveling with them, any problems would escalate out of control. "I'll go with Lenny and Dakarai. Not Sims. If Sims goes, I'm out."

Sims leaned across the table, the knife hovering near Zita's throat. "You'll go with who we say you go with."

Dakarai dragged Sims back to the bench. "Don't be stupid. Put the knife away."

Sims threatened Dakarai with the knife. "Taka's the stupid one. Bringing Zita here."

"What is it you boys are hoping to find at the plantation?" Zita asked.

Taka smirked and lowered his voice. "We're looking for the Imperium Wand."

The Imperium Wand. *A wand of great power. I would love to get my hands on that. Maybe I will help them.*

Zita looked at Taka. "Dad never had the Imperium Wand. And if he did, it wouldn't be at the plantation, he would have hidden it at the castle."

All the old men looked at Taka.

He said, "It's at the plantation."

"How do you know? Who told you that?" Zita thought through the people who might know this information. It would be a short list. The Grand Wizard, a couple members of the Council of Nine, such as Titan, Finn, or Ishwa. Ishwa was dead. Finn would know not to tell Taka, they weren't close. She hadn't seen Titan in five years.

"I'm not revealing my sources."

Why wouldn't Dad have taken the wand to the castle instead of leaving it unattended in a country plantation? It made no sense. "Dad wouldn't leave something so powerful so far away."

"My source is impeccable and assures me that's where the king left it."

Could Taka's informant be a woman? After Mom died, her father had a handful of women he dated and two he almost married. If any of them were still alive she wondered if one of the women still lived at the plantation. That could explain it.

"I'll go to the manor, but when we don't find it. Then you can go back to your source and tell him he's wrong."

Taka leaned in toward her; the man smelled of sweat and desperation. "My source isn't wrong."

Zita cocked her head, "Whatever. What should I do with it when I find it? It's a powerful wand, will you trust me handling it?"

"Your task is to break through the magic. Then Dakarai can bring the wand back to me."

Zita asked, "Then what? You'll release me, right?" She had to get away from these thugs as soon as possible.

Taka raised a mug of ale. "It's decided then. You leave in the morning."

CHAPTER 4

Dakarai and Sims led the way to Lord Haskell's manor house in Oak Ridge, a village a few miles from Velidred Castle. Zita rode her horse a few paces behind the two men. She hadn't slept since the tavern meeting, after which they took her to a village cabin where they bound her, and Dakarai made sure to block her magic. She wasn't happy Sims had joined the group. She worried who might have seen her leave with these thieves as they rode from the village.

The ride to the plantation followed forest trails and across a couple of large hills that worked the horses. Zita had summered at the manor as a little girl but hadn't been back since her mom had died. The house didn't hold memories, fond or otherwise, and she always wondered why her father had kept it.

She thought back to the rooms in the manor, trying to decide where her dad would place something as valuable as the Imperium Wand. Her first thought had been that there was no way her father ever owned the Imperium Wand. Zita still believed this and thought it senseless going to the manor to look for it. Even if she could access the location, Dad wouldn't let someone just take it. There would be traps, both physical and magical, any of which might kill her or leave her in a horrible physical condition. Maybe someone warned Taka that King Haskell had protected the staff, and that's why he had sent Zita.

Taka had concocted a great plan. If she acquired it, then Taka had its power available to him. If it caused someone to die by the very act of retrieving it, then Taka would eliminate a potential enemy.

They didn't push the horses and thus arrived at the manor in the early afternoon. Taka had outlined a plan to find the safe when they reached the manor, but they wouldn't break into the safe until the next day. He didn't want Zita double crossing the old men and taking the wand for herself.

When they reached the house, they gave the horses to a servant still serving the manor. Zita didn't recognize the older man, and she wondered if the cook that had always found a way to sneak a cookie into her hands still worked there. Dakarai allowed Zita time to wash the riding dust from her body, before they all sat down for a meal. Mabel, the cook, came into the dining room with dishes of food.

She asked, "Little Zita, is that you? You've grown into such a beautiful woman."

Zita smiled at the friendly face. "Thank you, Mabel. I didn't know if you would recognize me. It's been so long."

Mabel said, "You look so much like your mother, now more than ever." She looked at the men at the table with Zita and scowled. "Have you come to live at the manor now?"

Zita looked around the dining room and wondered why she hadn't thought to come here after her father lost the battle at the volcano. She shook her head, "No. There's something Dad left here . . ." She looked at the others, "for me."

They spent a few moments catching up. Mabel related stories from her childhood and warm memories of her time here flashed through her mind.

Then they ate the delicious meal that Mabel had prepared. After Dakarai threw down the last bone of barbequed anouora, he leaned forward in his chair and stared at Zita. "I'm going to release the wall between you and your magic. I'm prepared to hurt you if you try anything."

Zita had wondered if they planned to release their hold on her. She examined Sims and decided he wouldn't be a threat, but what power did Dakarai wield? She knew her father's magic outpaced Gadiel's henchmen and Zita suspected her magic would, too. With a deep breath she tried to relax. She'd wait until she had the wand before pressing her power against the thugs.

She nodded at Dakarai and felt the magic flow back into her body. She hadn't realized the addiction she had for it and sat at the table allowing the power to encase her body.

Dakarai said, "Let's find the safe."

Zita pushed her chair from the table and stood. "Taka thinks it's in the master bedroom. I'm sure Dad didn't put it there, but let's see."

The three walked upstairs to the bedroom. A modest house at best, it featured just a few bedrooms. The master bedroom measured only twice the size of Zita's miserable lodgings at Velidred Castle. The room should take a couple of minutes at best to search; they would find nothing and then . . . what, go back to Taka and the castle?

Excitement built within Zita as she climbed the stairs; her pulse beat faster and adrenaline rushed through her body. Upon reaching the room, she stopped at the doorway and scanned the walls and furniture. Not much had changed since she had been here. The curtains were different as was the blanket covering the bed, but otherwise it looked much the same. The room had a dusty, almost moldy scent as if it hadn't been cleaned thoroughly in the recent past.

Dakarai pushed her into the room. "Start looking."

Zita growled back at Dakarai, and then she tried to calm her body. Doing magic while stressed could lead to unintended consequences, and she knew if they did find the safe, Dad would have left little magic traps to kill or mutilate the perpetrators.

Zita searched for peace within herself, closed her eyes and took a couple of deep breaths. Then she began the hunt for the safe. She didn't want to rush the process. *Look for magic, examine walls for traps, and keep my body whole,* she willed.

Sims yelled out from the hallway, "Hurry up!"

"Do you want to come in here and stand between me and where I'm searching? That way you can get blasted with the acid or the attacking knives."

Dakarai pointed at the other thief. "Sims, go downstairs. I'll handle her."

"Get me if she finds it."

Dakarai waved him away.

Zita examined the walls one by one. Dad didn't trust anyone; why would he leave something this valuable in the bedroom? Any one of the women he dated might accidentally find it. Even if Zita found the safe, it could be empty by now. A woman who had tricked her father might hold the wand.

Half an hour later, she had finished searching the walls and began a search of the floor. The early excitement at maybe finding one of the great treasures of this era had turned to tension and fear. Her stomach had tightened, and she found herself holding her breath. Sweat formed on her forehead, and the room seemed to get smaller.

The last woman who had slept in this room had covered the wooden floor with a large rug. Zita dropped to her hands and knees and peeled back the edge. She ran her hands over the wooden floor and felt magic radiating from the floorboards. She nodded at Dakarai.

"Did you find it? Is it the safe?"

"I don't know. There is magic here. It might be a trap in case intruders enter the room. Maybe one of my dad's friends hid her jewelry here. I don't know."

Dakarai came closer. "Let me feel the magic. Maybe I'll get a different reading than you." Dakarai dropped to his knees like Zita. "Yeah, definitely magic. Though the protection is fairly simplistic. Stand back, I'll spring the trap and we can take a look at what's here."

Zita crawled backwards next to the wall.

Dakarai rolled his hands in a circle over the spot.

Zita felt heat radiate to her position by the wall. "I don't know what you're doing, but you better stop."

"Don't worry, I got it."

Zita's hair stood up on her neck as if lightning threatened to strike. "No! It isn't the treasure."

"Yeah, it's the safe, I feel it calling me." Dakarai continued rolling his hands and chanting magic incantations.

A huge hole opened in the floor and Dakarai fell to the room below. He landed on his back with a loud bang as he struck the dining room table.

Zita stood in the corner of the bedroom and watched the floor close back up. She smirked and stood. With a straightening of her shoulders, she adopted her perfect princess posture, and called from the room. "Are you okay?"

Dakarai moaned, but then movement came from below her, and he tramped back up the stairs.

After another hour of searching, they had found nothing. Every few minutes Dakarai would arch his back and rub a spot on his lower spine with his knuckle. They tried the other bedrooms with no luck. They inspected all the rooms in the house and found a few magic odds and ends, but no safe.

Using that much magic for so long had left Zita exhausted. She collapsed into a chair. "Much as I suspected, there's nothing here."

Dakarai pounded his fist on a table next to a couch. "It must be. Our information source assured us it's here."

"Tell me the name of your source. Maybe I can vouch for their trustworthiness on an important matter like this."

Sims said, "We'll never tell you that. You'll use the information to try to find the real location when we can't watch you."

"Whatever. I'm just trying to help. It doesn't matter to me if you find it."

"It had better matter to you, because if we don't find it, you die," Dakarai said.

"What can I do? You're telling me where to search. Actually, I don't think my dad ever owned the Imperium Wand, so you may as well kill me now."

Sims rushed at her with a knife, and Zita used air to throw him against the wall.

Dakarai tried to block Zita's magic and she set a shield.

"Ah, nice. Your shield will protect you, but you don't have any recourse to additional magic. The shield will continue to use up the magic you have within you and when the shield runs out of power, you'll have nothing." Dakarai said, "I suggest we don't wear you down completely. It might take a few days to get you back to a point where you can search some more."

Zita examined her magic and Dakarai hadn't lied. He had shielded her from additional magic, and she only had the reserves that were within her at the moment. She should conserve her magic for later. Maybe they would find the wand after all. "I'll drop my shield, but if that thug comes at me again, I'll kill him with my bare hands."

Sims bared his teeth. "You'll die, Princess."

"Dad bested you. I'm sure you'll be no problem for me."

Sims leaned toward her and growled.

Dakarai stepped between them. "Stop it. Both of you."

Zita rubbed her neck, trying to work out the tension between her shoulders. "Where next?"

Dakarai scowled. "Are there any outbuildings?"

"The gardener's shed and the barn. Do you really think King Haskell," she emphasized *king* for Sim's benefit, "would put something this valuable with the horses?"

Dakarai shook his head.

Zita said, "Your source. Who is it? It might help me think of something."

Dakarai looked at Sims and then back at Zita. He rubbed his palms over his eyes and knuckled his back.

Sims grabbed Dakarai by the arm. "Don't tell her. Taka will kill us both."

"If we don't find the wand, he might kill us anyway." Dakarai pushed Sims away. "Listen, I want to retire. Taka said I could retire when I found the wand. We'll spend as much time as necessary to find it."

He turned to Zita. "Our source is an old maid that used to be your mother's lady-in-waiting. Back when young Princess Noreen first dated your father. She's old, and maybe she doesn't remember well, but she assured us it's on this estate."

Zita's brain went into overdrive. *Who were her mother's maids?* "Caitlin?"

Dakarai sighed, "Yes."

Fond memories came back to her of Caitlin. A loyal servant to her mother. She had served as a wonderful confidant and aide to Zita after her mother's death. The servant had been with her mother as she grew up at the Goodwin Castle and must have traveled with her to the manor before her dad and mom married. What would she know that others didn't? She suspected her mother had found out about the wand at some point. Would she tell Caitlin an important fact like that?

That meant her father had the wand before they married. She couldn't imagine how the young Baron Haskell could have acquired the magical artifact.

Zita thought of places the wand might be, now that she knew the source of this fruitless search. Her dad and mom were young; they were at the manor, but Dad didn't trust the people in the manor, so he didn't put it there. Someplace outside the house, but still on the property was more likely.

Then a thought struck her. She wished Dakarai didn't have her magic blocked, because she suddenly had an idea that she might know the wand's location.

"You've thought of something." Dakarai smiled.

"Maybe. I can't be sure, but my grandfather would bring my mom out to the manor to see Haskell when they were still both rather young. Kind of like they were dating."

"Go on."

"Dad built a treehouse in one of the old trees. I remember Mom showing it to me and telling me that they sneaked their first kiss in the treehouse."

Sims threw his knife at a wall and it sank into the wood with a loud thwack. Taking two belligerent steps forward, he wiggled the knife free and said, "Let's find us a treehouse."

CHAPTER 5

Zita looked up at the treehouse at the back of her father's manor with trepidation. The boards set up in a large oak, weren't so much a house as a platform with twelve cracked boards and a few missing nails. The sight of rusty nails made Zita question the safety of the structure.

While the men were better dressed for climbing since her long skirt would get in the way, Zita knew she didn't have a choice. Besides, the excitement of finding the Imperium Wand drew her onward.

Zita said, "Help me up into the tree."

Dakarai and Sims raised her onto their shoulders and with a slight jump, she grabbed the board that looked most likely to hold her weight. It held, and she pulled herself onto the platform. The treehouse smelled of damp wood, and insects had eaten little trails into the lumber.

Zita peered back toward the barely visible house from the platform. She imagined in the summer when the leaves were nice and green it'd be a great place to smooch with your betrothed without the parents and servants watching. She thought of her boyfriend, Erik, once again and smiled at the fond memories. Then she focused on the task that had placed her on the questionable platform, twelve feet off the ground.

She yelled at Dakarai, "Release the block and let's find that wand."

"No funny business."

He released the block, and Zita took a deep breath as she enjoyed the flow of magic. She worked slowly, searching for invisible traps and triggers her father might have set to entrap or kill people that might want to make the wand their own. It didn't take long on the small platform before magic popped.

"Something is here. Do you want to climb up to see?"

"No, you do the search, and I'll wait down here and pick you off the ground."

Zita huffed. *Yeah, this might just kill me.*

Zita found one trigger and intercepted the trap. A hundred knives magically appeared from the canopy of leaves, but Zita pushed it away with her magic. They planted themselves in the ground with repetitive thwomps. *Dad, you don't need to kill me today.*

Zita located a second trigger, cleverly disguised as a spell to release a pod of butterflies. *Come on Dad, do you really expect a wizard wise enough to go for the Imperium Wand to believe you protected it with butterflies?* She expected something wicked.

She took her time unraveling the layers of magic threads tying the trigger. It took concentration to identify the proper threads to pull to prevent triggering the bait. She took a deep breath and felt the air grow still around her as if someone had erected a cylindrical wall around the wooden structure.

A knot formed in the threads, forcing her to slow down and focus all her attention on circumventing the next pitfall. Her hair fell into her face, and she looked back toward the manor and blew the air from her eyes. Her hand slipped, and she lost one end of the magic threads. The thread curled in on itself, ticked once, tocked, emitted a clack, and then the butterfly ruse released a burst of poisonous gas. She reacted too late, and the gas accumulated within the narrow cylinder surrounding the platform. The toxin built up within the enclosed space.

Zita held her breath as she tried to locate a way to push the corrupted air out of her space. As her lungs cried out for her to take another breath, she worked through a couple of spells she thought might work to blow the lid off the container, but she needed to chant the spells, not just think them. She hoped her lungs contained enough air to say the words, without taking another breath.

With great effort, she remembered to speak without breathing in, and she chanted, "Sopre a tampa," a powerful wind blew the top off in a loud whoosh of air.

Zita forced a gust of wind to blow the poison up through the top of the cylinder away from her position on the platform. She had worked fast but still coughed for three minutes as she struggled to find oxygen to breathe.

It took another ten minutes to figure out how to remove the transparent cylinder and free herself from the enclosed death trap.

After thwarting three more traps, her confidence grew. The number of traps implied that this indeed held the safe's location. She yelled, "It's here."

"Did you find it?"

"Not yet, but I'm sure it's here." She located another trap. "I can't believe he put so many traps in. It's just luck we even knew about this place. Plus, as his daughter it should recognize me and I should be able to get around them." She grew tired, the stress of making a fatal mistake weighed heavily on her mind. How many more traps would she need to disarm?

"Your father didn't trust too many people."

Zita smiled as she found another magic thread to pull. "I'm not surprised since he hung around with you and Gadiel his whole life."

Dakarai laughed.

She rubbed her shoulders and repeated a chant she had used multiple times that day to loosen her dad's magic traps. This snare felt different, though. She felt her arm tingle as she continued her examination. The trap had changed just as she released the trigger. It didn't behave the same as the others. It should have released its spell and simply discharged harmlessly to the ground. Instead, something clicked and snapped. Then the boards below her exploded upward and catapulted her into the sky.

CHAPTER 6

The blast triggered by her father's magic blew Zita through the air. She landed with a thud on the snow-covered ground ten feet from the oak. She was so dizzy her head hurt, and a loud ringing filled her ears. Struggling to come to her senses, she looked up at the treehouse and saw Dakarai straddling two boards of what remained of the treehouse.

"You found the safe," he announced.

Yay me, she thought as she gingerly took stock of her injuries. Her neck and head hurt, yet she remained in one piece. She rubbed her temples, trying to gain control of her battered body.

Sims stood over her and barked out a laugh. He pointed his knife at Zita. "Guess you're not so smart after all."

Dakarai waved his hand toward Sims and the knife flew twenty feet away. "What are you doing? We still need her to open the safe."

Sims scowled at Dakarai and stomped off to get his knife.

Zita sat on the ground a few more seconds and then struggled to her feet. Another blast like that, and Sims wouldn't have to stick a knife in her. She realized she needed a strategy to get away from these two if she expected to live after finding the wand. It might be wise just to let Dakarai have the wand if it meant saving her life.

King Haskell had embedded the safe into the floorboards of the treehouse. Not necessarily a fancy or elegant method to hide something so valuable. Zita wondered if her dad's skills weren't that great when he originally hid the safe, and he kept adding layers of traps as his skills improved.

Dakarai used magic to move the safe to the ground, before climbing down to stand beside Zita. With a wave of his hand, Zita felt her stream of magic close off, and an emptiness encapsulated her. She stared at the safe as the ringing in her ears grew louder and shriller.

Sims walked up to the heavy metal box and said, "This is it. We'll get the money Taka promised us, and then we can leave this two-bit region. I'm going to take my money and go to the beaches.

Zita shook her head. "Do you really think Taka is just going to let you walk away? He's just like Gadiel. He'll keep promising you freedom until you die. I bet he won't even give you all the money he pledged to you two."

Sims growled.

Dakarai said, "That's enough. We'll take the safe into the house and open it there."

Zita looked at what remained of her father's treehouse and mumbled, "Yeah, so we can destroy the manor, too."

# # # #

Zita dropped to her knees on the expensive rug that protected the wooden floor, and knelt in front of the safe. Her chest tightened as she took a deep breath to calm her nerves. Guessing from the number of traps in the treehouse, she'd have to be very careful if she wanted to stay alive. She didn't feel ready and expected nothing but trouble opening it. Even if they managed to get it opened, nothing guaranteed the wand had remained in there. If they found the safe empty, then what would the old men do to her?

Dakarai looked nervous as he scraped his hands through his thinning gray hair over and over.

Yeah, he understands what we're attempting. His nervousness increased Zita's own tension, and Sims bounced up and down on his toes. She needed a plan to stay away from Sims after she opened the safe.

She asked Dakarai to allow her to touch her magic which called to her just outside her reach.

He hesitated.

Sure, she thought. *He's worried I'll get my magic, grab the wand, and then exterminate these two rats.* It sounded like a grand idea, but she didn't see it playing out like that. Until she found a way to prevent Dakarai from blocking her magic, she didn't really have any choice but to follow through. If she used the wand incorrectly, it might just kill her.

Dakarai said, "Okay, I'm releasing the block, but you better behave. I've created traps in the room forcing you to stay in here until I tell you to leave. You understand?"

She scowled at Dakarai and nodded. *Of course, you did.*

The magic poured into her like a huge rush of water and she jerked in surprise. This was more than he had given her yesterday at the treehouse, meaning he had the power to limit how much she received.

She focused on the safe. It seemed an old-fashioned model but with a complicated metal locking mechanism and a handle to pull open the safe door. The lock itself must not be guarded by a magic trap, because she had seen Sims playing with it this morning before breakfast.

Zita placed her hands on the safe's metal surface and chanted a spell to find traps. Nothing. She wondered if she matched her father in intelligence. He had been a powerful wizard. Maybe this process would have been easier with the Helmet of Justice. Too bad, she didn't have it with her.

The safe radiated energy. A trigger waiting for some fool to do the wrong thing. The next incorrect move by Zita might cause the box and the house to explode into a million pieces.

Carefully, she ran her hands over all the exposed surfaces. All good, just magic humming around the safe. *Or is that still the ringing in my ears from yesterday's explosion?*

"Do you hear a humming?" Zita asked.

Sims said, "Nope, I don't hear anything but you wasting our time."

"Yeah, I hear it." Dakarai nodded. "Magic. Be careful, we don't want to lose the safe."

Zita rolled her eyes. She tried to think of her dad as a young man her age. What would he be thinking back then? But this trap could have been set by her dad, either as a boy or even the last year before the eclipse. She didn't know.

She took a deep breath and chanted a different spell to identify triggers. Still nothing happened. *At least it didn't explode. It might be possible Dad never thought anyone would find it.*

She sat crossed legged on the rug and ran her fingers over the safe.

Sims took out his knife and twirled it in his fingers.

Dakarai gave Sims a look of irritation, but Sims ignored the other's narrowed eyes and kept on with the knife.

An idea came to Zita. Despite their differences as Zita grew older, her father adored her mother. She thought the door could be opened with an incantation that included something about her mom. What did Dad call her? *The Princess of the Gods.*

Zita looked at Dakarai. "Here goes. Be ready."

Sims pocketed the knife.

Dakarai bent his knees as if assuming he'd have a chance to run if this turned bad.

She made the same incantation as before, but ended with, "Remove the triggers, traps, and cages, and release the lock for the glory of the Princess of the Gods and all her needs."

They all held their breaths.

The safe's locking mechanism began to move. A metal pin with a jagged edge pivoted left in a slow methodical motion. The process stopped for five seconds. The flat bronze metal on the top rotated outward and then extended up, pushing downward a rounded pin. Again, it appeared the mechanism had finished its movement until two long rounded metal stems connected by a flat golden edge extended until they fell from the locking mechanism.

Zita expected the safe to open automatically with the magic controlling the door, but it didn't. She looked at Dakarai who hunched his shoulders. Zita edged her body away from the safe.

Sims jumped in front of Zita. "Get out of the way you fool." He grabbed the handle, turned it, and pulled.

Zita threw herself to the floor, shielding her eyes.

The top of the metal chest opened.

Nothing happened.

Sims pulled out a scroll and threw it at Zita. A second scroll landed on Zita's back. Lastly, he pulled out a box.

Zita saw the box and reached for it with magic.

"Not so fast, little princess." Dakarai said, blocking her.

Sims opened the box and pulled out a wand, a simple walnut stick with ancient markings carved into the handle. He raised it into the air.

Zita stared at Sims and the wand. A twitchy feeling pulsed from her extremities and her eyes narrowed as she watched the non-magic user wave and point it at different objects in the room.

Dakarai walked over to Sims and took the wand. He placed it back in the box. "We're done here."

"Do we kill her first?" Sims asked.

CHAPTER 7

They reached Velidred Castle before midnight, taking care to not rush the horses in the dark. Dakarai and Sims raced to see Taka and to present the wand to him. Zita followed after them, but Dakarai stopped her on the castle's second level, one floor down from Taka's chamber.

Dakarai said, "This meeting isn't for you, we can't have you causing trouble with a powerful wand in the mix. Back to your servant's quarters."

Zita retired to her little chamber off the kitchen hallway. Despite sleeping poorly the night before, she lay on the bed, worried about her future. She expected Taka and Sims to come in and demand something from her, or worse, come to kill her.

In an effort to keep her mind off of her current problems, she opened one of the scrolls from the safe that she had scooped up. She wondered what her dad had considered important enough to keep in the safe with the Imperium Wand. The scroll had been wound tight and took a little finagling to loosen. The parchment paper felt brittle and delicate to the touch, and Zita worried she might rip the paper if she mishandled it.

She heard a gentle crackling as she manipulated the page; a subtle earthy aroma drifted from the paper scroll. As it opened, a smaller scrap of paper fell to the bed. Zita picked it up, and despite the nearly illegible penmanship, read.

Haskell, this curse could be used to summon a moon god to bring punishment or justice upon someone who has wronged you. Be careful. I have researched the curse and I believe it is a true and faithful curse which presents no wrongdoing to its handler and wielder.

Be sure to keep this curse's location a secret. It is a valuable and powerful magical artifact that must be protected. Use it wisely and with care.

An indecipherable signature had been scrawled on the bottom of the note.

She had never heard of her dad using a curse like this, and she wondered who had given it to him. He had many enemies and few friends. Maybe an enemy had sent it to King Haskell to trick him.

Zita unrolled the scroll again and read its contents. A symbol of a red moon over an erupting volcano stood at the top of the page. She had been taught by her castle tutor that the symbol represented an illegal spell. The first section, written in a flowing script, detailed where to go and when to cast the spell. Then, in neatly printed letters she saw the curse. The bottom of the paper contained warnings.

The moon must be full and not almost full.

You must have a direct line of sight to the moon during the entire casting of the spell.

You must have magic; this will not work for a commoner, or someone whose magic is blocked.

Though it's not absolutely required, Gadiel found it worked best when he cast it in a cemetery.

Zita's heart raced as she saw Gadiel's name. She knew he had a relationship with the goddess of the Velidred Moon and wondered if this was how he came by it. Gadiel had some success manipulating people, but his minor magic skills left him inept at throwing a curse like this.

Zita read through the scroll again and thought about her options. At the moment, she didn't have any magic as Dakarai and Taka kept her blocked, even after they returned to the castle. How far did the block work? She could take a long walk away from the castle and see if the block held. To keep Taka from getting too worried about her, she could head back to her mother's crypt. *A place to go to cry.*

She needed to know if the curse would work for both Prince Krunal and Taka. She smiled at the thought of a two-for-one curse. Kill two enemies with one mighty curse.

Zita dropped the scroll on the bed and opened the second scroll. No special note dropped out of this one. Instead, she read about the Crystal of Zaraboth, a powerful object that allowed the bearer to control entire kingdoms and even nations. At the bottom of the scroll, she recognized her father's handwriting.

This is too difficult to retrieve. Alpherge the Great died in his quest. Saved me the trouble of killing him.

Zita took the scroll detailing the Crystal of Zaraboth and placed it under her pillow. Then she picked up the curse and studied it some more. She would feel better about it if she knew how it had come into her dad's possession.

The prospect of using the curse excited her and she decided she needed a walk. Her room didn't really have any great hiding places. This seemed as good as the wand and she didn't want to lose it. No one knew she had the curse at the moment, so they shouldn't be searching her room.

Still, she grabbed a knife and ripped open a seam in the mattress and shoved the scroll inside the straw. She pushed the bed up against the headboard and hoped no one noticed the tear. Then she headed quickly to the cemetery.

CHAPTER 8

Zita wandered around the cemetery and every few moments took a pulse of her ability to reach a stream of magic. Nothing happened as the block persisted. At her farthest point from the castle, she felt a tiny thread of magic. Not enough to do anything with, but the knowledge encouraged her. Maybe she just needed to walk a few miles out of the village.

Zita heard a couple of people talking, and she noticed Lenny and Sims coming toward her. She tried to access enough magic to create a shield, but the trickle left her without protection.

Sims stepped in front of her and asked, "What're you doing out here, Little Princess?"

"I'm visiting my mother's crypt. Is that not allowed?"

Sims pulled a knife. "Your mom's gravesite is a hundred yards that way." He pointed the blade in the direction of the crypt. "Did you forget where she's buried? We can help you find it." He forcefully grabbed her arm.

She backed away and yanked her arm from his grip.

"Taka doesn't want you too far from the castle. He says he might need you and wants you to be available to him." He reached for her arm, and again she resisted.

"Don't touch me. If you want me to go back to the castle, then lead the way."

Lenny came up behind Zita and before she could make a move, he twisted her arm behind her and pushed up on the hand moving it toward her head.

Zita strained against the pain and stood on her tiptoes to reduce her discomfort. "Stop. That hurts."

Sims smiled.

"We need you back at the castle." Lenny pushed her in that direction.

Did Taka have someone watching her, or did the magic block notify him in some way? She would have to be careful.

# # # #

Over the next few days, Zita found one of Taka's three henchmen following her wherever she went. Two days earlier, it had been Sims' turn to watch her, and he tripped her in the hallway when she went for lunch. Later, he sat beside her as she ate chicken and peas with the servants. Just as she reached for a slice of chicken, he plunged his knife into the meat and crammed a huge chunk of it into his mouth. The uncouth and dangerous man scared her.

Lenny seemed to get angry for no reason whatever. She didn't know what his problem was. On his night to watch her, he just barged into her room as she read a book by the fireplace. With no knock or notification beforehand, he interrupted her solitude.

Zita asked, "What do you want?"

"I had to verify you were still in your room."

Zita shook her head. "You've been sitting outside my door for the last two hours. I poked my head out twice and there you were. Where do you think I disappeared to?" She waved her hand to include the small room with no windows and only the single door.

"You know magic, and I don't trust you. As long as I'm responsible for you, then I'm going to check in on you."

Zita wanted to yell and scream at the old man but knew that might lead to a beating or worse. She couldn't afford to irritate him too much. She scowled at him instead. "Well, here I am."

Dakarai's turn came the next day. He generally treated her okay. He entered her room unannounced and they spoke about her father and other magic artifacts he might have possessed and hidden.

Zita sat on the edge of her bed. "I didn't even know he had the wand. I would have taken that for myself months ago if I had known. I'm even thinking of going back to the manor and living there once Krunal becomes king." She said the last line in an attempt to see if Dakarai would give up their plans for her, or tell her when they might kill Prince Krunal.

"So, there are other magic items at the manor."

"I didn't say that at all. I just want to get away from you thugs." Zita wondered if he remembered that she took the scrolls from the safe. Were these questions, feelers about those items? He might have told Taka about the scrolls and wanted to know where they were.

"Oh, it's not bad here at the castle," Dakarai said.

"Maybe for you, but you took away my magic. I'd kind of like it back."

"Sorry, Princess, but we don't trust you." His eyes drifted to the corners of the small room searching for something.

"Did you misplace something?" Zita stood and walked nearer the fireplace. She couldn't have him thinking she had hidden the scrolls in the bed.

Dakarai looked at the bed, but he must not have seen any bulges or misshaped sections to the mattress, as he came and stood by Zita.

They didn't say anything for a few seconds and then Zita asked, "When do you guys plan to murder Prince Krunal?"

Dakarai grabbed the front of her tunic and pulled her close. "Don't ever say those words out loud again. To anyone. I will kill you in a moment."

She backed away, pulsing her hands above her shoulders in a pacifying manner. "Understood."

He left the room, slamming the door as he exited.

# # # #

The next day, she walked in the marketplace, looking at new shoes. The smell of leather permeated the small shop. Lenny stood outside the vendor stall while she spoke with the cobbler about a pair of new shoes she'd like to buy for the coronation of the king.

Prince Krunal had announced that he would be made king within the next month. The news incensed her, but she couldn't do anything. Taka had been silent on his plans. It bothered her that she didn't know if he planned to take action before the coronation or sometime after.

Zita had no reason to dislike Krunal other than he wanted to be king at a castle she thought of as hers. Taka's leash on her pulled at her discomfort, making her just as angry at Taka as at Krunal. The twenty-four-hour surveillance by Taka's thugs began to wear thin. She had to take action.

She expected the Velidred Moon to be full the following night, and she still didn't have a plan to escape the castle, find the proper place to say the curse, and then act. Velidred wouldn't be full again before the coronation, so she had to risk leaving tonight in hopes of being ready in time.

The banging of metal against metal from the nearby blacksmith shop seemed to jar her every thought. She couldn't think with all the noise around her, but she needed answers.

She asked the cobbler, "Where are your parents and grandparents buried?"

A surprised expression crossed his face. "Why?"

"I was just wondering if everybody in the village had their loved ones buried in the village cemetery near the mountains or somewhere else." So far, the same question had provided the same answer yes, in the common Velidred village graveyard. Zita had determined that the graveyard would be too close to the castle and would not work for her purposes.

"That's a strange question from a royal like you. He pointed in the direction of the royal graveyard. We aren't all lucky to have our family members in the imperial burial ground like your mother." He pulled out another shoe pattern and showed it to her. "How about this one?"

This shoe had a pointed toe and a slight heel, but she was searching for something more practical. She shook her head.

He put the design back in his trunk of samples and dug through the trunk. "My mother came from Tanuku and my father is from Crossroads. There is a cemetery on the trail leading up to the Village of the Stone Warriors. Both of my parents are buried there." He bent his head as if thinking of them for a brief moment.

Zita said, "Yeah, I'm familiar with that area." She remembered it from trips to the mountain village. A simple place, with modest gravestones and only one crypt. No gate blocked the entrance and thirty massive stones encircled the small funerary grounds. She tapped a finger to her lips. "That might work."

"This one?" The cobbler held out the shoe with wide toes and a small heel and handed it to Zita.

She smiled and nodded. "Yes, that's perfect." That wasn't what she meant at all, but, yes, that would work.

CHAPTER 9

It was nearly midnight and Zita's nerves were tingling all over her body. She lay trapped in her chamber in the castle. She had only a day to get to the cemetery near Tanuku and say the curse.

It was Sims' turn to watch her tonight, which wasn't the worst-case scenario. Lenny would have been the easiest to get past. He was the oldest of the three and the palsy in his hand seemed to be getting worse. But if it had been Dakarai's turn, she would have had to forget the plan completely because even if she had escaped the castle, he would be able to follow her and reset the magic block.

Zita had a chance with Sims, but his short temper and quick desire to pull a knife scared her without her magic for protection. At supper, she had sat next to one of the stable boys. She slipped him a gold coin and convinced him to saddle a horse for her after the bells tolled midnight. More gold coins jingled in her pocket for the men at the gate.

Her immediate goal was to escape the castle and get on the road to Tanuku. Then she hoped to distance herself enough to beat the magic block before Sims found her and stuck a knife in her gut. She had watched his movements over the previous three nights and noticed he had a habit of going back to the kitchen each night at midnight to scrounge up food. He never stayed away for long, but she thought it might be enough for her to get out to the stables.

The bells chimed twelve times to mark midnight, and Zita counted to thirty. Then she pulled open the door and peeked in the hallway for Sims. He wasn't in his normal spot, so hopefully he had gone to the kitchen on his search for food.

Zita exited the room, gently closed the door, and hurried to the stables. She felt her heart beating fast as she crossed the courtyard. She didn't dare turn around to see who might be watching through a window or from the tower. Taka himself might be standing outside admiring the nearly full moon of Velidred even at that moment.

The stable boy should meet her with a horse saddled and ready to go. It'd be a simple transaction and a quick walk of the horse to the gates. When she reached the stables, though, her plan fell apart. The boy couldn't be found, and no saddled horse waited for her.

Zita shoved open the stable door, and an earthy smell of hay, manure and horse urine emanated from the enclosed barn. She whispered the boy's name. "Jeremy, where are you? Are you in here?"

No answer.

A horse snorted and another horse neighed.

Why did I rely on a boy to do an important job for me? She'd have to do this herself, and she proceeded to check the stalls for a suitable horse. She prayed Sims hadn't noticed she'd left the room.

The first two horses were too big and feisty. The third seemed to be gentler but was a massive horse, and Zita thought it might be difficult for her to saddle the beast. As she tried to make up her mind, someone entered the stable carrying a lantern. Quickly, she ducked down in the stall.

The horse in the stall with her stomped its foot.

Someone whispered, "Zita, are you in here?"

Finally, the boy. "Yes. You're late. Help me."

The stableboy rushed over to her. "No! Not that horse. She's too hard to handle. There's another one over here."

"You better not give me a plow horse."

"No, no. Of course not." She saw the boy's face flush. "This one will be perfect for you."

Zita helped the boy saddle the one he chose, a chestnut-colored mare with a white smudge on the rump. It didn't look like a runner, but she hoped to leave the castle before Sims knew she had left. Dad had taught her the dangers of running horses in the dark, but she hoped the big red reflection from Velidred Moon would give them enough light to move at a good pace.

"This one is called Moon Stepper."

The boy hadn't done her any favors by not having the animal already saddled, but she liked the horse's name as she led it out of the barn and walked it to the gates. The empty castle bailey spooked Zita as her horse clipped-clopped on the snow, exposed grass, and an occasional stone. She knew in her heart that Sims, Taka, Lenny, Dakarai and every castle guard would come running in a moment if they heard the noise the horse was making.

By the time Zita made it to the gates, her insides quivered in anticipation of being caught. She fingered the necklace with the turtle pendant her mother had given to her on her birthday years ago, as she pulled out two gold coins for the guards. Her hands were wet with sweat as she fingered the coins, and she hoped she didn't lose them in the snow.

The taller of the two said loudly, "A little late at night for a princess to go for a horse ride."

"Quiet!" she whispered. With a quick flick of her wrist Zita tossed a coin to each. They caught the coins with a practiced motion.

Then the second guard whispered, "Velidred moon is a lovely time for a ride, My Lady." He opened the smaller gate door, and Zita walked Moon Stepper through the opened arch and continued to walk her twenty feet from the gates. There Zita mounted the mare and slowly maneuvered the horse away from the castle.

She knew better than to trot away from the guarded walls. Then everyone in the castle would know someone was leaving, and she'd heard of people who had left at night meeting their demise with an arrow to the back. *Take no chances. Nice and steady.* So far it didn't seem as if Sims realized she had left.

A quarter mile away, she found the main road to Tanuku. It wasn't a big highway, but enough people traveled it daily to keep it free of bushes. Big pine trees grew to her right and she waited until she reached them before encouraging Moon Stepper into a trot. She brushed her hand across the animal's neck. "Nice and easy girl."

Horse and foot traffic in the winter-time snow rutted the road. They couldn't go too fast, but there were enough ruts, foot-prints and horse prints to disguise which way she went.

She yearned to reach out for magic, but worried doing so might notify Dakarai or Taka of her location. *Patience*, she thought. She would have plenty of time to test for magic when she reached Tanuku.

Zita rode through the night, frequently looking behind her to check for any followers. Every mile or so she doubled back on the road for a few hundred steps to help disguise her real destination. When the Velidred Moon set, the darkness brought on more fears of being captured, but she couldn't hurry. Every sound in the night quickened her heartbeat, and her neck muscles ached in their stiffness.

She traveled through daybreak and reached Tanuku at mid-day. The small village didn't offer much, but it did have a small tavern. Zita tied up the horse behind the building. By now, the alarm of her departure had been sounded and she hoped to stay hidden. The Velidred moon would be full tonight and if she could make it to midnight, she would have the power to stop Krunal from becoming king and get her magic back from Taka. They both would pay.

She enjoyed the warmth and smells of the tavern. The roasting meat above the fireplace sent out amazing aromas of spices and sweetness. A cook in the back could be heard stirring a pot of soup, the sound of the ladle clanging softly against the pot while someone whistled a familiar tune.

As Zita warmed up with hot cider and lunch in a dark corner of the room, she studied the curse written on the scroll, trying to memorize it as much as possible. She might not have enough light to read it at night and needed to be prepared for any potential interruptions that might present themselves.

She didn't notice the spiritualist, Forest River Blossom, come into the tavern until the woman sat down opposite Zita. "What do you have there?"

A flush of adrenaline tingled through her body, and she quickly rolled up the scroll and shoved it in her coat. She looked around the room to make sure no one else had entered with the spiritualist. *How could I have been so reckless not to keep an eye on the door?* "Some reading from the castle library." She lied.

"That symbol at the top of the page would force the castle library to burn it immediately. That's the mark of evil and all documents with that mark are considered dangerous to the crown. You should hand it to me."

No way would she hand the scroll to Forest River Blossom. "Yeah, I found it in a little mountain village past

Crossroads and I'm taking it to the Grand Wizard. I just stopped in here to warm up before returning to the castle."

The small woman smiled at Zita. "My people watched you ride in on the path from Velidred."

Zita's chest tightened. She hadn't thought about the troublemaker Forest River Blossom for a long time. Whatever she did, she couldn't allow the spiritualist to take the scroll. She thought she had the curse memorized, but what if she missed a word or added a word that didn't belong?

Forest River Blossom said, "I received a message from friends at the castle this morning. I'm supposed to report back to them if I see you in the village."

Zita hated this woman. Why hadn't her father killed Forest River Blossom when they were younger? The woman had been a thorn in Zita's side for a long time now, always spouting prophecies about her death.

She rubbed the back of her neck and pushed strands of hair away from her face. The spiritualist had her trapped, and would likely return her to Taka's control. Zita asked, "Did you tell them you saw me?"

"Not yet. Now tell me why you're here and what evil curse is in the scroll." Forest River Blossom's voice oozed honey and charm.

Her only recourse was to lie. Make the curse sound bad, but not as bad as its reality. She felt her face heat up as the lie formed on her lips. "Taka has found a way to block my magic. I paid someone in the village for this curse that will help me break the block." She hoped that would be enough truth to keep the spiritualist from taking the scroll.

"I see. That sounds pretty drastic. A curse to break a spell. I've never heard that one."

Zita bared her teeth and rushed the words, "Well, that's what it is."

Forest River Blossom nodded. "If it's as benign as you say it is, then you'll have no problem showing me the document." She reached out her hand.

Her fists were tight in frustration and with a strained voice said, "I'm not giving you the document. I have to break this spell. Taka is forcing me to do evil things. He wants me to kill Prince Krunal." *There's a truth that might work for me.*

Forest River Blossom gasped. "We can't allow that to happen. Give me the document and I'll send a message back to Velidred about Taka's plan to kill the prince. I'll make sure the document is destroyed."

Zita shook her head trying to regain the calm she felt before Forest River Blossom had arrived. Her jaws ached from the strain of the last few days.

"I'll notify the castle, then, that you've been found. We've taken your horse, and it's too cold for you to walk back to the castle."

Zita sighed and rubbed her eyes.

The spiritualist just sat there with her hand outstretched across the table.

"Can't you let me just say the curse and then I'll give you the document?"

The woman leaned in close to Zita. "Nope, it needs to be destroyed. These never work the way you think they will. It might remove the magic block, but it could just as easily kill a friend. The way I see it, you have few enough friends to take that chance."

Zita hated this woman, always sticking her nose where it didn't belong. "If I give it to you, then you'll promise not to let the castle know I'm hiding here?"

"I can promise I won't send that message, but the castle has many eyes and ears in Tanuku. Someone else has already sent the message."

This can't be true. She's only lying to force me to give up the curse.

Forest River Blossom continued, "I can hide you. There are people on their way right now to return you to the castle. Let me help you. I'll hide you and protect you."

"I don't need protection from the curse." Zita pressed her hands tight against the table. "I need protection from Taka and his thugs."

Forest River Blossom slowed her speech and emphasized each word, "My dear after looking at this curse. You need protection from yourself."

A bell rang in the distance.

"It seems someone is here from the castle already. You can give me the curse or I'll let them know where you are."

This can't be happening. This close to freeing myself from Taka and taking back the castle. Zita felt her throat constricting as she stuck her hand in the jacket and pulled out the curse. She fantasized adding Forest River Blossom to the people she planned to curse. She handed the scroll to Forest River Blossom.

The spiritualist opened it and glanced quickly at the scroll. Her mouth went slack and the blood drained from her face. "This is the evilest curse of all. This curse will make you a slave of the Velidred Moon Goddess. Promise me, even if you ever see a copy of this document, you will never say this curse."

Zita's heart thudded dully in her chest. "Yeah." Her hands went limp as she slumped in her chair, "You have it. Can you hide me now?"

CHAPTER 10

As night fell on Tanuku, Zita found herself at the home of two elderly women. Forest River Blossom had taken her through the tavern's back door, across three backyards, and planted Zita with the women. Forest River Blossom's last words were, "Don't let her out of the house after nightfall."

Zita sat on a bench at a table across the room from the two women who spoke about dead husbands and former lovers. They were funny to listen to, but Zita needed to leave for the cemetery. Even though she had told Forest River Blossom she didn't know the curse, she thought she could remember it. At the very least she wanted to go to the cemetery and check out the surroundings.

A couple of hours later, the time had come to leave for the graveyard. She thought it might help if she somehow manipulated the two women to come with her. She asked, "Have you two ever wanted to have your husbands speak to you from their graves?"

The first woman, a tall, elderly gray-haired woman named Helga said, "Oh, I doubt my husband, Lars, would have anything interesting to say."

Ingrid, the second woman, seemed intrigued by the idea. "Do you have a way to bring my husband back to the living?"

"They don't come back in their bodies, just as ghosts that you can talk with," Zita said. "I bought a little spell in Velidred, and the seller assured me it worked. We can try it out tonight if you want. There's a full moon, so we'd have a lot of light."

Helga crossed her arms. "No! Forest River Blossom was adamant and left explicit instructions that you stay in the house after nightfall."

"I'm sure she meant to make sure I didn't go off unattended. She wants to protect me from animals and people that might want to do me harm."

"I always wanted to see Gunnar one more time before I die." Ingrid lifted her hand toward her friend. "Come on Helga, let's go see the boys."

Zita felt a flutter in her belly, and she gently bit her lower lip. Yes, she had one convinced, but could she convince the second woman?

She licked her lips. "Are they buried in the graveyard up the hill as the trail runs to the Village of the Stone Warriors?"

Ingrid had been stitching a torn tunic. She looked up from her work. "Yes, of course."

Zita rose from the bench. "Let's go up and see the gravestones. You can tell me stories about your husbands as we walk. It isn't far, is it?"

Helga winced as she repositioned herself in her chair. "It isn't far for a youngster like you, but my hips ache even when I'm sitting, and I can't imagine walking that far at night, in the snow. It's all uphill."

Ingrid put down her stitching, rocked forward a couple of times, and used the momentum to propel herself to a standing position. "I think it'll be fun. I want to ask Gunnar a couple of things. Let me get some warm clothes on and Zita and I will walk up to the cemetery. I haven't been for a night walk up the mountain in years, and Velidred should be full tonight. A lovely red this time of year."

Zita felt a rush of adrenaline race through her body. She wanted to squeal with excitement and do a happy dance, but tamped down her glee at convincing one of the women to join her. With a sense of calm and purpose she pulled on her stegox jacket and some homemade mittens the women had given her.

Helga struggled to stand, her hips obviously bothering her. "I don't think you should be doing this." The woman finally made it to her feet and stood across from Zita.

Ingrid pulled a hat over her head. "Don't worry about anything. I will escort Zita to the gravesite, and then we'll come right back here. Forest River Blossom doesn't even have to know we went." She patted Zita's hand. "Isn't that right dear?"

"I promise we'll return in no time."

Helga gingerly sat back in the chair and shook her head. "I think you're making a mistake."

# # # #

Zita searched left and right as they walked through the village. It'd only take one of Forest River Blossom's informers to stop their progress. Zita was also concerned about being seen by Taka's thugs. In the back of her mind, she wondered who Taka had sent to find her in Tanuku.

Lenny she could handle and even Sims if her magic worked. She still hadn't tried her magic in case Dakarai or Taka were close enough to discern if she used it. She'd wait until she reached the burial ground and then use the magic suggested by the scroll.

The scroll. She shouldn't have let the spiritualist take it. She repeated the curse a couple of times in her head. Yes, she remembered it word for word. Zita wasn't going to let Forest River Blossom scare her out of saying the curse. What did the old woman know about magic curses? Nothing, she acted as a spiritualist and no more.

Ingrid walked slowly through the village. The full moon of Velidred cast an eerie red glow about the snow, and lit up the village like it wasn't even nighttime. Zita wanted to throw Ingrid over her shoulders and run out of the village or maybe just sprint up the mountain. The old woman wouldn't be able to keep up, so she had to make it look like she was just going out for some fresh air with the woman.

They finally reached the trail that led to the Village of the Stone Warriors, and Zita breathed a sigh of relief as some of the tension left her shoulders. At the slow pace they walked, she hoped they made it to the graveyard by midnight, otherwise her plan would fail.

The tall mountain pines cast shadows over the path. As they walked, the shadows became shorter, but it wasn't midnight yet.

The winter air felt crisp, dry and still, and no clouds darkened the sky. Zita enjoyed the fresh pine scent the cold air seemed to have enhanced. The temperature had dropped significantly and Zita shivered for a moment. The fresh clean air, without the smells of burning fires or the habitations of people, felt invigorating to Zita, and it rejuvenated her for the night's adventure.

Ingrid stopped for the hundredth time. "I just need to catch my breath a moment. I forgot how steep this mountain path is."

"How close are we to the cemetery?" Zita asked.

Ingrid looked up the hill. "Not far. I believe the path takes only a couple of more turns, and then opens to a meadow."

Zita wanted to sprint up the mountain side and get to her destination, but she felt compassion for her accomplice and waited for the elderly widow to catch her breath.

Ingrid's memory proved right. After two turns in the path, they reached the journey's end. Giant, ancient stone monoliths encircled an open space where gravestones poked out of the snow and a large crypt stood in the center of the cemetery. Zita felt a sense of power and energy building within her.

Ingrid exclaimed, "Oh thank goodness, we made it. I was beginning to think I should turn back."

Zita breathed heavily from the exertion up the mountain, but she increased her pace into the cemetery as excitement bubbled up within her. A glance at the moon's position gave her confidence it wasn't midnight yet.

What a wonderful night in the mountains! Zita saw her breath in the air as she entered the necropolis. She wanted to run to the crypt and shout for joy as she imagined a new life after saying the curse and destroying Taka and Prince Krunal.

As she walked to the crypt, her senses were on high alert for anything that might prevent her from achieving her goal. No one but the old ladies knew her journey's end. Not even Forest River Blossom would guess this as her destination.

No one had walked to the cemetery since the last snow, and Zita's steps were the only ones that led through the opening between two of the stone sentinels and to the crypt. She watched Ingrid struggle through the deep snow toward her location.

Ingrid finally reached the crypt, wiped snow off the steps and sat. "I haven't done anything like that in a long time. I'm worn out."

A stegox's roar sounded in the distant mountain tops. Zita knew that on a clear cold night like this sound traveled far, and the animal could be many miles away. She studied the Velidred moon, watching it for minutes at a time as it made its way across the sky, waiting for the right moment to start the curse.

Ingrid said, "Should we be nearer Gunnar's gravesite to talk to him?"

Zita looked around at her surroundings. She needed a good sight line to Velidred Moon and this meadow cemetery looked perfect. The stone monoliths seemed to make a focal point with the crypt and a feeling of awe and reverence surrounded her.

Zita pointed at Ingrid. "Stay right where you are and don't make a sound."

"Oh, you're bringing Gunnar right to us, here. You're such a nice young lady, not making me clomp to his gravesite in the snow."

Zita reviewed the curse in her mind and remembered what else she needed. "Are there candles in the crypt?"

"Probably dear."

She rushed to the crypt, which, thankfully, wasn't locked, and opened the door. She found a wooden box half-filled with candles. She grabbed ten candles and ran back to the front of the crypt and set them in a circle in the snow.

A bell from Tanuku rang in the distance. Midnight.

Zita lit the candles with magic and stood in the center of the glowing ring. The feeling of the magic encouraged her excitement.

A voice cried out in the forest. "Zita, I know you're out here. I felt the magic. Where are you?"

Her worst fears were realized. Dakarai. Someone who could block the magic she needed to converse with the god of Velidred and enact the curse. Did she have time?

Zita pointed at Ingrid and whispered, "Stay quiet." She pulled a small vial from her coat pocket. It contained stegox blood she had bought in the Velidred village. She splashed the blood in small droplets in a circle around her. Her chest thudded with a rapid heartbeat so fast it couldn't be healthy.

She recited an incantation from her mother that increased magic when enclosed in a circle of blood and candlelight.

"Where are you, little princess?"

Did she still have time? She feared the danger of interrupting the curse. Her head felt like a feverish timebomb as she tried to remember the curse.

Zita stared up into the night sky and raised her hands skyward. "By the power of Velidred, I call upon the ancient goddess of the red lunar empire. Hear my curse and come forth from the dark shadows of midnight."

She fired a burst of energy at each of the thirty monoliths, one at a time. A bright red light sparkled at the top of each rock structure as the blast hit it.

Dakarai's voice could be heard, "Look! Over there above the tree line, where the red glow is happening. Hurry."

So, he wasn't alone. She had to hurry; as she didn't know how much time she had with her magic. Looking across the meadow, she saw Dakarai, Sims and Lenny crest the hill and reach the open field.

Ingrid sat up a little straighter. "Is that Gunnar?"

Zita felt as if every sense in her body had come into sharp focus. Her stomach roiled in huge waves of bile and distress as panic rushed through her body. She needed more time to say the curse and deliver the magic within it.

Zita lowered her hands to her sides, took a deep breath, and raised them toward the big red moon that dominated the sky. "Oh, Goddess of Velidred, bring forth your power and your wrath. Smite my enemies with your divine fury. May they feel the full weight of your celestial wrath. So be it!" She fired an explosion into the night sky with reds, yellows, and blues filling the crisp meadow air with color.

Dakarai and the others ran across the meadow.

He has to be close enough to block my magic. I can't let him win. Zita dropped to her knees and her voice went higher as fear of Taka's wrath overcame her. "Oh, great goddess of Velidred, manifest yourself in this mortal realm, and take me as your loyal and faithful servant."

With one last rite to perform, she grabbed a candle, and threw a dash of incense at it. "Smite my enemies, Taka and Prince Krunal. May your light shine through eternity."

Zita didn't know what to expect. Did the curse happen immediately? She expected to see a luminous spirit appear, direct her, and maybe answer her questions. Nothing happened. Dakarai got close enough to Zita to block her magic which extinguished the red fires on the monoliths.

Her breath hitched as her heart shrunk within her chest. Taka had won. She hoped that Taka and Krunal lay on their deathbeds, their last breaths leaving their bodies at that very moment, but she suspected that this curse was as fruitless as the one to bring her mother back.

Dakarai snuffed the candles with magic. As a sign that her own life would be shortened by her association with Taka and his thugs. A painful lump formed in her throat as she bowed her head. Sims pulled her to her feet and jerked her arms behind her back. Lenny slapped her across the face. "That's for leaving the castle."

CHAPTER 11

our days after returning from Tanuku, Zita stood on the rock floor of the castle tower as the red Velidred moon peeked over the horizon, casting long shadows framed in red. The wind whistled through tiny holes in the castle walls and she pulled her stegox coat tighter around her body.

A voice said, "Mistress, I have found you. I have come to serve you."

Zita jumped when she first heard the voice as she thought she was alone. She searched the shadows for its owner, but there was nowhere a person could hide.

Zita was no person's master any more. As a young princess in the Velidred Castle, though, she was master of many. Now, she was a captive prisoner under the desert wizard Taka's control. How had she fallen so far? She convinced herself no one was near to her.

An owl hooted nearby, and she thought she saw a shadow of a bird pass in front of the moon.

"Mistress, I am here."

A woman's voice. But where? She searched the nearby shadows, looking for the source of the voice. Who called her? Stepping lightly in the crunchy snow covering portions of the brick floor, she searched for the person calling her. A person couldn't hide here.

The woman said, "What is your command for me?"

Zita's heart raced, and she probed the surrounding area. "Who's speaking?"

She heard the muted voices of the guards, but they were far from Zita's location.

"It is I, Luna Rosso, the Velidred Moon Goddess. Mistress of Aloheno."

Zita rotated a full three-hundred-and-sixty degrees, looking for the troublemaker. "Sims, is that you playing a trick on me?" She saw no one.

The hair on her neck stood on end. Could this be direct communication with the Velidred moon goddess? Zita stared at the moon.

"Ah, you have found me, Master."

Zita tensed her muscles and furrowed her brow. In the cold, dry air, the moon loomed large over the horizon, seeming within a reach of her hand. She didn't know what to say. Zita dropped eye contact with the moon and studied the castle walls, looking for someone pranking her. She stood on the wall by herself. Alone. She heard nothing but the normal sounds of soldiers walking their beats, and the groans and creaks of the castle.

If she ignored the voice, maybe it would go away. Sims would eventually get cold and force them back inside the castle walls.

"Mistress."

Zita didn't want to look at the large red moon. She swallowed back the fear taking hold of her. If she refused the moon, then maybe she would stay free from this manifestation of its craziness.

"You are my master now. I can read your thoughts. I can help. Look at me."

She peeked at the moon and thought she saw a large face, a woman's face, that dominated its surface. Zita opened her mouth to shriek, but she lacked the ability to make a sound. The blood drained from her head, turning her pale face ashen white. Every part of her body told her to run, but she stood rooted to her position as if she were a part of the rock structure. She wondered if this weird experience manifested from the radiation poisoning she had received from the Helmet of Justice which she had found at the Ice Castle. *Erik told me I had made a full recovery.*

"I'm waiting."

Every muscle in her body tensed, ready to run as she looked behind her and around her. Velidred's glow turned the snow crimson.

The moon called her. "A quick look."

Zita lowered her voice to a whisper. "What do you want?"

"Look at me. Let me see your face." The voice was soft and warm like a mother speaking with her young daughter.

She glanced at the moon. The red surface of the moon reflected the sun's rays. Zita studied the craters. Sharp shadows edged across the moon's surface. Maybe the moon's face was an illusion created by the shadows, but with the voice in her head, she wasn't so sure.

Zita struggled to disengage with the moon, to pull away, or stare across the snow-covered plateau. The moon's power made it impossible for her to simply blink her eyes. She found herself hugging her arms about her, a stiffness spread across her neck as she strained to disengage. The moon had somehow hypnotized her.

The Velidred moon held her in its powerful grip.

She stared at the moon.

Zita didn't know how long she stared, but she couldn't take her eyes off the moon. Cold had seeped into her skin. She brought her gloved hands underneath her armpits and hugged her body to maintain body heat.

When Velidred had moved a tenth of the way across the sky the voice said, "I have marked you. I am yours to command. We are bonded"

Zita had no clue what that even meant. *I can command the Velidred moon goddess? To do what? Is this an effect from the curse? But the curse had failed. Dakarai reached me too soon.* She licked her lips.

Then the moon goddess said, "Thank you, Mistress. The contract is complete."

A knot formed in her stomach as adrenaline flooded her body. "What contract?" Zita shouted.

The moon remained silent.

Zita pressed her lips together as her jaws tightened. "I didn't agree to a contract with you. What does this mean?"

The moon didn't answer, and the wolves howled as if they laughed at Zita.

The emptiness of space and the night time quiet on the plateau spooked her. Zita wrapped her cold arms around her body. "What did you do?"

CHAPTER 12

Zita couldn't believe it. Her heart thundered in her chest and she wobbled on the edge of hyperventilation. Velidred had manipulated her into some magical spell and now she had committed to a contract with the goddess of Velidred, a contract she didn't understand or comprehend. This had to be the worst possible outcome of her relationship with the moon.

She raced back to her room and grabbed the mirror hanging above her vanity. Zita pulled at her eyelids searching the whites of her eyes. There wasn't enough light. The candle she grabbed flickered in her trembling hand.

Another search of her eye while holding the candle close to the mirror and her face, and Zita couldn't determine if she had contracted the Corruption of Evil. The same evil spell that her father's mentor had used to control people.

What caused Velidred to talk with her? This could be a result of the curse she intoned in the mountain cemetery, but that happened a few days ago. She expected something to happen immediately and Krunal and Taka to die at the same instance she said the curse.

If the curse caused her present condition and now Taka and Prince Krunal were to die suddenly, she might be blamed. She had hoped that she would incant the curse, they would die while she traveled many miles away, and no one could blame her. If they die while she was in the castle…

Zita pondered the implications of the goddess of Velidred being her Master. Luna Rosso had already shown that she could communicate with her. There wasn't a way to escape the voice and commands of the Velidred moon goddess. *The voice said I am the master.* Yet she knew it wasn't true. She had entered into a contract with the goddess of Velidred, which is what Forest River Blossom had warned her about.

She needed more information and she worried about her eye. A red mark in the eye could be a sign of the Corruption of Evil. As her first course of action, she needed to see if the curse she chanted worked hand in hand with the Corruption of Evil. She needed a hand mirror and more light than she could get here in her room.

Zita evaluated her options. She could wait for morning, find a hand mirror, and check out her eyes on the castle walls. At least she'd have the light needed to evaluate her eyes' status. But she knew she wouldn't get any sleep tonight if she waited till morning. Maybe she could find a sympathetic ear from one of the other wizards, but who might be up at this time of night? She thought of a couple of wizards she knew well enough to visit that worked late into the night. The wizard Ixis or another older wizard named Qatar might help.

Zita decided to visit the wizard Ixis, who had a room in the castle. When she left her room, Sims followed her through the halls as she ran to Ixis' office. She knocked once on the closed door and entered. The desk and two benches were a messy pile of stacked scrolls and flat paper.

Ixis looked up from the scroll she studied and narrowed her eyes. "What does the little princess want?"

Zita gazed at the floor and whispered, "I have a problem." She stopped talking.

Maybe Ixis wasn't the best person to ask about this issue. Zita realized that Ixis might blame her for her twin brother's death, even though it was Kestrel who had fired the blast that killed Master Wizard Ishwa. Still, as King Haskell's daughter, she'd be easy to blame.

Zita steadied her feet and said, "I think I have lunacy from the Velidred moon."

"Ha." Ixis' face broke into a big grin. "Lunacy, you say. Have you been reading scrolls written by Nilsen? I think he's the one with lunacy, not you. Let me guess, you're afraid you'll die in the next two years, and you'll never reach your twentieth birthday. Is that it?"

Zita didn't respond to Ixis' amusement because she feared the problem was even bigger than lunacy. Chills ran through her body as she looked at Ixis, and her fingers shook. She forced herself not to whimper.

Ixis studied her for a moment. Then walked around the desk and put an arm around her. She guided her to a bench positioned against one wall. After moving some piles of paper to the floor, they both sat on the bench. "Let's talk. What's really wrong?"

Zita cleared her throat and blinked at the tears pooling in her eyes. "I'm worried about more than lunacy. I think I have the Corruption of Evil. I don't know how it entered me. We had it locked in the Sword of Freedom. Erik wouldn't purposely release it on me. I doubt he even knows how."

Ixis' eyes widened, and she shook her head. "You were able to remove the Corruption of Evil from Gadiel?"

She nodded.

"Let me examine your eyes."

Zita dabbed a sleeve across her face to soak up the tears that had flowed.

"We're scientists as well as wizards. Maybe you got poked in the eye and you just think it's there." She grabbed Zita's chin and produced a magic light. "Open your eyes."

Ixis pulled Zita's head back and forth shining the light as she examined her eyes.

"It's only in the right eye." Ixis seemed deep in thought. "Hmmm. Limited to just one eye. Interesting." Ixis manipulated Zita's eyelid to peer into her eye better. She talked while conducting the examination. "No one knew how Gadiel came about this evil curse. Many guessed his age at over two hundred years, but I found evidence that dated him back to as many as three-hundred and seventy-eight years."

Zita felt something crawling across her eye. She wanted to blink, but Ixis held the eyelid open, moving the light while examining the eye.

"Hmmm." She released her grip on Zita's eyelid and softened her tone. "The scorpion lives again."

"No. It can't be!" Zita tried to jerk her head back, but Ixis held tight to her chin. "We locked it into the Sword of Freedom." A range of emotions seared through Zita's body. Gadiel had somehow used the power of the scorpion that roamed on his eyes to manipulate people. Somehow when the red scorpion traveled from the corner of his eye to stand guard over his black pupil, he could force others to follow his will. Zita feared the Corruption of Evil and what it might do to her, but would she now have the ability to manipulate others as she saw fit?

Ixis asked, "When do you think it infected you?"

"I don't know. It might have been when we released the stone warriors. Toward the end, I felt magic flow into me. I wasn't hurt or anything, I just felt different." There was no way Erik had released it on her on purpose. "Can you pull it out of me? I don't want to die."

Ixis shook her head. "I'd have to consult with the Council of Nine—"

"No! Don't tell them. The Grand Wizard will lock me up in the dungeon. He already hates me."

"As members of the council, it is our responsibility to follow protocol when we come across magic aberrations. I agree that we need to remove it as soon as possible. It gives you power over people and helps you manipulate things to your gain."

Zita regretted her decision to talk with Ixis. She didn't need Council of Nine members poking at her eye and trying untested techniques to remove the corruption. She needed to leave the castle, find Erik, Al, and maybe Kestrel. They could perform the same task that encased the Corruption of Evil in the Sword of Freedom the first time.

"I'll speak with the Council of Nine, and we'll find a way to help you," Ixis said. "It's a dangerous curse."

Zita shoulders drooped. "There's more."

Ixis cocked her head and raised an eyebrow.

"I might have signed a contract with the goddess of Velidred, Luna Rosso."

Ixis bit her lower lip as if deep in thought. "Velidred talks to you?"

"Yes."

"Do you feel that Velidred can control you and make you do things you don't want to do?"

Zita didn't want to believe the moon had that kind of control over her, but maybe Luna Rosso could control her. "I don't know."

Ixis walked back around the desk and flopped into her chair with a concerned expression plastered across her face as she scratched the back of her neck. "A low-level thief with some profitable illegal business enterprises, Gadiel had limited magic, but he could control people, a control that seemed to emanate from the Corruption of Evil."

Zita's skin seemed to crawl and felt raw.

Ixis put her elbows on the desk and rubbed her eyes. "Gadiel's political power grew stronger when he gave your father, King Haskell, the Fire and Ice challenge. With Haskell's magic and Gadiel's ability to manipulate people, Gadiel became a force despite his weak magical skills."

Is there a way I can control the Corruption of Evil and become even more powerful than my father? Zita thought.

"If you were responsible for Gadiel's death, then that ability might be you accepting the students he proctored through the experience. When he died someone close would 'inherit' the people he administered the Fire and Ice challenge to." Ixis sighed and dropped her hands to the desk and leaned forward. "What concerns me is your magical power is significantly greater than Gadiel's. I don't know what that will mean if the Velidred moon goddess is truly able to control and assist you."

Zita moaned, "You believe that she will be able to control me. What can I do?"

Ixis tapped her index finger against her lips. Zita waited a minute as Ixis pondered.

Zita asked, "Is there a cure? We can get Erik and the Sword of Freedom, grab Alpherge and you three can suck it back into the sword where we stored it before."

Ixis tugged on her bottom lip. "We can't do that right now. It's winter. It's difficult traveling to where Cugbert is helping the people."

"I know the general area where Erik and Cugbert are right now. I'll go find them, or we can send a messenger."

"Well . . ."

Zita's stomach felt like a thousand knives were cutting through her from the inside out. "What is it?"

"The mountains are deep in snow even this early in winter. The snow is much higher than here in the meadows. There's no way to get into the mountains at this time of year."

"I'm sure I can find a mountain trail and go locate Erik. You don't have to come with me. I'm sure I can find a wizard that can perform the procedure." Heat flushed through Zita's body as anger built within her. She lowered her voice an octave. "I need to find Cugbert and get this fixed."

Ixis steepled her fingers, wriggling them back and forth. "Wait for spring. It'll give me time to study you. I think it'll be interesting to see what powers you manifest as the corruption gets stronger within you."

"You want to study me like a guinea pig?"

"I research things. That's what interests me." She walked back to Zita, sat on the bench with her and took her hands. "It'll be okay. We'll work through this together."

Zita threw her hands apart, breaking Ixis' grip and stood. "You are not using me as a guinea pig. I'm leaving the castle and finding Cugbert and Erik whether you want me to or not. You can't let me die here."

She turned to leave the room, and Sims greeted her at the door, a knife in his hand. "You aren't leaving the castle."

Zita pushed Sims back into the hallway, not even worried about the thug's threat. She wandered the castle halls as Sims followed her like a hungry coyote.

She couldn't stop thinking about the Corruption of Evil and the curse of the Velidred moon. She tried to calm her pounding heart by taking deep breaths. Velidred had tricked her. Zita wasn't Luna Rosso's master; but her servant. She had to find a way to reverse this curse. The library must have a scroll, manuscript or book that would help her remove it. Why hadn't she listened to Forest River Blossom?

When Eric, Al and Zita had removed the Corruption of Evil from Gadiel and stored it in the Sword of Freedom, Gadiel died ten days later. She needed the corruption removed as soon as possible. Maybe if she had it removed in a day or two, then she could live a long normal life.

Zita needed to hide the scorpion in her eye from others until she found out more information about the evil curse. She took deep breaths, trying to calm the panic rising in her throat. Ixis would notify the Council of Nine soon and then she would lose her life. She couldn't scream or cry out. She couldn't let others know about the scorpion until she learned more. Within her tightly closed fists, her fingernails cut into her palms. *Think!*

CHAPTER 13

Zita hurried to the library. First, she wanted to do more research to see if they discussed the Corruption of Evil or had additional information about Velidred lunacy. She snuck into the room and raced to the stacks of scrolls. She grabbed a few off the storage cases on the shelves. Zita needed a scroll that told her everything about the corruption, but she found nothing. *Maybe it's a singular event. Only Gadiel had it, and now only I have it.*

After two hours of pulling scrolls and manuscripts and reading them, she found very little about lunacy. It seemed most of the knowledge on the subject came from a researcher named Nilsen. Others pretty much parroted Nilsen's research.

An article by a woman named Schmidt discussed lunacy and the fact that magical healers, scientific healers, and wizards had found no known cure for lunacy. But at the bottom of Schmidt's research, she mentioned an old tribe in the desert, the Sahrakinlari, that held the belief that a magical object of great power, the Crystal of Zaraboth, potentially had the power to heal lunacy.

Taka was a member of the Sahrakinlari, but would he help her? She didn't know a lot about the crystal and she found additional documents that talked about the ancient magical object.

Schmidt did quote three other researchers that disagreed with her on the power of the Crystal of Zaraboth to help heal lunacy. They were also quite adamant that the crystal existed, though it was unattainable in its present form.

She thought it best to talk with Taka and see what he knew of the Crystal of Zaraboth. If she acquired the crystal, maybe that would remove the risk of lunacy, the Velidred curse, and the Corruption of Evil.

Zita went to Taka's chambers, but he wasn't there. She asked Sims where else his master might be. He waved his knife at her. "I'm not your servant, find him yourself."

Where else could the desert wizard be? The Council of Nine members had a chamber at the top of the castle where they congregated. Zita had been there when she lived here in the castle as a princess, but Prince Krunal had cut off that privilege. She'd have to send a servant with a message and hope that Taka responded.

Zita wrote out a cryptic message about her need to see Taka. She didn't need every servant in the castle knowing her plight. She needed him to respond and meet with her now.

She waited in the castle hallway for at least half-an-hour before the servant returned with Taka's response. She unfolded the written note. *Meet me in my chambers before dinner tonight.*

Zita returned to the library for further research. Not much had been written about the Crystal of Zaraboth. She found information that suggested the magic artifact was guarded by three to five gatekeepers. Making your way past the gatekeepers proved no guarantee you could capture the object. You needed a vessel to hold the crystal, the Anticletus moon had to be in new moon status. The object hadn't changed ownership in centuries.

In a fit of anger, Zita swept her arm across the library table scattering the scrolls she had piled on it. They toppled off the table, bounced and made a loud ringing sound as the metal rods hit the floor. Every indication led to the likelihood that the Crystal of Zaraboth was untouchable. The scrolls hadn't talked about who owned it or how they used the object. It seemed very powerful, since it had been used in the past to win wars, take over kingdoms, and in one instance open a portal.

She gave up; the crystal wasn't the answer she needed. She trudged down to her room, flopped onto her bed, and stared vacantly at the ceiling, fear eating at her stomach. She flitted in and out of sleep dreaming of the moon goddess placing a chain around her neck and leading her around the planet in great leaps each day.

# # # #

Zita awoke to the sound of someone knocking on her door. Lenny stood outside the door when she opened it.

"Taka is ready to see you."

The smells of dinner preparation drifted down the hall. The savory odor of caramelized onions and a spicy, slightly smoky hint of meat being cooked over a fire. She needed to make sure she ate dinner tonight, it smelled delicious.

If Taka couldn't help her, then she would find others who might. Before leaving, she grabbed the second scroll from Haskell's manor that contained information about the Crystal of Zaraboth.

She stopped at the opened door when she reached Taka's chambers, and Taka motioned for her to enter. Lenny followed her into the room. "Close the door," he said.

She shut the door and sat on a bench. A tapestry hanging on the wall behind Taka drew Zita's attention. It showed a desert landscape with a person in the middle of the landscape kneeling and looking up at the sky. In the sky above the person, liquid poured out of a teapot onto the kneeling person. Angels and rays of sunlight surrounded the kneeling person.

Taka said, "Ixis tells me you have a problem."

Zita slowly nodded her head. The box containing the Imperium Wand lay open on Taka's desk. *Did he really just leave it out in the open, an important magic object with reputed great powers?*

"Let me see your eyes." He leaned in close and produced a ball of light. He made some noises as he lifted each eyelid and poked his finger in her eyes a couple of times.

"Hey stop. That hurts." Zita pushed him away.

"Yeah, it looks like the Corruption of Evil. It's a good thing I have your magic blocked. The Council of Nine will have to vote on whether to permanently remove your magic."

Zita bolted to her feet. "You can't be serious. I'll never allow that."

"We can't have someone with your magic capability using the Corruption of Evil. None of us would be safe. Even Gadiel using your father as a magic weapon against his enemies was harmful enough."

Zita's chest tightened as she backed toward the door. Her eyes darted between Taka and then as realization of the problem came full force on her. It didn't matter whether she had lunacy, the Velidred curse, or the Corruption of Evil, they couldn't afford that someone with her power would have the Corruption of Evil. The Council of Nine wouldn't help her, study her, or allow Erik and Al to try to save her. She wouldn't be allowed to live much longer.

She raised the scroll in her hand. "We can get the Crystal of Zaraboth and get rid of the Corruption of Evil."

"That's an impossible dream. No one has been able to use that crystal for years. We're not sure the owner is still alive."

"Won't that make it easier to get?" Zita struggled to think of a solution that didn't include them taking her magic away.

"Forget the crystal. It won't help you." Taka raised his hands shoulder level in order to placate her. "Relax Zita. It isn't that bad. I've known a few wizards that had their magic confiscated. It doesn't hurt, and you can live a long happy life. We'll find you a nice boy, maybe a royal from another kingdom. Get married, have kids, and you'll be happy."

"You know that's not how it works, Taka. I've seen wizards that lose their magic die within months. Months!" She spit the words at him.

Taka motioned at Lenny. He held Zita by the shoulders.

"I've spoken with the Grand Wizard and two other members of the Council of Nine. We're going to move you to the dungeon for now. It'll be safer for you there and less likely you'll escape. I hear it's well-guarded."

Zita's jaw tightened as she thought of spells she would blast at him if she had her magic. Her throat constricted at being thrown in the dungeon with the murderers, political enemies, and the sick. She laughed to herself. *Yes, sick people like me.* She struggled against Lenny's tight hold on her.

Taka crossed his arms and gave a sad shake of his head. "I thought we could use you until the prince had died. It doesn't matter. Even in the dungeon, I'll make sure you're blamed for his murder."

"You can't do this to me."

Zita jammed her elbow into Lenny's side and the old man tumbled to the chamber floor. She flung open the door, and ran into Dakarai and Sims. Dakarai held her tight, and Sims laid his ever-quick knife against her throat.

She stilled and glared at Taka as he exited his chamber. "Throw her in the dungeon and then come back here. We have to make a plan for the prince. Don't kill her, Sims. She'll die without you having to murder her."

The sound of her heartbeat thrashed in her ears as she thought about her short future. Her skin felt clammy, and her breath came in huge rasping gasps. Her options were limited, and the best she could hope for was finding some way to run away. She looked at her captives and knew without magic her chance to escape were hopeless.

Dakarai walked her down the hallway, a light grip on her upper arm. As they walked, she heard a voice. No, not a voice. A thought seemed to filter to her brain. *Wow, out of all the ways I thought this might play out, I never imagined they'd kill Zita.*

Zita looked at Sims. "Did you say something?"

Sims said, "Keep moving, Princess. You're not going to trick us."

Were those Dakarai's thoughts? Zita wondered how she could hear his thoughts. Maybe she could use them to her advantage. "Dakarai, you're right. You can change what's happening here. Let me go. Restore my magic. I'll run into the mountains or to the ocean, and you'll never see me again. I'll give you this scroll that contains instructions on how to capture the Crystal of Zaraboth. You can have great power to control armies and make loads of money."

Sims moved closer to the scroll as his eyes took on a shiny appearance. "It's ours when we toss you in the dungeon, Little Princess."

Zita stopped, wriggled out of Dakarai's grip, and squared off against them, holding the scroll as a weapon.

Sims stepped right, faked, and then poked her in the side with his knife. "Don't even think about it, Princess."

She moved away from the sharp jab. It wasn't a deep cut, but the knife broke the skin. Zita bounced off the wall and stumbled toward Dakarai, catching herself with her hand on Dakarai's shoulder. She felt a connection to his Fire and Ice Challenge tattoo on his shoulder. A strong connection.

Gadiel had sent electrical charges into her body when he wanted to punish her. These weren't driven by magic but were a result of the ancient Fire and Ice Challenge. Remembering this, Zita thought of a thousand tiny knives digging into Dakarai's shoulder. He suddenly went to the floor in pain. His eyes widened and he swallowed hard as the color drained from his face. Satisfied, she kicked him in the gut.

Sims came at her with his knife.

Zita felt the magic. Her magic. With Dakarai injured, she could break through the magic block. The first thing that entered her mind was the sand blast that Taka had shown her a few months earlier. She had failed using it before, but she needed protection from Sims, so she reached out her hand, palm showing, toward him.

Sand blasted from her fingers, flying into his eyes. Too late, he covered his eyes with his arm. She saw the weakness in his knees and kicked his kneecap hard. Sims went down on top of Dakarai who let out a whimper when Sims landed. Zita thumped Sims' head with the scroll and ran.

CHAPTER 14

Zita needed to get out of the castle and as far from Taka and his gang as possible. She didn't know where to go, but she couldn't stay in the castle.

Her heart pounded as she ran down the castle stairs and outside into the castle bailey. She'd do anything to have a horse, but she didn't have time. She'd have to exit the castle walls before the general alarm sounded.

Clouds covered the sky, and despite a red glow from Velidred moon, the light didn't reach the ground. The darkness covered her and she sprinted to the gate still holding the scroll in her hand ready to use it as a weapon if necessary. She yelled at the two guards at the gate, "Let me out now."

The guards were slow, but eventually a door opened, and Zita sprinted into the Velidred Village. She had no friends in the village to hide her and she thought of other places she might hole up. She stayed on the path that led onward to the shops of cobblers, blacksmiths and bread makers.

A thought crossed her mind that she could check out the blacksmith's shop and search for a horse waiting to be shod in the morning, but she didn't need the locals looking for her, either. Halfway through the village she heard the alarm. Taka had notified the king's guards, and they would begin to search for her. She couldn't hide in the village.

If she wasn't in the village, then the guards might think she had sprinted to Tanuku or some other village farther from the castle. They would find her easily on the road. Where could she shelter until the guards got tired of the search and Taka stopped worrying about her?

Zita ran through the village and continued until she saw the path to the cemetery. Her mother's crypt might provide a suitable hiding place. She hadn't taken a jacket with her in her hurry to leave the castle, and her arms were already chilled. Her mother's crypt could keep her warm. Except, Taka would think to look for her there. A crypt, but not her mother's. Let them search the village, fields, and roads first, and then she would make her escape.

She turned on the path to the cemetery, making sure she stayed on the already worn path through the snow. She reached a suitable crypt and verified no one had followed before sneaking into the chamber and shutting the door. The room was dark, but she feared using her magic to light candles would alert Dakarai and Taka of her location.

Zita sat in the dark, her insides quivering as she played with her necklace. She needed a plan to escape Velidred, remove the curse of the goddess of Velidred, and remove the Corruption of Evil. Blowing out a series of short breaths, she gained control of her trembling. If she could find Erik and Al, then they could come up with a solution. Erik still had the Sword of Freedom, and together they could solve her problems one at a time.

The first place to look for Al would be the Village of Crossroads. He had planned to work on his magic training at the building Ishwa used to train the warrior wizards for Prince Krunal's army. Al should be there, and his friend, Sherry, would be close by, too. She had proved to be a smart woman and would have ideas on how to find Erik.

Zita rubbed her arms; the chill of winter seeped into the crypt chamber. She thought of ways to get to Crossroads. Since she hadn't left the trails to go into the forest, the castle guards would stay on the roads. Maybe early in the morning she could head off into the forest walking in the general direction of Crossroads. It might take her a couple of days, but she could make it. She felt her bare arms. *If I don't freeze to death.*

She fell into a restless sleep where ghosts and ethereal spirits and a large face on the Velidred moon chased her around the cemetery. A sound of something hitting the roof of the crypt woke her. Her stomach involuntarily clenched as she realized they had found her. Zita ran her hand through her hair and cocked her head to listen. The crypt had no back door or exit other than the entranceway. It wouldn't be one guard; it'd be five guards and Sims, Lenny, and Dakarai.

Nothing. No more sounds. Something had hit the crypt. She waited in the dark for something to happen. How much time had elapsed since she came into the burial chamber? She rose from the cold hard floor and waited to be captured.

Time passed, but in the darkness, she didn't know how long. Why weren't they coming in? She couldn't wallow in self-pity. The cold had settled in her limbs and she thought the dungeon might be warmer than this tomb. Zita opened the crypt door. A heavy snowfall covered the building, but she didn't see anyone in the cemetery with her. Suspicious, she crept from the grave waiting to be attacked.

Then she noticed the limb that had fallen from a tree above the crypt. A large dead branch, overloaded with wet snow, had landed on the roof. That's what woke her. The falling snow settled on her shoulders as she stood, trying to determine what to do. If she ran to the forest, maybe the heavy snowfall would hide her tracks. She could get deep into the forest, and the guards would never find her.

Determined, Zita ran across the cemetery. She reached the fence that enclosed the dead and pulled herself over. The wind blew snow into her face, but she continued into the forest, running—more like leaping—through the deep snow.

She jumped, landed on a hidden log, slipped and splashed into the snow. The exertion of running and fear of being captured had kept her warm, but the cold snow made her realize the danger she was running into was just as deadly as the danger she ran from. On a clear summer day, it would take twelve hours or more to get to Crossroads. On a cold snowy night, in deep snow with temperatures below freezing, lost in the woods, this decision could be life threatening.

Zita stood, brushed off the snow and continued plowing a path to Crossroads. She stopped worrying so much about her tracks being seen as she noticed the trail she made behind her. The deep snow made it difficult to tell if the path had been created by a deer, fox, stegox, or human. It didn't matter, she must continue. Certain death lay behind her, a chance for life and healing lay ahead.

The snow continued to fall and accumulate. Zita's hair was soaked with snow, but she couldn't stop. After an hour of steadily pushing through the deep drifts, she heard water flowing below her. She had arrived at a ravine.

She stopped and evaluated her options. Ideally, she could find a bridge and cross over at that point, but that meant possibly exposing herself to the people searching for her. The river wasn't fully frozen, since she heard it splashing and gurgling. She didn't know this river or if there were places just upstream to cross safely. Despite a steep drop to the river, she saw a number of trees that grew along the hillside which might help slow her down without plummeting to her death into the icy water.

She mapped out a path in her mind that would get her to the water with the least chance of breaking her neck. Zita slowly worked her way down to the water's edge. She had to slide down the steep side of the ravine, grabbing small trees as she worked her way to the water. She searched the river when she reached it. The river had frozen in the slow-moving pockets along its side, but water ran rapidly in its center. The distance across had to be eighteen feet or more, but the light didn't allow her to determine its depth. If she got soaked, she would die. She couldn't chance crossing here. There had to be a better location that would keep her from getting wet.

Zita moved up the river looking for safer places to cross. In fifteen minutes, she found a spot that looked promising. The water pooled in this area and five large stones seemed nicely spaced and flat enough to chance a dry crossing.

Her feet were numb from her trek through the snow, and she had to stretch her leg to reach the first stone. It had a slick feel to it from the snow that clung to its top. It was large enough for both feet and she stopped to assess the next step. The next stone was closer, but only large enough for one foot, she would have to step on it and continue on to the next step.

Screwing up her courage, she managed the first step and reached out with her foot for the next. She landed nicely and lifted her first foot to join this one when the rock moved. It wasn't a rock at all, but a giant turtle. It lifted its head and moved into deeper water. Zita reacted quickly and jumped for the next rock, missed her landing and skidded into the water. She splashed hard into the water with her shoulder hitting a rock. The scroll flew from her hand and landed in the snow close to the other side of the river on a layer of ice.

She screamed as she landed in the icy cold liquid. The coldness of the water took her breath away, and she lay motionless as she tried to gain control after her involuntary reaction to the landing. With a mighty push off the bottom of the rather shallow river, she scrambled to the other side of the river as fast as possible. She managed to retrieve the scroll, still mostly dry.

Zita burst from the water and rested a moment. She could feel the little body heat she had left oozing from her body. *I can't rest. I must find shelter and start a fire.* With determination, she tried to climb out of the ravine. The trees were farther apart, and she kept slipping in the snow.

Her heart beat as if it wanted to jump out of her body. She found a handhold on a small tree and pulled herself up. The next grew just out of reach so she stood on the first and jumped to grab the next. Her hands were numb and even though she grasped at the limb, she couldn't manipulate her fingers to hold the grip.

Zita fell back to the previous tree and slapped her fingers against her body, trying to get enough blood into them to hold the limb above. Her wet clothes didn't help warm her fingers. She wiggled her fingers until she thought they might hold a grip on the tree and tried again. With a mighty leap she reached the tree and only by wrapping an elbow around the tree did she maintain her position.

She looked up the ravine embankment. It was still farther than she wanted to think about to the top. She identified the next tree to grab, but when she reached it, her fingers slipped, and she slid back down the ravine wall. She lay next to the river looking up. Her body ached, and what didn't ache felt numb. She had no strength to get out of the ravine.

The loss of body heat, no food for at least twenty-four hours, numb fingers and feet, she knew death awaited her at the bottom of this ravine. She wondered if the mountain wolves or the guards would find her body first.

She had hoped to see Erik once more but now realized that she'd never see him again. If she slept a few minutes, she'd have the energy to get out. Zita closed her eyes. The cold enclosed her, like a comfortable cocoon. The river gurgled, a peaceful sound that soothed her worries. *Yes, relax and release the tension. Everything will be okay if I just sleep.*

CHAPTER 15

A wolf howled in the distance, followed by a responsive howl that seemed closer. Adrenaline pumped through Zita's body as she pushed herself to a standing position next to the snow-covered riverbank. What was she thinking? Sleeping here would result in her death; she must find shelter and make a fire. The certainty of that knowledge sent a flash of heat through her body.

With renewed effort she grabbed at trees and pulled herself up one tree at a time. She moved away from the slippery areas where she had been before. She forced her numb fingers to hold tightly to the trees she grabbed. Ice clung to her wet hair and scratched against her face as she swung her body for the next tree.

Despite slipping a couple of times, at each setback, she renewed her efforts to find the path to the top. The last tree before the ravine top grew higher than she could reach. She knew that she had to make it out of the ravine right now if she expected to live. There was no way she would be able to climb the fifteen feet a second time. She searched for something to hold onto above her head, but found nothing. She evaluated if she had the ability to jump up and over. Her feet felt numb and unusable and her ankles felt stiff. With a mighty effort, she jumped grabbing for anything that she might be able to use to pull herself up higher.

It seemed as if time slowed as she reached for a handhold only to have more snow come down on her wet tunic as the drift she had mistaken for a rock disintegrated. She reached up again, feeling gravity begin to pull her body back to the river. Her face scraped against a rock. She frantically swiped her hands on both sides of the ground above her.

Zita found a shrub and held with one hand. As her numb fingers began to slip, she grabbed the rim with her other hand. Breaths of relief and effort blew in large visible clouds as she manipulated her legs over the top of the ravine and rolled onto the level snow. She lay on her back and gasped for air. Her body shivered to overcome the cold. Ice had formed on her wet clothing, and she felt the numbness in her fingers advancing up her arms.

Zita hoped she had traveled far enough from civilization to use magic. It took great effort to move onto her hands and knees. Why had she left the warmth and comfort of the castle? She crawled to a nearby tree and used it to help her stand. Once on her frozen feet, she set her jaw and searched for dry firewood. By searching the trees, she found a number of dead limbs that she could shake off the tree and make them fall to the ground. She knew nothing of winter survival skills, but she found a large boulder, bigger than her body, not far from the ravine. Sitting next to it allowed her to get her body out of the wind. With no other choice but to use magic, she stacked the wood and was relieved to find she was able to light a fire.

She listened for sounds of anyone that might be following her, fearing someone lurked in the woods waiting for the right moment to capture her.

Zita leaned toward the fire trying to warm her extremities as her eyes fluttered closed from fatigue, hypothermia, and lack of sleep. She placed her hands as close to the fire as she dared as no feeling was left in them. Despite fatigue gutting her body, she feared sleeping would lead to death.

It snowed for another two hours. Then the sky lightened to a dull gray as the sun tried to shine through the clouds.

Her head jerked and she awoke with a start. She could feel her hands and feet, but the cold had seeped back into her body. She looked at the fire. Another round of snow had dampened the wood and it had become a large smoke signal, a beacon to anyone who might be looking for her.

Zita snapped to alertness despite stiff, sore muscles. *How could I have been so stupid to let the flame go to smoke?* Kicking snow onto the fire pit, she put out the smoldering wood. She looked around the area and saw all the tracks she had made which would help anyone figure out she had been here. Her clothes had dried in most places but she needed to move to not be found. With a sigh, and holding back tears, she moved quickly away from the ravine.

She traveled hours without stopping. Occasionally she heard voices in the forest, but couldn't identify if they were people on the road or guards out searching for her. Crossroads had a higher elevation than Velidred, leaving Zita feeling like she was walking uphill the entire way. The constant rise in the land assured her she was headed in the right direction.

Hunger stabbed at her stomach, but she continued walking. It wasn't safe to stop and look for food. She would eat when she found Alpherge. She tried not to remind herself of the yummy food the castle kitchen staff had been preparing as she escaped.

When she did stop to rest, she scanned the area to make sure no one followed. Looking back at where she had been, her footprints made it obvious someone had been tramping through the woods. The guards would have no trouble following her, and if they were on horses, it wouldn't take long to catch her.

The cold made it difficult to walk as her knees stiffened. As the early winter night came on, Zita found a small cave large enough for her to sit inside. She stopped, cleared out some leaves and found some wood. She lit a fire and stoked it with the driest logs she could find. Her limbs shook from the cold, and as her fingers warmed, it felt like a thousand needles poking her all at once.

Zita had to rest. She couldn't keep walking through deep snow like this all night. It wasn't safe. She had no way to know how far she had traveled. One mile? Sixteen miles? She hoped she was close to Crossroads, but she just didn't know. She imagined the guards right behind her. Sleep called her, but was it safe to sleep?

She placed large logs on the fire she had tucked in a corner of the cave where good airflow pulled the smoke out the mouth of the cave. She hoped the light was unseen from outside. The fire heated the rocks and Zita became comfortable. She curled up at the back of the cave and fell into a deep sleep.

Zita woke thinking she had heard a woman's voice. *What woman would chase after me? It doesn't sound like Ixis.* The fire had burned down to embers, casting a soft red glow on the cave wall and ceiling. Darkness still reigned outside the cave, though she could tell that the Velidred moon had not completed its night-time journey.

Hunger pains jabbed at her stomach. She needed food if she expected to reach Crossroads. In all her training at the castle no one had taught her how to survive in the wild. She heard an animal howl but didn't know if it was wolves, coyotes or even the dangerous stegox. Tension built in her neck as she worried if she had chosen an animal's lair as her resting place.

The voice said. "Are you hungry my child?"

Zita felt an ache in the back of her throat and chills raced through her body. They had found her. *The guards must be outside. I should have paid better attention to create an escape route before they arrived. Now I'm trapped in this cave and they have me surrounded.* She huddled in the far corner of the cave rocking slightly as she searched for a way to escape.

"You're safe my child. I'm the only one that knows your location. Come out of hiding and we can begin your training."

The knot in Zita's belly tightened as she mentally ran through the possibilities of who had tracked her to her current location. The person sounded more friend than foe, but she knew no one who lived in the forest. Whoever this part of the forest belonged to, she needed to know more about this person, but she also had to be prepared to run. All this would be easier if she wasn't starving. Maybe the woman had food.

If the voice sounded female, then it wasn't Dakarai or Taka, so Zita could disable the person with magic and then go on the run once more. Her mind told her running out in the snow once more would be the smart thing, but her body sounded the alarm about not having eaten in the last twenty-four hours and that she was still not dressed for the cold. She needed to confront the person and see what might happen.

"If I come out of the cave, you won't try to capture me, will you?" Zita searched the area near the cave entrance, but the darkness gave no clues.

"Come my friend. You're in no danger here."

Who is this person? Zita struggled to stand in the small cave and walked to the entrance on tired, sore legs. She poked her head from the cave, expecting to see a lantern, or twelve soldiers with glistening swords, but she saw no one.

Two moons, Velidred and Anticletus shown in the night sky, casting dull shadows through the trees.

"Where are you? Present yourself," Zita shouted into the night sky in a raspy dry voice.

"Look up, my child. It is I, Luna Rosso, the goddess of Velidred, come to help you in your time of need. We have plans to make, and we need you to learn and grow."

Zita backed into the cave, "No, stay away."

"You are hungry. You'll make better decisions once you are fed. Let me teach you the powers you possess and how to master them for your benefit."

This has to be a bad dream caused by fatigue, cold, dehydration, and hunger. The moon can't speak with me. I don't have lunacy disease.

"Come out of the cave. We'll talk."

Her skin felt raw as she debated whether to converse with this dream or to run through the snow. Her stomach rumbled. *Maybe this dream can help find me some food.*

Zita cautiously stumbled out of the cave.

"There you are. This experience is always more intimate when I can see my servant. Let's start by catching food."

Zita snorted. She'd never caught food in her life. *What does this deity expect me to do, trap a rabbit and eat it?*

"Ah. You don't know the powers I impart to you, yet. That is why you must learn and practice these skills. It took Gadiel a long time to master the skill sets I'll teach."

She didn't know if she should sit or stand or run. "What do you want me to do?"

"There is a rabbit not far from you."

"Where?" Zita asked.

"You don't have to speak. We don't want to scare the poor creature."

Zita's muscles quivered as she processed the goddess of Velidred being able to read her thoughts.

"Sit where you are and the rabbit will visit with you in a minute or two. When it gets close, look it in the eye and think of the rabbit desiring to come to you. A simple command. Come to me."

She looked at the snow and hesitated before sitting down. *Maybe if I follow the directions this dream will end sooner.* Zita waited. It wasn't long before a gray rabbit with a white tail approached her.

Zita closed her eyes.

"You have to open your eyes. Wait until the animal looks at you, then imagine my symbol, the scorpion talking with the animal. Then invite it into your lap."

She rolled her eyes but opened them and looked at the rabbit. It hopped closer to her and then sat a moment staring at Zita as it wiggled its nose. She thought of the scorpion crawling across her eye and almost screamed at the thought. Then she told the rabbit to come to her.

The animal seemed to be considering its choices, go to Zita or run off into the forest to find food. Then it hopped over to Zita and she caught the animal placing it on her lap.

"That's it. You have caught tonight's dinner."

"What do you mean, dinner? Do you expect me to cook this cute little creature?"

The goddess of Velidred said, "I never did like working with royalty. They don't like to get their hands dirty. Yes, I will help you prepare it so you have something to eat. Otherwise, you die."

It took a while for Zita to get up the courage to prepare her meal but two hours later she sat in the back of the cave licking the last juicy remains from her fingers.

The moon goddess spoke once more, "Sleep now, my child. Get warm and rest during the day and I will guide you to your destination at night."

"Are you crazy? I need to move during the day when I can see where I'm going."

"You must trust me. I am your protector."

Zita thought about listening to the moon goddess. She might be two hundred yards from the entrance to Crossroads. With a little luck she could find Alpherge in an hour, warm up and be free of Taka and the others. "I must go and find my friends." *Or I might be five miles, yet.*

They went back and forth like this for a number of minutes until fatigue and cold returned to Zita, and she crawled back into the cave with some more wood for the fire.

Full of rabbit, she slept well, and at night fall the moon goddess awakened her. "It is time to travel. The guards have found your tracks. They are tracking you."

Zita peeked out of the cave, her heartbeat driving the fear that gripped her chest as her legs tightened preparing to run. A cold wind had picked up and Zita crossed her arms when she came out of the cave. She had been comfortable and wasn't prepared to go back on the run. The snow had drifted in places and it took her a second to get her bearings and continue on the path that she thought led to Crossroads.

Coyotes howled in the distance. Zita plowed through the snow again. She would zigzag through the trees, sometimes finding deer trails to follow and other times having to backtrack to make it around a fallen tree. The process slowed as she tired. Luna Rosso offered directional information when Zita got turned around, but she continued toward the Village of Crossroads.

About three hours before sunrise, the Velidred moon had almost set. In the distance, Zita heard the howl of dogs. Or was it wolves? She wasn't sure, but it seemed to be getting closer. If dogs, then the guards were hot on her trail, and she needed to move faster.

Zita hurried through the forest, occasionally glancing behind her. As she ran, she tripped on a log in the path in front of her and landed face down in the snow. When she rubbed the snow out of her eyes, not ten feet away a wolf stared her in the eyes. She held back a scream as fear gripped her stiffened body. She willed herself to be still.

Four feet tall, its gray fur was streaked with brown. The yellow-eyed wolf stared at Zita with rising interest.

If not the guards, then wolves, Zita thought. Fatigue racked her body, but she felt the acceleration of adrenaline kick in as she planned an escape. The wolf facing her growled, and then she heard an answering growl behind her. Wolves. Not a single wolf. They travel in packs.

Zita looked to the setting Velidred moon and thought to the god of Velidred. "Can you help me?"

"Use the power I taught you with the rabbit. It works every time."

What if it doesn't work? She glanced around to see five wolves walking slowly toward her, their hackles raised. Her gut told her to run, yet they had encircled her, and she had no clear path to safety.

The Velidred moon dropped behind the snowy mountains rising above the forest.

Zita shook her head. *Is this the punishment I get for killing that rabbit?* She forced herself to focus on the lead wolf, or, at least, it was the one in front of her. She got the scorpion in her eye to move and she stared at the animal.

The wolf stared at her and growled.

She told it to go away, but it didn't. It growled again and moved a step closer.

Zita concentrated harder as her breathing increased, and she felt her heart beating hard in her chest. Her body trembled as she tried to command the animal to leave her alone.

It advanced again.

That's it, she thought. *I can't control the scorpion. I'll have to use old fashioned methods.* She hoped that the guards weren't close enough to find her, because her solution meant making a lot of noise.

Zita used her magic to send a fireball at the animal. It exploded on the wolf in a loud bang and she heard a yelp and the animal darted off back into the forest.

The other wolves growled at her and then followed their retreating leader.

Zita relaxed with a smile on her face. *Well, if the new way doesn't work, then I'll use the old-fashioned methods.* The adrenaline from the confrontation with the wolves had warmed her and she felt prepared to do another mile or more.

Then a male voice cried out in the forest, "She's close. After her, but be careful, she's using magic."

Guards! Zita felt the blood rush out of her face and she plunged after the retreating wolves through the forest.

CHAPTER 16

Zita thought her heart would leap out of her chest as she raced through the forest, not worrying about her tracks, the noise she was making, or her direction. Her leg muscles cramped from lack of adequate nourishment and from being in the cold for so long, but she pushed through the pain. She continued to look behind her to see if the pursuers were in sight.

Beads of sweat built on her lip as she ran, but she couldn't worry about how she looked. She must continue to run until she reached safety, but she didn't know where to find safety. She worried she might be wandering around in a large circle as she had no sense of direction. Even if she found Crossroads, the guards would find her right away.

Zita searched for places she could hide. She remembered she might be able to hold off a number of king's guards if she could use her magic, but what if Dakarai tracked her with the guards? He would find her the moment she engaged her magic. The Velidred moon had set and Luna Rosso couldn't help now, which led Zita to think hooking up with the spiritual deity wouldn't provide her much protection.

She ran on, looking for some way to escape her pursuers, and then she noticed another ravine coming up. It wasn't very deep, five feet at most, channeling a quick running creek, racing down the mountain.

An idea struck her. She jumped into the ravine staying on the bank of the creek and found a good size rock that she tossed into the creek. Using the shapeshifting skills Gadiel had taught her, she shapeshifted into a wolf. She jumped to the other side and ran in circles near the creek, and then she leaped out of the ravine and made her way through the forest. She found a spot a hundred yards away where it looked like she could hide and catch her breath.

The guards stopped at the ravine.

"Look, I see her footprints. There!"

"But they stop."

"She must be running in the creek."

"Which way?"

A deep male voice commanded, "Half of you go up the creek, the other half follow the creek downstream. She can't stay in the water for long. If she does, we'll find her dead before morning."

Zita heard voices going off in different directions. She waited for a while before continuing on in the wolf's body, not wanting to alert the guards to her deception. An hour later, she had made good time and distance. Shapeshifting into the wolf's skin had warmed her, but the shape was unsustainable for long periods in her current state of fatigue. She wished she had thought of this earlier. With a sigh, she transitioned back into her human body.

After more walking, fatigue had settled into her whole body, and she knew she couldn't go on like this much longer. Zita stopped and rested more often, her extremities aching from the cold. She leaned against a tree and took in huge gasps of air. She settled down to rest. Rubbing her numb legs in an attempt to get warm blood into them, the clang of metal and people's voices shattered the quiet of the woods. It could be the guards fixing something as they rested from their search, or it might be the sound of a village. Could it be Crossroads? Excitement coursed through her exhausted body at the thought of safety and warmth.

She slogged through the snow in the direction of the sound. If she found Crossroads, then she had won, but if she found the guards, she would surrender. She couldn't continue in her present condition.

Zita hurried to the edge of the forest and peeked out across the frozen, snow-covered meadow. Her face beamed in the sunshine and the lightness of victory pounded in her chest. The most beautiful sight she had ever seen—majestic mountain peaks hooded in white—climbed to the sky. At the base of the mountains, she saw Crossroad's fortified walls.

She had made it. Tears welled in her eyes and froze where they leaked over the edge and streaked down her face.

She knew she wasn't out of danger yet. The village walls stood a half a mile from her present position, and it appeared that a line of people, horses and carts were waiting at the gates. She narrowed her eyes as she watched the guards examine every person trying to get into the village, and couldn't believe how fast her joy faded. They were checking every person that came into the village.

There had to be a different way into the village. A horse and wagon with two men on the buck boards bounced in the deep pot-holes in the road from Velidred as they headed toward Crossroads.

Zita thought she might hide in the back of the wagon with the goods the men were carrying. The guards wouldn't see her back there and she could jump off after entering the village. It would be perfect

She waited in the tree line until the wagon passed her. She didn't see anybody else behind the wagon, so she left the safety of the forest, and tramped through the snow to reach the road. It took her longer than she expected and when she looked back, the tracks she had left were plain to see.

The king's guards would know she had entered Crossroads, but she saw no other choice. She had nothing left in her body, and reaching the mountain village was her only hope at survival. She hurried to reach the wagon, slipping and sliding on the snowy, icy road. Moments before the wagon reached the waiting line to get into the village, she slipped in next to the left side of the large wagon, walking next to its back wheel.

She examined the wagon bed for room to hide among the cargo. It didn't look good. There were two barrels of alcohol, four boxes of foodstuffs, a cage of chickens and something wrapped that looked like a bolt or two of fabric. She couldn't hide here; she'd stand out to anybody that looked inside the wagon. Why didn't these men cover their goods with a tarp she could hide under?

Zita pressed her lips together as she searched for a solution. The line moved slowly toward the castle gates. She saw the guards remove tarps that lay upon the wagons. It's just as well she didn't try to hide under a tarp. Her muscles tensed as the cart neared the village entrance.

Other travelers tucked into line behind her. She refused to look behind her, for fear of being recognized by someone. Best they didn't see her face.

She peered under the wagon. There wasn't much there to prevent her from being seen. The wagon wasn't fancy in any way. Just a simple box structure sitting on top of a single framing log. There did seem to be a little distance between the box and frame. Maybe she could slip in between those and hide. Were the guards looking under the wagons?

The wagon driver made a clicking sound and the horse moved forward. She had to make a decision or be seen by the guards. Zita ducked under the wagon as it moved and waited until it stopped. Then she tried to position her body along the log frame. She had miscalculated the amount of space available to her as she squeezed onto the narrow log.

She thought she had positioned her body perfectly for the trip into the village, but as soon as the wagon began to move, she wobbled on the log. The wagon hit a rut in the snow and the box above her hit her in the head. She bit her lip to keep from screaming.

The wagon stopped and she saw the village guards begin their search. They interviewed the two guys on the buckboard who convinced the guards they hadn't seen a woman with black hair and green eyes. She hoped no one behind the cart had seen her hair or recognized her in any way. Zita looked down at the ground stifling a cough as her dry mouth begged for water. She held firmly to the wooden frame.

A man asked. "Why are you looking for this person?"

"Haven't you heard? The castle guards claim she killed Prince Krunal. King Haskell's daughter, little Princess Zita, is a murderer."

Zita felt light-headed as blood seemed to rush to her face. Taka had killed the prince and blamed her. Now they wanted her for murder which would prevent her from going back to the castle ever again.

The driver said, "We finally have peace in this section of the world, and Haskell's ugly hand reaches from the grave to squash it."

"Yep, I hope the Council of Nine finds her and executes the murderer."

"I look forward to being in town to watch that. Whoa." The driver pulled on the reins when the horse yanked forward a little.

An itch formed on the back of Zita's neck, but she had no way to reach it without falling from her perch.

The guards finished their questioning of the driver and passenger and started their search of the wagon-bed. Boots slid along the snow next to her as the guards looked for uninvited passengers. Her stomach quivered as the cough caught in her throat became more persistent. *Hurry up guards, I can't stay out here much longer.* Her frozen hands had trouble holding maintaining their grip on the log that she had wrapped her body around.

When the guards reached the back of the wagon Zita peeked back at them. *Good,* she thought. They aren't looking under the wagon.

Staring beyond the guards, she saw a young girl, probably not even a teenager, holding her mother's hand. Zita gasped as the girl looked directly at her and pointed.

One guard asked, "Which tavern are you delivering the whiskey to?"

The driver called back, "The Blue Stegox."

"Did you hear that, Henry? I'm having dinner tonight at the Blue Stegox."

Both guards laughed.

"I hope you find the princess. It'll be a blessing to the goddess of Velidred to see her hang."

Zita's stomach wanted to empty itself, dizziness taking control of her. All of a sudden, she had a thought. Why was she bothering to ride this carriage into the village gates when she had the ability to shapeshift into a dog. Too late now, she feared the noise she'd make getting off the wagon would bring unwanted attention. She had to hold on and prevent the guards from finding her. She shook her head at the girl, praying she would keep her mouth shut and not tell her mom or the guards about Zita's hiding place.

CHAPTER 17

One of the guards smacked the back of the wagon-bed. "You're cleared."

Zita breathed a sigh of relief when the little girl put her arm down as the family moved forward.

The wheels lurched into another rut, and Zita got smacked in the head once more.

She tightened her hands on the wagon post to prevent her being knocked to the ground and leaned low over the rail as the wagon jerked back and forth. She watched for holes where the wagon-bed might bounce and tried to predict them so she could keep from getting knocked off her hiding spot.

The sounds of an active village increased as the wagon passed the village gates. People talking and industrious blacksmiths pounding their metal filled Zita's ears.

With the wagon's movement over the uneven road surface, Zita watched the moving landscape of the ground undulating below her. They traveled some distance into the village before stopping.

Zita's entire body seemed to be frozen onto the log, and that kept her from falling in the yellow puddle of snow and horse manure beneath her. It had definitely been easier to slip into the position than to slide out. She tried to lean left, but her back was stuck. Maybe the wagon-bed's position had changed or had been angled to reduce the amount of space available to her. When she tried to unmount on her right side, her arm had wedged into a position that made it impossible to move it.

The men began unloading the goods and the wagon bounced up and down as one of them jumped onto the wagon-bed. Zita slid left as it bounced up and fell into the yellow snow. Some kids standing on the boardwalk laughed at her as she crawled from beneath the wagon.

The wagon men didn't seem to notice her, and she moved toward one of the shops to get her bearings. She thought her best opportunity for help would come from Master Wizard Ishwa's old training center. That's where she had heard Alpherge went after they rescued the stone warriors. She still needed to get to the training center without alerting the guards to her presence in Crossroads.

Risking recognition, Zita had to ask a couple of the residents who were doing their daily chores to get directions to the training center. She maintained her gaze on the ground as she asked, hoping they didn't notice her green eyes. They seemed to think she was a homeless person, and she made progress and finally found it.

When she reached the building, it was only a burnt-out shell. Zita felt lightheaded as her hands dropped to her side, and her posture slumped. The hope of finding her friend Alpherge had driven her to this place. She stared with an open mouth at the destruction of her hope for sanctuary and safety. Where did they set up the new training facility?

If she had to wander around the village for any length of time to find the new training facility, someone would spot her and report her to the guards.

Her options were limited. *Who will know where the new magic training center was located? The Magic Shoppe owner will know, but he'll also recognize me. Can I trust the man?* She knew he didn't like her father because laws enacted by her dad limited the number of magic items the man could sell. There were no other options, though. She couldn't ask every person in the village where to find the center. She had to sneak to the Magic Shoppe and hope for the best.

The shop wasn't far, and after a couple of wrong turns she found the place. When she opened the door, a little bell rang on the counter, operated by magic of course. The dark shop felt warm, and she moved to the fireplace in the corner of the room. Being out of the wind brought her great joy, but the heat from the fireplace absolutely thrilled her. She listened absentmindedly to the crackle of the fireplace, and watched the ascent of burning incense drift in the air.

Zita stood facing the fireplace and didn't notice the man that walked up behind her.

"May I help you?" a man's voice startled her.

Zita turned quickly. She wished she had a hooded cloak to hide her face. She averted her eyes as she recognized the shop's owner. She dropped her head a little so her long hair could hide most of her face. Zita looked at the soiled smelly clothes she wore. *Maybe my disheveled appearance will help me hide.*

"I'm looking for the magic training center," Zita said. "I want to become a student."

The small man sniffed the air. "I don't believe they are taking on new students at this time. They told me to send any students back home."

She had a small hitch in her breath as her chest restricted. "I've come a long way, maybe they can provide room and board for a small price, and I'll return home tomorrow."

He studied her as he lifted a single eyebrow. "You look familiar. What's your family name?"

Panic rolled through her body as the thought of being recognized by the man worried her. She needed a convincing lie. "My cousin is Alpherge Greystone. People say we have a slight resemblance."

The shop owner put a finger on his lower lip and shook his head. "No, that's not it."

Her eyes narrowed. "Just tell me where the building is and I'll leave you to your work. Let them tell me they don't want to see me."

His eyes flitted over to a picture lying flat on his counter. The word's "Wanted for Murder" written in large font at the top of the page.

Zita's muscles quivered as she recognized a poorly drawn penciled picture of her. She felt the scorpion move across her eye. She didn't dare let it take control. This man had stature in the wizarding world and would lead the guards right to her.

She asked, "Where did you say I can find the building?"

Heat flushed through her body and she tensed her still-tired muscles ready to run once more. She expected this man had plans to capture her and call the guards. To defend herself, she prepared to throw up a shield to protect her from any magic traps the man might use to delay her departure.

The shop owner walked behind the counter and rummaged through some paper. Then he pulled out one of the documents and plopped it on the counter. He unrolled the pages and a map of the village of Crossroads appeared.

She glanced behind her to verify no one else occupied the room with them, and she felt some relief from the building tension in her body.

Moving his fingers over the map, he finally stopped at a location. "You are here. The training center is three blocks this way in an abandoned stable. It used to be a red building, not so much anymore."

Zita looked at the man's wrinkled face. "Thank you!"

"Be careful, Zita."

She felt a sharp stab of tension in her neck. The man recognized her. Would he let her go or not? She stared at the man, but his face gave her no clue if he planned to capture her as she left the shop.

She hurried out of the shop and turned left. She thought it lucky that the magic training center's direction was opposite that of the village gates.

In a few minutes, she knocked on the training center door, thinking back to the first time she had visited Wizard Ishwa's facility. She had come here with Alpherge, Erik and Sherry as they searched for Lily, though her purpose then had been to send them back to Earth. That plan failed, and after that she strove to hinder their plans, to make them too late to save their friend Lily. Zita had failed in both goals. The blind wizard Ishwa had known who she was, though she didn't know how he had figured it out.

Later on, Zita had been the one who alerted Kestrel of the location of the training center which eventually led to Ishwa's death. She didn't realize they had burned of the building. She hoped that wouldn't prevent the wizards who trained here now from allowing her sanctuary until she could figure out what to do. She had a target on her back and had to watch out for people who believed the lies Taka had disseminated.

She waited for the door to open while she watched for people who might recognize her. Eventually someone came to the door. It opened, and there stood Alpherge. Zita wanted to jump into his arms and hug him. The face of a friend.

Al asked, "May I help you?"

Zita pushed to get into the building as she whispered, "It's me. Zita."

Al must not have recognized her, because he didn't move, using his tall body to block the entrance. She wasn't surprised. She had to have lost weight, her hair fell disheveled across her face, and she smelled like horse piss.

"Zita?" Al's eyes went wide as an expression of disbelief played across his face.

"Yes. Let me in." She shoved past him into the room.

As her eyes adjusted to the dark room, she recognized two wizards, Jayanti and Blayze. These two had been held captive in her father's dungeon, and Blayze had been a thorn in her side from the very beginning.

Al shut the door and walked over to her. "What are you doing here?"

Blayze approached her with a scowl on his face. "Forget that; why did you kill Prince Krunal?"

"I didn't. I'm being framed by Takatavara."

Blayze laughed. "Why would a long-standing member of the Council of Nine kill the prince and then blame you?"

A fire burned in the large brick fireplace, and Zita gravitated to it, her fingers and toes already tingling in pain. "Because he wants to be king. I helped him find the Imperium Wand and now he wants to take over Velidred Kingdom."

Jayanti said, "The Imperium Wand is a legend."

"It is real and apparently my father had it in his possession. Taka forced me to find it for him." Zita looked up at Al; the teenage wizard towered over her. "You have to believe me. I didn't kill the prince."

"Doesn't matter if we believe you or not." Blayze said, "If someone saw you come in here and we don't give you to the guards, we'll be just as guilty as you."

Jayanti nodded. "You've put us in a bad position."

"Give me a day or two to get my bearings and figure out where I can hide."

Blayze shook his head. "No, we should report you immediately to the authorities. We're at risk of being hanged with you."

Zita stared into Al's eyes. Surely the big dope would believe her and protect her. She felt the red scorpion crawl across her eye.

"What's wrong with your eye?" Al asked.

Zita shut her eyes. It's nothing. I injured it while running in the forest at night.

"Maybe we should call in the healer." Al said.

"No! No healers; it'll be fine."

Zita wondered if the Corruption of Evil might help her convince these people to help her. Sure, it worked on the bunny, but not the stronger minds of the wolves. She would need to hone her skills with it, but not now, not today.

"Can you at least let me bathe and help me find some clean clothes?"

Blayze held his hand over his nose. "Yeah. We will have to burn your clothes, both to keep any evidence of you being here and because you stink. It smells as if you have been sleeping with horses."

"No, I've been running for my life for the last two days. I need your help and protection. I promise I didn't kill the prince. He was making things better in the castle. I had no need to kill him." She hoped they would buy that lie, because in truth, she was happy he was dead, just sorry that she had been blamed for it.

Al looked at the others. "Can we protect her for a couple of days."

"No," Blayze answered quickly.

Jayanti looked at Al, Zita and Blayze. "We should help her for a few hours, anyway. We know the Velidred castle is known for being dishonest in situations like this."

Zita said, "Yes, and they are lying now."

Blayze shook his head. "We can't let her stay here. It's too dangerous for us."

Al stood closer to Blayze. "She's our friend and actually helped us in the dungeon. Without her, you and Jayanti would both be dead."

"It's not right," Blayze said.

"Let's wash her up, get a meal in her, and then we can send her on her way," Jayanti said.

Based on his expression, Blayze wasn't buying it, but he nodded slightly.

Jayanti took Zita's elbow to lead her to the baths. "Oh, you're so cold. We'll make a warm bath for you."

# # # #

Alpherge stood next to a bookshelf that contained scrolls, books, and bottles of potions in the Wizard Training Center's small conference room. His staff stood in the corner of the room. He needed to find out if Zita had killed Prince Krunal. The prince had been King Haskell's enemy, so it made sense that Zita held animosity toward the guy, but at the celebration after they had rescued the stone warriors, the prince and Zita had spent time talking and appeared to have been friends. Prince Krunal had agreed to allow her to stay in the castle while she studied magic with a couple of the elders there.

Blayze shrugged a warm cloak over his shoulders.

Alpherge asked, "Where are you going?"

Blayze said, "I'm going to get the guards. There's a bounty on her head, and the training center can use the money." Blayze adjusted his coat a little tighter.

"We can't turn her in. They'll kill her without a trial," Al said. "If a member of the Council of Nine accuses her of murder, there's no way anyone would believe her side of the story. That could just as easily be you."

"It's dangerous for us to protect her. All it'll take is for one person to see her and say something." One of Blayze's eyebrows twitched. "The guards might be on their way toward us already."

"Give her time. A day to warm up and tell us her side of the story. She's my friend. Let's give her the benefit of the doubt until we know more."

"No. It's too dangerous." Blayze put his hand on the door handle and twisted the handle.

Al tried to think of something to say to make Blayze stop. He hoped Zita was innocent, but once the guards got her . . .. "Wait."

"For what? We have a murderer in the house. You might be next."

Al grabbed Blayze's arm, "I spent time with her in the mountains. She didn't kill the prince."

"How can you be sure? I'm in charge of the house, I won't allow her to stay here."

Al stared at the fireplace at the flickering flames.

"Then we'll send her on her way, but let's feed her, warm her up, and get her the proper clothes to travel in the winter. We'll send her to Kestrel's place in the mountains."

Blayze smirked and rolled his eyes. "You're worried that if I give her to the guards, she'll die. After this last snow, she'll never make it into the mountains. It's either she dies in the winter mountains or at the Velidred castle."

Al felt his blood pressure rise. There had to be some solution that would help Zita in the short term. Beads of sweat built on his forehead in the warm room. Blayze had never liked Zita, and they always seemed to have differing opinions on all things magic. She had saved his life before, and he thought it important to cut her some slack until they heard her whole story. Plus, he wanted time to check out her eyes. Something about them unnerved him.

Blayze opened the door and took a step outside.

Al grabbed his arm and pulled him back into the room. "Not yet. Give her six hours to rest and then you can go get the guards."

"We shouldn't."

"Six hours. We owe her that much." That wasn't much time, but maybe she could convince them of her innocence, and then that would present other solutions. Al knew of a secret compartment where they might be able to hide her. Surely the others would allow Zita to hide there. But Blayze was right, if one person had seen Zita enter their building, then they would all be branded as accessories to her crime.

CHAPTER 18

Two hours later, Al, Jayanti and Blayze sat across from Zita in one of the small training rooms. Al fidgeted on the bench, bouncing his leg up and down as he leaned forward, his elbows on the table, across from Zita. He wanted to check out her eye; he knew something wasn't right. It was too soon to give her up to the castle guards, but he needed to know more about what he suspected he saw in her eye.

Zita had washed up, received clean clothes and been fed. Angry red scratches marred her face from her journey through the snowy forest. She fingered a necklace, a magical focusing device that Al knew her mother had given her.

"We can't allow you to stay here." Blayze shook his head.

"I know." Zita rubbed her palms over her eyes, then looked pleadingly at Al. "Just a few days, so I can make plans. I'm willing to chance hiking into the mountains in winter, but I need time to rest and get my strength back."

Before Al decided, he wanted to weigh the pros and cons of letting her stay. He couldn't just kick her out into the cold. He had to offer her some form of hope. Like Zita, he also wanted a day or two to find the right solution to hide her from certain death.

"Please help me; you don't know what I've been through the last few days." Zita recounted all the things that had happened and how Sims and Dakarai had forced her to find the Imperium Wand. "Dakarai and Taka can block magic."

Jayanti leaned in closer to Zita. "I've heard of that incantation, but I've never known anyone who could cast it."

Zita said, "I think Taka learned it from the desert-people and taught Dakarai."

Al raised his eyebrows. "The desert-people?"

"Nomads of the desert," Jayanti explained. "Taka is from there. Two hundred miles east of here there is a mountain plateau that gets little rain. The Velidred Mountain Range pulls all the moisture out of the air and the plateau is dry."

Blayze looked at Jayanti and then back at Al. "You two are just delaying the inevitable. We must send her back out into the village."

Al rubbed the back of his neck and felt sweat forming on his body. "We agreed on six hours."

"A number of our trainees have seen her. Any one of them might have snuck out of the training center and be bringing guards over here right now." Blayze's eyes were cold and hard as he slammed his palm onto the table. "As soon as this meeting is over, I'm personally finding a guard."

Al jumped at the noise when Blayze hit the table, and he felt his fingernails biting into his closed fist. He looked at Zita. "What else can you tell us?" As he stared into her eyes, he saw the scorpion crawling across her iris and settling onto the wide black pupil. "You have the Corruption of Evil!"

Jayanti gasped.

Zita grabbed her stomach as if in pain.

Blayze stood up. "She's trying to manipulate us. Isn't that what Gadiel used to do?"

Al remembered back to his time with Gadiel. The old businessman did force Al to do some things he didn't want to do. Most especially, the Fire and Ice challenge that almost killed Al and then the tattoo on his shoulder that marked him as Gadiel's. Once the old man had died the power over him had stopped.

"I'm not trying to manipulate you. I don't have Gadiel's power. That's why I came to see Alpherge." Zita reached across the table and grabbed his hands. "You must help me. You, Erik and one of you," she nodded at Jayanti and Blayze, "can use the Sword of Freedom and suck the evil out of me."

Blayze stood and moved away from the table. "Why are we even waiting? Of course, the Corruption of Evil forced her to kill the prince. We would expect nothing else. She's as sure as confessed to his murder. We must turn her in before she manipulates us to believe her."

Zita shook her head. "I don't even have control over it. Alpherge, you believe me, don't you?"

Moments of doubt trembled through his body. The Corruption of Evil might have forced her to kill the prince though he really didn't know how it worked. Was it something that controlled her or just allowed her to control others? "How did it happen?"

Zita rubbed her hands together. "I don't know. I think something happened when we rescued the warriors. As we closed off the magic, a discharge of energy struck me. Maybe I have the Corruption of Evil, but I don't know how to use it to my advantage. It definitely didn't make me kill the prince."

"I'm not sitting here with her." Blayze stepped back two paces. "She'll have me barking like a dog."

Jayanti pointed at the bench. "Don't be stupid. I don't think it works like that. Sit down."

Blayze backed toward the door.

"Please help me get rid of it. We took it from Gadiel and we thought it was encased in the Sword of Freedom. I need your help."

"Erik has the Sword of Freedom. He's somewhere in the mountains. There's no way he can get down here before

Spring." Al got up from the bench and went over to Blayze. "Come on, sit back down, and help us figure this out." He pushed the older wizard toward the table.

"I'm not going down with you three. I'll see you all rot in the underworld before helping you."

Al held tight to Blayze as he forced their leader back to the bench.

Al asked, "Can you promise not to use that evil to manipulate us to do your will?"

"I don't have that power."

"You wore the Helmet of Justice when we removed the evil from Gadiel. Where is that now?" Al asked.

Zita snorted, "I sent it with Finn to his place in the mountains. We figured it would be safest with him."

Al pursed his lips. "Without the Sword of Freedom and the Helmet of Justice, we might not be able to help you."

Zita looked at her hands crossed on the table. "I read in a scroll in the Velidred library how the Crystal of Zaraboth might be used to remove the Corruption of Evil."

"Impossible!" Jayanti said.

Blayze shook his head. "Even if it was real and not just a legend, how could we even find it?"

Al looked at the wizards in the room, "I believe it is real. Master Wizard Ishwa told me my grandfather, Alpherge the Great, died trying to retrieve it. If a mighty wizard like my grandfather couldn't get it, what chance do we have?"

Zita pleaded with Al, her feverish, over-bright eyes making the scorpion dance, "You have to do something to help me."

Al wanted to help Zita. Erik, his friend from Earth, liked Zita, even though they hadn't seen each other since Erik went back to studying to be a Pankratios priest. Still, he knew Erik would want him to help Zita, but he didn't know how.

"She's manipulating you Al. Don't listen to her." Blayze moved toward the door. "I don't care what you say. I'm getting the guards. If you don't want her to be caught, get her out of here before I get back."

"Blayze, come back!" Al shouted.

Blayze walked out the door and slammed it shut.

Al's chest tightened as he thought of his choices. He glanced at Jayanti who stared at Zita's eye. "Come with me," Al grabbed Zita's arm.

"Where are you taking her?" Jayanti asked.

"It's best you don't know. Do you have a cloak that we can use to hide her face?"

"I can find one." Jayanti slowly rose from the bench.

"Hurry! We don't have much time. As it is, the guards will know she's with me." Al felt a heaviness in his stomach. He shouldn't be taking this risk. If Zita had murdered the man who would be king, it would heighten the stakes if he got involved with her.

Al grabbed his cloak and ran with Zita into the kitchen. They grabbed food that didn't require special storage and stuffed it into his pockets.

"You don't have to take this risk. Let me go on my own."

"No, we're going to hide you, but we have to be prepared to go on the run."

Jayanti came into the kitchen with a cloak. "Here, this should help."

Zita threw it on and gave Jayanti a hug. "Thanks."

Jayanti nodded. "Don't worry Al, I won't tell the guards that Zita is with you."

Al grabbed Jayanti by the shoulders. "Tell them the truth. Let's limit the number of people who will be in trouble if we get caught."

He pushed Zita out the back door and grabbed her arm. "We go west, away from the village gates. The guards will be coming in that direction."

Zita asked, "Where are you taking me?"

Al smirked. His strategy would get his best friend, Sherry, in more trouble with the Crossroads village officials. She had been doing everything possible to keep the people happy, and she wasn't going to be pleased to see Zita with him. "Don't worry about where we're going, just keep up."

They ran two blocks west and then headed north. The guards blew whistles in the distance and Al hurried. He heard Zita sucking in air behind him, but they needed to be clear of the area before the guards reached the training center. *Why did Blayze have to get so high and mighty? They could have hidden Zita for two days or even a week with no problem.* Al knew his actions forced him deep into the conspiracy now, no matter what happened after this.

CHAPTER 19

When Al and Zita reached Sherry's place, they were breathing hard in the crisp, cold mountain air. Al figured Sherry would be livid when he told her the problem. This might be the fight that broke up their relationship, which had been on rocky ground anyway since Al hadn't spent much time with her. He hoped she would be happy to see him.

The guards were blowing their whistles, and the piercing sounds echoed off the buildings and distant mountains.

Al knocked on the door, but didn't wait for a response. He opened the door and pushed Zita into the room.

Sherry sat on the floor with a young girl who attended her little school when Al and Zita entered the small cabin.

Al had hoped her teaching would be over for the day, and they could talk, but it looked like Sherry was still tutoring a child. Teaching the young boys and girls of Crossroads had gotten her arrested for crimes against the village, and it wasn't until she helped the village get clean fresh mountain water that they allowed her to educate the local children.

"Zita, what are you doing here?" Sherry asked.

And there it was. Now the little kid knew who was with Al. They couldn't hide here.

Sherry rose from the dirt floor, where letters and numbers had been scrawled into the dirt, and gave Al a quick kiss. "What's going on?" She looked between Al and Zita.

"Let me explain," Al said. "We need somewhere to hide." He almost said Zita, but he realized that he couldn't go back to the training center. They both needed a hiding place now.

Sherry's nostrils flared and she raised her hands skyward. "You can't hide here. It's a one room cabin."

Al ran a hand through his hair. "Yeah, I see that."

Sherry looked down at her young student. "Let me take Ruby home. I'll be right back." She packed up Ruby and huffed out the door.

"She's right." Zita shook her head and moved toward the door. "We can't stay here."

"Wait, Sherry is better at thinking in difficult situations. Let's wait for her to return. Maybe—"

"She isn't going to have a solution." Zita bit her lower lip. "The only solution is for me to run into the mountains and hope no one finds me for the next ten to twenty years."

Al muttered to himself as he tried to think of somewhere to hide her. He sat down on the bench by the kitchen table. The cabin was cool. Sherry didn't make much money from her teaching and couldn't afford much wood for heat.

Zita rubbed the back of her neck, twisted her necklace in her fingers, bounced a foot, and rocked in place as they waited for Sherry's return.

Whistles still sounded in the village as the Crossroad's guards continued their search for Prince Krunal's killer.

Al felt the tension in the air. They didn't know if Sherry would return first, or the guards would figure out where he took her. His own feet restlessly bounced on the dirt floor.

The door opened and cold air blasted into the cabin. Al jumped up and instinctively formed a shield. Thankfully, Sherry entered.

Sherry asked, "Did you kill the king?"

Zita's voice rose in pitch, "No. I'm being framed by a wizard named Taka."

There had always been some tension between Zita and Sherry. Al began to regret bringing her here.

"If they think Zita is with you, where do you think they'll look first?" Sherry asked. "Right here! Al, I've been educating these kids for just a few months, and you're going to ruin everything."

"Can you recommend where I can take her?"

Sherry put her hands on her hips. "Take her to the guards, and make peace with them."

"I can't do that. She's innocent."

"So, your best solution was to get me involved?" Sherry's face reddened to almost match her fiery hair.

Al felt his throat tighten, and he lowered his gaze to the floor. He realized bringing Zita here had only made things worse. "I'll find someplace else." He turned toward the door.

"Wait, I have a plan." Sherry squeezed her lips tight and looked at Zita. "It probably won't work, but it's the best I can think of at the moment. We can go to Triponca and visit my friend Paxton. He has hidden people for years at his house."

Al didn't like the idea that the first person Sherry thought of was Paxton. He got the feeling that Paxton liked Sherry. Feelings of jealousy arose in his mind, despite the merits of her idea.

Zita nodded, "Lead the way."

"Not so fast. He lives up in the mountains, and we can't just take the road. The guards will be searching along the roads between Crossroads and every little village within ten miles. I'm going to send him a message. You two go on toward Triponca. Maybe he can send one of his workers in our direction with a horse and meet us. If the guards see us, we don't stand a chance."

Al grunted, "Okay." His brain numbed as he thought of Paxton saving Sherry one more time. Another bad decision on his part. He felt like everything he did failed his friend.

The whistles sounded closer than before.

Sherry lightly touched him on the shoulder, "Go, now. When you reach the road to Triponca, hide in the woods until I can get there."

Sherry didn't give him a peck on the cheek or any sign that she was okay with this decision. Al pushed Zita out the door, and they turned to the village gates that faced Triponca.

Sherry's shout stopped them. "No, not that way. Go south. There's a small gate that's only manned by one guard. Use magic or whatever you need to exit through that gate."

They headed south as Sherry ran toward the village messenger service.

Al wondered if she would actually come with them. She could just say she hadn't seen us, but then he remembered Ruby. The little kid would remember. Sherry had committed to Zita's cause whether she wanted to or not.

Zita and Al kept their faces hooded and hurried to the southern gate trying to go fast without being noticed by any villagers that might see them. Al kept looking left and right trying to move his eyes without exposing any of his face. He hoped no one would automatically recognize him, since he carried his staff. They stopped when they neared the gate, and hid behind a corner of a building.

Five guards were stationed at the gate.

Zita whispered, "How do we get past that group?"

"You heard Sherry, use magic."

"I'm afraid to use my magic. Dakarai and Taka have the ability to sense when I use it, and then they might identify where I am."

Al shook his head, his unsettled stomach jumping with acid. He couldn't just blast the guards; they were trying to sneak out, not notify every guard in the village of their whereabouts. He kept looking around, sure that someone tracked his every move.

Al considered sending Zita to the gate and having her use her scorpion powers to trick the men into letting them go, but she claimed she couldn't wield that power. He had seen the scorpion flit across her eye but maybe she hadn't learned how to wield it.

Zita said, "I don't know what you're planning, but maybe you can cast a spell to muffle any sound we might make before you blow something up."

Whistles sounded closer, like they were moving in their direction. The guards must have given up at the magic training center and the noise had alerted men at this gate.

Great, thought Al. He racked his mind trying to come up with a spell that could help them get past the guards. With an idea in mind, Al asked, "What noise would the guards make if they were to find you?"

"Are you going to turn me in?" Zia asked.

"No, but we could blanket the area with a muffle sound spell and then cast a spell to make the guards at the gate think that we've been found. They'll leave their spot and then we can escape."

"No, that'll take too long. More guards will be at this gate in just moments. Do something."

Al saw a teenage boy looking at him and Zita. Al cast the muffle sound spell, "Obvolvere sonitum."

The whistles of the approaching guards stopped. Zita raised her eyebrows and nodded at Al.

Then Al called out, "Volatilia caeli volant, volant." Which roughly translated to "Birds of the sky, fly, fly, fly." He pushed out his hand and birds dashed from the sky at the guards. Then he waved his staff. "Follow the birds." He didn't think the spell would work.

The guards hadn't heard the birds coming, then suddenly, they were engulfed with winged pigeons swarming around their heads. With another wave of Al's hand, the birds flew down a side street that ran along the castle wall. The guards chased after the little birds.

As soon as they were out of sight, Al and Zita hurried to the gate only to find that the guards had placed a heavy chain and lock to secure the gate. Zita pointed down the street. "More guards are coming."

There were magical solutions to manipulate a lock like this. Al had used them at home when playing D&D with his friends. Now, his mind went blank. Nothing came to him.

Zita said, "Open the gate!"

"I can't think of the right spell." His mouth turned dry. The guards would arrive any moment and they would throw Al into the dungeon with Zita to await their execution.

"Are you serious? You've been doing magic how long, and you don't know any pick lock commands?"

"I know a lot of different spells; I just can't think of the perfect incantation right now."

Zita looked back at the advancing guards. "Get out of the way." She pushed Al to the side and placed her hands on the lock. "Glas oscailte!"

Al watched as the lock opened and the chains flew off the door. Zita pushed open the door where three guards waited on the other side. They pointed spears at the two wizards.

Without thinking, Al threw up a shield and produced a strong wind which he directed at the guards. They tried to fight against the wind, but it blew too strong and created an opening that Zita and Al managed to escape through.

They charged across the snow-covered road which ran alongside the Crossroads' Village walls. Al had planned to run down the road thinking it would be faster, but Zita grabbed his arm and pulled him into the forest with her. A quick glance behind and Al saw seven guards chasing them.

Al felt like his heart wanted to jump out of his ribcage as they sprinted into the forest. He realized he should have listened to Blayze and just turned Zita over to the guards. His breath came in huge bursts as they jumped fallen limbs and ran around bushes. Al was no athlete and wouldn't be able to keep up this pace for long.

Zita pushed him to his right. "Watch out for the large boulder." They moved right just as an arrow whooshed by them, missing them by inches. "Crossbows!"

He wanted to throw Zita to the ground and just let the guards catch them, but fear and adrenaline drove him deeper into the forest. The guards were probably trained to run in deep snow and for long distances, but Al suspected he would exhaust his capabilities in the next twenty yards. They needed a new plan to escape.

"How are your shapeshifting skills?" Al asked.

"They're fine, but we can't shapeshift now. They'll know it's us and just kill us with an arrow to the chest."

"Can you turn us into an inanimate object like a log on the forest floor?"

"We can't run away as logs."

Al wheezed, "We want them to see us, but not realize they are seeing us."

"Oh, you want to become invisible."

"Yeah, can you do that?"

Another arrow swooshed over their heads and planted itself into a tree.

Zita said, "An arrow will still have the power to kill us if we shapeshift into logs."

"They won't know it's us, if we do it right."

Zita shook her head. "Our footprints will just stop where we fall."

"We'll make them think we climbed a tree and are somehow flying from tree to tree. I'll make noises." He barely got out that last sentence as his lungs cried for air.

"We can try. There's a large birch just behind those three pine trees. Go behind the pines then dive into the snow and try to get under the snow. I'll shapeshift you as you are in the air. Make no noise or we're both dead."

They ran around the pine trees and were momentarily hidden from their pursuers.

"Okay here goes." Al ran toward the birch tree and at the last moment dove past it, sliding six feet as he plowed through the snow. When he landed his whole body felt stiff. He couldn't move. If they found Zita and killed her, would her spell last forever and he'd be a log until his body disintegrated or he starved to death?

Quiet fell on the area for half a minute before the guards showed up. They stopped at the birch tree, and were breathing as hard as Al had been just moments before. He wondered if he still breathed as a log.

"Where did they go?"

"Looks like they ran up the tree here. The last tracks lead right to this tree."

Al used magic to make noises in the trees to sound like a squirrel was scurrying along the branches. He hadn't had time to study the forest to know if other trees were close enough for Zita and him to navigate from this lone birch.

"Sounds like they're running along the canopy."

"I don't see them. Are they invisible?"

Yes, we are, Al thought.

The soldiers milled around the area, many gasping for breath. They walked near Al. One guard kicked a log, which was Al. He swallowed hard, trying not to cry out in pain. He hadn't imagined it would hurt if someone kicked him when he imitated a log.

"I don't see them. We should head back to the gates."

"What do you think we'll tell the mayor?"

One man plopped on top of Al's back almost causing Al to grunt from the force of impact. He hoped nobody else used him as a couch or he'd be in big trouble.

Another sat down on Al's legs squeezing them against the ground. He lit a cigarette and began smoking. "We'll tell them they're wizards, and we lost them, because they used their wizard skills."

Al struggled to stay silent as the weight of the men seemed to increase each moment.

The men talked between themselves for a few minutes. One of them had checked out the pine trees and even walked toward the sounds Al had sent through the trees.

Eventually, he commented, "They're not here. I don't know where they went. Let's go home boys."

The two guys sitting on top of Al struggled to their feet. The one threw his cigarette butt onto Al and the lighted end burned him slightly before the wet snow snuffed it.

As they had just about left the area a guard asked, "What are you doing George?"

All of a sudden, Al felt a sharp pain go through his thigh.

"Practicing my arrow shooting."

"Come on. We can practice somewhere warm. It's time for an ale."

Al heard the sound of the trigger mechanism releasing a second arrow which glanced off his shoulder just inches from his neck.

"Ha! You missed it."

"I'll get it this time."

Where will the next arrow hit me? Al's heartbeat thrashed in his ears. *I should have listened to Blayze.*

CHAPTER 20

Al's body had grown cold as he lay in the wet snow after shapeshifting into an inanimate log. He willed with all his might for the guard not to shoot another arrow at the log—the log that wasn't a log, but his flesh and blood body. He closed his eyes hoping the arrow wouldn't hit any major organs or arteries or for sure he would die.

The guard released the arrow and Al heard it fly. A loud thwack sounded in the forest. He didn't feel as if he had been hit and he breathed a silent sigh of relief, followed quickly by the realization that it might have struck Zita. She lay as a nearby log in the snow, and if the arrow killed her, Al might die anyway since he didn't have the ability to shapeshift back into a human by himself. He felt panic begin to set in waiting for the soldiers to leave.

"Pick up your arrows, it's time to go back to the village and warm up."

Al felt a foot on his rib cage as the man pulled the arrow out of his leg. He forced himself not to gasp at the pain when he removed it. The man stepped over him and picked up the arrow that had missed Al's neck. They tramped off back to the village. He wondered how long he would live and hoped the animals wouldn't disembowel his body at night.

How long should I wait to call Zita? She has to still be alive; I can't die like this.

A couple of minutes passed and Zita walked over to him.

"Are you okay?" She asked.

"No. Hurry up and transform me back into a human. A guard shot me in the leg with an arrow."

Zita said a few words and Al shapeshifted back into his human form.

His leg hurt and he sat up to check the injury. Blood oozed out of the wound and dripped onto the snow. He pressed his hand onto the injury to stop the bleeding. *This is it. The arrow hit a vein and I'm going to die. I should have agreed with Blayze and turned Zita over to the authorities.*

"Move your hand and let me look," Zita said.

"No, it's over for me. Run to the meeting spot with Sherry. Don't let her get caught. Maybe send Paxton over to retrieve my body in a couple of days when it's safe." If it took Paxton more than a couple of days to find him, then maybe the vultures would pick at his flesh once the smell of death had begun. *Will they start feeding before I died?*

"Come on. It can't be that bad." Zita bent in the snow to check on the injury. "Move your hand so I can examine it."

Al moved his hand.

"Yeah, it's a jagged wound with a lot of blood."

"I knew it." He stared at the blood that had pooled on the ground. "I'm going to die."

She dabbed at the site with a cloth, pressing it hard and then releasing it. It's just a surface wound."

"No. I'm sure it's over for me." Al thought about his life choices to this moment. He'd never see Sherry ever again. "Do you think a tourniquet would help?"

"Give it a few more minutes and see if it clots on its own. If not, then we try more extreme measures."

Al took shallow breaths as he worried about his leg and how this would affect him long term. Maybe, he would live, but be forced to go to a crazy doctor that used rusty instruments and would recommend to have his leg amputated.

"Relax. I won't let you die." Zita ripped material from her tunic. She wrapped the strip around Al's injured leg. "That should hold. Come on. We need to get to the meeting site before Sherry thinks we've been captured."

# # # #

"Just keep moving." All the walking, running, and hiding over the last few days had left Zita's body empty. A numbness permeated her mind as they crawled over another downed tree in the forest. How had she fallen so far? It was her father's fault.

They traveled through the forest with Al using his staff to help him walk. The wound hadn't clotted completely, and it dripped blood onto the forest snow.

Al said, "If the guards come back to the location where they lost us, they're going to see our tracks and see that one of us is injured."

Zita whacked at a low hanging tree branch and said through gritted teeth, "Don't worry about that. Move!"

Two years ago, she had been a pampered princess. She could walk to the village shops and buy whatever she wanted, jewelry or clothing, it didn't matter. She lacked for nothing. Then her father had decided to bring the children who had escaped to Earth back to this planet. Nothing was the same, and Zita hated what her life had become. Now, guards hunted her like an animal for a crime she didn't commit.

They stomped through the snow parallel to the road but far enough away not to be easily seen. They had walked for an hour and sunset neared.

Al whispered, "Get down, soldiers are coming."

Zita crouched low in the snow as voices drifted from the road. This was the third time soldiers had passed them. They would never leave the road, but searched the forested areas.

"Over there!" One soldier pointed in Zita's direction.

The group's commander said, "Set up to release arrows."

Zita's pulsed quickened. They were sitting ducks at this distance. They had been so careful. It had to be Alpherge. His height must have given them away.

The commander shouted, "Release."

The twang of strings releasing and the whirring of arrows flying through the leafless forest canopy upset the quiet twilight.

Three deer bounded past Zita's position heading in the direction they had just traveled.

One soldier laughed. "That's not our killer, unless she turned herself into a deer."

Zita waited to move until the soldiers continued on toward Crossroads. She stood searching for any guards that might have stayed behind, but saw no one. She touched Al on the shoulder.

The sun's remaining rays colored the horizon with a red-orange hue. A stegox howled in the distance.

"I have to stop." Al stopped and looked at his leg. "My leg is hurting too much."

"We can't stop, we have to keep moving. If we miss the meetup with Sherry and Paxton, then what will we do?" Zita felt a tightness in her jaw. This was the tenth time Al had stopped because his leg hurt. Her whole body hurt, even her hair follicles caused her pain. They couldn't keep stopping.

"Give me a second to rebind the cloth."

They stopped as Al unwound the blood-covered cloth strip. She thought the injury had clotted, but it must have reopened while they jumped over logs and rocks. The blood once again trickled down his leg.

Zita began to realize another problem they were going to have. Stegox had very sensitive noses to animals that were bleeding. The trail of blood would lead the animals right to them. Plus, it was winter time and food might be difficult to find, which meant they'd be hungry.

"I can't re-use this cloth." He waved it in the air. "It's too covered in blood."

Zita squeezed her eyes shut. She regretted having to tell Al about the stegox because the big guy worried about everything, but he needed to know. She grabbed his cloak and pulled him to her.

"Listen!"

A stegox roared west of them. Then another roared from the south.

"Yeah, what are those?" Al asked.

"Those are stegox."

Al's shoulders slumped.

"They have great noses for blood."

Al's mouth gaped.

"Rip off a piece of cloth from your tunic. Wrap your leg as fast as you can and then we have to move. Those animals are fast when they know easy, injured prey is near."

She had never seen Al move so fast. He ripped off a jagged strip of cotton, wrapped it around the injury leg, and tied it tight.

"Okay. It's fixed. Let's go."

They hurried through the forest. Zita tried to determine if the stegox were gaining on them each time she heard them roar. She worried that with darkness coming they might miss their meetup spot with Sherry. It's not like they could yell her name to find her. The guards were just as likely to hear them as Sherry.

Zita wondered how they were all going to meet. First, they needed to find Sherry, but even after they found her, how would they know where and when to meet Paxton? This plan seemed even more unlikely to work than her original plan to get Alpherge to help her. She wouldn't last another night in the forest.

They continued to sneak through the forest as darkness fell upon the sky. The Anticletus moon had risen and the Velidred moon peeked over the horizon. Anticletus provided a white light bright enough to produce shadows in the trees. Zita hoped it stayed dark enough for them to stay hidden in the forest.

"We should move closer to the road," Al said. "How else will we find Sherry?"

They heard voices coming from the road.

"Quick to that holly bush over there." She dropped behind the bush and listened.

Guards stood at the intersection of the road from Crossroads and the road to Triponca. There were five of them and they had created a fire to keep warm while they guarded the intersection.

Al whispered, "This is where we're supposed to meet."

"Where is Sherry?"

"I don't know. It's not like she could just waltz down the road. She had to get out of the village and probably run through the forest like we did."

A stegox roared in the forest behind Al and Zita. It seemed to be fewer than a hundred yards from their position in the forest.

Zita's legs went weak, dropping her to her knees. She felt light-headed as she rocked back and forth. Would it be easier to give herself up to the guards or get eaten by the stegox?

Al leaned over to her. "Are you all right?"

She shook her head and loosened the collar of her cloak. Fatigue had finally won.

"Get up. We can't stay here. There's a stegox behind us. We have to move."

"I know. You'll have to wait." Did he really think she was that stupid? Yes, they were trapped, but they had no options.

Al grabbed her arms and pulled her to her feet. Then he pushed her through the forest. "Keep moving, we'll go past the intersection and wait for Sherry that way." He pointed in the direction he thought they should go.

"What about the stegox?"

Al shook his head. "I don't know."

They walked a couple hundred yards and stopped. Zita wiped snow off of a stump and sat.

Minutes passed and then half-an-hour. No sign of Sherry. The two stegox seemed to find something more interesting than Al at the moment, which made Zita happy. But where was Sherry?

Al paced back and forth, fiddled with his bandage, and shook out his hands.

Zita whispered, "Stop pacing. You'll step on something and give us away to the guards. Where's your girlfriend?"

"I don't know."

Then they heard it. A whistle like a summer bird. A bird that only sings during the day, never at night.

Al tried to imitate the whistle, but wasn't even close.

Zita asked, "What are you doing?"

"I think that's Sherry."

"Are you sure?"

Al looked at the packed snow where he had paced back and forth. "No."

"Then shut up. It might be a guard."

A twig snapped nearby.

"Quiet."

Twenty yards away a stegox roared.

Zita jumped from her seat on the stump and looked at Al. She pointed in the opposite direction from the animal. She whispered, "We have to move."

Just as she started to follow Al, something touched her shoulder. Zita jumped at the touch, but luckily didn't release the scream on her lips.

"There you are." Sherry whispered.

Al turned to Sherry and hugged her. "We have a stegox following us. We have to go."

Sherry nodded and pointed in the direction they were already planning to go. "We'll go another hundred yards in that direction and then turn toward the mountains. We'll have to cross the road, but the guards probably won't be able to see us, or they'll think we're animals or something in the dark.

Al led, Sherry behind him, and Zita in the rear. She kept looking behind them for the stegox.

They reached the spot Sherry recommended and talked about how they would cross the road. As they stood at the edge of the forest Sherry whispered, "I recommend we go one at a time."

Zita looked in the distance. The fire roared bright and she counted the five guards at the intersection, but she couldn't make out any faces. Despite the bright moons in the sky, she thought the guards wouldn't know if they were humans or animals. Maybe the roar of the stegox would keep the guards close to the safety of the fire.

Zita nodded.

They decided to send Al first. He limped across the road and disappeared into the trees on the other side. Sherry went next and Zita didn't see any movement from the guards. They didn't even look in their direction.

Zita looked both ways on the road. It was still clear. One last glance at the guards who still seemed more interested in the fire than them. She hurried to cross the road. The roar of a stegox suddenly came from five feet behind her. Startled, she screamed.

"There she is. Get her!" the guards yelled.

The stegox roared again.

Zita ran across the road.

The thudding of the stegox's paws on the road followed Zita to the other side.

"Go! Go!" Zita reached the others, waving both hands as she sprinted past them.

Al screamed like a little girl, while Sherry grabbed his arm and pulled him away from danger.

The teens dashed through the snow, which became even more difficult as the landscape changed from forest to scattered boulders. Snow had drifted around the boulders and Zita found herself scrambling through waist high patches of snow. Her legs were useless in this landscape.

The stegox roared and jumped onto Zita rolling them both into a deep snowdrift. She felt her heart stop. One of its big claws, the size of a dinner plate, lay on her chest preventing her from moving. She looked up into a long snout and mouth full of yellowed teeth, drooling onto her face.

Defeat and fatigue had settled over her, and she lay unmoving in the snow. She had heard of survivors of stegox attacks, but she didn't have the will or strength to fight back.

A blue flame shot through the darkness and struck the stegox in the neck.

The beast rose to its hind legs to a height of ten feet.

Another lightning bolt struck its belly, and it roared in response to the attack.

Zita watched in amazement, but feared the huge animal might fall upon her.

Once more a magic fireball battered the beast forcing it to turn away from the magic and retreat into the forest.

Zita felt her heart start again, and she breathed. Al had saved her from the stegox.

Sherry grabbed Zita's hand. "Get up."

An arrow bounced off a boulder.

Zita forced herself off the ground. Her chest muscles seemed to tighten around her like a vise being cranked to crush her.

They made a lot of noise as they raced on, but it didn't matter, their lives were at stake.

She heard the sound of pursuit, but she wasn't sure if it came from the guards or a stegox.

A female voice called out to her, "Zita if you are in trouble just ask and I will help you."

Zita snorted. A female guard wanted her to slow down and talk with her so they could surround her and capture her. She wouldn't fall for that trap.

"How may I help you?" The voice asked.

"Leave me alone," Zita answered.

Sherry, who ran beside Zita said, "What?"

"I'm not talking to you; I'm talking back to the guard who wants to know if they can help me."

"I didn't hear a guard," Sherry said.

She jerked her head toward Sherry. "You didn't hear the voice that asked to help?"

"What voice?" Sherry ran next to her, sucking in air.

Zita looked up at the Velidred moon, just visible between a couple of bare deciduous trees. It wasn't full anymore, but it still reflected crimson light from the sun onto the snow.

"Can you stop the guards?" Zita asked out loud.

"You don't have to speak the words. I can hear your thoughts," Luna Rosso said.

Sherry said, "What do you want me to do?"

"I know!" Zita screamed.

"I don't like your attitude, but I will help you."

Zita looked back in the direction from where everyone was chasing them. She thought of the advancing guards. Then she heard a crash in the forest as if two trees fell at once.

CHAPTER 21

Men screamed in the distance.

"Did you hear that?" Sherry asked.

"Don't worry. Just go." Zita pushed Sherry in the back.

Zita followed Sherry and Al as they all ran uphill for twenty minutes. She couldn't be sure if the guards or the stegox were still pursuing them.

Sherry put up her hand for them to halt near a large stone. Zita cocked her head to the side, listening for the sounds of the guards. She heard nothing.

Between gasps, Sherry asked, "What happened?"

Zita didn't know for sure what to tell her. She wasn't sure of the moon goddess' influence on the planet. She asked for help, and then it seemed something happened. It had to be a coincidence. "I don't know for sure."

"Who were you talking to?"

Zita furrowed her brow and chose her words carefully. How much information did she need to tell Sherry at this time? She didn't want to scare her away. They still needed to find someplace safe. "There is a deity I pray to when I'm afraid. You heard me praying, because I was scared."

"Well, your prayers were answered," Sherry said.

Indeed, they were answered. Zita looked at the Velidred Moon. She felt a prickling of her skin that ran up her back.

Al asked, "What do we do now?"

"Wait for a signal."

Great, more waiting for someone to rescue me or believe me. Zita sat in the snow, too exhausted to care about the melting snow wetting her tunic and cloak. Her whole body was sweating from bounding uphill through the snow.

Al asked, "Do we know what the signal is?"

"I don't know for sure we'll get a signal. When Paxton and I were working together on the aqueducts, we had developed a whistle to find the other person when we worked deep in the forest together."

"Was that you that whistled at us in the forest?" Al asked.

"Yes, that's the signal."

Al developed a sullen look. "I see." He crossed his arms in front of his chest.

What's his problem? thought Zita.

They waited in the dark as the moons journeyed across the sky. Zita thought about all the things that could still go wrong. Paxton might decide not to help them, or to not even show up tonight. Paxton might find them and then the guards would jump out and grab them all. They could reach Paxton's farm only to discover the guards waiting for them, because they intercepted the message that Sherry sent. Zita chewed on her lower lip. So many things could go wrong.

A stegox roared, but Zita could tell it was far away and wouldn't be a danger to them.

Sherry sat in the snow with Al. They held hands.

Zita sighed, thinking about how nice it would be to sit with Erik right now. He would have the Sword of Freedom, and then they could rid Zita of the Corruption of Evil.

A bird warbled in the distance.

Strange for that bird at this time of year, thought Zita. She searched the dark forest for the bird.

Sherry sat up. She cupped her hands around her mouth and forced out a similar sound to the warble.

A response came from the direction of the road.

Sherry stood. "That's Paxton," and headed through the forest toward the sound.

Zita whispered, "Are you sure it's safe?"

A shadow formed in the darkness, a man.

Sherry ran to the man who wrapped her in a hug.

Al sneered and kicked up some snow.

Sherry held the man's hand and walked him back to the group. "You all remember Paxton?"

The man wasn't much taller than Sherry and he smelled like a pine forest.

Al shook the man's hand, and Zita waved.

"I have a sled and two horses up the hill. They're hidden behind some bushes. Follow me."

# # # #

Al bounced along on the wooden sled Paxton used as a utilitarian transport vehicle to haul lumber or supplies during the winter. Paxton had the foresight to pack blankets on the sled, and Al huddled under a blanket while Sherry sat next to Paxton as he guided the horses. Zita sat in a precarious position near the side of the sled. They didn't encounter any guards as Paxton guided the horses up the steep mountain road to his farm.

When they reached the house, they cleaned up, were fed hot stew by Paxton's staff, and gathered close to the roaring fire in the large, stone fireplace.

Al sat by the fireplace and wanted nothing more than to find a bed to fall asleep in for a number of days. He felt exhausted from running through the forest and freezing in the cold mountain air. Sitting this close to the fire, he found himself nodding, on the edge of sleep. His leg had been tended to, but the injury ached.

Paxton looked at Sherry. "So, what is this about?"

Sherry held a warm cup of cider in her hands. She rolled her eyes and nodded in Zita's direction. "I'll let Zita answer that question."

Zita looked at Al, Sherry and Paxton. "I've been accused of a crime I didn't commit. The wizard Taka has killed Prince Krunal and has convinced the castle guards that I killed the prince. You have to believe me; I didn't kill him."

"That's a serious accusation. Why didn't you just let the guards capture you, and then explain what happened and who's to blame?" Paxton asked.

"I don't trust Taka. He'll fabricate evidence to make it look like I did it. He's a sneaky old wizard. I have no idea how he killed the prince."

Sherry asked, "Do you think the guards will come here looking for us?"

Paxton nodded. "I'll hide you like we did in the fall. Though for something this serious, they may be more diligent in their searches of my property."

Sherry looked over at Al. "I can't believe you brought her to me. You've ruined everything for me. There were three more new students that joined the school just this week. I had started training a local intern to take over some of the younger students, so I could work exclusively with the older and smarter kids. All that work I did the last four months is ruined; I'll never be able to go back to Crossroads."

Al's stomach dropped with a feeling of dread as he pulled his knees to his chest, and a flush crept across his cheeks.

Paxton sat beside Sherry and held her hand. "We'll figure something out, together. You can teach school here in Triponca. We have kids here, too."

Sherry stared into Paxton's eyes and squeezed his hand. "I'm going to have to stay hidden for a long time until the people at Velidred either find Zita, or she clears her name. And they may still accuse me of being an accessory to the crime, even though I obviously have an iron-tight alibi. At least until that big lug showed up at my door."

"I'm sorry!" Al yelled. "I thought you could help Zita. And look, you did. We're all safe." He muttered under his breath, "You should be happy."

"Happy?" Sherry shouted back at him. "You've ruined my life here on this planet. A planet I don't even want to be on, and you say I should be happy. Ha." She buried her face in Paxton's shoulder.

Paxton rubbed her back.

Al wanted to shoot a fireball at Paxton. *How dare he touch my girlfriend in an affectionate manner like that?* He picked up his staff. The staff his grandfather, Alpherge the Great, had made and passed down to Al. He wanted to rant and rave and explain to Sherry his decisions, but he knew it would only damage their tenuous friendship.

A sob escaped Sherry.

Paxton patted her on the back. "I'll protect you."

Al snorted at the comment. He stood and said through gritted teeth, "I'm going to bed."

CHAPTER 22

The next morning Zita walked into the kitchen to find some breakfast. The aroma of freshly cooked food smelled like a dream come true for Zita. The sound of bacon sizzling on the stove made her mouth water. She found Al and Sherry on opposite sides of the table, ignoring each other as they pushed eggs and bacon around on their plates. She needed to tell Al and Sherry something, but it wouldn't be received well in their present animosity.

She took her plate of food and sat in the living room next to the large fire. She needed to make some decisions. She needed rest, and Paxton's home seemed like a good place. He said they could hide there, but she didn't know at what cost. She didn't even know whose side he favored. Was he a friend of her father's, or did he support the Kallurian army? She'd have to find out if she could trust him.

She needed more information on the moon goddess. The woman wanted something. Zita knew it wasn't a coincidence the trees fell on the guards. Somehow, Luna Rosso had the ability to make things happen on the ground. She wasn't just a distant deity.

The moon goddess had told Zita that she would train her. To do what? She still wasn't sure if her problems stemmed from the moon goddess, Velidred lunacy, or the Corruption of Evil. They all seemed to have happened concurrently, and Zita needed someone to interpret it all for her.

Paxton entered the room. "Did you sleep well?"

Zita put her hot cider on the table. "Yes, I can't thank you enough for taking us all in. You are truly a wonderful friend."

"Sherry is a close friend; I couldn't let her and her friends suffer in the cold."

Al rolled his eyes.

"I see." Zita leaned forward. "Do you include Erik Anderson in your list of friends?"

"Yes, absolutely!"

Erik Anderson had led his friends, Al, Sherry and Lily through a portal that connected Earth with the planet Aloheno. Zita and Erik were dating, if you could call it that, and her stomach got that fluttery feeling when she thought of him. "Have you seen Erik recently?"

"It's been at least a month or two. Before the first big snow, he headed out with Cugbert to tend to the mountain population. Who knows what little mountain village they're trapped in this time of year."

"Is there a way to get a message to him?"

Paxton slowly shook his head. "I doubt it. The birds have trouble flying in this extreme cold and it's even colder where they are."

Zita's shoulders slumped when she heard the news. She dropped her head to her chest and closed her eyes. She needed Erik now. And he needed to bring the Sword of Freedom. There must be some way to get a message to him and bring him here.

"I'm sorry if that news disappoints you. It's always been like this in the winter. I was surprised when I received the message Sherry sent. Like I said, it's unusual."

Zita raised her eyebrows. "So, we could try?"

"No. It's impractical. I only have a handful of birds that I use for emergencies. And we don't have a clue what village Cugbert and Erik are helping in."

She sighed as her previous enthusiasm crashed back to reality. Her cause was hopeless. She'd have to hope she didn't die of lunacy or the Corruption of Evil until spring arrived. Could she stay until spring?

# # # #

Two nights later, Zita lay in bed on the cusp of falling asleep when a voice called out to her, "Zita, don't sleep, it's time for you to enhance your skills."

It had been a relaxing day and she almost felt normal again after those many cold days and nights in the forest. Paxton was a gracious and kind host and made sure she was fed, and his housemaids stoked the fireplace in her room each night which kept her warm. She needed to think about and make decisions of her next steps.

The warm fire had lulled her into a comfortable feeling of contentment, and she closed her eyes once more, searching for sleep.

"My child, you don't have much time to learn these things. They'll be here in a few days and you must go with them when they ask."

She sat up straight. "What? Who's coming?"

"Taka and his men have decided to find the Crystal of Zaraboth, and they will need your help. I need to prepare you for acquiring this object."

Zita felt a sinking feeling in her stomach. She wanted nothing to do with Taka and his men. *How dare they go for the Crystal of Zaraboth? It is mine.* She rubbed her forehead and closed her eyes. He would just take away her magic and control her once more. "I won't do it."

"Quiet, child. You don't have to speak the words."

Zita shook her head. "Yeah, I know I just forget that you aren't real."

"I am real."

Zita felt a tingling sensation in her right foot. It forced its way up her leg, seemed to circle her stomach region and then exploded into her head like a migraine headache. She hugged her knees and rocked in place as the pain increased. She couldn't let the moon goddess come into her head like that.

"Do you agree that it's time to train with me?" the moon goddess asked.

She moaned and grabbed a fistful of her hair and pulled, trying to corral the pain circling her brain. "Stop torturing me." Zita said the words in an emotion-choked voice. "I'll listen and train."

The pain subsided, but Zita still grasped her knees tightly as she tried to breathe.

"That's better. Get some warm clothes on, and go outside. We'll start with some simple commands that you can practice on your friends."

"If I practice commands that will hurt them, like you hurt me, then they won't be my friends for long. It's nice here. Can't I just listen to the commands and practice them on Taka when he shows up?"

"No! You'll need to be skilled in this magic because the road ahead is difficult and dangerous."

Zita shook her head and put on warm clothes and a hooded cloak. She tiptoed through the quiet house and went outside to stand on the snow-covered porch. The blowing north wind picked up snow and sent it as stinging needles through the air.

The Velidred Moon captured her attention as it shone just above the tree line off to the Northeast.

"You see me, and you look more rested than the last time we spoke. You must learn to control your ability to influence people with the Corruption of Evil. Imagine my disappointment that you couldn't control the wolves. They are such simple-minded animals.

"I feared them."

"There is no need to fear animals or humans. I am by your side and will protect you in every way. I have a task for you to help complete our arrangement, but you must be skilled in my ways."

Zita moaned wondering what more she needed to do to complete her arrangement with Velidred. Could her relationship become worse than it already was?

Luna Rosso proceeded to instruct Zita on using the Corruption of Evil to control others. An hour passed quickly as they conversed, and Zita attempted the commands given her. A rabbit came to the porch and Zita practiced coaxing the rabbit to follow her orders. She stared at the rabbit and as they locked gazes, she felt the scorpion crawl up her iris to her pupil. The thought of it sent a shiver up her spine.

She convinced the rabbit to come and sit in her lap. She stroked the soft fur as the moon goddess educated her more.

A coyote walked through the snow and foraged under bare shrubs near the house.

Luna Rosso said, "Now we will practice forcing animals to do things they don't want to do."

Zita grumbled. "Will you hurt this cute little bunny?"

"Not me my dear. That is your job."

After a few minutes of instructions, Zita set the bunny so she could make eye contact. The animal's nose twitched.

The bunny seemed enthralled by the scorpion, and it stared at her without blinking.

Zita didn't want to do it but feared reprisal. She commanded, "Go. Visit that coyote. It is hungry and you are its meal."

The bunny didn't hesitate. It jumped off Zita's lap and hopped near the coyote. As it got close to the coyote, Zita thought it might run away, but it jumped closer until the coyote noticed it. The coyote attacked the rabbit.

She averted her eyes and felt sick to her stomach at the crunch of bones.

She worked on her skills as Luna Rosso sent her a different coyote to practice with. She stared at the animal and said, "Come to me."

"You don't have to say the commands out loud," Luna Rosso said. "If your target is looking at the scorpion, they will obey without you speaking."

Could it be that simple? The coyote acted reluctant, but Zita concentrated harder and it came closer and closer. She marveled at the power she could wield. These were just small animals, but they listened to her and did her will. She continued to use the scorpion to pull the coyote to her. With the coyote only a foot away from Zita's out-stretched hand, the back door opened.

The noise startled Zita. She didn't want the others to know what the moon goddess had her doing.

Al came a few paces onto the back porch.

She avoided eye contact with Al.

The coyote lost concentration and scampered off.

"What are you doing out here in the cold?" Al focused his attention on where the animal had run into the woods. "Was that a coyote that scampered away? It's a good thing I came out and scared it away."

Luna Rosso said, "Practice on the wizard."

"He is my friend." Zita responded in her brain.

The tingling sensation formed in Zita's foot.

She raised her hands, "Okay. I'll practice."

The tingling stopped.

"Are you okay?" Al asked.

"Sit down next to me," Zita commanded.

"I can't stay out here long; I just came to the kitchen for a glass of water. I'm not dressed to be outside like you."

Luna Rosso said, "Get him to stay outside with you for thirty minutes, just using the commands I taught you."

"Am I strong enough to dominate a human?"

"Practice."

Al sat down next to Zita.

Zita stared at Al's eyes and she felt the scorpion begin to move across her eye. She didn't feel like she controlled it. The creature seemed to have a mind of its own. Or did Luna Rosso force it to do her will?

Al looked out over the wind-swept landscape.

Zita said, "Look at me!"

"Yeah?" Al turned his head toward her. "What's up?"

Zita started a mantra in her mind. "Stay outside with me. Ignore the cold." She looked at Al and he seemed to be staring at the scorpion. *It's working! I can manipulate Al.*

Al stood, "Nope, it's too cold for me. I thought you had enough cold those nights in the forest. I figured you'd be hunkered down next to your room's fireplace. I'll see you in the morning."

He moved fast and stepped back into the house.

She hung her head at her failure to influence Al. How could Luna Rosso expect her to manipulate others when she had trouble with a mope like Al?

"That's okay. You just need to practice," Luna Rosso said. "A wizard is a tough target. Practice on the housemaids during the day; they have a more willing brain for manipulation. We are done for tonight. Come out and see me tomorrow night so we can talk more."

Zita enjoyed the power she had gained over the animals but didn't feel it translated well to humans. The moon goddess had to understand that animals didn't have the same brains as men and women. She couldn't expect Zita to immediately control other people with her new power. Certainly, influence like this takes time to master. If Luna Rosso expected Taka to arrive in two days, Zita had to gain proficiency in her skills.

CHAPTER 23

Al sat at the kitchen table the next morning, eating his second bowl of oats. He had waited at the table for an hour before eating, hoping Sherry would show up and they could talk. He admitted that Paxton had it pretty good here. The farmer seemed to have a lot of food, a competent staff and a comfortable life.

Al could understand why Sherry was attracted to the farmer. Even though he had to be ten years older than Sherry, the man had created a life for himself that Sherry would enjoy. Al wondered if he should settle down and find a career on the planet. Maybe Sherry would think differently of him if he resolved to act like an adult and buy a house and make some money. *Doing what? I could be a wizard for hire, assuming that's an occupation here.*

Zita entered the kitchen.

"How long did you stay outside last night?" Al asked. "It was freezing out there."

"I just wanted some fresh air, and the view of the Velidred moon over the snow-covered field and frozen lake mesmerized me."

"Yeah, it was pretty." Al agreed.

She held something in her hand, the scroll that she had carried into Crossroads with her. He was surprised she hadn't lost it in the forest when they were running from the guards or dropped it in the snow when she turned them into logs.

He nodded at the scroll. "Is that special?"

"I don't know. It talks about the Crystal of Zaraboth."

"You don't want anything to do with the crystal. It killed my grandfather." He thought back to the story Master Ishwa told him about, how in their search for the crystal in hopes of defeating King Haskell, something had happened, and his grandfather had been disintegrated. The group of wizards had to return home empty handed.

"I'm trying to decode what the scroll says about the crystal. There are tips that may prove useful in capturing and controlling it."

"Good luck. I'm not as skilled as my grandfather, and I would never think of trying to capture it."

"I'm interested in it because it might help me with my Velidred moon lunacy. They say it might keep me from dying in two years."

Al tilted his head and smirked. "It will probably kill you sooner, so you won't have to go through a long slow death."

She unrolled the scroll on the table, and Al moved his bowl to the side. She pointed at a line on the scroll. "It says here to expect four gatekeepers protecting the crystal."

"It's my understanding that you need specialized magical objects to defeat the gatekeepers," Al said. "It's also winter time, in case you haven't noticed, so we might need to wait until summer to plan a quest for the crystal."

Zita said, "I can't wait until summer."

"That's what always gets me in trouble is thinking I don't have time to wait. It's only a few months. Then we can search for the magical objects."

Zita stared across the table at Al.

Al looked at the red spot that moved across her eye and felt a quiver of angst in his stomach. He wondered how much power she had. He suspected Gadiel had perfected his use of the power over many years. Zita couldn't have had the Corruption of Evil for more than a month. She shouldn't have the ability to manipulate him.

Her lips moved as she stared at him.

Al glanced at the document. "Can you really read these words?" The document contained half words and half symbols. One symbol, a half-moon, colored red, he thought might represent the Velidred Moon. A round blue object could symbolize the Anticletus moon. The scroll showed a blank circle, but he didn't know if that represented the third Aloheno moon called Pantaleon, or the new moon status of one of the other moons.

He looked at Zita, her face all pinched as if deep in mental work. Her lips were pursed tight and she had narrowed her eyes as she stared at Al.

All of a sudden, she relaxed her expression. "I can't read all of them."

Zita pointed at the blank circle on the scroll. "This is definitely Anticletus in new moon status. Notice the tiara right behind the moon. It refers to the Crown of Anticletus."

Al raised his eyebrows. The teens had learned when they arrived from Earth that Sherry was actually the magical item known as the Crown of Anticletus. Sherry had shown her power when they rescued the stone warriors, and Zita must know that key point.

"Okay. What else does it say?"

She placed her finger on a word written in script. "This is roughly translated to mean Great Wand."

"Yeah, where is that? Even if we interpret the meanings of this scroll, we won't necessarily have the resources to acquire the needed items. I remember Ishwa saying that they had to make some shrewd deals to find the objects they used. And they failed."

"I think it means the Imperium Wand, and I know where to find it."

"Where?"

Zita said, "Taka has it back at the castle."

"And how do you plan on getting it from Taka? I thought you said he prevents you from using magic." Al wanted to touch this magical item and see what power it contained, but he kind of feared Taka's ability to block magic usage and manipulate Zita.

"I haven't figured it all out yet. We need to decode all the symbols first."

Al pointed at an object that he thought looked like a bowl. It seemed the image showed that water flowed into the bowl. "What do you think this is? It looks like maybe we have to find a waterfall and bring it with us."

Zita studied it for a few minutes. "I don't think it's the water that's important but the bowl or vessel is what we have to bring."

"Should we get Sherry to help us? She's smart."

"No!" Zita shouted. "Let's just you and I work on it first. No need to involve her any more than she already is."

At that moment, Sherry walked down from her room upstairs. Al remembered that earlier he had thought about settling down with Sherry, but now his thoughts led to the fun of a quest for the crystal.

He watched her speak with one of the kitchen staff and then she came and sat at the table. She avoided looking at Al, but she did examine the scroll. "What are you two doing?"

Al opened his mouth to say, "Planning a quest," but decided to let Zita do the talking.

Zita quickly rolled up the scroll.

Al looked at her, and she shook her head. He looked at Sherry, who quickly averted her eyes. He glanced at the person preparing Sherry's breakfast. He said, "Master Ishwa believed that the Crown of Anticletus was needed to capture the crystal."

Zita turned on him and glared at Al with cold black eyes. She pivoted and left the kitchen.

Sherry gazed at Al.

He sucked in his cheeks with a wheeze. "Zita's document explains how to get the Crystal of Zaraboth. She thinks it will help heal her lunacy."

Sherry said, "And you immediately thought how much fun it would be to go on another adventure with Zita after ruining my life in Crossroads."

His mouth went dry as he thought of a way to respond. He felt his cheeks turn red. *She thinks I don't love her, just because I'm trying to learn my way on this planet.*

"I didn't think about the effect my coming to see you the other day would have on your life and career. I'm sorry."

"That's all I hear from you. You're sorry you went to see Finn instead of looking for me while I suffered in a jail less than a mile away. You're sorry you left Lily and me alone as you went on a quest with Erik."

She turned her back on Al.

He didn't know what to do. Should he touch her shoulder, take her hand, or apologize, again? He just sat there. She must realize they had been able to rescue the stone warriors only because they found the items at the Ice Castle.

The maid brought over a plate of warm food for Sherry and set it on the table.

Sherry looked at the plate, glared at Al, then pushed the plate away and walked out of the room.

Paxton came into the room just as Sherry left. He watched her leave and then stared at Al. Paxton shook his head.

The maid glanced at Paxton and then the plate of food on the table. "Should I take it to her?"

"No, that's okay, I'll take it to her." He picked it up, and grabbed some eating utensils before walking out of the room.

Al sat and lowered his head into his hands.

CHAPTER 24

Zita spent the next three days working on her skills with the Corruption of Evil and practicing on Paxton's housemaids. Her first problem was getting them to look her in the eye. They would make eye contact, but then drop their eyes to the floor as they waited for Zita to say something. Or else they would scurry off to make the bed or find out what clothes needed care. She decided that she needed to learn how to force the housemaids to continue to stare at the scorpion.

The moon goddess had taught Zita commands to coerce animals and humans to respond to her eye. She hadn't realized how adept at manipulating people Gadiel had become, yet the moon goddess seemed to want Zita to learn it all in a day's time.

In the morning Brigid, a housemaid, came into Zita's room. "Good morning."

Zita mumbled, "Good morning." As the servant opened the curtains, Zita covered her eyes with her hands and rolled over on her side facing away from the window, wishing she could keep sleeping.

"Breakfast is prepared. Should I tell them you'll be joining them this morning?"

"Yes," She murmured.

"Very good." The woman began to walk away.

"Wait," Zita called out. She had spent over two hours working with Luna Rosso the night before and needed to practice. Brigid seemed the friendliest of the maids assigned to her, and Zita felt she'd be a good test subject.

Brigid stood at the foot of the bed staring at Zita.

Zita sat up and blinked her eyes a couple of times. Then she made eye contact with Brigid. When the scorpion moved, it didn't seem to bother Zita as it had in the past. She made a mental command as she looked at Brigid. The command allowed her to gain control of her test subject and get the person to maintain eye contact. The command worked.

Brigid eyes stayed focused on the scorpion. Her pupils seemed to dilate into large black balls completely covering the woman's blue irises.

Zita knew she had the woman in her control, but then she realized she didn't know what command to give. Brigid stared at the scorpion as Zita tried to come up with a suitable request from the woman that would prove Zita had control.

"Strawberries and cucumbers." Paxton probably didn't have either this deep into winter. Zita could find out how much desire to follow her commands her power imparted to the servant.

"What?"

"For breakfast. I would like strawberries and cucumbers." Zita smiled and shooed Brigid out of the room with a flutter of her fingers.

Brigid left.

Zita prepared herself for the day by putting on wool stockings, a wool skirt, and wool jacket. She missed the clothes she had worn at the Velidred Castle when her dad held power—the silks, satins and velvets. She hadn't worn lace or ribbons in what seemed like ages. Even though her room felt warm in Paxton's house, other parts of the home tended to be cold. The wool was more practical here. She glanced at herself in the mirror and when satisfied, headed toward the kitchen.

When she reached the kitchen, the farm workers were in a bit of a frenzy. It appeared Brigid had stepped out of the house to go get something for Zita. Despite the others telling her the items were unavailable at this time of year, Brigid left the house determined to retrieve the requested ingredients.

Paxton stopped Zita. "What did you request of Brigid?"

Zita blushed for a moment. Had her attempt at using her power on a human worked? "I asked for strawberries and cucumbers. Why do you ask?"

Paxton rubbed his eyes with his hands. "I don't know what got into the girl. She walked into the kitchen and asked the cook if we had those items, and when told 'no,' she walked out the door without putting on a jacket or anything. I sent someone after her. Did you put a spell on the girl?"

Zita worked hard not to smile at the news. She had her first success manipulating a human with the Corruption of Evil. "That sounds so inappropriate. I used to have those foods in the castle on a regular basis and I felt in the mood for some fresh fruit and vegetables. Cucumbers were the first thing that came to mind."

Paxton shook his head. "Our stock of food isn't as diverse this time of year as at your father's castle. We have apples that are still mostly fresh, will that do?"

"I'm so sorry. I forgot myself. Yes, apples will be fine."

"Thank you," said Paxton. "I apologize for our level of comfort here at my humble home."

"It isn't a problem. Will the girl be back soon?" Zita felt some remorse at sending Brigid on this wild request, but the victory of forcing a human to her will gave her a rush.

"We aren't sure. She seemed to be in a hurry, but she's never acted this way before."

Zita asked, "Would you like me to help look for her? I can't imagine what made her think that my request required this much attention."

The kitchen cook stood over a large cauldron hanging above the fire. As she stirred, the aroma of a simmering stew filled Zita's senses. The cook looked at Zita and scowled, her brows drew closer and her face tightened.

Zita thought she would have to practice on the cook when her skills improved. She would be a worthy adversary as the woman obviously didn't trust her. Zita lifted one side of her lips in a partial smile.

CHAPTER 25

After lunch, Al and Sherry sat by the fire in Paxton's study. The fact that she stayed in the same room surprised him and he felt a little nervous about what that might mean. He sat in a high-backed padded and upholstered chair. The decoration at the top of the chair had the shape of a wolf's head engraved into the wood. The armrest repeated the wolf motif.

Sherry relaxed on a wooden couch and pointed to a porcelain vase on the fireplace mantel. "Paxton mentioned that your grandmother gave that vase to his mother. Your grandmother's had an artist create the item."

The vase top was rimmed in gold, with red art work across its neck. The bulb of the vase showed dragons flying across a forest landscape with an azure waterfall flowing in the background.

Sherry said, "He considers it his most prized possession, and he says it reminds him of his mother."

Al looked at it and thought of his own mother. He wondered what his grandparents were like, and what Paxton had done to deserve such a valuable gift.

Al had been thinking of Sherry and his own desire to maybe settle down. He blurted, "I might be able to find work as a wizard here on the planet."

Sherry crossed her arms. "Does this mean you don't plan to go on another quest with Zita."

He sat up straight. "It's not in my plans. I'm ready to settle down and become a working wizard. I'm not sure what kind of jobs wizards perform, but there must be some way I can earn a living without working the fields or banging on metal as a blacksmith."

Sherry almost smiled, "I can honestly never see you as a laborer of any kind."

Al pretended to look offended, but he knew it wasn't in his DNA to be a laborer. Even after going to the Ice Castle and working with the animals, he hadn't added any muscle to his thin frame.

Al looked at the floor. "Maybe we can brainstorm ways I can use my skills on this planet." He wanted to see her laugh, so he lifted his staff and pointed it at the fireplace. "I can walk around the village each night lighting fireplaces to keep people warm."

Sherry shook her head. "I don't know if people will pay for that service. The populace seems to have figured out how to light a fire on their own. During the summer, Kestrel helped us by taking down trees like a lumberjack."

"That's it." Al stood with staff in hand. "I'll be Lumberjack Al." He walked around the room pretending to shoot magic at trees and yelling out, "Timber."

"Sit down, you crazy nut. I'm just happy that you understand it's time for you to be an adult. At least on this planet. If we were home on Earth, we'd be planning for college, but here, we're adults."

For the moment Al felt happy she sat in the same room with him, and they had a conversation about life together on this planet.

Paxton ran into the room. "Quick! Three riders are heading to the farm. You must hide. Where's Zita?"

Al felt his breath catch in his chest as the realization that he was still a criminal on the run hit him full on. "I think she's in her room."

"Go get her, and bring her back downstairs." Paxton grabbed Sherry's hand. "We must hide you."

Sherry yelled, "Hurry Al."

Al tilted his head to the side as he watched Sherry head off with Paxton. He wanted to be the one protecting Sherry and wasn't happy Paxton had her hand in his. He wrinkled his forehead, and with his staff in hand ran upstairs to find Zita.

He burst into her room. She lay on the bed with her scroll rolled out before her but turned around as he entered. "Don't you know how to knock?"

"There's no time for niceties. Some men are coming up the path; we must hide." Al nervously played with the staff. "Come on. Hurry."

Zita got up from the bed and hurried off down the stairs, following Al. When they reached the bottom of the stairs, they heard a knock on the front door.

Al groaned, "They're already here. Move. We gotta hide."

Zita grabbed his hand. "Wait, it might be Taka. I left the scroll on the bed. I have to go back and get it."

"There isn't time. You have to hide."

Paxton walked through the room, heading toward the front door. He pointed at his right-hand man. "Magnus, take them to the secret room."

"I have to go upstairs and get something." Zita cried.

"No, there isn't time."

"I can't let Taka have it." She took the first step on the stairs but Al hauled her back.

"Leave it."

Zita looked up the stairs.

Magnus hurried over to corral Al and Zita toward the secret room.

She escaped from Magnus and raced up the stairs.

Al looked at Paxton and Magnus.

Paxton stood at the bottom of the stairs, sweat forming on his brow. His lips were drawn tight and he appeared angry at Zita's actions. He pointed to the kitchen. "Follow Magnus into the kitchen.

Magnus led them through the kitchen where two women were preparing the next meal. Al wondered if they could keep their mouth shut about their secret hiding place, but he knew that they weren't the first fugitives Paxton had hidden. They reached a small closet containing food stuffs and unused pans. On one wall stood small jars of pickled vegetables. Magnus reached behind two large jars and unlocked a handle. Then he pulled back on the handle and the shelving rotated into the room.

Sherry stood in the dark and pulled Al into the room with her. Zita followed.

"What took you so long?"

Al looked at Zita. "She left the scroll on her bed and went back for it."

Sherry bit her lower lip in worry.

Magnus put a finger over his lips and said, "Quiet. The room isn't soundproof." He left the room and shut the door leaving the three of them in darkness.

# # # #

Zita waited in the dark hiding place in Paxton's pantry, her pulse beating rapidly. She should have thought to grab the scroll. She couldn't afford for Taka and his thugs to get it. Who knew what they would do if they found it. She had deciphered some of the hieroglyphics and she felt confident she could interpret the rest if she had enough time.

A tiny hole in the wall showed them a view into Paxton's study. Zita looked through the hole and watched as Paxton led Dakarai, Sims and Lenny into the study.

A shiver of fear ran up Zita's back. *Dakarai will know where I'm hiding. He's going to find me, take away my magic and have me killed.* She fingered her necklace in the darkness.

"Where are they, Paxton?" Dakarai asked. "I know you're hiding them."

Paxton shifted in his chair, "Hiding who?"

"Zita and her companions. Those teenagers."

"It's my understanding that Zita is wanted for the murder of Prince Krunal." Paxton stopped a moment. "I supported Krunal during the war. I wouldn't hide her; I would be the first person to hand her back."

Dakarai sneered at Paxton and nodded his head and raised his eyebrows at Sims.

Sims pulled a knife and stood next to Paxton.

Zita heard Sherry stifle a gasp. *Can I trust Paxton not to give us up if he's tortured? How much pain would Paxton take to protect me?* She realized that he probably didn't care about Zita at all, but he would protect Sherry at all costs. She had seen the way he catered to Sherry's wants and despite her relationship with Al, there appeared to be some feelings in Sherry's heart for Paxton.

Sims held the knife to Paxton's throat.

Dakarai asked, "Where are they?"

"I don't know who you're talking about."

Sims slid the knife a slight inch across Paxton's neck, drawing blood, but the slice wasn't deep.

Paxton didn't flinch. "Look. These people you're looking for aren't here. I don't harbor killers and thieves. This is a friendly farm that has served our community for three generations. Many of the families in this area saw you enter the village. If you kill me, there won't be any doubt who murdered me. They'll end up hanging you with Zita."

Sims looked over at Dakarai as if for the signal to plunge the knife further into Paxton.

Zita wondered if she should just give herself up. Paxton didn't deserve to die because of her.

Dakarai shook his head at Sims. "Maybe you'd let me search your rooms. A maid of yours could be hiding the murderers without your knowledge."

Paxton nodded. "You're free to search all the rooms in the house. There's no one here."

Sims asked, "Can we search the house, Boss?" He stood ready to rumble through the home.

Zita could imagine the damage the thug would do to Paxton's beautiful home.

Dakarai studied Paxton.

Paxton didn't flinch; he just stared at Dakarai.

Dakarai raised his voice, "Zita, I know you can hear me. We want the scroll you took from your father's house. We know it contains secrets to capture the Crystal of Zaraboth. Taka wants it."

He waited.

Zita could hardly breathe.

"Taka has agreed to let you go, if you give yourself up. Give us the scroll and you're free from all charges of killing Prince Krunal."

Zita's muscles quivered and she clenched and unclenched her hands. She wanted nothing more than to release a fireball or use some other spell on Dakarai and his gang. Anger threatened to take over her senses. Maybe her skills with the Corruption of Evil could help her overpower Dakarai now. She wanted to scream out that Taka killed the prince.

Zita walked over to the door. The time had come to confront Dakarai. She had the skills.

Al grabbed her arm.

She wriggled to get away, but Al didn't release his grip. She wanted to use magic, except Dakarai stood there only a few feet away.

Dakarai yelled again, "Five seconds, Zita. Come out now and you will be exonerated for murdering the prince." He counted down the seconds.

Al held tight to her arm. Zita shook her arm free and went back to the hole in the wall to watch.

Dakarai nodded at Sims.

Sims plunged the blade into Paxton's shoulder. He moaned and dropped to his knees. Blood ran down the front of his shirt.

Sherry gasped as Paxton slumped to the floor.

Dakarai looked directly at the wall behind which the three teenagers hid.

He stood there a second before turning to Sims. "Okay. We'll let Taka know that Zita wants to die."

"I thought we were supposed to get the scroll. We're supposed to search the house."

Dakarai stared at Paxton, who lay panting on the floor.

"No. We know where it is. We'll come back for it when we're ready to travel to the crystal. Let's go."

Sims breathed deeply, looking disappointed at not being allowed to rough up Paxton some more or to ransack the house. He pulled the knife from Paxton's shoulder which caused the farmer to flinch and groan.

Dakarai said, "We'll find our way out."

As Sims made his way out of the room, he ran his hand along the mantel above the fireplace pushing knick-knacks to the floor, and when he reached the expensive porcelain vase, he picked it up and smashed it to the wood floor where it crashed in a cacophony of a hundred broken ceramic pieces.

CHAPTER 26

Zita watched the thugs leave, and heard the banging of the door as it closed, signaling they had left the building. She wondered why Dakarai didn't make a move to take action against her today. The man knew where she was hiding in the farmhouse. Everyone knew where they were after the loud gasp Sherry made when Sims stuck the knife in Paxton. Didn't the woman know how to keep her trap shut? She had to make decisions on how long to stay at Paxton's place.

When it was safe to leave the secret hiding place, Magnus opened the door. Sherry rushed out of the hiding space first and raced to Paxton's chair in the study where he lay bleeding from his neck and shoulder. She took a cloth from a nearby table, kneeled, and pressed it to Paxton's shoulder.

When Zita and Al reached them, Sherry pointed at Zita. "If Paxton dies, I will hold you responsible."

Paxton pulled her arm down. "It's okay. They purposely didn't kill me. I'll be all right." He pressed his hand against Sherry's where she held the cloth.

"They want the scroll, which means that Taka is planning on going for the crystal," Zita said. "We have the scroll, and within a few more days I'll have interpreted all of the hieroglyphics. Then we can get the crystal before Taka."

Sherry glared at Zita.

Al stood six feet from the rest of them as he wobbled back and forth on his feet, as if trying to decide whether to go on a quest with Zita or to stay.

"You heard Dakarai," Sherry said. "Give the scroll to Taka and then they will exonerate you. We'll all be free. I'll be able to go back to Crossroads."

"I don't trust Taka," Zita said.

Paxton removed Sherry's hand, pulled the blood-soaked cloth away, and grabbed another cloth to hold against the stab wound. "Unfortunately, I agree with Zita. I know people like Dakarai and though they may say they'll release her we can't trust them. The scroll won't be enough for them. They'll just ask for more and threaten other people we love."

Sherry pointed to the broken porcelain on the floor and tears welled in her eyes. "They broke your precious vase. I'm sorry I brought these horrible people to you."

"It's okay". He stared at Sherry. "You all are okay, that's what is important."

Sherry put her hand on Paxton's hand and glared once more at Zita.

"I need to work on figuring out the rest of the symbols on the scroll. Taka and his thugs will be back before you know it." Zita pointed angrily at Sherry. "They know we are here, and Dakarai knows where the secret room is located. Because you couldn't keep your mouth shut."

Sherry gaped. She looked at Al, but he just stood there, speechless. "Aren't you going to say something to her? Are you on her side?"

Al's mouth dropped open, but he remained silent. His eyes darted back and forth from Zita to Sherry.

Sherry got to her feet, red ringing her eyes. She approached Al. "You better figure out whose side you're on, Wizard Boy." Then she pointed at Zita. "I'm not the one in this room that killed Prince Krunal. I've just about had enough of your bad behavior. I might decide to turn you in to the authorities myself."

Zita wanted to use magic to put Sherry in her place, but she feared Dakarai had stayed close to the house and it might be dangerous for her. She moved closer to Sherry, "I didn't kill the prince. They are framing me, and now we're in danger because you couldn't keep your mouth shut."

Sherry didn't back down. "I wasn't in any danger until you came into my life." She poked Zita in the chest. "Leave us alone. Take your scroll and your princess problems far from here."

Adrenaline rushed through Zita's body. She felt the scorpion start its move across her eye. She hoped the scorpion had the power to smite Sherry right where she stood.

They stared at each other.

Zita used the powers Luna Rosso had taught her, and tried to manipulate Sherry, but the redhead didn't seem to be affected by her power. She thought it might be her own roiling anger making her unable to control the power.

Sherry broke her gaze and looked at Al. "Are you coming with me or staying with Zita?"

Al stood motionless in the corner of the room.

Sherry seemed disappointed. She walked slowly from the room, heading toward the stairs that led to the bedrooms.

"What can I do to help you Paxton?" The metallic smell of blood, and the salty, musky ammonia scent of someone who had been perspiring drifted up to Zita as she moved closer to Paxton.

"It's nothing. My staff can help bandage my wounds. I'll be okay. I've had worse from Haskell's minions." He motioned to Magnus. "Help me out of the chair."

Paxton's calmness after the attack surprised Zita.

It took a moment and a couple of grunts from Paxton to get on his feet. Then he nodded to Magnus, "Ask Molly to help you clean this mess." Paxton slowly walked out of the room as he called the cook's name.

Zita thought back to her dad's brutality against his enemies. Taka was cruel repeating her dad's rise to power. Eliminate your enemies and show strength against others, so no one will rise against you. She should take that stance, be more like her father. Retrieving the crystal will be one more step to power. She could use the Corruption of Evil to get the crystal, kill Taka and take over the Velidred throne.

"We have to work on deciphering the symbols on the scroll. Al, I need your help. Follow me."

CHAPTER 27

Three days later, Al stood examining the scroll which was laid out on a table Paxton had set up for them in the study. Al and Zita had made great progress in teasing out the secrets and deciphering the symbols and ancient words written in Devanagari script. There were still two points that had eluded them. Day after day, Al watched Zita get more worked up and antsy about the project.

Taka's thugs hadn't returned, and the tension increased each day, wondering when they might show up at the door.

Zita walked back and forth in front of the fireplace repeating the object's name shown on the scroll. "Gigas Llagosta. Gigas Llagosta. What does that mean?"

Paxton had found an old wizard living nearby who had offered the name Gigas Llagosta to the strange insect shown on the scroll. The insect stood on its hind legs. Its middle legs held some kind of cloth and its upper legs held weapons.

The old wizard described the insect as large, but didn't remember if that meant a foot tall or ten feet tall. He also hesitated on committing to one insect or multiple insects with the same abilities.

"Zita. Sit down. You're driving me crazy."

She stopped her pacing. "We have to come up with a plan to defeat all the gatekeepers."

Al remembered that the old wizard had called the strange insects, gatekeepers.

The old wizard had enough background in the Devanagari writing that he managed to give them the names of the gatekeepers. Along with Gigas Llagosta, their adversaries included Ixinite, Xalawad Furioso, and Geirhild Hlifsteed. So, there were four gatekeepers guarding the Crystal of Zaraboth. Each was worse than the one before it. They would have to defeat all of them to succeed in their task.

Whoever had created the scroll had identified four magical objects that might help them succeed. The words, "might help them succeed," didn't give Al much comfort.

Al struggled with the decision about whether he should go with Zita and search for the crystal or stay and settle down with Sherry. She had stopped coming into the study ever since the attack on Paxton, and she would raise her hand any time Al tried to talk with her. He couldn't understand what her problem was. She spent more and more time talking with Paxton which didn't make him happy.

Zita said, "How do you defeat a giant insect?"

"If I was on Earth, I would spray it with insect spray." Al laughed at the idea of spraying a giant flying insect.

Zita looked confused.

"Ignore that comment."

"We should be able to defeat it with magic. How much power do you have in that staff you carry?"

Al said, "I'm getting better, but people keep pulling me out of my training." He gave Zita a pointed look.

"We're running out of time." Zita sighed. "Taka is going to retrieve it before I do, and he has the Imperium Wand."

The Imperium Wand appeared to be a critical tool to achieve their goal. It seemed to be the proper tool to defeat Xalawad Furioso. Plus, they still hadn't determined what kind of vessel to bring. One day, Paxton had pulled out all the pots, pans and bowls in the house and Zita compared them to the image drawn on the scroll. The object seemed to be more like a ceramic planter decorated in blues and yellows than a pan, pot or bowl. Zita went through them all and decided that Paxton didn't have the right one.

"How do you plan to get the Imperium Wand? If it is so critical to our success, then won't we have to join forces with Taka to beat the gatekeepers?" Al rolled his shoulders to relax the tension out of them.

"There must be some way we can steal it from him. He had it on his desk at the castle for anyone to just pick up. We could sneak in and grab it without him even knowing."

"It probably has a tracking beacon like my staff. I just call it and the staff will come to me. And if someone tries to steal it, the staff will make a noise and let me know it's being stolen. But you already know that, don't you?"

Paxton and Sherry entered the room. Sherry had a smile on her face.

Al glanced at the couple. *She doesn't even talk with me, anymore and she waltzes in here with Paxton with a smile on her face.*

Zita nodded. "Yeah. How trustworthy do you think Taka is? We could offer to trade him information if he joined us in our quest."

Paxton said, "Like I said before, Taka isn't trustworthy and any alliance with him will end in disaster."

Al looked at Sherry, and she turned to face the fireplace. Al rolled his eyes as a pang of jealousy shot into his chest.

"I have good news. I received a message from my cousin, Kestrel." Paxton waved a small piece of paper in the air. "He's coming to the farmhouse with Lily. They should be here in two days."

Al thought that explained the smile on Sherry's face. Lily was her best friend from high school. Being of royal blood, Kestrel had the resources to travel even in this weather. Maybe with Lily here, Sherry's coldness would warm a little.

"And I have good news for Zita, too." Paxton continued. Sherry glanced briefly at Al then at Zita. "Kestrel managed to make contact with Erik. He's on his way here, but it might take him a week to arrive."

The news lifted Al's spirit, and it seemed a heavy burden lifted from his shoulders. He drummed his hands on the table for a few beats and shouted, "Yes!"

Zita's face transformed from a tight controlled look to smiling eyes that seemed to sparkle.

"That's great news," Al said. "With me, Kestrel, and Erik with the Sword of Freedom, we can remove the Corruption of Evil from you, Zita."

Sherry snorted, "Yeah and she can see the man she loves for the first time in months. Al, it isn't always about a quest or magic. Sometimes it's two people that touch hands, stare into each other's eyes and share memories together."

Al looked to the floor. He was trying to do those things with Sherry, but she hadn't spoken with him the last three days. How could they stare into each other's eyes when she wouldn't even stay in the same room with him? "Yeah, you're right," he mumbled.

Zita closed her eyes and swallowed hard.

Al wondered if she had changed, and might not let them remove the Corruption of Evil from her. She had to let them manage the evil before it became worse. Surely, she wanted the same result.

Sherry grabbed Paxton's arm. "We have a few things to get together before Lily and Kestrel arrive. I want to brighten up the rooms with some decorations. She escorted him from the room.

Al collapsed into one of the wooden chairs in the room as he thought of Sherry and Paxton and his own feeble attempts to get closer to Sherry. He felt like she enjoyed crushing his heart in a wine press.

Zita said, "We have to figure this all out, tonight."

"Why? It'll be even easier with Kestrel here. He can provide more insight into the hieroglyphics."

"I don't know if we can wait another two days to begin our journey."

Al ran a hand through his long hair. "What's the rush? Even if we were ready to go now, which we aren't, I would wait the extra days for Kestrel. His magic strength is probably back at full strength, and we could use his flight ability to allow us to spy on Taka, or even to scope out the castle where the crystal is located."

"I get this feeling in my gut that Taka is going to make his move soon and we should go with him, even if the others haven't arrived."

"That's crazy talk. We'll wait for Kestrel. Even wait for Erik. He has good ideas, and can probably solve some problems for us. At the very least, he can heal us if we get attacked by these gatekeepers."

What's her rush? Al thought. *Does she know something about Taka that she isn't telling us?*

CHAPTER 28

The moon goddess had told Zita that Taka planned to begin his quest to capture the Crystal of Zaraboth in two nights. She had twenty-four hours to finalize everything and get a head start on him. There were still so many unanswered questions. She didn't feel ready to leave.

She resumed stalking back and forth in front of the fireplace while Al continued to study the scroll.

Zita said, "Do you think Taka has all the tools to capture the crystal?"

Al remained seated in the wooden chair in front of the table. "We have the scroll that details all the guardians. Taka doesn't know all the magic objects he needs. Like this flower with the seven petals in the picture. Does he have that?"

Zita became animated and jabbed her finger angrily on the scroll. "See these seven stones?"

Al nodded.

"They are the guardians to the Castle of the Sacred Flowers. The seven-petaled flower is at that castle."

"Yeah, but I don't know how to find that castle."

Zita didn't know its location either, but the moon goddess told her not to worry about it, she could help Zita find it. Her stomach churned as angry bile bubbled like a fiery volcano of molten lava. She knew they weren't ready, but the Velidred moon goddess kept pushing her every night. She *must* acquire the flower before Taka.

"Listen," Al said. "Taka can't have everything he needs. We have the Crown of Anticletus. The defining magic item that will allow us to capture the crystal. If Taka goes to capture the crystal without the crown, he'll disintegrate just like my grandfather. We have time to do this right. Let's wait a week for Kestrel and Erik to get here."

That's why Zita and the moon goddess were working so hard on her mastery of the scorpion and her ability to manipulate people. She needed to convince Sherry to come with them. Given the amount of time Sherry spent with Paxton, she didn't see Sherry making the decision to travel with them on her own.

Zita asked Al, "Can you persuade Sherry to be ready to come with me tomorrow night?"

"We can't let you go that soon. Look at the scroll." He gestured toward the table. "There's more information we need to coax from it."

"Taka is heading for the crystal in two days. I have to beat him there. Sherry is needed."

Al shook his head. "You've seen the way she's treated me the last three days. She's not coming with you. I'm not even sure if I'm joining you. Plus, where are you getting your information about Taka's plans?"

Zita walked behind Al.

He twisted his neck to look at her.

Zita touched Al on the shoulder and she felt the tattoo from Al's Fire and Ice Challenge. Of course. Gadiel had proctored Al's induction into the mystical group, and that meant Zita could control him. She didn't need to wait for the big dork to agree to her demands. She could force him to act immediately with her connection to his tattoo. She had tried to manipulate him with the scorpion, but she only needed to touch his tattoo. A flush of excitement from this power rushed through her.

She wanted to at least give him a chance before pressuring him. She changed her tone from begging to a position of power. "Talk with Sherry and force her to come on the quest with us."

Al dropped his shoulders. "Let me talk with her first and see what she says. I'll meet you in the study after dinner."

Zita would let Al sit on the information until after dinner. Then she would either pressure Al or pressure Sherry. No matter what, she planned to leave with the Crown of Anticletus by tomorrow night.

# # # #

Al did not like the way Zita's tone had changed. It was like she had figured out a way to get Sherry to travel with her without Al's assistance. Had she mastered the scorpion? He needed to talk with Sherry before dinner; it was a conversation he didn't want to have. Maybe the two of them could convince Zita to wait until the others arrived.

Al stared, head in his hands, at the scroll without really reading any of it. He knew so little about this whole process. The scroll talked about finding the Crystal of Zaraboth in the Red Castle. He had no clue where to find the Red Castle. They also needed a map to find the Castle of the Sacred Flowers. He doubted his ability to persuade Sherry to take this trip with Zita. She was too cozy with Paxton, so getting her away from him would go a long way toward making Al feel better about his own relationship with her.

Twenty minutes later, Al had found Sherry sitting on the porch wearing a heavy cloak with a mug of hot chocolate in her hands. Al didn't know how Paxton had acquired chocolate, but it reminded him of how the farmer could provide for Sherry much better than he could ever imagine on this backwards planet.

Al stepped out on the porch. "Can we talk?" The wind had died down and the porch overhang provided enough shelter that it was almost comfortable on a cold winter day.

She looked at him, and he almost thought she would get up and go back into the house, but instead she nodded her head at an empty chair.

Al really didn't know how to broach the subject with her. He imagined her leaving in a huff or crying about something that Al couldn't fix.

"Well?"

"Um," Al started. "It's like this." He took a big breath and let it all out in one quick long statement, "The scroll says we need the Crown of Anticletus to capture the crystal. We need you. What do you say, will you come?"

She looked disgusted with him. She flinched and curled her lip as she responded. "We haven't talked in three days and this is the first thing you want to say to me? Will I give up everything I've worked for these last few months just to follow you and Zita to the ends of Aloheno looking for another treasure?"

"Well, it's just—"

"It's just what? Another adventure, a quest, or another chance you can squirm away from any real responsibility and go have fun. That's all you've ever done since you came to Aloheno. Oh, look, I have magic. See you." Sherry stared at the lake.

Al's chest tightened as his fears of how this conversation would play out came true.

"I thought we were talking about settling down," Sherry said. "Working side by side to make this world better. Remember? You would find a job using your magic, and I could go back to teaching. No more drama. No more adventures. We can be adults doing adult things."

Al leaned toward her. "I want all those things."

She scowled; her face flushed. "Ha! You don't even know what those words mean."

"That's not true. I've been trying to open the portal so you could go back to Earth. You know—all those luxuries on Earth like hot showers, cars, and movie theaters. All the things you say you miss. Every step I've taken is for you, and you know it."

She put up her hand and turned her head away from Al.

"Listen Sherry, we need you to go with us to capture the crystal. It requires the Crown of Anticletus."

"Why should I? You've ruined my life in Crossroads. I think I'll stay here with Paxton. I can educate children here in Triponca. That's assuming I'm not arrested and hanged for helping you and Zita escape."

Al ran his hand through his hair. There it was. She just told him that their relationship was over. She'd rather stay with Paxton. He thought there might be another option open to him. "Listen. I want to stay here with you, but Zita is determined to leave tomorrow night. Help me convince her to stay until Kestrel and Erik show up."

She shifted toward Al, and confusion creased her brow. "Why wouldn't she wait for Kestrel? They were friends growing up and I would definitely expect her to wait for Erik. She begged us to find him just a few days ago. Now we know he's coming, and she wants to leave early?"

"Yeah, I don't know what her problem is, but she seems worried about Velidred lunacy, Taka getting to the crystal before her, and I know she has the Corruption of Evil. Help me keep her here for a few more days. Can you do that?"

"Okay, but be assured that I'm not going with you." She gave him a flat look and crossed her arms across her chest.

Al's tension released. She wasn't completely in, but he hoped Sherry could help talk sense into Zita, allowing them to make decisions about the crystal as a group. It wasn't all settling onto his shoulders.

# # # #

After dinner, Zita examined the scroll once more as she waited in the study for Al and Sherry. They were actually talking with each other during the meal and she hoped it meant that Al had convinced Sherry to go with them. She needed to leave and find the seven petals and the Red Castle. She would rather wait for Kestrel, but the moon goddess had convinced her to leave immediately.

A few minutes later, Al, Paxton and Sherry entered the study. She smirked when she saw Paxton come with them. Did they think Paxton had any chance to change her mind? She figured he'd be just as easy to manipulate as his staff.

Al looked at Zita and then at Sherry and Paxton, who were sitting close to each other on a couch. No one said anything for about a minute. Zita felt the tension in the room as the darkness seemed to close in about her.

Sherry motioned at Al with her hand.

Al cleared his throat. "We made a decision."

Zita didn't say anything.

With a glance at Sherry, Al said, "We're planning to wait for Kestrel, Lily, and Erik. We'll be stronger as a group."

Tightness settled in Zita's jaw as she realized she'd have to force them to cooperate. The moon goddess made it seem so easy, but she knew how hard she'd have to work to get them to agree with her.

"That won't do," Zita said. "I need Sherry to come with me. I don't have time to wait for Kestrel."

Al stood, wringing his hands. "We want to help you, but you're thinking irrationally. Maybe it's the Velidred lunacy affecting your decisions, but it's in your best interest to wait."

"Sherry isn't ready to go with you." Paxton chimed in.

Zita scowled, "You have no say in this decision."

"Leave him alone, he's been helping you for over a week now," Sherry said. "Don't be so ungrateful."

Zita felt the scorpion start across her eye.

Al moved to stand between Sherry and Zita. "Leave it for another day."

"Out of my way. I'm leaving with Sherry, and you can't stop me."

"No, I'm staying here with Paxton." Sherry stood and moved toward Paxton. "I'll never go with you."

Al blocked her way, but Zita knew what to do.

She placed her hand on Al's shoulder which proved difficult because the young wizard was much taller. Al's branding from the Fire and Ice experience pulsed. She delved with her mind into the brand.

Al stepped back a step and sucked in a deep breath. She felt his heart stutter and then restart beating. He glared at her. "What did you do?"

"Since Gadiel died, I own you and your Fire and Ice tattoo." She remembered the control Gadiel had over her and his ability to cause her pain at times without magic and without touching her. She still needed to work on her ability to control at a distance, but she knew just a slight touch would be enough.

Al raised his hand and called, "Staff come." His staff flew into his hands.

Zita laughed. "Your staff won't stop me. Convince Sherry to come with me before I hurt you and Paxton."

Al turned to face Zita and placed the staff diagonally across his frame, separating them. "Sherry, leave the farmhouse. Find someplace to hide."

Sherry stood next to Al and crossed her arms. "I'm not letting her bully you. I've had it with ungrateful bullies. You remind me of the thugs in Crossroads."

Zita moved closer to Al to regain the contact she had lost when he moved.

He stepped back another step, pulling Sherry back with him. Paxton moved up to stand with his friends.

Zita took a deep breath and exhaled. Her hand shook as she looked up at Al. "If Taka gets the crystal before me, I'll never be able to use it."

"We keep telling you, Erik can help," Sherry said.

Paxton said, "As long as the weather stays decent, Erik will be here soon. Everything will be okay."

Zita shook her head and then looked at Paxton. She chanted silently as she gazed into the farmer's eyes. The man didn't know enough to look away, and Zita had guessed right that he couldn't withstand the Corruption of Evil.

Paxton moved to the couch. "I need to sit."

Sherry looked at Paxton and then returned her attention to Zita. "What did you do to him?"

She feigned surprise. "I didn't do anything. He must be tired and wanted to sit."

Paxton had a glazed expression on his face.

Sherry's mouth slackened, as her eyes widened in disbelief as the scene unfolded before her.

Al pushed Sherry in an attempt to get her behind him but she fought him.

"Run and hide. Zita has the Corruption of Evil and is willing to use it on us to get what she wants."

"I'm not hiding."

Al groaned.

Zita attempted to use the scorpion to manipulate Sherry, but it wasn't working. She didn't know if Sherry had more ability to fight her because of her power as the Crown of Anticletus or another reason.

Al moved toward Zita. "Stop it." He attempted to push her to the floor.

Zita grabbed Al's shoulder and sent a charge of power into his tattoo. "I need to leave and you're going to help convince Sherry to come with me."

"Never!" Sherry and Al said simultaneously.

Then Zita added more power to the tattoo and Al crumpled to the floor.

Sherry had a dazed look when Al went down.

Zita cheered internally for a moment because Sherry didn't have the sense to run. She moved toward her where they stood face to face. With a touch of her hand, she directed Sherry to face her. It must have been the physical touch that allowed Zita's scorpion power to work. With a little chant, Sherry submitted to her.

Sherry yelped, and her posture stiffened.

Zita directed, "Grab a cloak and some food we can travel with. Meet me on the back porch."

"Yes, master." Sherry left the room.

Zita leaned to Al. "Stay down until after we leave or next time, you won't move for a month. Do you understand?"

Al used magic to enable a shield.

"The shield won't help you." She touched his shoulder and watched for five seconds while he lay on his back, kicking his legs uncontrollably. He looked like an overturned beetle.

When she released him, Al breathed heavily and tried to crawl backwards, banging into chairs and table legs to escape.

Zita smelled Al's fear as he tried to move away. "Don't come after me, or I'll make our next encounter worse."

Al collapsed into a quivering bundle of sweat.

CHAPTER 29

Thirty minutes later, Al heard the farmhouse's kitchen door slam shut. It took him another two minutes to manipulate his body to a standing position. The pain of the electric charge still fired through his body. He glanced at Paxton who still sat with glazed eyes. Al hoped the spell would dissipate soon. They were going to have to leave immediately if they wanted to rescue Sherry.

Al limped to the back door, but couldn't see anything in the dark of night. He grabbed his cloak and checked outside. He followed tracks in the snow to Paxton's barn. When he opened the barn door, he didn't see anybody. A quick search revealed that Zita had stolen Paxton's two horses. The farmer only had the two.

He called Sherry's name in the darkness, but heard no reply. She had been kidnapped by the crazy, green-eyed former princess. He trudged through the snow back to the farmhouse, defeated.

An hour later, Al had revived Paxton to his former self. Luckily, Zita's spell only lasted a short time.

Sitting across the table from Paxton, Al said, "They left on your horses. Can we get horses from other farmers to rescue Sherry?"

Paxton shook his head. "This is a poor community. The other farmers in the village have one or two horses, but they will be reluctant to release them to us at this time of year. The snow increases the chance for their horses to be injured."

Al stared at Paxton. "Look, you want to rescue Sherry as much as I do."

Paxton nodded.

"We'll go after them, but I can't withstand Zita's power. You saw what she can do with one touch of my tattoo. I hate to do it, but we have to wait for Kestrel to get here. He'll provide more magic power."

"Tomorrow morning, I'll go to my neighbors and see if I can find a horse for you."

"Aren't you coming with me?"

"I'm useless against all your magical powers, and I have a farm to run. It's been chaotic since you three arrived, and it's best if I stay at the farm. I don't trust Taka and his thugs. They'll be back and I need to be here." He touched the knife wound in his shoulder.

Al felt heat in his cheeks. It felt shameful the way he and Zita had disrupted Paxton and Sherry's lives. And now, Zita had run off with Paxton's work horses. He knew Sherry and Paxton were close, but he hoped if he could save her, he might be able to win her back.

"I promise to find Sherry and bring her back, and return with your horses." But he feared he was in over his head on this one. He would wait for Kestrel, but could they wait another few days for Erik? He stared into the fire.

# # # #

Al watched with excitement around two o'clock the next afternoon when Paxton returned from a trip into the village leading two horses. He walked out to the barn as Paxton led the animals into separate stalls.

Paxton said, "I found these two old mares. They aren't much to look at, but they're hard-working farm animals. You'll have to rest them more than younger horses, but they'll get you where you need to go."

Al didn't know much about horses, but even he thought the animals looked a little worn. They didn't have much choice. "Why two horses?"

Paxton shoveled some hay into a stall. "You need to wait for Erik before you go after Sherry."

"But that will put us five or more days behind them. Do you think that's wise?"

"He has a calming influence on Zita."

Al agreed with Paxton's comment, but he wanted to rescue Sherry as soon as possible. Maybe this time she would realize how much he loved her.

They finished settling the horses, and as they walked into the farmhouse, Magnus ran into the kitchen. "Those guys are back. You need to hide."

Paxton stood unmoving, a grave expression on his face. "No, I can't leave you all in the house with those monsters. I have to face him."

Al called his staff to him. As he caught it, he promised, "I'll stand with you. I owe it to you."

With a voice devoid of emotion, Paxton said, "They'll be happy to kill you as easily as me."

Al hadn't been this afraid since his first time in battle against King Haskell's warrior wizards. Time felt like it had slowed to a crawl as they walked into the study to wait for Taka's thugs.

Dakarai walked in first, followed by Sims and Lenny, and someone Al hadn't seen before. The man wore a cloak with fur at the collars and carried a wooden wand. Taka?

"Gentlemen," Al said as he threw up a shield.

Dakarai laughed.

Al's shield disintegrated. He attempted to throw a fireball at his adversaries but realized that Dakarai or Taka had taken away his magic. How did Haskell's warrior wizards not use this ability when they attacked the Wizard Ishwa and the wizard warriors he trained?

"Where is she?" Sims asked.

Al shook his head. "She left last night. Took Paxton's horses and a housemaid."

Sims walked over to Paxton and pulled his knife. "Is that true, farmer?"

As Sims got closer to Paxton, the blood drained from the farmer's face. Sims wasn't a nice man and Al couldn't see any reason for Sims to spare his friend's life now that Zita wasn't there. Fear filled Al's shoulders.

Paxton said, "I'll be happy to show you our secret room and you can verify she isn't here."

Sims put the knife under Paxton's chin. "You better not be lying to me."

Al couldn't let Paxton be killed. "He's not lying."

"Why didn't you go after them?" Sims pushed up a little on the knife and Paxton lifted his chin higher.

"We couldn't, they took the horses." Al shrugged.

Sims laughed. "I had heard this boy wizard was someone special. You can't even protect your friend." He drew blood under Paxton's chin.

Paxton grunted.

"Leave him alone. We've told you all we know."

Dakarai said, "Have you? Where's the scroll?"

"She took it with her."

"Where is she going?"

Al hardened his stomach as if he planned to pounce on Sims, but realized he had no chance against the thugs and the two wizards. Sims had the knife poked hard under Paxton's chin. Sherry would never forgive him if he did something that killed Paxton. He thought about leading Taka on a wild goose chase, but worried what might happen to the farmer if Taka caught him in a lie.

He took a deep breath. "Zita said she needed something called the Imperium Wand. She thought she could find it back at the Velidred Castle."

Dakarai stared at Al and shook his head. "No, she knew better than to go back to Velidred. We would have crossed her on the road."

Al felt the stare penetrating his soul. *They are going to catch me in this lie and I'm done for.*

"Sims, convince our wizard friend here about the need to not lie to us."

Sims sneered and pushed up on the knife where blood dripped from Paxton's chin.

Paxton stood defiant against his attacker.

"Stop it. I'm telling the truth. Zita said she needed the Imperium Wand to defeat something called a Geirhild Hlifsteed."

Taka smiled. "Our friend does know something after all. What else is needed?"

"How should I know? Zita didn't share any information with us. She had a scroll up in her room, but she would hide it every time one of us entered the room. She used magic to hurt one of the housekeepers who found the scroll lying on her bed. We thought the woman would die."

"I want to talk to this woman."

Al took a deep breath. *I can't continue these lies; Taka will kill me when he finds out.* "The woman quit. She said she didn't see anything on the scroll, and Zita is crazy. We haven't seen her since." He felt heat flush in his face. Surely, Dakarai or Taka could sniff out his lies.

Sims turned to Taka, "I can finish the farmer off with one twist."

Taka raised his hand. "No, not yet. He's still useful for the moment." Taka tapped his wand on his shoulder as if in thought. "Is there anything else Zita said, or comments she made, that might be helpful."

Al looked at Paxton, who stayed stoic throughout the torture Sims exercised. Maybe he should throw Taka a truth, something they hadn't found an answer to. "Zita did something strange."

Taka leaned in closer.

Al looked at the floor and thought about the best way to present this fact in a way that Taka wouldn't be able to use the information. "One day, Paxton and I were sitting at the kitchen table and Zita entered the room and started going through all the bowls, pots, and pans. Like she needed a specific size bowl or something."

Taka threw his head back and laughed. A full belly laugh that came from his core. "Yeah, don't worry about that. I have that lined up already."

Al stood silent.

"What else do you know?"

"That's it. We were still doing research, and somehow Zita knew you were coming. She disabled us, and took the house maid with her. Told the woman to pack some food and saddle the horses."

Taka asked, "She knew we were coming?"

Dakarai piped up, "Like I said boss, she has the Corruption of Evil. She's a crafty little wizard like her dad. We'll have to be careful around her."

The blood pounded in Al's brain. He hoped Taka believed his lies. That might be the only thing that saved them.

"Tell me. Why did Zita take the housemaid?"

Al stiffened. Could he continue to lie convincingly to this master wizard? He pressed his lips together, biting his inner lower lip to calm his nerves. "Simply a woman who lived in Crossroads. Zita and I hid in the woman's home and then took her with us to Paxton's. The farmer agreed to let her stay on here as part of his staff since the Crossroads patrol would have figured she helped Zita escape." Al shrugged like it was no big deal.

Dakarai asked, "Why didn't Zita take you? You have magical training and are the wonder kid, the grandson of Alpherge the Mighty."

Al sucked in some air, "I don't know. She crippled me with her magic, and she must have figured I wasn't worth the trouble of another mouth to feed on the journey."

Taka nodded and rolled the wand around in his fingers. He contemplated something.

Al hoped they would leave. Sims still held the knife to Paxton's throat.

Dakarai looked at Taka. "Boss?"

Taka stood silent for two minutes staring at Al.

Al wasn't able to keep eye contact; he set his gaze on Taka's feet. Sweat beaded on his forehead as the room seem to heat up from the number of people in it. Al's inability to lie convincingly or the wood burning in the fireplace seemed to play a role in his discomfort? His throat felt constricted and he believed smoke from the fireplace had stopped going out the chimney and was backfilling into the room. His breathing became ragged. He rubbed his hands together as his anxiety increased each second Taka stared at him.

Taka walked to Al and raised his chin so their eyes met.

Al stared into the man's brown eyes burnished with gold. He wondered if Taka could hear his heart pounding against his ribcage. At least Taka would kill him with magic, and he didn't have to bleed out from a knife wound from Sims.

"Let's go. She's got a head start on us." Taka pushed Al back against the wall.

Sims pushed the knife further into Paxton's chin.

Paxton struck Sims' knife hand with a hard chop of his hand. The knife clattered to the floor.

Paxton jumped on Sims and they both went to the floor, knocking over a table. A lantern burning on the table crashed to the floor spilling oil.

Taka walked out the back door.

Lenny jumped on Paxton and flailed the younger man with his fists.

The oil caught fire and a flame flared.

"Stop it." Dakarai pulled on Lenny. "I said, stop." Lenny stopped pounding on Paxton and rose slowly off of the pile of sweating bodies.

Paxton released his hold on Sims and struggled to his feet, grimacing when he pushed off with his injured shoulder. He kept his gaze on Sims despite the fire burning nearby grew stronger each moment.

Sims rolled over to all fours and scowled at Paxton. Sims' mouth and nose were bleeding. He slowly got to his feet. He bent down and picked up the knife.

Lenny stood between Paxton and Sims. Lenny pushed Sims to the door. "Let's go."

The wooden table legs began to burn.

Sims said, "I'm coming back for you, farmer."

The men left the farmhouse.

Paxton grabbed at his knees, as his breaths came in huge gulps of air.

CHAPTER 30

The fire spread across the wooden floor and a couch began to burn as Paxton rallied his staff to extinguish the flames. They brought buckets of water, and Al helped throw water on the table and floor. His magic returned before they had completely extinguished the fire, and he called out a chant to snuff out the remaining blaze.

The room stank from the burned hide covering the couch.

Al grabbed the wet hide and turned it over to see if it might still be burning. The water had saturated the hide and it smelled like a wet dog. "I'm sorry Paxton. This is all my fault. If I had turned Zita over to the authorities in Crossroads, you wouldn't have been impacted by this."

Paxton held his hand over his shoulder where the knife wound had reopened and a ring of blood darkened the bandages. The man who usually smiled at life's struggles looked like he had reached the end of any kindness he could offer Al.

Al hung his head, disappointed at all the trouble he had caused Paxton.

Paxton ran a wet hand through his hair. "My great grandfather originally built this home over a hundred years ago. Watching the room go up in flames broke my heart." He walked to the couch and shook his head. "My grandfather built that couch. Oh, we've had to repair it a couple of times, but the frame is still the same." He picked up one end that wasn't burnt and pushed the couch away from the charred wood beneath it.

"Do you think Sherry will be safe?" Paxton asked.

"That's why I told Taka she was a servant. Then he won't need her."

"Which means she's disposable."

Al gasped. "You're right. I just made it worse for her. Sims won't hesitate to stick a knife in a simple servant." What had he just done to his girlfriend?

They heard horses clomping at the back of the house and worried that Taka had returned. Al raced to the windows to see Kestrel and Lily dismounting as Paxton's stable boy held the horses' reins. Lily's face beamed when she saw Al. Seeing his old high school friend from Earth brightened his mood. *Now with Kestrel here, we can make plans to rescue Sherry and help Zita.*

Al embraced Lily in a tight hug. She had come through the portal from Earth with Al and his friends. Zita's father had kidnapped her. Al, Erik and Sherry had to rescue Lily. "I'm glad you're here."

"I can't wait to see Sherry. Where is she?"

Al's heart thumped in his chest. How could he break the news to Lily that Zita kidnapped? He rubbed his hands over his face and took a deep breath. Avoiding answering the question, Al grasped Kestrel's arm in a tight squeeze the way Kestrel's family and tribe exchanged greetings.

Lily expressed concern, "Is she okay?"

Paxton stepped out on the porch. "Let's get your things and go inside." He motioned for one of his hired hands to fetch the guests' belongings as he opened the door for Lily and his cousin, Kestrel.

They settled down at the kitchen table while the cook warmed up soup for the cold-weary travelers. Al related the story of Zita and the trouble they had gotten into because he had wanted to help her.

Lily gasped every time the story got worse, and she broke down and cried when she heard of Sherry's current situation.

Kestrel said, "It hasn't been long. We can rest a couple of hours and go after them."

Paxton shook his head. "Not so fast. Zita is highly unstable at the moment. We should wait for Erik before chasing after Sherry."

Lily grabbed Kestrel's arm. "We must do something. We should head out immediately."

Kestrel looked at Lily and then at Paxton, who did a minor shake of his head.

"Waiting for Erik would be better."

"We can't wait another few days for Erik." Lily's voice betrayed the anguish she felt for her friend. "I beg you."

Kestrel took her in his arms. "It's best we wait."

They talked some more about what they might need to find Zita and Sherry, and then Kestrel said, "I have an idea. Let me fly over the travelers and get their positions on the journey. With a little luck, I'll be able to tell you how far they've gotten. I've heard the snow isn't as bad in the valley, and maybe they'll be safe from Taka until we get moving."

"That's a good idea, but you'll have to fly high enough for Taka not to take your magic from you. He has a spell that blocks magic, and his thug Dakarai also knows the trick." Al had never heard the full story of how Kestrel gained the ability to transform into a falcon. It seemed like a unique skillset, even for this planet.

"I heard desert wizards had learned to block magic, but they don't share that knowledge with other wizards," Kestrel said. "I'm surprised the Grand Wizard still let Taka stay in the castle. Usually, you had to teach others extreme magic before you were allowed on the Council of Nine. I'm interested to see what my father has to say about this. What do you think Taka's range is with this spell?"

Al said, "He has the Imperium Wand, so that might be more powerful than you or I can imagine."

"Hmm." Kestrel stood, arched and knuckled his back. "I have to walk around a little and get my land legs back."

"Let me walk with you. It's been a long journey." Lily rose and walked to Kestrel's side.

Al heard Lily whisper to Kestrel, "Will it be safe for you to fly so far after our long journey? You're still recovering from your magic sickness."

Kestrel grimaced but didn't say anything.

Al hoped that Kestrel's full strength had returned. Their journey to rescue Sherry would be difficult, and Al didn't think he could beat Taka or Zita by himself in a magic challenge. Kestrel needed to be strong, mentally and magically, if they hoped to beat Taka and Dakarai.

# # # #

Four hours later, Kestrel relayed the news after his reconnaissance mission. "Zita and Sherry have a good lead on Taka, but it looks like Taka and his thugs are moving faster. I think Zita will make it to the Castle of the Sacred Flowers before Taka catches her."

Al pursed his lips in thought as his chest tightened. If only there had been some way for him to have stopped Zita from leaving. Then he remembered Taka arriving. Zita would have been forced to leave with Taka and she still would have taken the Crown of Anticletus.

Lily asked, "Once at the castle, will she be safe?"

Kestrel shook his head. "No. That's just one stopping point in the journey. If we expect to follow, we'll need to stop and pick up a flower petal, too."

Lily squinted her eyes as her face tightened, obvious signs of worry about her best friend from high school.

Al asked, "How long do you think it will take them to reach the Castle of the Sacred Flowers?"

Kestrel bobbed his hands up and down as if he were juggling imaginary balls. "Two days, maybe three. Four at the most. Their horses seemed to be struggling in the deep snow. Taka's mounts looked stronger and more capable."

Paxton snorted, "My work horses aren't suited for this type of journey at all. They were good farm animals, but not for long distance travel."

"They will get out of the deep snow in a little over a day, depending on how many miles per day they are pushing the horses." Kestrel said, "That'll make it easier on the horses. It didn't look like they were carrying a heavy load."

"I fear that once they get past the snow-covered trails, they'll try to push harder." Paxton ran his hand through his hair. "That'll increase the chance to injure the horses. They are bred for slow steady work with a proper amount of rest and a good diet, not a fast-paced run over long distances."

"How do we plan to catch them?" Lily asked.

"We will try to be smart about it. The horses Paxton acquired for Erik and me are hardly better suited for the journey." Al looked over at Kestrel, "Do you know where to find the Red Castle?"

Kestrel said, "I've never been there. My father has talked about it in the past. It's located just past the desert."

Al glanced at Paxton. "Do you have a map that might show us the Red Castle?"

He grunted, "No, there's no need to have a map of that area of the world. It's outside of my district."

"In the morning, I will fly back to my father's castle," Kestrel said. "I'm certain he has a map that will help us. We can't go wandering around the desert with no idea of where we're headed."

Lily touched his arm, "That's a long way to fly. Will you be all right in the cold for that long?"

Kestrel patted her hand. "I'll be fine. I will rest overnight and return the following day. Hopefully by then, Erik will have arrived and we can leave the next morning."

They talked late into the night about the tools, magic items, and the steps required to reach the Red Castle in time to rescue Sherry and try to heal Zita of the Corruption of Evil.

"How's Zita's mindset?" Kestrel asked.

Al shook his head. "She's bending more each day to be controlled by the Velidred Moon Goddess. We are losing time each day we wait for Erik. Zita might not be able to be saved by the time we find her. The power of the scorpion might be too strong to defeat."

CHAPTER 31

Zita yelled back at Sherry for what seemed the hundredth time in the last hour. "Hurry up. You need to keep pace with me." She pushed the horses hard in hopes she could get to the Castle of the Sacred Flowers before Taka caught up with them. Sherry seemed to be purposely holding back her horse.

"My horse doesn't want to move faster." Sherry kicked her heels against the horse's side, but the horse didn't increase its speed. "It's tired. We should stop and let it rest."

"We don't have time to let it rest." Zita had been clenching her teeth so tight her jaw hurt. The frustration with the horses and the deep snow seemed to make everything worse. She had tried to use the power of the Corruption of Evil to motivate the horses, but earlier her horse had almost fallen over. She had run it to exhaustion.

Zita groaned, "Okay, let's get down and walk them for a couple of miles."

"They're hungry and thirsty," Sherry said.

The redhead had been stating the obvious for the last ten miles. Sherry had brought food for Zita and her but hadn't considered what the horses would eat. The deep snow along the road hid the grasses and whatever else horses might eat.

They walked until Zita's toes turned cold. "Okay, let's mount." She got up on the horse and watched as Sherry struggled to mount hers. The non-athletic woman made the simple act of riding a horse like a battle against monsters.

Sherry eventually mounted, and they continued on the path down the mountain.

Four hours later, almost at noon, a strong southerly breeze had pushed the clouds from the area. The sunshine felt good on Zita's face and she had hopes that things would get better. They had reached a part of the road that ran into a valley far below. The snow had begun to melt and small waterfalls cascaded down the side of the mountains.

Zita's mood improved as the day progressed. They had traveled far enough south for the snow to be less deep. The sun was melting the snow on the road and there were patches where they walked on bare dirt. The horses seemed to do okay with the muddy road. Their speed increased, and an hour later she saw the first patches of green. They reached a meadow where green blades of grass poked out of the snow, and small sections were completely clear of snow.

They found a creek and gave the horses a rest. The sunshine on Zita's back seemed to loosen the tension across her shoulders and neck. She closed her eyes and enjoyed the sun. Maybe the snow would be gone soon, and they could make better time than they had in the high mountains.

Zita hadn't slept well the last three nights worrying about Sherry escaping her control. Whenever the Anticletus moon rose, Zita sensed Sherry looking for a way to escape. As the Crown of Anticletus, Sherry had a strong affinity to the moon. Whose moon magic had the most power, Anticletus or Velidred? She couldn't imagine what might happen if Sherry escaped. She hoped to use the Earth girl as a bargaining chip with Taka. Realistically, she supposed Taka could take Sherry and prevent Zita from doing anything about it.

They had to move on. Soon they would reach an area without snow, and they could gain distance over her pursuers. She assumed Taka was chasing her, but she couldn't wait for him to catch up to see. She press the horses to move faster.

They gave the horses two hours to eat, drink and rest, and then they re-mounted to journey further. The rest had helped, and Zita felt at this pace they could be at the castle early the next day, get their seven-petal flower, and head to the desert before Taka caught them.

The path became rocky and the horses slowed. The landscape was rolling hills, with snow at the summits, and in the valley shadows.

Sherry yelled for Zita to stop. She had dismounted and examined her horse's leg. "Zita, you need to look at this."

"What is it now?" Zita shouted.

"My horse is limping."

Zita's mind went numb. This couldn't be happening. They needed to move forward, faster than anybody that might be trying to chase them. "Let me look at it." Zita dismounted and examined the animal. She walked it around a small space and watched it walk. The animal definitely favored the one leg, not putting any weight on it.

Sherry asked, "What should we do?"

Zita stood close to Sherry. "You are going to get onto the horse and make it walk."

"But it's injured. These are Paxton's horses. We are responsible for them; we have to take care of them and return them to him."

"We're never going back to Paxton's. You're never ever going to see Paxton again. Do you hear me? Get back on the horse and force it to move." She felt the heat of anger pour through her body.

Tears formed in Sherry's eyes. Zita had never seen the woman cry. Sherry was one of the strongest women that Zita knew and worked hard to make things happen no matter the circumstances or pain of doing so.

Sherry sat on a nearby rock and began balling. "I'm tired. I hate you. I hate this planet. I'm not going another step, and you can't make me."

"Oh, I can make you, and I will force you to continue. Believe me, if we continue on just another day, we'll reach the Castle of the Sacred Flowers. They will feed us, and we can rest in real beds, and have a nice hot bath." Zita hoped for all that. She had no idea what she'd actually find at the castle.

Sherry continued crying with her arms wrapped around her shoulders.

Zita just let the woman cry. She actually felt like crying too. It had been a horrible journey, and even the times she had tried to sleep, the moon goddess had wanted her to practice her lessons. Fatigue and travel weariness had settled in, and she wondered if they would make it to the castle the next day.

The Anticletus moon had risen in the sky and Zita gazed up at it. Then she heard a voice. "Release me. I'm your friend. Let me go, and let me return to Paxton."

Sherry was using the Crown of Anticletus. She wasn't tired or crying. The redhead was manipulating the crown to force Zita to release her. Zita felt she should release the girl. *Sherry doesn't belong on this planet. Let her return to her friends and continue on the journey alone.*

"Yes, you are right." Zita nodded and smiled.

Sherry stood. "Is it okay if I take your horse?"

Zita felt hesitation. She couldn't let Sherry take the healthy horse. Something was wrong with that idea, but she acquiesced. "Please, take mine. I'll make do with this horse."

Sherry walked over to Zita's horse and mounted.

Watching with rapt attention, Zita let Sherry click her tongue and the horse moved back in the direction toward Paxton's place. Zita walked toward Sherry as the scorpion crawled up Zita's eye. She raised her hand. "Wait." She needed to regain control, before Sherry got beyond her reach.

A blue glow encapsulated Sherry and her now-visible crown reflected onto Zita.

She struggled for control in this battle between the Corruption of Evil and the Crown of Anticletus. If only the Velidred moon had risen, she knew she could gain control.

Sherry walked her horse away from Zita who continued to hurry toward Sherry.

Zita's muscles quivered in anger at this turn of events. Her captive was taking control of the situation. No, she must stand firm. Release her own power. The Corruption of Evil placed a wall between her and Sherry's commands. Then her anger really kicked in. She ran over to Sherry, pulled her off the horse, and slapped her across the face, sending the girl to the ground.

The sound of the slap echoed off the mountains.

Zita said, "Look at me."

"Never."

Zita grabbed Sherry's hair and forced her face toward her own. "I demand you to look at me."

A whimper emanated from Sherry. She closed her eyes.

"Open your eyes."

"I will not."

Then Zita felt it. She had the power to force Sherry to obey without having the girl stare into her eyes. The Corruption of Evil proved stronger than Anticletus. Zita had the power over her redheaded adversary.

Sherry opened her eyes, and Zita recognized the fear in that encapsulated them.

Zita touched Sherry's arm and commanded, "Get up, and get back on your horse. We're moving. Now." Then she sent an electric shock of a hundred tiny lightning bolts through the girl and watched as she shook and kicked her heels.

Sherry's horse didn't last another mile, making Zita furious. They were forced to abandon the horse near a stream, and they were left with them both riding the single horse. This became a horrible situation in Zita's eyes. Her horse already struggled, and the added weight of the girl and the food she carried would force them to walk slower, and require more breaks to rest the animal.

They traveled together for another few miles, and then walked the animal to give it a chance to rest. The Anticletus Moon had begun to set which allowed Zita to relax her control over Sherry.

The fight for power had forced them to lose time, Zita compelled Sherry to continue on their journey. Zita worried that the next day the Anticletus moon would be in new moon status, potentially giving Sherry her greatest power. She imagined they would reach the Castle of the Sacred Flowers at the same time Sherry's power reached its zenith. She hoped Taka was still a couple days behind.

Zita did not feel comfortable stopping overnight to rest. She let Sherry sleep on the horse while Zita walked it during the darkest part of the night when only the Pantaleon Moon shone in the night sky.

The next morning, they were officially out of the mountains and the land leveled. The warm southern wind had dried the landscape, making the walking easier. Zita knew they were getting closer to the Castle of the Sacred Flowers and felt confident they would reach it before noon.

She looked back and saw four figures on horses following the same road they traveled, but still high in the mountains.

Her heart skipped a beat, and adrenaline rushed to her core. Could that be Taka and his thugs, and could she beat them to the castle? Her mind raced, trying to calculate the time necessary for Taka to catch her.

Zita couldn't take a chance, so she jumped on the back of the horse behind Sherry, and forced the horse faster. She set a brisk pace.

CHAPTER 32

Zita saw the seven obelisks in the distance as black monsters. They were known as the guardians of the Castle of the Sacred Flowers. They rose twenty-five feet into the sky. When they reached them, she saw that they were obsidian stone. She had observed and touched obsidian at the Velidred Castle, but she had never seen blocks of the stone like this. Each stone seemed to be a single piece with a ten-foot by ten-foot base.

She looked at the mountains in the distance. None looked like volcanoes, yet she knew obsidian came from volcanos. Where had these originated and who had transported them to this location? The Castle of the Sacred Flowers awaited, a mile away from the seven stones.

They traveled on toward the castle. The drawbridge had been lowered, and they didn't know if it was always down or if the residents of the castle saw them coming and lowered the bridge. They walked over it into the castle bailey, a large courtyard, to discover it filled with many houses.

Zita yelled, "Hello, is anybody here?"

Silence.

No smoke drifted from chimneys. She heard no blacksmiths banging, children playing, or any normal noise you'd find in a village surrounding a castle. The keep stood on a motte within the bailey, a tall hill difficult to navigate while guards had the opportunity to shoot arrows at any invading force Yet, it appeared no one guarded the keep.

Sherry asked, "Now, what do we do?"

Zita scowled at her, "We continue up to the keep." Fatigue from walking and traveling at night had sapped her every strength; she had no desire to climb up the hundred or more steps to reach the castle doors. She wondered if she had traveled here all to no avail. Could it be that no one lived in the castle, and there were no seven-petal sacred flowers?

Zita shouted again, "Hello!"

They searched the homes near the castle steps, looking for anyone who could help. From the condition of the homes, the cold fireplaces, barren cupboards, and beds without covers, she surmised no one had been here in a long time.

Zita found a place to hide the horse, although she had hoped to find hay or oats, but saw nothing to feed the animal. She hoped if Taka came, he wouldn't steal her only mode of transportation. On second thought, maybe if she hurried and acquired the flower petals, they could hide in the village and steal Taka's horses.

They started the long journey up the stairs to the castle. About half-way up, she turned to look back at the stone guardians, to see if she could spot Taka, but it looked clear as far as she could see. *Good, maybe they had time to get in and out with no trouble.* The Anticletus new moon rose in the east. She must hurry, before Sherry tried to escape again.

Zita was sucking in huge gasps of air before she reached the keep doors and had to catch her breath. She found two huge wooden doors carved with battle scenes. She pulled on the handle, but the door didn't budge. Zita turned around and sat down, looking out into the meadow below. If they couldn't get into the keep then they couldn't go after the crystal. Taka would capture her and make her a slave.

Sherry arrived at the top of the stairs, out of breath like Zita. "Why aren't you going in?" she wheezed.

"It's locked." Even though Zita felt angry, she didn't have the strength to yell at Sherry for asking an obvious question.

Sherry tried the door with the same result as Zita. "What's this cord for?"

"What?" Zita asked.

Sherry pulled the cord and a bell rang on the other side of the door.

After the pealing had ended nothing happened. The door stayed closed. *This is where it ends then.* A sound of steps echoed behind the wooden doors.

Zita struggled to her feet.

The door pushed open, and a woman wearing a white robe greeted them, "Hello. We've been expecting you."

Zita exchanged a look with Sherry, who shrugged her shoulders. *If they were expecting us, couldn't they have been at the door when we arrived?*

A woman introduced herself as Davina and escorted them into a large foyer where three women waited with hot steamed hand cloths, a tray of apples, strawberries, grapes, and orange slices, and a tray with silver chalices of water.

Davina said, "Please clean your face and hands, and help yourself to the refreshments."

Zita cleansed the dust from her face, neck, and hands. She asked, "Who are you, and where is everyone?" She indicated the town at the bottom of the motte.

"We will have someone share our history with you later. Please, come into our antechamber and refresh yourself."

Davina led them to another room with chairs along the wall and a table with benches in the center of the room. Tapestries hung on every wall. They showed different scenes of women working. One with a background of red with figures in white thread showed women stomping on grapes and making wine. Another with a green background and white thread showed images of women milking cows. The last had a background of white that displayed three women making bread in the kitchen stitched in red.

Zita didn't know exactly what to think about the tapestries. Velidred Castle had multi-colored tapestries with images of men in battle, slaying their enemies. She wondered if a queen ruled here in a matriarchal society.

Sherry sat at the bench while eating the grapes and oranges they had been offered.

Zita sat across the table from her and sipped tentatively at the chalice of water. She worried it might be poisoned, a trick from Taka. Could he have already arrived? But it tasted fresh and didn't make her sick, so she downed the remaining drink.

She asked, "Who rules here in this castle?"

"You will learn that information," Davina said. "Please relax. There is time."

"There isn't time," Zita pleaded. "I'm being chased. I need to get a seven-petaled flower and leave. Please help me. Evil men are pursuing us." The woman surely would help them, if she knew the dangers of the men behind them.

Davina stood at the head of the table near the door with her hands together as if in prayer. "I'm not the person who can offer you the sacred flower."

"Can you introduce me to the person who is responsible for that transaction?" Her father had always told her to ask for the people that could help and not to be shuttled around from one incompetent bureaucrat to another.

"I assure you; we will give you an opportunity for the flower, but it is still early. There is a ceremony, and the high priestess is busy at the moment."

Zita stood and the red scorpion moved from the corner of her eye to cover her iris and pupil. "I command you to take me to her immediately."

Davina smiled, "We have seen your kind before. Your evil magic has no power here. The obsidian guardians have jurisdiction here and will always protect us. Please enjoy the refreshments. I will return." With those words, Davina turned and left.

Sherry said, "Enjoy the fruit. It's really fresh." She picked up a grape and popped it in her mouth.

Zita wanted to stomp, stamp, and scream, but she forced herself to relax. Maybe the priestess wouldn't be long and they could get on with the ceremony. She had more water and ate some of the fruit.

They waited half-an-hour and Zita began pacing the room. The lack of sleep weighed on her and she had to keep moving. "When will that woman return?"

"I'm sure she'll be back soon. Sit and rest. You must be tired," Sherry said.

"I can't rest until I have the flower, and we're back on the road toward the Red Castle."

"It's nice here. We should spend a whole night resting. It'll do us good and the horse could surely use the time."

Zita stopped her pacing and stared at Sherry. "You don't realize the danger we're in. Taka might kill you. He'll take away my magic. I can't be captured by him."

Sherry stopped talking.

An hour later Davina returned. "Please follow me."

"Where are we going?" Zita asked.

"The priestess would like to meet you."

Finally, Zita thought. "Lead the way."

Davina led them across the foyer and down a great hall where at every fourth door stood a woman wearing a white gown who stared at the door across from them.

Sherry asked, "What are these paintings about?"

Zita hadn't even noticed the paintings lining each side of the hallway.

Davina stopped at a painting of a woman with black hair and sky-blue eyes. "That is the High Priestess, Marian, who led our community two-hundred and seventy-three years ago. Many of the portraits depict the women that have inspired us to be better humans."

She pointed across the hall to a painting of a black spiral on a white background. The spiral began finger-wide and as it plummeted into the center, the width of the spiral decreased and ended in a dot. "This is a meditative image that our members use to reach a point of inner peace and harmony with the world."

Sherry stopped at another geometric work with many colors. "I've seen images similar to this before. What are they called? Their name escapes me."

Davina said, "We call them mandalas. They represent inner peace and harmony for the world."

Zita thought the abstract picture looked like a flower petal. This journey to the ceremony had begun to take too long. "Enough about the paintings. We need to hurry; we don't have much time."

"Oh." Davina said, "It's that devastating need to be somewhere other than where you are at the moment that makes our meditative community important to the world. We have found that people are thinking too much about the future and not enjoying the present moment."

Sherry stared at Zita as if she was guilty of engaging in this behavior.

Zita bit back, "Don't look at me. I just want to get the flower petal and leave. Is that asking too much?"

Sherry and Davina exchanged a glance.

Zita motioned them forward. "Okay, I get it. Can we see the priestess now?"

They continued on in silence, passing more portraits and symbols until they reached a doorway. Davina ushered them inside the room. They stepped into a humid room with a rough stone floor. A round pool, large enough for swimming, was built into the center of the room with steam rising from its surface. Three women wearing gray linen robes stood along the walls.

Davina said, "These initiates will help you during the initial cleansing ceremony. Take off your old clothes and they will wash them and make them ready for you after your visit with the priestess." She pointed to the far wall. "There are clean towels there. When you are finished bathing, change into the white robes that you must wear to see the priestess."

"This is too much." Zita huffed. "Men are chasing us who mean to kill us. We don't have time for useless rituals."

Sherry scowled.

"This is the first of five rituals you must complete to see the goddess," Davina said. "If you refuse this, I'm instructed to show you out the front door."

Zita looked at Sherry, Davina and the girls along the wall. Her face flushed and her nostrils flared. She wanted to just run from this place. Five rituals! That could take all day. Didn't this woman know the importance of leaving with the flower before Taka found them?

"How do I know you won't steal my scroll?"

Davina said, "Your scroll will be safe. There is a steep price to pay for stealing in our community."

Zita huffed.

Davina walked out of the room.

Sherry moved to the wall where she sat on a bench and took off her shoes. Then she removed her clothing and wrapped a towel around her body as she approached the pool.

Zita hurried to remove her clothing and cover herself with a towel. She settled at the stone lip of the pool and placed her feet in the water. The warm water felt just right. She moved her feet in the water a few times, dropped the towel, and submerged. Her tired, dirty body responded to the warm water and she relaxed involuntarily.

One of the initiates removed the travelers' soiled clothing and left the room.

"We'll probably never see our clothes again."

"Relax Zita. The water is nice. It's not as nice as a private bath at Paxton's place, but we needed a chance to wash."

An initiate lit three incense burners and placed them around the edge of the pool. The other girl brought two bars of soap.

Sherry grabbed one of the soaps and tossed it to Zita. She caught it and sniffed. It didn't even have a fragrance. She needed to capture the crystal and take over the Velidred Castle. Then she could bathe alone.

The warm water was releasing the tension she felt in her shoulders. After washing her body and hair, she submerged completely. As she luxuriated in the water, Zita couldn't feel the presence of the moon goddess of Velidred. She wanted to drink in this moment of peace from the demanding deity.

Davina returned. "Please, if you will dry yourselves and put on these white robes."

The girls complied.

Davina led them to another room where two more initiates stood in front of desks with mirrors. "They will brush your hair for presentation to our priestess."

Thirty minutes later, Zita felt like a princess again. Her hair had been arranged on her head in a style she approved, and the woman had cared for her fingernails and toenails.

When Davina arrived, she said, "The next ritual is the blessing of your body with oils."

"But we're nice and clean now," Zita said. "Are you going to oil our bodies?"

"Nothing like that. It's a simple ceremony, you will see."

Davina led them to a third room, a circular room without windows. It was fragrant, like flowers. Two large candelabras with twenty burning candles each lit up the room. A man stood behind a table next to a statue of a woman with her hands raised, as if in a blessing. The statue appeared to be made of pure gold.

Zita tried to estimate the value of the statue. The presence of a man in the room surprised her. One old gentleman with graying hair with all these women didn't seem right. He wore a blue robe. His beard was streaked with gray and black.

With a deep voice he spoke, "Kneel before me."

Zita raised her eyebrows. "Kneel on the hard stone floor?"

Davina pursed her lips and nodded to the floor.

Zita acquiesced and went to her knees. *How dare they ask a princess to kneel before a common worker?*

Two initiates entered the room carrying censers with billowing incense. They stood next to the man and swung the censers in small arcs filling the room with the fragrant smoke.

The man raised his hands and spoke. Zita recognized the language though she didn't understand the words. The man must hail from the Southern Islands off the coast of Hepanon. He chanted, he sang, he whistled, and he spoke. Zita's knees and back began to hurt from kneeling.

When the man stopped talking, he removed a small container from the table. He walked in front of the table and stood before Zita. "I mark you as an initiate of the goddess of Pantaleon." He bent toward Zita, rolled his thumb in the container and smeared oil onto Zita's forehead in the shape of a circle, and placed a single dot in the middle of the circle.

Zita snorted thinking about what the moon goddess of Velidred might do when she found out the man had marked her as an initiate of the goddess of Pantaleon.

"Quiet." The man commanded.

He applied the oil to Sherry's forehead.

Zita suddenly felt warmth rush through her body. She wobbled in her kneeling position. Her body didn't feel right; it was as if two forces struggled internally within her. The pain of kneeling became too much. She attempted to rise but she fell into darkness.

CHAPTER 33

Zita woke and found herself in a bed in a dormitory-type room with many beds. She looked to her left, where Sherry sat up in a bed next to her. Zita's mind raced to figure out what had happened that landed her in this room. She blew out her cheeks as she surveyed the room.

Sherry said, "Oh good, you're awake. We were worried about you."

"Where are we?"

Sherry pushed her red hair off of her forehead. "We are in a healing room."

"To heal from what? Did they poison us?"

"No. You are of the moon goddess Velidred and I'm associated with Anticletus, so we are incompatible with Pantaleon. I've been informed that we cannot become initiates of the Pantaleon moon goddess."

Zita harrumphed and sat up in bed, "That's okay because I didn't want to become an initiate. I just wanted the seven-petaled flower."

"Davina told me we can't have the flower unless we become initiates. You would have to leave the Velidred moon goddess behind, and come into the graces of Pantaleon."

Zita forehead throbbed with pain. She pounded the bed with her fist in frustration. "The moon goddess of Velidred will not release me. If I had the power to be released from her entrapment, I would have gotten rid of her long ago."

Sherry shrugged her shoulders. "Now what? We'll have to leave without the flower."

"We can't leave without the flower. We can't capture the Crystal of Zaraboth without it. Did you try to reason with Davina? Tell her the urgency of our needs?"

"I didn't try anything. Davina sat by my side when I woke, and this is what she told me."

Zita stood. "I'm a princess and there is always a way to get what I want. I must see the High Priestess." She wobbled unsteadily on her legs, tried to correct, and fell back to the bed in a tangle of legs and arms.

Sherry laughed. "Easy there. It takes a few minutes to get your legs under you."

"I'm sure the incense contained some poison gas that knocked us out. This is all a ruse to keep us here. They probably won't let us go now. We'll have to serve the priestess forever like those other girls we saw in the hallway."

"No. Davina made it clear that as soon as we are able, we can exit the building."

Just at that moment Davina entered the room with three initiates. "Oh good. You're awake. Once you regain your balance, these women will escort you from the castle."

Zita rose quickly to her feet. She felt a moment of vertigo, closed her eyes, took a deep breath, and then steadied her stance. "You can't just kick us out of here. I came here for the seven-petaled flower. I won't leave the castle without it."

"Only approved initiates have the ability to handle the sacred flower," Davina said. "If you tried to handle it, you might die."

"Ah-ha. I might die. You said 'might,' which means I might have the ability to handle your sacred flower," Zita said. "I must be given the opportunity to take the flower with me. My needs are great. Please let me have an audience with the High Priestess."

The initiates all recoiled in horror. Their reactions ranged from bulging eyes to moaning.

Davina shook her head. "You cannot go further in the five rituals; you will not survive. The Velidred moon goddess has placed a claim on you."

Zita approached Davina. "I'm a princess. I have the right to see the high priestess as an ambassador for the kingdom."

Davina smirked. "You *were* a princess. Now, you are a commoner with a powerful adversary."

Zita needed a new plan of action as Davina wasn't able to be manipulated like most people she had met over the years. How did the woman even know of Zita's past and present? Her father, King Haskell, had taught her that if bullying and the power of your position didn't work in your favor, then sometimes, a last minute grovel might prove effective.

Zita bowed her head. "Oh, mighty gatekeeper to the High Priestess of the Castle of the Sacred Flowers, please grant my request to visit with the High Priestess, I beg you. Evil men are chasing us."

"That is not allowed. You must leave."

Zita touched Davina's hands. "Please. You have great power over me. Have compassion and let me talk with the high priestess. For just a minute."

"No."

Zita took one of Davina's hands and kissed the back of it a number of times. The woman's hand felt soft and smooth, her nails were impeccably manicured. Zita had seen commoners beg with her father numerous times to be forgiven or to keep themselves or a family member from being executed.

"Please. Oh, powerful one. Have mercy on me. The Velidred moon goddess has placed a curse on me. If I could, I would do everything in my power to remove this curse. Surely, you and the high priestess can help me."

Zita kissed Davina's hand a few more times. She sensed Davina considering her request.

Davina frowned, delicately slipped her hand out of Zita's grasp, and rubbed her hands together. She glanced at Sherry and then the initiates. "Okay, I will ask the High Priestess, but you won't be happy with her answer." She turned and hurried out of the room.

Zita kept her head down and smiled.

# # # #

It took an hour for Davina to return. Zita had paced about the room, the initiates following her every movement. She wondered what the three girls would do if she left the room. Would they follow her, manhandle her and return her to this room, or forcibly remove her from the castle? She couldn't take a chance of leaving without seeing the High Priestess.

"I'm surprised, but the High Priestess has granted your request. She will visit you in the west tower overlooking the lake. This is an unusual move for the High Priestess. I hope you know what you're doing."

Zita smiled. Yes, she knew exactly what she planned, and she would leave here with the sacred flower.

"Follow me."

"Sherry, are you coming with me?" Zita asked.

Sherry shook her head.

Zita followed Davina and the three initiates through the castle hallways. The women were silent, so Zita also held her tongue. They ascended three flights of stone stairs, and eventually they reached the meeting room.

Davina knocked. Zita heard no answer, but then Davina opened the door and entered the chamber. Zita followed her into the room. The initiates stayed outside in the hallway. She wondered if they were allowed to converse with the High Priestess. Davina shut the door.

Zita expected a larger space than what she saw. There were no desks or tables. A window to her left allowed light into the chamber. To her right stood an empty suit of armor. A red curtain hung from the ceiling before her. It wrapped around the space shaped like a half circle. An image of a bird had been embroidered into the middle of the curtain.

Davina took a deep breath and pulled a cord that opened the curtain in the middle. A bell rang.

A large pile of feathers lay before her on a dais. When the bell sounded, the feathers began to move, like a flag unfurling in a slight breeze. The feathers stretched out into wings and a human figure stood before Zita, a woman dressed in a silver garment that hung loose around her shoulders and bosom but ended at her hips. Below that she wore a tight-fitting pair of pants that seemed molded to her body.

The woman fluttered her wings slightly and then stood, examining Zita. The woman had flawless black skin, matte black hair that hung just below her shoulders, a tall lithe frame and dark brown eyes.

Davina said, "I introduce to you, Gormlaith Boru, the High Priestess of the Sacred Pantaleon Religion. Please bow."

The woman's beauty and her pure white wings stunned Zita, and she barely heard Davina's request. It took her a moment to understand, and she immediately went to her knees. As she stared at the ground, many thoughts flashed through her mind. Could the priestess fly like Kestrel? Did she always show her wings or could she manipulate her body to look normal? The woman had to be at least six feet tall, and on the raised dais, she towered over Zita.

Gormlaith Boru spoke, but Zita didn't understand anything the woman said. The words were sung like music, but they came from a language Zita knew nothing of.

"You may stand." Davina took Zita's hand and helped her to her feet.

Zita stood, feeling slightly disoriented. She didn't know if the priestess had magic capability to cause this or if Zita still suffered from the oil ceremony.

Gormlaith sang again in her beautiful clear voice.

Davina interpreted, "What is your request."

Zita had practiced in her mind how she planned to manipulate the priestess and now her thoughts were jumbled and didn't make sense to her. She stared into the priestess' eyes and her words seemed to spin within her mind. She needed to focus on her needs, as she couldn't leave here without the sacred flower.

Zita spoke in a soft, shaky, halting voice, "I—need a—sacred—flower."

Gormlaith sang, but her voice sounded harsher as if she reprimanded Zita.

"Only initiates are allowed to handle the flowers," Davina interpreted for the priestess.

Zita felt her lips purse tight and she challenged the priestess. "My needs are great. There are men trying to destroy my kingdom, and I must have the Crystal of Zaraboth to take back my home."

Gormlaith sang, and Davina spoke back to Gormlaith in a harsher voice than the fluid angelic sounds of the priestess.

Zita wondered if the priestess could understand her but used the interpreter technique to keep her off-balanced.

The two went back and forth in conversation for many minutes. The priestess' eyes had turned cold and hard. Her nostrils flared at some of the words Davina used.

A flush crept up Davina's face as the priestess said something in a sound clearly meant as a rebuke. Davina swallowed hard and addressed Zita. "The priestess has made her proclamation. You cannot have the flower."

Zita couldn't just walk out of here without the flower. It had taken so long for these ceremonies that Taka must be at the castle. Her shoulders curled forward as she realized the truth. She had to convince the priestess of her need.

"When I leave here, there is a man waiting for me. He's expecting me to have the flower." Zita looked at Gormlaith with as humble and obeisant expression as possible. "He'll kill me if I don't present him with the sacred flower. Please have mercy on me."

Gormlaith sang for a good three minutes.

"You are correct," Davina said. "Your adversary stands at this moment at the castle gates, but he is not allowed to enter because he is a man."

Zita said, "But your priest at the oil ceremony is a man."

Davina didn't wait for the priestess, "He serves a purpose. Taka wouldn't agree to the contract terms that our priest has agreed to."

"You can't release me to a man who will kill me as soon as he sees me without a flower. Without the flower I'm nothing to him. You must help me."

Davina interpreted the priestess response, "You must turn your requests to the deity of Velidred. You have bound your life to her. She will have to help keep you alive."

Zita's hands trembled. The Velidred goddess had been a demanding god to her, and she feared what her reaction might be to the Pantaleon mark on her forehead from the oil. "You must help me."

Gormlaith sang her response that even though Zita couldn't understand the words she heard the note of finality.

"The priestess has heard your plea and will help you with your foe," Davina said.

Zita's eyes brightened and she smiled.

Davina continued, "You will be deposited outside the town walls. We will delay Taka and his men to give you a chance to escape."

Zita's mouth slackened at the news. She needed more than a chance to escape. She needed the sacred flower. A pleading glance at the priestess confirmed Davina's words. Gormlaith pointed to the door.

Zita felt lightheaded as disbelief of the final verdict punched her in the gut. She would leave without the flower.

Davina closed the curtain hiding the priestess.

Then Zita saw Davina shimmering and her own body felt strange. The next thing she knew, Zita stood outside the walls next to the black obelisks guarding the castle. She felt numb as her shoulders slumped in despair. She stared back at the castle. The portal Davina had opened to transport her closed, and Zita stood in the hot sun with no horse and without the Crown of Anticletus.

CHAPTER 34

Al rode his horse toward the seven tall black stone monuments dominating the blue sky. The sun shone on him and his friends Erik, Lily and Kestrel. They had been riding for four days, and the soreness in Al's legs seemed to get worse each day. He always thought riding a horse would be fun, despite his fear of the animals, but four days of riding had him wishing for the cars back home on Earth.

They had found one of Paxton's horses on the trail. It had died or been killed. The stench of death kept them from investigating the cause of the animal's demise. They wondered what had happened to its riders. Were Sherry and Zita still alive?

Al pointed at the castle in the distance. "Is that it? The Castle of the Sacred Flowers."

Kestrel responded, "According to my father's maps, yes."

A quiet cheer swept over him. They hadn't stopped for food or rest very often, and the southern air was so hot he felt they deserved a longer rest. He hoped it wouldn't take them too much time to find the seven-petaled flower, but he craved a break from riding. He worried about what they might encounter at the castle.

They hurried the horses forward. When they got between the black stones and the castle walls, Al looked over at Kestrel. "Do you feel that?"

Kestrel said, "Yes. My magic has been blocked."

"Should we be worried?"

Kestrel shook his head. "No, let's go forward. It's my understanding that the inhabitants of the castle are peaceful." His facial expression didn't match his words; his lips were pressed tight.

Al glanced over at Kestrel. "What aren't you telling us?"

He rubbed his cheek with his hand. "I've heard conflicting reports over the years. Women from villages take a journey to the Castle of the Sacred Flowers and they never return. Rumors have it they are made slaves by the castle owners. Girls just entering their teen years are kidnapped and are never seen again. The castle inhabitants are blamed. And I've seen with my own eyes women who claim they escaped from the castle cult. They have been driven crazy. We can't understand a word they say."

Al looked at Lily. "Will it be safe for Lily?"

Kestrel seemed to search for the right words as he hesitated to answer. "I think it'll be okay. We'll be with Lily the whole time."

Lily chirped, "It's going to be fine boys. We'll go in, meet the leaders, get the flower and leave. I'm hoping they are kind enough to feed us. I'm tired of that chew leather you guys call beef jerky."

All the guys laughed.

Al looked at the open gates to the castle bailey. "Do you think Sherry and Zita were able to get a flower and leave?"

"We don't even know for sure they made it this far before Taka captured them."

They rode slowly into the village. The deserted homes left Al feeling a mixture of curiosity and fear. He blinked his eyes and tilted his head to view the castle on top of the hill. He felt his pulse increase with each step the horse took.

"I don't like this silence," Al said.

"Yeah," Erik said. "Like everyone disappeared."

"We don't have any weapons other than that sword you carry. We'll have to be ready for hand-to-hand combat with any monsters," Al said.

Kestrel said, "I don't think we'll encounter any monsters in the village."

Al felt a cold breeze on his neck and turned to look behind him. The village seemed empty, but he felt as if someone followed him or watched him.

"Kestrel, how is your ability to fly while you're in the village?" Al asked. "You might be our only hope to get the message out that we've been captured."

Lily said, "Okay, I don't know what you're doing, but stop it. We're going to be okay. Stop scaring me."

Al wanted to stop scaring himself. The silence within the village and all the empty homes kind of spooked him. He couldn't imagine traveling through the village at night. He didn't believe in the undead on Earth, but he wasn't so sure here on Aloheno.

Kestrel said, "I'm confident my ability to change into a falcon is still valid. Come on guys, let's go get the flower, if it's still here, and hurry on to help Zita and Sherry."

They all agreed and encouraged their horses to a faster pace. They reached the hill formed at the base of the castle and hobbled their horses near a house where a small patch of grass grew.

Al recognized the difficult climb up the hill was a defensive arrangement, tiring soldiers who tried to reach the inner wall. And the castle guards could fire arrow after arrow downward to eliminate their enemies. Al searched the castle windows for a guard aiming an arrow at him.

They reached the keep door, and Erik found the rope for the bell. "I guess we ring first, before inviting ourselves in."

The sound of the bell faded into silence.

They waited.

"Is it lunch time?" Al asked. "Maybe we'll have to come back later."

Kestrel put his arm on Al's shoulder. "Relax. Someone will come. I'm sure the castle is occupied."

They heard a slight noise, and then one of the large wooden doors swung open. A woman appeared at the door. "Hello, my name is Davina. How may I help you?"

They all looked at each other, and Erik said, "We are here to request a seven-petaled flower."

Davina looked into Al's eyes, and then she did the same for Erik and Kestrel. Then she took Lily's hand. "I'm sorry, but men are not allowed into the castle. Only women. Please come with me." She pulled on Lily's hand. Lily hesitated and looked at the boys with questioning concern in her eyes but followed Davina inside.

Erik said, "Wait, we need to talk about this."

The door closed.

"Shouldn't we go after her?" Al asked.

Erik unsheathed the Sword of Freedom. "I'm game. We can't let them make Lily a slave."

Kestrel stopped them. "Listen. I don't want to see Lily in there by herself, but she might be our only hope at getting the flower or finding out if Zita has it. If we barge into the castle, they might not give us anything. I think we should wait out here for her."

# # # #

Davina directed Lily into a room with a table full of food and drink. Despite her hunger and a deep uneasiness in her stomach, Lily felt uncertain whether she should eat. The things Kestrel had said about the women in the castle becoming slaves left her off-balanced and concerned.

Lily asked, "Would it be possible to have some of this food sent to my friends at the gate? It's been a long journey and we're all a little hungry."

Davina nodded and then clapped her hands. Two women wearing white robes entered the room. Davina directed them to take some food out to Lily's friends.

Knowing that her friends would be fed and not just asked to leave the premises gave Lily hope for her mission. She realized that she was the only person in their group able to acquire the seven-petaled flower. Lily sat down and enjoyed the fresh fruit that had been prepared.

Lily ate like a queen, and when full, Davina escorted her to a large room with a round pool where she could bathe. After days on the dirty horse and dusty road, the water felt relaxing. She remembered she had to stay true to her goal. She could see how women could be lulled into joining this cult, or whatever it was. It didn't seem too bad to her compared to some of the dangers this planet had held for her and her friends since they had arrived.

The bath complete, Davina escorted Lily to a room where a man stood behind an altar. A number of candles on candelabras provided plenty of light to the room. The experience unnerved her as it hadn't been that long since King Haskell tried to sacrifice her on a similar altar on the Velidred Volcano.

Lily said, "I didn't think men were allowed."

Davina explained, "He is a priest of Pantaleon."

"Oh, my friend, Erik, is a first order priest of Pankratios. Is that the same thing? Maybe Erik can come inside."

"No, they aren't the same type of priests. Your friend will have to stay outside. Please kneel."

Davina gently pushed on Lily's shoulder, and she dropped to her knees.

Two initiates entered the chamber with incense billowing out of censers that they gently.

Lily took in the sweetly scented smoke, a mixture of fear and curiosity running through her mind. She hadn't seen any knives or swords nearby, so she felt somewhat comfortable about the proceedings.

The priest spoke in a language Lily didn't understand, so she just closed her eyes and listened. When he had stopped talking, he took a small container of oil and spread some onto Lily's forehead.

Lily felt the man draw a circle on her forehead, and then smudge a spot or a period in the middle. It seemed the combination of incense, oil and kneeling had left her light-headed and she swayed a moment.

The priest stared at Lily and then pointed at her forehead.

Davina walked around in front of Lily and gasped.

Lily asked, "What is it?"

"Nothing, my child." Davina motioned to one of the girls holding the censers. "Take the girl to a private room on the third floor."

As the girl led Lily out of the room, she heard Davina whisper, "Who are these women?"

The priest mumbled something in his strange language as Lily followed the initiate down the hall.

Lily touched her forehead and it felt strange, like the oil had hardened. What had happened in that room? Something had gone wrong. She felt a tingling in her fingers and toes, and her previous steady nerves and bravery weakened.

The white-robed initiate walked her through a hallway where Lily saw more robed women standing before their room doors staring at paintings on the other side of the hallway. The women didn't seem to notice Lily as she passed. All the women looked pale, like they didn't get much sun.

The initiate led Lily up two sets of stairs, and then they turned a corner to another corridor of women standing in front of doors staring at walls. Again, the women were pale in appearance. Except one, standing three doors away.

CHAPTER 35

Excitement charged through Lily, as she raced to the red-headed woman standing in the hallway at the Castle of the Sacred Flowers. She waved her arms in the air, too excited to shout out the woman's name. The woman's ruddy complexion convinced Lily the initiate hadn't been at the castle for very long.

The woman stared straight ahead mumbling something through closed lips.

Lily ran up and stood in front of the woman. "Sherry?

It took a moment for the woman's eyes to focus on Lily.

Lily thought for a moment she had made a mistake, because the woman took so long to acknowledge her. Then it all clicked into place.

The red-headed woman's eyes sparkled as a wide grin replaced the woman's mumbling tight-pressed lips. "Lily, is that you? Davina told me you were coming, but I wasn't sure if I should believe her."

Sherry focused her gaze on Lily's forehead for a moment, and then embraced Lily in a tight hug.

Lily whispered, "Are you a slave? Do we need to help you escape?"

"No. I've been waiting for you." Sherry laughed. "They sent Zita away, and the High Priestess said I could stay here, protected by their magic."

They hugged again and laughed with excitement. "You're free from Zita, that's great news."

"Did Al and Paxton come with you?" Sherry gazed down the hallway.

"Al, Erik, and Kestrel came, but boys aren't allowed inside the keep." Lily grinned. "Isn't that wild?"

Sherry forced a weak smiled.

Lily wondered if the news that Paxton hadn't joined the quest to save her disappointed her.

The initiate that had escorted Lily this far grabbed her arm. "I'm sorry, but we must continue to your room." The initiate looked at Sherry with a pouty bottom lip almost as if she wished her friends had come to rescue her.

"Are you sure I can't stay here with my friend?"

"Not at this time. Davina instructed me on where to take you, and I will be reprimanded if I disobey."

Sherry and Lily hugged once more before the initiate led Lily away.

They placed her in a room just a few doors down from Sherry. It had a bed, a small table and an open window. Sunlight filtered through the window.

Lily asked, "How long will you keep me here?"

The initiate shrugged, "I don't know."

"Did I do something wrong at the ceremony?"

The initiate glanced at Lily's forehead and immediately looked at the floor. "No. I don't think so. I'm sure Davina will be with you soon." She peeked at Lily's forehead again before she left the room.

Lily swallowed and searched the room for a mirror. What had happened? She touched her forehead. It felt like they had placed hot wax on her forehead and it had dried. She tried to grab at an edge, but it didn't peel back. Whatever this issue with the oil, she couldn't let this stop her from getting the flower. The rest of the team depended on her receiving or taking the flower, so they could capture the crystal. Her stomach fluttered in confusion.

Lily sat on the edge of the bed for a few moments, trying to collect her thoughts. She wished Kestrel, Erik, and Al were with her. Sherry needed rescuing. Lily knew she couldn't leave the castle without taking her best friend with her. She hoped the oil on her forehead didn't mean that she couldn't get a flower. If it did, she would find a way to steal one, though she had no idea where the flowers were stored. Maybe Sherry knew where to find them. She could rescue Sherry first, and then the two of them could search for the flowers.

She waited for what seemed an hour, maybe two before Davina returned. Lily had lost all track of time as she sat on the bed pondering what might be next.

Davina said, "The High Priestess has informed me to continue the Pantaleon initiation ceremony."

Lily asked, "You must tell me what the next step in the process is, or I won't go with you."

Davina looked at Lily's forehead and seemed to ponder her next words. "The next ritual is purification by incense."

"The last ritual had incense in it, wasn't that enough?"

Davina smiled slightly, "This one is different."

"Is it dangerous?"

Again, Davina looked at Lily's forehead before shaking her head. "It can appear dangerous, but you're in no danger.

Lily placed her hands on her hips. "What's wrong with my forehead?"

Davina turned toward the door. "Come with me; we are ready for the next ritual."

Lily waited a moment. Her breathing accelerated as if she had danced hard the last five minutes. Anytime adults wouldn't tell her what was going on, especially on this planet, bad experiences followed. She thought about running out the door, away from Davina, grabbing Sherry, and racing to the exit. Could she remember how to get out of the castle?

Davina led her in the direction of Sherry's room, but Sherry had left her position and didn't stare at the wall anymore. Lily peeked in the open door to the room but found no sign of her friend. Now she had to locate Sherry again if they were to escape.

Davina directed Lily to a long narrow room with twenty-foot-high walls, a vaulted ceiling, and opened windows high on the walls. Despite the open windows, dusk had begun settling on the castle, and the room's light came from a single candle in the middle of the room. The darkness gave the room an eerie atmosphere.

Six initiates walked into the room carrying large, golden censers. The incense hadn't been placed in the censers yet, as no smoke rose from the containers.

Lily's nervousness increased; her muscles twitched in anticipation of impending disaster.

Davina came and stood next to Lily. She placed a hand on Lily's shoulder. "Relax. No harm will come to you during this ceremony." She pointed at a door at the far end of the room. When I tell you to go, walk at a slow pace to that door. I will be there for you."

Lily looked back at the door she had just entered from. She could still make a run for it. She touched her forehead. "If I keep doing these rituals, the High Priestess will give me a seven-petaled flower. Right?"

Davina pursed her lips. "I'm not allowed to lie. Doing so will force me to do penance. I think you'll receive your flower, but . . ." She trailed off to silence.

Lily took a deep breath, a twisted knot forming in her stomach. With another glance at the door across the room, she nodded and hesitantly said, "Okay."

Davina motioned to the initiates holding the censers. They huddled together and lighted the pieces of coal in the censors' bowls. The initiates swung the now-lit censers to accelerate the burning. Then they huddled together again and placed a blend of incense on top of the burning coal. Once heated, they swung their incense burners as they walked across the room.

As the smoke increased in the room, it became more difficult for Lily to see the door on the far side of the room. The smoke rose toward the open windows. The sun had almost set and Lily thought she saw smoke or maybe fog coming into the chamber from the open window.

Lily looked at Davina with apprehension. As her vision in the room faded from the accumulated incense smoke and the slight burning in her eyes, she began to use her other senses. The smoke swirled about her arms and legs feeling cool to the touch. The sweet and savory smell of different herbs played about her nostrils.

Davina touched Lily's back and Lily jumped.

"It's okay, child. You may begin walking to the other door. You won't be harmed."

Lily hesitated.

Lily rubbed her hands on her white robe in nervousness. Davina said she wouldn't be harmed. She took in a small breath, afraid to suck the incense into her lungs. She wished Kestrel could be there to hold her hand.

Lily looked back at where Davina had been standing, but the woman had disappeared. The windows high above the room were obscured by the incense. A door shut behind her and she heard the sound of a key turning in a lock. She had no choice; she must move forward.

With a moment's hesitation, she took faltering steps on the smooth stone floor. She remembered the intricate pattern of circles and triangles that had made up the floor's pattern. Each step she took required her to stop, and pat the air around her. She didn't want to run into one of the initiates with the incense burners. The only sound she heard came from her own breathing.

A dark shape walked past her, and the smoke swirled about the figure as it disappeared into the darkness. As she moved forward, the smell of the smoke changed, became thick with sweetness. She heard feet shuffle by her and the scent of wet dog lingered in the air. The hair on her neck and arms lifted as she felt a rush of coolness.

Lily stopped, rooted to the spot, afraid to go further. The smell brought back memories of when she had been bitten by an Irish Setter as a ten-year-old. A shrill noise sounded to her right. A bird of prey or a strange animal found only on Aloheno. She didn't know.

Her heart beat like a speeding train intent on going faster than the engine could handle. She felt weak in the knees. She pleaded with herself to go on. *I'm the only person that can retrieve the magic flower. I must continue.* She thought of Kestrel and knew he would be waiting for her when she finished her quest.

Lily cautiously took the first step, then gained enough confidence to take a second step. A third and fourth step reduced the trembling in her hands. Then a low guttural growl sounded on her left. She stopped again. She swayed a little to her right to avoid the animal she expected to bite her.

More than anything, Lily wanted to whimper and cry. She had no illusions that she was the bravest person in the group. No one could match Sherry's bravery. Lily just wanted to have friends and stay alive. Two more steps and she bumped into an object.

Lily stopped. At first, she thought she had bumped into one of the initiates, but upon further inspection, she identified it as a statue. She touched it, and a shock of electricity forced her hand back.

The stone statue appeared to be a robed woman with wings. But where had it come from? The room had been completely empty when she arrived. She stared at the statue's eyes and they came alive and opened, glowing blue.

CHAPTER 36

Lily squeaked and her heart pounded on her rib cage. She pushed forward despite the fear building within her. She tried to step to the right of the statue, still trying to avoid the animal roaming the room with her, but she hit the wall. She took small steps to clear the statue's left side and headed in the direction she hoped to find the door. A glance behind her confirmed the statue hadn't followed.

An animal brushed across her arm. A hairy animal with shining yellow eyes. It continued past her in the same direction she walked. Davina had told her she couldn't lie, and she said Lily would be safe. Lily took a deep breath, trying not to cough as the incense tickled her nose and throat. She continued.

She shuffled silently so the animals roaming with her might not hear her. Lily thought after fifty steps she should be at her destination. She worried she might have gotten turned around when she reached the statue, and had begun walking in circles.

Chanting began around her. First a chorus of female voices, and then a single male voice joined the chant. That must be the priest that placed the oil on her forehead.

Lily stopped. Had she reached her destination?

Then multiple male voices joined the chanting, but that shouldn't be happening. If all these men were in the room with her, then why couldn't Kestrel, Erik and Al have come with her? She hadn't reached a door, so she continued her slow pace to her destination at the far side of the room.

A gong sounded. Low and steady. A warm pleasant tone. She walked another step and the gong pealed again, a higher note than the first. The chanting continued, matching the tone of the gong. The singing and tones made Lily feel lighter and more confident. She strode forward as the peal of the gongs increased, joined by rhythmic tapping on a xylophone.

Lily stopped and absorbed the music. It made her want to dance, bringing to mind her dance lessons on Earth. Her feet felt like they had lifted off the ground without conscious thought. She twirled in the smoke surrounding her body and watched the smoke whirl and swirl in intricate patterns.

As she swayed and spun, letting the music take her body into familiar motions that always left her with a feeling of joy, her mind jolted. *Wait. I can't keep spinning; I'll lose my direction.* Her breath caught in her chest as she spun once more trying to find her way. *Which way should I go?*

She stood in the dark smoke staring at a single spot of light seemingly far in the distance. Davina had directed her to go to the door at the opposite end of the chamber, but she now found herself lost in the smoky room. When she started her journey, a single candle burned in the center of the room, but she didn't know if she had passed the candle yet or not. All the turning, sounds, animals and statues left her not knowing which way to go.

The music seemed to come from behind her, so she turned in the direction of the music. *Yes,* she thought, *I must continue through the music to reach the door.*

She strode forward among the singing men and women, through the sound of the chimes and xylophone, toward an unknown finish line. A colorful flash of light shone dimly through the incense. An animal howled behind her; the piercing sound forced her to hurry her steps.

A rainbow of colors broke through the darkness, and in the middle of the rainbow, multi-hued colors changed shapes and positions, as if she were looking through a life-size kaleidoscope. She continued toward the shifting colors.

When she came within ten feet of the colored light, Davina appeared by her side. She clapped her hands and the music stopped. The smoke from the incense burners seemed to be sucked out through the room's windows.

Lily looked behind her to the door she believed she started from. A single candle burned in the center of the room. There were no animals, no statues, no singers, and no birds in the room with her. She gazed at Davina with a questioning look.

Davina said, "It is more emotional than real."

Davina took Lily's hand and they exited the room.

Lily enjoyed the fresh air in the castle hallway. "Where are you taking me now?"

"It is time for you to meet the high priestess."

"Will I get a flower for my troubles?"

Davina looked at Lily's forehead and shrugged.

Lily didn't know what had happened in the room where the oil had been applied, but she refused to believe she wouldn't get the flower despite whatever caused the problem with her forehead.

They hurried along the hallway until it widened. Two large wooden doors, engraved with many images of men and women stood on one side of the hall. Davina escorted her into a small chamber on the opposite side.

"Wait here, the high priestess will be informed of your availability, and you will have your audience with her."

She touched Davina's arm. "Do you know if my friends are okay? It must be dark by now. Will they be safe?"

"They are well. Don't concern yourself with them." Then Davina glided from the room.

Lily stood in the small room; a six-foot bench along the wall was the only furniture. She tried to make sense of the recent ritual. The smell of the wet dog had reminded her of her neighbor's spirited dogs who loved to run in the rain and splash through puddles. It brought back memories of her childhood on Earth. She thought back to her Aunt Carol who took her into her home after her parents had died. They had died here on Aloheno and Lily had no memory of her parents.

Lily paced back and forth, a chill in the air settling in her neck causing her to hug herself. She worried for her friends and wondered about the statue of the woman with wings.

A knock sounded on the door and Davina entered. "We are ready for you. First you must change out of your white robe and wear this garment." Davina handed her a silky, purple robe.

She changed into the new robe and took a deep breath. Purple reminded her of the color of kings; maybe the garment could bring her luck.

They exited the small room and walked across the hall to the large doors. Davina knocked, and an initiate from inside pushed open the door.

As Lily entered the room, the fragrance of flowers greeted her. Flowers of every type, color, and shape stood along the walls, forming an aisle to a dais at the far end of the room. The room had a large and airy feeling, with high ceilings and tall windows. A hundred candelabras stole the darkness of night. A polished marble floor led to the dais where a large golden throne, highlighted with black, surrounded a tall thin woman standing regally on the dais.

Davina said, "I introduce to you, Gormlaith Boru, the High Priestess of the Sacred Pantaleon Religion. Please bow."

Lily went to one knee and bowed.

A bell sounded and Davina took Lily's elbow and helped her to her feet. With a slight push in the small of her back, Davina moved Lily to the dais.

The woman's stunning beauty took her breath away. Lily moved hesitantly toward the dais. A range of emotions smothered Lily.

Gormlaith stood patiently as Lily approached the throne.

When Lily reached the dais, she dropped to her knee and bowed again. "I am Lily. I have come to seek your help."

The High Priestess nodded. "I have been expecting you. Please, sit."

Lily waited for the High Priestess to sit and then sat on a cushion at the foot of the throne.

Gormlaith waited for a moment.

Lily worried about castle protocol. Would it be okay if she spoke first?

Gormlaith said, "Tell me about the help you seek, and I will determine your need and our ability to meet them."

This comment took Lily back a moment. She had expected Davina to tell the priestess her desire for the seven-petaled flower.

Lily thought about her response. She wanted to be respectful, but clear that the need demanded that the priestess agree to the request.

"My friends and I are on a quest to obtain the Crystal of Zaraboth. Our friend, Zita . . ." Lily hoped it would help if she called Zita a friend, though after what she had done to

Sherry, maybe Zita had returned to being an enemy. ". . . needs it for her own plans, but we want to help her get it in hopes of helping to heal our friend."

Gormlaith nodded as Lily spoke. Her facial expressions led Lily to believe her request would be denied. The High Priestess said, "You, Zita and Sherry are an interesting combination of women. I denied the flower to Zita, and I cannot give it to you if your goal is to give it to Zita."

A spike of adrenaline rushed through Lily's core at the news. Denied! She must find a way to convince the woman of the strength of her need.

"Let's talk about you. Your blood line is of royal blood like your cousin, Zita."

Lily nodded.

"But you escaped Aloheno before King Haskell determined your whereabouts. How do you feel now that you have returned to our planet?"

"It's all very interesting and scary for me. I have met Prince Kestrel, the Falcon Prince, a kind and caring man."

Gormlaith stood like someone had poked her. "The Falcon Prince?"

"Yes. He's my dear friend. Do you know him?"

"I have never met him, but I'm familiar with his story. Is he one of the men escorting you?"

Lily perked up at the question. A chance to be with Kestrel while being questioned by this woman might help sway her to their request.

Gormlaith motioned with her hand and Davina came to her side. They whispered and Davina looked surprised at Gormlaith's words.

Davina said, "But it's not allowed."

"I demand it." Gormlaith answered.

Davina bowed and left the room.

"Your experience during the rituals has surprised me," Gormlaith said. "The statue of the woman with wings, you awakened her."

Lily's eyes widened. "I didn't do anything. I just . . . bumped . . . into . . . the statue."

You saw the woman's eyes. Yes?"

"Yes, glowing blue eyes, emanating a mysterious light. Doesn't that happen to everyone who encounters the statue?"

"No!" The woman said sharply. "Nothing about your experience here and your reactions to our ritual is normal."

Where before, Lily thought bringing Kestrel in might give them a better chance to receive a flower, now it seemed she had upset the woman more than she expected. "I didn't try to do anything." She said meekly bowing her head.

"Yes. Of course. Your experience with the statue leads me to believe you have powers closely associated with the moon of Pantaleon. You have the ability for compassion and kindness and can encourage that in others. The fact that you released the stone statue from its captivity means that you are in tune with nature and can connect to the natural world in unique ways."

The information overwhelmed Lily. Had she really released a person from captivity? She wondered if she had powers like Erik, the ability to heal others.

"Your abilities need to be honed. This is something we wish to help you with."

"Okay?" Lily felt reluctant about agreeing to anything at this time. She needed to get the flower so they could continue their journey. "I willing to come back at another time and get training from you. That could be interesting."

Gormlaith shook her head. "No, my child. Now that we know who you are, we cannot allow you to leave us without the necessary training."

The comment floored Lily. *I'll not be able to leave. They'll make me a slave just like the other initiates. I must go with Kestrel.*

Lily asked, "Can you tell me about this thing on my forehead? Is it possible to rub it off?" She rubbed her forehead with her palm.

Gormlaith pursed her lips. "That thing," she scowled, "represents the sacred symbol of Pantaleon, and has been a symbol of its people for thousands of generations. It cannot be undone. You must wear a scarf whenever you are outside the castle, so others cannot see it."

All these revelations surprised Lily, and she felt her chest tighten as if someone had squeezed a corset around her bosom. Lily glanced around the room looking for some way to escape though initiates guarded the doorways. She couldn't stay here for education, or so people wouldn't see her forehead. It didn't matter, she had to leave this place, with or without the flower. Her friends would have to find some other way to acquire the needed magical object.

Davina re-entered the room and the high priestess nodded in her direction.

A gong sounded and the tone reverberated off the stone walls and vaulted wooden ceiling.

No one in the room moved.

Then the sound of a flock of birds echoed outside the opened windows. Large winged creatures flew through the windows into the room and landed all around Lily.

She gasped and felt the blood drain from her face. Her arms and legs shook.

The winged creatures transformed into men and women. They moved away from Lily to stand along the chamber walls. The creatures kept flying into the room until over a hundred men and women surrounded her. For some their wings disappeared completely, while others flapped their wings until they folded and tucked in around their bodies.

Lily sat motionless, afraid to move.

A man stepped forward in front of Lily. He gave her an apprising look and turned to the Priestess. "Is it true? You have found the thief of my wife's soul."

CHAPTER 37

The winged humans who had entered the room through the open windows had settled their wings into a closed position, and the chamber had grown quiet. Lily clutched her cold fingers together still thinking of ways to escape. The winged people stared at her and she gazed down to avoid their stares.

A single tone sounded in the room and the door where she had entered opened. Davina escorted a blindfolded individual toward the dais. At first, Lily didn't recognize him, but then she recognized Kestrel. She bolted from her position before the throne and ran across the room to her boyfriend's side.

She grabbed Kestrel's bound hands, and he tightened his fist around Lily's hand. "Kestrel, are you all-right?"

"Yes. I'm fine."

He didn't look okay. His face showed signs of fighting.

Kestrel stopped the procession and shouted, "What do you want from me, High Priestess?"

The men and women standing along the walls started whispering to each other, creating a buzz in the room.

Gormlaith raised her hands. "Quiet."

The room slowly came to silence.

"Release the boy's blindfold."

Davina glanced around the room uneasily. She hesitated in removing the blindfold. She stared at a man with gray hair, who shook his head.

The gray-haired man stood along the wall. He stepped from the wall and unfurled large white wings. "Stop. Don't release him."

Gormlaith challenged, "Sir Frederick, do you dare to disobey your high priestess?"

"This usurper is not of the bloodline. He has no right to be in this room."

Gormlaith sighed. "That's true. He is not of the Pantaleon bloodline, but he is of royal blood, which entitles him to an audience with the high priestess."

"Not while we are here. Kestrel gained his wings by accident. He experienced an event that he had no right to see. He prevented my wife from reaching the heavens to spend eternity with the true goddess of Pantaleon. Now she will rot in a worm-filled grave." He fluttered his wings in anger.

Others in the chamber fluttered their wings.

Davina shouted, "Quiet!"

Gormlaith said, "I will not be bullied by the likes of you, Sir Frederick. I'm sorry about your wife, but he was just a young boy. You know how they like to see the event."

The fluttering of wings caused the chamber to grow noisy.

A woman left the wall and stood next to Sir Frederick. "I voted against you being high priestess because of poor decisions you've made in the past. And now you are making another bad decision."

Lily held tight to Kestrel's hands. She thought about slipping the blindfold away from his eyes, but this confrontation scared her.

"You voted against me because my bloodline isn't as pure as yours and Fredericks. Even though I'm five generations removed from my non-winged ancestor, you still hold me in contempt. I won't be bullied by your kind, Kami. Now return to your positions by the wall. Both of you."

The winged-humans took up fluttering their wings again, but Kami and Sir Frederick stood their ground.

"If you remove his blindfold, we must kill the boy." Sir Frederick pointed at the door. "Send him back outside, and be done with this."

Lily gasped. Maybe they should escort Kestrel back outside to Al and Erik. She could go with him. Maybe they could get past the guardian without the flower.

"We must talk with him. Did he gain wings because of his bloodline?" Gormlaith said, "We will study him and convert him into the religion." She nodded at men by one of the doors.

Three younger men, all with black hair and whose wings did not show, walked over to Sir Frederick and Kami. The tallest of the three took Sir Frederick's arm, but the elder man shook off the clasp.

Sir Frederick's nostrils flared and he said, "Don't do this Gormlaith. You have no right to allow this boy into this room." He took Kami's hand and walked with her back to their position by the dais.

Gormlaith flicked her wrist and the young men returned to the wall.

Lily sighed in relief. With the way some of the winged-people felt about Kestrel, she didn't feel safe.

Gormlaith nodded at Davina.

Davina looked back over at Sir Frederick, who hesitated and then nodded.

Gormlaith spoke, "Davina of the Decatur tribe, I am the high priestess and in charge of this proceeding. Ignore your father's request or I will ban you from the castle."

She removed Kestrel's blindfold.

Kestrel blinked and then stared at Gormlaith.

Davina pushed on his shoulder. "Bow before the High Priestess, Gormlaith Boru."

Kestrel hesitated and then obeyed.

Gormlaith said, "You may approach." She beckoned with her fingers. "Both of you."

Lily held onto Kestrel's bound hands as they approached the throne. She looked into Kestrel's eyes, which had become large brown orbs that looked intensely at Gormlaith. She squeezed his hands and he squeezed back.

When Kestrel reached the dais, he bowed again.

"Sir Frederick is right," Gormlaith said, "now that you have seen this congregation, our by-laws state that we are to kill you."

Lily's breath hitched and she felt her chest tighten. They wouldn't force Kestrel to come into this room only to kill him, would they? She didn't know how, but she would find some way to save him.

"I didn't come in here of my own volition," Kestrel said, "you dragged me into your throne room. If I'd known death was the consequence of coming, I would have fought harder."

"Sir Frederick is right. You have stolen the wings from one of our own as they flew into the heavens. I should strike you dead right now."

The room erupted in a fluttering of wings and whispered agreement. "Kill him."

Kestrel didn't flinch.

Gormlaith said, "Show me your wings."

"Release my hands."

"It is forbidden."

"Then I cannot show my wings. My skills aren't as practiced as your own."

Gormlaith's posture went stiff, and she spoke through clenched teeth, "Don't test me, boy."

Kestrel hunched his shoulders. "You prevent me from following your command and then are mad at me for not following your command."

Lily wondered if Kestrel had the ability to produce his wings while his hands were bound. She had never seen him change into a falcon while his hands were tied, but she didn't think it necessary for them to unbound his hands.

Gormlaith stepped down from the dais, and long beautiful white wings unfurled around her. She approached Kestrel.

The three young guards hurried from their position by the door as their wings also unfurled.

Gormlaith raised her hands to halt their progress, but they continued to her side.

"Are the priestess' guards not listening to her, too?" The anger built with Gormlaith's voice.

The tallest said, "We are commanded to protect the high priestess from all dangers."

"The people in this room are testing my patience." She moved to stand in front of Kestrel, the guards close by.

"You are safe with me. I have no desire to harm you." Kestrel nodded at Lily. "We are only here to acquire a sacred flower for our quest for the Crystal of Zaraboth."

Sir Frederick shouted, "Kill the boy now. That is sacrilege. This boy with ill-gotten wings and the girl with the mark of Pantaleon are chasing the crystal. We must prevent them from leaving this castle."

A chant built again, "Kill them."

Kestrel stared up at Lily's forehead, his own forehead tight with a questioning expression.

Lily shrugged.

Gormlaith raised her arms to silence the room. It took a while, and the guards seemed ready to take action against those still talking. Finally, it quieted enough for Gormlaith to approach Kestrel.

Gormlaith said, "Before I release your hands, I need to ask you questions necessary for you to become a member of the Pantaleon Moon Religion."

"There is no reason to ask those questions," Kestrel said. "I have no desire to become a member of this cult."

A gasp erupted simultaneously in the room.

Lily closed her eyes for a moment. This was no time for Kestrel to be argumentative. Didn't he see that these people wanted to kill him? She squeezed his hands once again, but he firmed his stance, his gaze focused on Gormlaith.

"I see. You realize that attitude might force me to acquiesce to Sir Frederick's desires," Gormlaith said.

"My father will be angry to hear of my death."

Sir Frederick shouted, "I wasn't happy to hear of my wife's eternal death at your careless actions."

"You're placing me in a dangerous position." Gormlaith looked disapprovingly at Kestrel.

Kestrel leaned toward Gormlaith and Davina tugged on his collar back to a vertical position.

"Oh' favored High Priestess of Pantaleon. I beg of your mercy and forgiveness. You have invited me into your castle." Kestrel smiled. "I've enjoyed your meals outside the castle with my friends, and now you have kidnapped me and threatened me with death. I've done no wrong in the castle."

Gormlaith reached out to touch Kestrel's hands, and the guards pulled her back.

The leader of the three said, "We can't let you touch him. Let Davina do it."

Gormlaith glared at Davina with cold, hard eyes. The warmth that Lily had seen in the woman's face had disappeared. Had Davina summoned the other winged humans without Gormlaith's consent? They seemed to be at odds with each other.

Davina looked at Sir Frederick, who made no sign of consent or dissent. She reached down to Kestrel's hands and untied his restraints.

Kestrel rubbed his wrist where the bindings had cut into his skin. He nodded, "Thank you."

She pursed her lips.

Kestrel said, "Now that you are willing to treat me like the royal member that I am, can we sit and discuss our needs and yours like adults?"

Gormlaith returned to the dais and throne chair. She curled her wings into her body and sat.

Kestrel and Lily moved closer to the dais and sat in front of the priestess.

The guards took a position surrounding the two teenagers.

Lily had difficulty swallowing as she glanced at the guards. They didn't have any visible weapons, yet she knew that she and Kestrel had to be careful around the priestess or there might be trouble. She hoped Kestrel had magic available to him to protect them if things went wrong.

"Why do you want the Crystal of Zaraboth?" Gormlaith asked. A frown furrowed her brow.

"It's my understanding that Zita wants it to return to power on the throne of Velidred. My friends and I are worried about her use of that power. She is heading to the Red Castle with a person who is known to have killed Prince Krunal. One of them will die. We think the crystal will be safer in our hands than in either Taka's or Zita's."

"I see. What do you plan to do with it if you are able to conquer the guardians and the other two searching for it?"

"Lily's friend, Al, thinks he may be able to open the gateway to Earth with the crystal, and Lily and her friends can return to their families."

Sir Frederick moved from the wall, "Those are lies. They will return and take down the obsidian guardians and destroy our treasured religion."

Kestrel shook his head.

Gormlaith refused to respond to Sir Frederick, though she squinted through cold eyes at Kestrel.

"I am sorry that I upset Sir Frederick's wife's flight to the afterlife." Kestrel looked truly sorry. "I would take it back if I had the power."

Gormlaith nodded in Kestrel's direction.

Kestrel said, "We have no desire for power with the crystal. Our little group only wants to prevent evil people from getting the crystal. Please help us to achieve our goal."

"I'm sorry, but we won't be able to let either of you go." Gormlaith looked sad.

Lily's heart beat against her ribs with a force so strong she knew that Gormlaith heard the sound. She stood and raced to the dais. "You must let us go."

The guards stopped her before the throne.

Gormlaith said, "We will let you have your freedom, but you both have many years of training ahead of you." She stood and approached Lily. She took Lily's chin in her hands. "You remind me of your father. A great man who died to King Haskell's desire for power. This imprint on your forehead places you as a member of the Pantaleon religion, and will lead you to one day become a candidate for high priestess within this castle."

This set off a storm of whispers and wing fluttering. The noise rose so loud that Lily couldn't think. It sounded like a million cicadas were enclosed in the room.

Sir Frederick's voice shouted above the others, "This is preposterous. You have committed treason with your words."

Lily didn't know what happened, but suddenly, strong arms grabbed her waist from behind and lifted her into the air. She shrieked in fear as she soared toward the ceiling.

CHAPTER 38

Lily tried to look at the winged creature that had lifted her into the air, but couldn't see enough to identify it. "I demand you put me down on the floor."

Kestrel said, "Don't worry, I have you. If we can escape through that window, we'll be safe."

Hearing Kestrel's voice helped calm the anxiety racing through her body. She knew that Kestrel would save her. She glanced toward the open window, seeing freedom in the open night air.

Lily leaned back into the comfort of Kestrel's arms as a tingling of relief rushed through her core. She looked down at the commotion happening on the floor of the castle throne room as she soared into the air. Sir Frederick argued with Gormlaith. The other winged humans debated with loud voices in small groups. Many raised their wings as their anger increased. Her body shuddered at their speed to the ceiling.

Then she felt a jerk and heard Kestrel moan.

Kestrel's grasp around her waist loosened, and she screamed as they plummeted to the chamber's marble floor.

Suddenly her body jerked as a pair of strong hands grabbed her around the waist to stop her fall. Although she had felt safe when Kestrel carried her into the air, now she felt confusion at being captured by the flying guard. A distressing moan escaped her lips when she saw Kestrel lying in a heap on the marble floor. She feared the guard might accidentally drop her, and she might also fall to her death.

The guard flew to the floor in a tight spiral and let Lily's feet find purchase. He held her arms tightly behind her back.

Her mind reeled at she realized they had failed.

Lily's body tensed as anger held her in check. They had no right to hold her. She didn't ask to be a member of their religion; she just requested a flower. She struggled with her captive, but he gripped her arms tighter.

"Let me go."

"It is not my decision. You tried to escape, now you will be accountable to the High Priestess."

She wriggled, but it didn't help.

The commotion in the room hadn't settled down at all as the beings, circled into small factions, as they yelled and waved their hands at each other.

Kestrel hadn't moved since he hit the floor where two guards stood over him.

Lily yelled out, "Kestrel. Are you okay?" A cold chill ran up her back as she leaned toward Kestrel.

He didn't move.

Sir Frederick stood in front of Gormlaith. "They tried to escape. You must put them to death. We can't trust these two to become initiates of the religion."

"I won't talk about this until you quiet your people." Gormlaith signaled with a minute wave.

The initiate standing to Gormlaith's right raised a tall staff with cloth wrapped around the top and struck a large gong hanging from a metal stand.

The noise in the room settled a little, but a couple of groups still argued.

The woman smacked the gong once more.

Finally, the room resolved into silence as the lingering tone reverberated off the stone walls.

Gormlaith stood, surveying the room with tight eyes. She settled her gaze on Sir Frederick. "We will not kill these young people. Sometimes initiates are scared. We must train them in our ways."

Lily shouted, "Let us go. We have no desire to become initiates in your religion."

Gormlaith stared down at Lily.

Lily felt small, like she had when her aunt had corrected her when she spilled milk on the floor trying to fill her bowl of cereal. The high priestess had the look of someone who didn't like it when people disobeyed her commands. Lily worried about their fate.

She screwed up her courage. "At least let me help my friend. Your goons tossed him to the floora."

The man behind her squeezed her arms tighter behind her back and pulled her upright.

Gormlaith moved a hand and two initiates ran to Kestrel's side and knelt beside him.

He still hadn't moved since he fell, and Lily feared he had already been killed. His wings lay at an odd angle to his back.

Sir Frederick said, "I warned you about these two before we began. Neither should have been exposed to our process."

Gormlaith's back stiffened and her face reddened. She spoke through gritted teeth, "The blond-haired woman before us has the mark. Are you blind to the mark of Pantaleon that is embedded in her forehead?"

"A magic trick of treachery and deceit."

"You know magic doesn't work while the obelisks guard the castle. The mark is real. We must respect our traditions."

"You know that no one respects the old religion as much as I," Sir Frederick said. "Our traditions are important, but no one has worn the mark in over twelve-hundred years. The Pantaleon moon goddess has picked our leaders for hundreds of years. Put the child to death, or I will talk to the council to arrest you for high treason."

"We must give her an opportunity to go through the initiate training," Gormlaith said. "We don't know the meaning of the mark. Let us study her and help her realize her divine fate."

Lily listened to the conversation as she watched the initiates attend to Kestrel. He still hadn't moved and her stomach roiled with bile. She tried to stay strong, but she dreaded her future if Kestrel died. She only half listened to Gormlaith's comment about some divine fate. Her legs trembled with uncertainty.

Gormlaith continued, "I understand that you expect your eldest daughter to take over the position of priestess when I retire, but that isn't in our hands."

"This girl is a threat to the old religion. She isn't from this planet and might become a target for the forces of evil." Sir Frederick countered.

The crowd murmured.

Sir Frederick continued, "We can't allow her to use the power of the position of High Priestess to push off the old guard and bring forth a new order."

When the man said she wasn't from this planet, Lily's attention shifted back to the conversation dominating the room. The crowded room had warmed and Lily raised her arm to wipe sweat from her brow. She lifted her shoulders and scowled at Sir Frederick. "I am from this planet. I was born on Aloheno."

This brought a louder response from the others.

"The next high priestess should come from the members who were raised from birth within the castle," Sir Frederick said. "We can't allow this woman to usurp our ways. Who in here knows what beliefs she might bring with her from Earth? She associates with an undesirable."

Gormlaith lowered her voice, "Your reactions to this are understandable. You grew up with the old ways and are afraid of change. When the woman entered the castle, we had no way to anticipate that Pantaleon's power would settle upon her, but despite our doubts and fears our moon goddess has spoken and we must listen."

Sir Frederick's nostrils flared.

Lily thought the man might explode.

He bared his teeth. "I will not accept this and will speak to the council first thing in the morning. Keep these two alive because I plan to be in attendance when they're executed." He nodded to a group of people that looked like family members, and they flew from the room. A scattering of others joined their flight.

Kestrel's arm moved and then the other. The guards quickly pinned his arms to the floor.

Tension released in Lily's chest as she realized her friend lived. She tilted forward to run to his side, but the guard held tight and didn't allow her to move.

Gormlaith smiled when Sir Frederick and his contingent exited the room. She raised her hand out to Lily. "Please."

Lily attempted to move, but the guard held her back. She snarled at him and he released her, but she first went to Kestrel. She knelt by his side. "Are you okay?" she whispered as she stroked his hair.

One guard had his knee on Kestrel's head which pinned him to the floor.

Blood dribbled through Kestrel's closed teeth as he looked into her eyes. "Yes."

Lily looked to Gormlaith to release Kestrel, but she made no movement. Lily placed her hand on Kestrel's black hair and then rose from the floor. *If they want me to become a high priestess, then I will act like a priestess.*

Lily pushed back her shoulders and walked like a queen, well, a queen like the ones she saw on the TV shows on Earth. She approached the High Priestess once more. "I repeat my earlier comment, I will not become an initiate of this religious order."

Gormlaith didn't seem fazed and stood triumphant on the dais, "It is not your decision to make."

"We didn't come here to become your servants. We're here to save Velidred, maybe this castle and possibly all of Aloheno. You can't deny us an opportunity to defeat Taka and rescue Zita."

Gormlaith smiled. "Your spirit for good reminds me of my childhood. Full of passion and the willingness to change the world. Those times are long past, I'm afraid. You will develop your powers and indeed will change the world, but for now you must learn to control the powers that the Pantaleon Moon Goddess will gift to you."

"I'm grateful for the opportunity to become a member of the Pantaleon Moon religion, but my friend needs me. She's in danger and we are the only ones who can help."

Gormlaith said, "In your present state you could put yourself and your friends in danger. We know so little about the mark. Sir Frederick correctly stated that we haven't seen the mark in twelve-hundred years. We must search through the archives to understand this momentous occasion."

"It's settled then, your library staff can search the archives while I continue our quest for the crystal."

Gormlaith shook her head, "You will stay here and train, then you'll be equipped to handle the powers you possess."

"I feel no powers." Lily brushed her hand across her forehead. "It's just a little wax and metal. Hand me a candle, with a little heat we can clear it all off. I should have thought of that before." She rubbed hard on the symbol.

Gormlaith said, "It's permanent. You *will* stay with us and learn to face the challenges the future holds for you."

Frustration built within Lily as her throat tightened. She forced the words out, "If you must hold me, at least let my friend Kestrel go free. The others will need him. And Sherry. Release her."

"Your friend Sherry has already been released and is with your friends outside the castle door."

A tingling of joy and hope swept through Lily's body. Gormlaith did have compassion. She might be able to convince the high priestess to release Kestrel and her. With Sherry free, she wouldn't have to try to rescue her friend as well. She smoothed her clothing with her hands and stood erect. "I request you release Kestrel and me as well."

Gormlaith looked at Kestrel with disdain. "Kestrel has committed a serious offense."

"He was just trying to help me escape."

"No!" Gormlaith said sharply. "The escape attempt meant nothing. We knew he'd make a play for the window and were prepared for the attempt."

Gormlaith stayed silent for a moment.

"What is it then? He hasn't been here long enough to hurt anyone. Why can't you release him?"

Gormlaith frowned and then looked down at the captured Kestrel. "Like Sir Frederick mentioned, Kestrel has committed a serious sin within our community, by taking over the ability for flight and preventing Sir Frederick's wife from reaching the afterlife. I cannot let him go. It might be impossible for me to keep from having to execute the boy."

Kestrel mumbled something, but the guard pressed harder on his skull, which silenced him.

Lily asked, "Are you going to execute him for something he did as a dumb kid? Didn't you do anything stupid when you were young? Have mercy on him. Sir Frederick is gone, release Kestrel and let us get far away from this castle."

"It's not that easy, my child." She snapped her fingers and the guards yanked Kestrel to his feet."

Kestrel moaned when they moved him. His arm looked like it had broken and both wings looked misshapen.

Lily moved toward Kestrel, but a guard stepped forward and grabbed her purple tunic. She thought with disdain about how her royal garment had done nothing to help. She wasn't royalty or a princess. Nothing but a prisoner.

She watched in horror as the guards marched Kestrel from the room. Blood dripped on his tunic from his mouth, and his posture had the look of a defeated man.

CHAPTER 39

Al sat with Sherry and Erik in one of the village houses within the castle bailey. A woman dressed in a white gown from the castle had come out with food in the morning and given it to them. They had been happy when the castle released Sherry late the previous day, and had waited at the castle doors until nightfall for Lily and Kestrel. When they didn't show up, the three found a place to bed in the village. Now the sun's location meant noon and they hadn't seen any more movement at the castle doors.

Erik asked, "Who were those winged creatures that flew into the castle last night?"

Al said, "I don't know. Maybe they are relatives of Kestrel, and they're all eating and partying and having a good time in the castle while we twiddle our thumbs out here."

"When that first group of winged creatures left the castle, they looked pretty angry," Sherry said. "I don't think Kestrel and Lily are having a good time."

"You heard Kestrel. This cult likes to steal girls and force them to participate in their cult. Kestrel probably tried to rescue Lily." Erik said,

"What if those winged creatures ate Kestrel?" Al asked. "Maybe the ones who left weren't able to get a piece of him."

"Don't say stupid things." Sherry said, "This is serious. They requested Kestrel to come into the castle, so, they probably didn't eat him."

"What do you think they would say? We want to roast you over a pit and eat your body. Kestrel wouldn't have gone in if they said that. No, they said, 'The high priestess requests your presence so she can speak with you about some important issues.' Those issues were if he tasted better with honey barbeque sauce or vinegar sauce," Al said.

"Stop it. They aren't eating him though they might be in danger. When Lily walked by me yesterday, she had a strange mark across her forehead. I don't know what it means."

"Show us. Draw it on the dirt floor," Erik said.

Sherry bent down and drew the circle and dot. "This is a symbol they traced on our heads during the oil ritual. When they drew it on my head and Zita's we had a bad reaction to it. After the ritual they sent Zita away and held me for observation or something. They didn't say why they released me earlier today."

Erik bent down to examine the symbol closer. "Maybe when Lily arrived, she looked more interesting. Are you sure you didn't have the same symbol on your forehead and they just wiped it off?"

"I'm sure. For me and Zita it was a smudge of oil that made us faint."

"And Lily has a shiny smudge of oil?" Al asked.

"Not oil. It's like they permanently affixed a golden symbol to her forehead. It shined to the point where I thought it might be glowing."

Al leaned forward to examine Sherry's forehead.

She pushed him away. "Get away from me."

"I wanted to verify you didn't have a growth coming out of your forehead." He leaned in again.

"Get back. We have to figure out how to get inside the castle and rescue Lily and Kestrel."

Al shuffled away from Sherry muttering to himself. "I wanted to get the information I needed to make a competent decision." He felt his ears turn red in embarrassment.

Erik said, "Al and I have walked around the castle twice, and the only entrances are guarded by at least two guards."

Sherry asked, "Can we overcome the guards?"

"I have the Sword of Freedom." He waved his sword in the air. "I've never actually used it as a weapon though. Its real purpose is to be used for healing, not fighting."

Sherry outlined the symbol she had drawn on the dirt floor with a square, "The guards might not know that. We may be able to bluff our way into the castle."

"They all had weapons and are probably better trained than I am."

Al bounced the bottom of his staff on the ground. "I have a weapon."

Sherry shook her head. "Zita said her magic didn't work. Does your magic work here?"

Al dropped his shoulders. "No, my magic hasn't worked since we came within the circumference of the obelisks.

Sherry handed the stick to Erik. "Draw out the castle exterior and mark the entrances you found."

Erik sketched the castle and drew an X at each entrance.

"Any clue what they were for? Like a kitchen entrance, to remove the waste, exercise the guards, or bring in armor?"

"I couldn't tell."

Al said, "We can't keep sitting here waiting for them to return. We have to get hiking to the Red Castle and capture the crystal. Taka and Zita are days ahead of us and we're just sitting here."

"I know!" Sherry's face flushed bright red, anger radiating toward Al.

Erik stepped between them. "Relax. We'll find a way to rescue them. We're smart. Right? There must be a way into the castle. Let's think some more."

Al sat in the dirt with his staff across his legs.

"We can create a distraction." Erik said, "Sneak into the castle, start a fire, and then check the rooms."

"We still haven't figured out where or how to sneak in."

"If we knew the kitchen's location, we could pretend to be delivering food supplies into the castle," Al said.

Sherry said, "We don't know its location, so off the list. Though it has possibilities. Keep thinking."

"We disguise ourselves as members of the staff. There must be one entrance we can pretend to belong to and convince the guards we are staff. Then we have free rein around the castle. Those women won't even know we're in the building," Al said.

"Are we even sure men are allowed into the building?" Erik asked, "Wait. We're making this harder than it has to be. Al and I can dress as women. We knock, they allow us in, and bingo, we can search for them."

Sherry snorted. "You two as women will never work. You both have beards, Al is over six-foot-five, and . . ." She paused for a moment. "The first ritual you'll experience is the cleansing ritual."

"I could use a good bath," Al said.

Sherry held her nose. "I know. But you don't understand. You have to disrobe in front of the women initiates. They stand there and take your clothes to be washed while you are in the building. So, do you plan to run around the building naked looking for our friends."

Al pretended to cover himself with his hands. "Okay, what's the next plan?"

They all laughed.

"How about those winged creatures from last night?" Erik asked, "The last one left the castle long after midnight. Are there any of those creatures waiting for us inside the castle?"

"There's no way for us to know. We didn't count them when they came in or when they left," Sherry said. "There could be many still in the castle guarding either one or both of our friends."

"We'll have to include that in our strategy."

"Listen." Al raised his hand.

They quieted. The occasional sound of creaking leather and wood along with the crunch of gravel and the rhythmic clip-clopping of horses sounded in the distance.

Erik said, "A horse and cart are coming."

"Here's our chance." Sherry whispered. "If it's a cart for the castle, then we can hijack the cart and they'll take us inside the castle."

They all jumped up and quietly went to the main road to check out the vehicle coming into the village. Six large horses pulled a wagon loaded with boxes, barrels and cages. Chickens squawked in the cages. Two men sat on a seat, one driving the horses and the other holding a large sword.

Al said, "Here you go, here's our chance."

Four men rode horses that followed the wagon.

Erik stepped near the wagon as it passed. "Hello, fine men. How is your journey?"

One of the men riding the horses rushed up to Erik and swiped at him with his sword. "Get away from the wagon." He twirled the sword in his hand.

Erik backed up and raised his hands. "Okay. No problem. I just wanted to say hi."

The man on the horse raised his sword. "Get back. These supplies are for the women of the castle. We are ordered to kill any person who gets in our way."

They all moved back from the riders.

Sherry whispered, "Okay, so we can't hijack the cart, but we can watch which door they use."

They followed the cart from a distance until the wagon reached a door. The two guards at the door knocked, and when the door opened, ten guards all carrying swords or spears came out to the cart. They forced the men away from the wagon and then checked the boxes and bags.

Al shook his head and whatever hope and excitement he felt before drained into self-pity. "Well, I guess we aren't getting in that way."

His friends agreed and they headed back to their cabin. They returned to the bench that leaned up against the wall on the outside of the cabin. The day had turned hot and it became more comfortable outside in the shade of the building than inside. A slight breeze kept them from getting too hot.

The wagon supplies had been unloaded and the men headed out of the village. The three teens watched the horses pull the wagon past the obelisks.

Sherry asked, "Do you think all the entrances are guarded that securely?"

Al said, "You said no men were allowed into the castle."

"Well, I suppose these men are required to keep the women safe. An old priestly guy placed oil on my forehead."

Al sat back and stared up at the castle. Fatigue had settled around his shoulders, and he felt like drifting off to sleep. The castle walls were steep, and the highest peak stood high above the castle grounds. The first windows started on the third floor and looked like they might be used for the guards to fire on any attackers. He closed his eyes and sighed. None of that knowledge would help them here. The guards would shoot them if they made a run for the windows.

A few seconds later, he opened his eyes. Hi gaze settled on the windows the winged creatures had flown into the night before. His pulse increased and his body became ultra-awake.

"Hey guys." He stood and pointed his staff up at the windows. "Those winged creatures flew from those windows up there on the fifth floor, in the straight part of the castle."

"Yeah." Erik mumbled.

Sherry sat up. "Go on."

"Do you see how if someone got on this first rooftop, they could scurry from rooftop to rooftop and end up just above one of those windows?"

"No, I don't see it." Erik answered.

Al pulled the wooden bench out from the wall. "Stand on this and look again."

Erik and Sherry both stepped up.

"Yeah, you might be right." Erik nodded.

Sherry leaned over to Erik, as she stood on her tiptoes. "Do you think they are connected? There might be some distance between the roof lines that we can't see from here."

"I'm thinking," Al said, "if we could get up there, we could use a rope or something to shimmy into the room where the winged creatures went in."

They spent the rest of the afternoon outlining a plan to get into the castle to find Lily and Kestrel. Sherry drew a diagram showing the rooms and hallways she remembered. She suggested a place she thought they might be holding Lily, but they still needed to get into the castle, and one or both might be in the dungeon. The setting sun blazed toward the horizon, shooting waves of red, orange and yellow to reflect off drifting clouds.

"I'm guessing Lily is still in the same room as earlier," Sherry said.

Al said, "If you can lead us through the castle to her room then we can rescue her. We'll need to find some rope if we hope to climb the roof and drop to the floor in that chamber with the open windows." His stomach began to feel like butterflies were fluttering around as he thought of climbing those steep roof lines to get into the window.

CHAPTER 40

Al, Erik and Sherry hurried through the village searching for rope and fragments that could be tied together. They hoped to find enough rope to shimmy down from the castle roof into the room the winged creatures had flown into. When they met back at the cabin they used as their headquarters, they had twenty pieces of rope. Al hoped it wouldn't be a problem that the rope scraps weren't of the same thickness.

He rummaged through the pieces trying to find the best combinations to hold their weights for their adventure into the castle chamber. He finally found seven pieces he thought might work, and he let Erik tie the knots. He had limited ability at tying knots and he didn't want to find himself thirty feet from the when one of them let loose.

After tying the knots, Erik and Al played tug of war with the tied rope sections, verifying the knots were tight. Finally, they had a strong seventy-foot length of odd sized ropes.

"I think this is going to work." Erik pulled the knot tight.

Al tried to pick up the pile of rope, but failed. He shook his head. "How are we going to get the rope up to the window? I can't even lift it."

Erik wrestled with it, and eventually got it over one shoulder. "There."

"We have to climb up multiple floors worth of roofline."

The sound of a flock of birds flapping their wings sounded outside. The three teens from Earth hurried out of their cabin. The winged creatures had returned.

"Oh, no," Al said. He wrinkled his brow and bit his lip. They might be doing something to Lily and Kestrel tonight. Were they going to be too late to rescue their friends?

After the commotion had died down and all the winged creatures had flown through the castle window, Erik said, "I counted forty-seven of them."

"Do you think we can take them?" Al asked.

"No."

Sherry said, "We won't even try, but we can eavesdrop on them and find out what their plan is. Grab the rope, we're going to the window right now."

Al stood. "Are you crazy?" The nice meal from the castle began to prompt distress and heartburn in his stomach. He rubbed his face in consternation. "You expect us to get on the rooftops and look down at the winged creatures? They'll fly out and throw us off the roof to our deaths."

Sherry went to him and held his hand. "Calm down. We'll sneak as close as we can, and then find a hiding place. Maybe we can hear what's going on." Nervously, she licked her lips.

"What if they are executing them? We don't want to watch that."

Sherry squeezed Al's hand. "Let's hope that isn't the plan. But maybe they'll tell us where they plan to put them or what they're going to do with Lily and Kestrel. It could be a ceremony where they provide them with the sacred seven-petaled flower, and we can know for certain they are being released. Then we won't have to rappel into the room."

Al didn't believe their friends were being given the flower they sought.

They waited another hour before starting their journey to the rooftop and window. The path that Al had scouted out had them only twenty feet from the castle's front door. They snuck past the castle door where Al had expected someone to jump out in front of them at any moment. It was a good place to stage an attack. The rooftop ledge lay about ten feet above them. If they could get someone on the ledge, then the rest of them could scurry up the rope.

For the first stage, Al stood under the perfect spot while Erik scrambled up onto Al's shoulders. Al's muscles tensed as Erik's shoes dug into his hips and sides as he struggled to find a footing to get to his shoulders. The roof overhang extended about three feet from the wall, so Erik couldn't support himself with the wall as he climbed. Finally, Al held Erik's feet on his shoulders as Erik strove to stand up straight.

Al readjusted his own feet to stay balanced as Erik swayed in a crouched position.

Erik whispered, "Stay still."

"Your boots are digging into my shoulders."

"Be still a moment longer and I'll reach the ledge." Erik's boot pinched Al's shoulder muscle as he placed his hand on Al's head for stability.

"Hurry."

Erik tried to stand, but immediately crouched back down.

"Are you okay?" Al asked.

"I thought I saw something or someone."

Sherry asked, "Are they guarding the rooftops?"

"I don't know. I'm going to look again. Wait a second, I want to see if it moved."

Al felt his breathing increase and his heart pounded against his chest. They were all going to be caught, and the winged creatures would rip open their chests and eat their hearts. Oh, and, just like Alaska grizzly bears, the creatures would eat their brains.

Erik's shoes dug into Al's shoulders once more, as he attempted to stand again.

Al wanted to scream out in pain as his friend's shoes hit a nerve in his shoulder. The effort to maintain his position had sweat pouring off his forehead. The pain increased and Al wanted to fall to the ground and die, but he knew they had to rescue their friends tonight.

Erik's journey to the roof line wasn't quiet. He squatted just a little and then jumped toward the roof. Both feet came off of Al's shoulders and then Erik's boot landed on and pushed off the top of Al's head.

Al looked overhead at Erik, still moving all his limbs at once as he scooted onto the roof. The roof had a steep incline to it, but Erik had moved to a corner section and sat looking down at Al and Sherry.

Erik leaned forward with his hands extended. "Okay, Sherry, you're next."

Al groaned as he realized he'd have to go through the same process with Sherry. He rubbed his shoulders trying to work some blood back into them. "Let's do it." He cupped his hands in front of his body and Sherry pushed off and made quick work to reach his shoulders. She seemed surer footed than Erik and quickly stood. Her weight proved significantly less and with a hand from Erik she reached the roof.

Erik said, "Throw a part of the rope up here and I'll drag the rest up."

Al dug out one end of the rope and loosened up what he estimated at over ten feet of rope. He tossed the rope up to Erik who missed catching it and the rope bounced noisily off the roof tiles and fell back to the ground.

They all stood still in their positions. Al looked up at the roof line for the winged creatures to come charging out of a window. All remained quiet.

"Throw it *toward me* this time." Erik held out his hands and squatted lower.

"That's what I tried to do last time." Al said under his breath. He prepared the rope again and tossed it right into Erik's hands.

Erik made quick work in bringing the rest of the rope up to him. Then he extended an end of the rope to Al.

Between being scared of heights and not having enough muscle to support his body, Al had always hated the rope climb at school. Now he feared being forced to climb up to a steep roof while hoping the winged creatures didn't throw him to the ground.

It took him a couple of minutes to work out the hand and foot combinations needed to actually climb the rope, but he eventually got close enough for Sherry to grab his hand and help him up.

Despite being only ten feet up, it felt to Al like he stood hundreds of feet off the ground.

Sherry took his head in her hands. "Don't look down. Look at me, or look at where we're going. You'll be okay."

Al shook his head. Then she held his head tight and kissed him, which sent a burst of adrenaline and joy through him.

They climbed the rooftop and reached a point where two buildings came close together but not close enough to share the same roof top. They were going to have to jump two feet across open air and they were at least three stories high.

The effort Al had already expended was causing his legs to quiver in distress. They couldn't seriously think that he planned to fly over that much empty air without a net or a cable securing him.

Erik jumped the distance. "Throw the rope."

Sherry and Al grabbed the bundle of rope and between them rocked it back and forth before tossing it at Erik. When Al tossed, his foot slipped and he began to slide down the roof. His heart thundered in panic as he reached out a hand.

Sherry grabbed his hand and held tight, stopping Al's fall.

When Al got his breath back, Erik had the bundle of rope and motioned for the others to jump across.

Sherry touched Al on the shoulder. "You're next."

"I don't think I can do it." Al stepped back from the edge and shook his head.

"It's only two feet. If you were on the playground and I drew a line two feet from where you stood, don't you think you could jump over to it."

Al shook his head. "I don't know that I could. Plus, it would be easier on the playground, where I don't have to worry about falling to my death."

"Erik will catch you. With your long legs, you don't even have to jump."

"My legs are shaking so much right now I can barely stand; there's no way I can step across this."

"This whole rescue plan was your idea, "Sherry said. "You can't give up."

Al thought of all the ways he might miss catching Erik's outstretched hands and slip off the roof, falling to his death. Or worse, he might not die, but be injured and live the rest of his life on this planet as an invalid. He gulped in huge breaths as he contemplated his next move. He wiped sweaty hands on his tunic.

"I've seen you accomplish so many things on this planet that you would never have done on Earth. It's only two feet, you've got this." She grabbed his chin and pulled him in for another kiss.

The kiss gave him momentary confidence, and he looked over at Erik. "Nope. Can't do it."

"I'm going to push you off the roof myself if you don't do this." Sherry reached out to Al.

With a deep breath, Al jumped. He landed stiff legged, and he bucked backwards windmilling his arms in the air.

CHAPTER 41

Al's breath came in huge gasps as Erik caught a part of Al's tunic and pulled him to safety. "Careful Buddy." Sherry joined them with a nimble jump across the gap. A few minutes later, they reached the castle's open window into the room they had seen the winged creatures flight through.

Al peeked through the window into the room below. Men and women filled the room. Some of them had wings showing but most did not. That explained it. The winged creatures were men and women like Kestrel that had the ability to fly.

Al looked at his friends, "What do we do now?"

Sherry placed a forefinger over her lips. "Listen."

A man argued loudly from the floor. "High Priestess, we have given you all the facts you need to make a decision on this case. The young boy is clearly guilty of the crime. He has admitted it himself. Make the call. He should be hanged."

The High Priestess raised her hands. "Sir Frederick, what you say is true. This young man has committed a crime against your wife and your family. We have heard his testimony. The incident happened while he was a young boy. He didn't maliciously try to harm your wife. Have you no mercy for an innocent child?"

"He shouldn't have been in the hallows that night. We warned the locals to stay away and this boy disobeyed. It is time to sentence the boy to death."

Others in the room spoke for the boy's death and a couple of the winged humans unfurled their wings and made a loud noise by beating them in the air.

Erik whispered, "Should we slide down the rope and rescue Kestrel now?"

"Are you crazy?" Al said. "We can't defeat all those crazy winged creatures . . . humans or whatever."

"We can't let him die," Erik said.

"Let's wait." Sherry moved closer to Al. "We might have a better opportunity later."

The High Priestess took a silver goblet from a white-robed initiate standing by her side. She drank deeply from the goblet and handed it back. She turned her attention back to the people standing in front of the dais.

With a glance at Kestrel, she said, "Kestrel comes from a good royal family that are our friends and make sizable donations to the Pantaleon religion each year. Remember any action we take could have repercussions for years to come."

"An eye for an eye." One man raised his fist.

The high priestess sighed. "I see."

She requested a quill pen and a piece of paper, and an initiate ran over to her with the tools. With a flourish and quick writing, she raised the paper above her head. "By the council of Pantaleon, I commit Kestrel, the Falcon Prince, to death by hanging at first light tomorrow morning." Her voice seemed to echo off the castle walls.

Sherry and Erik gasped.

Al couldn't believe the news.

Kestrel's head drooped to his chest.

The man in front of her said, "We should do it now. I don't want to travel back here in the morning."

The High Priestess raised her voice, "At first light. Now be gone from here. All of you."

An initiate struck a gong which resounded from the room's walls out the windows.

Male guards grabbed Kestrel's shoulders and forced him toward the doors.

The participants unfurled their wings.

"Quick, hide!" Al scrambled from the window.

"Where?" Sherry asked.

Al pointed to a section just beyond the windows where it looked most dark. Two of the moons of Aloheno reflected light onto the roof, but it just caused the shadow to be darker in that spot.

They rushed into the shadows, and even before they were all hidden, the men and women flew through the window and into the darkness.

The loud noise from the flying humans forced Al to clasp his hands over his ears as they flew away. Eventually, the flyers departed. Al and the others returned to the window.

Erik asked, "Do you see anyone?"

"A couple of initiates seem to be cleaning up feathers and taking away the high priestess' goblet and writing supplies." Sherry said, "The high priestess is just sitting on her throne."

Al stood over the window; his body numb with the knowledge that these people planned to kill their friend. He sat on the roof, afraid to stand when his head felt so lightheaded. He closed his eyes but felt like he might fall and quickly opened them again.

In a minute he looked back into the chamber, the initiates had extinguished the candles in all the candelabras. Only one candle continued to burn near the high priestess.

"What should we do?" Sherry asked.

Erik said, "We have to wait until the high priestess leaves the room, unless you want to try to capture her."

Sherry moved closer to Al and put her arm around him. "No, I'm not sure of her powers. She'll leave shortly."

It wasn't a few minutes; they waited over an hour before she left the room.

Al searched the room from above. "I don't see anyone. Should we start the rescue?"

His friends both nodded.

Erik tied off the rope around a couple of windows and dropped the rope into the throne room. They had brought more than enough and the remaining rope piled on the floor.

Erik said, "At least we don't have to drop a number of feet to the floor."

They scurried down the rope and soon all three stood in the room. Al was almost overpowered by the heavy, sweet scent of flowers growing in pots that lined the walls.

"What are all these flowers about?" Erik asked.

Sherry said, "I don't know, I've never been in this room."

Al asked, "Do you see any with seven petals?"

"There are hundreds of flowers, I don't have a clue which one might be the flower we're looking for." Sherry stooped toward one of the flowers and took a sniff.

It disappointed Al that they couldn't grab the needed flower. "Where to?"

Sherry led the way to the door. "We'll find Lily first because I think I know where she is, and she might know where they're keeping Kestrel."

They raced to the door, silently opened it, and stepped into the hallway. No guards stood watch in the hallway, and they snuck through the building, hopefully toward Lily's room. It seemed the people stitched into the tapestries watched their journey through the castle, and Al thought they looked at them disapprovingly.

They reached a set of stairs and Sherry said, "I know where I am now. We go down one flight, through another hallway and then up two more sets of stairs. Lily's room was at the end of the corridor."

Al kept expecting someone to jump out at them, or to hear guards shouting for them to stop, but the building was quiet. He wondered if it was maybe too quiet, but he thought the guards felt that all the entrances were guarded, so they weren't required to walk the building at night for security.

They followed Sherry, and after a minute, she stopped. "This is where they kept me. They placed her five rooms from mine and across the hallway."

She counted the rooms they passed, and finally, they reached the room where she thought they had secured Lily. "It should be this one."

"Should we knock?" Al asked.

Erik said, "Too dangerous."

"What if she screams. It might awaken the whole castle."

"Quiet." Sherry manipulated the latch and opened the door. "Lily, it's me. Sherry."

Erik and Al pushed in behind Sherry.

A woman dressed in white with a soft gold glow coming from her forehead sat on the side of the bed. She looked up at the three intruders.

"Lily?" Sherry asked.

Al wondered what magical symbol on her forehead caused the gold glow. He watched as beads of tears trailed down her face. The woman suddenly smiled and threw herself into Sherry's arms. They held each other tight.

Al had a momentary release of the tension he'd held. They had found Lily, and now hope bloomed at finding Kestrel. Al knew the danger wasn't over, but he felt joy at their current victory. A slight feeling of guilt ran through his mind for sending Lily into the castle to find Sherry.

After a moment, Erik released Lily.

"Where's Kestrel?" Lily asked.

Erik looked at Al and Sherry.

Al hunched his shoulders.

"We need your help to find him," Sherry said. "We think he's in the dungeon."

Al felt his muscles get heavy as if gravity pulled him harder toward the center of the planet. He didn't want to go back to a dungeon even to rescue a friend from death. Should they tell Lily about Kestrel's death sentence?

"We must rescue him, but I don't know where the dungeon is," Lily said.

Erik said, "It's got to be on the lower levels. Let's head in that direction until we see guards."

Al huffed and mumbled, "Great, let's find some guards."

"Wait!" Lily stopped them. "We need to grab a seven-petaled flower first."

"Where are they're located?" Sherry asked.

"Follow me." Lily led the way out of the room.

The symbol on Lily's forehead glowed and their ability to sneak around the castle might become more difficult with her leading the way. Al stopped and ripped fabric from the hem of his tunic.

"Come on, Al, what are you doing?" Erik asked.

Al finished tearing the cloth and handed it to Lily. "Put this around your forehead."

"Right, the Pantaleon symbol," Lily said.

Lily led them back to the throne room. She opened the door to the room with hundreds of flowers in it. "It's one of the flowers in this room."

Sherry snickered, "Yeah, but which one?"

"Watch." Lily unfurled the cloth wrapped around her forehead. The symbols glow lit up her face and Erik's and Sherry's. Al could see the concern on each countenance at the amount of light the symbol emitted. Was there someone outside who might notice the light from the room?

Lily walked slowly around the room. She stopped at a couple of flowers, but moved on. When she passed some red and white flowers, she halted. She turned back to the flowers.

Al watched in amazement as the flowers changed colors as Lily moved closer. The two colors of red and white transformed into seven colors each of seven petals. Each had a separate color. "This is it."

"Did you know this would happen?" Sherry asked and leaning in closer for a look.

"I suspected the symbol would have an impact on the plant we needed. I didn't know exactly what it would do, but

I had an idea it would do something. We got lucky. Let's grab it and go."

"Do we take the whole pot or cut the flower off its stems?" Sherry asked.

"I don't know," Lily said, "we better take the whole pot." She picked it up and they made a hasty retreat from the room.

They hurried to the lower levels until they reached the foyer, where the girls had first entered the castle.

Sherry said, "Be careful. They might place guards here. And remember how to get back here in case we split up. We might have to exit through those doors."

Sherry pointed across the foyer. "They took us over there when we first arrived, so we need to go the opposite way for the dungeons."

Al's hair stood on end just thinking about the dungeons. He had to toughen up if they were to find and rescue Kestrel.

They followed Sherry through a couple of hallways, and then she stopped them. She pointed down the corridor to where two guards sat on a bench.

CHAPTER 42

Al and his companions grouped together in a dark room, just a few feet from two guards who stood watch over the door to the castle dungeon. Al's heart beat fast and sweat beaded on his forehead. They had to rescue Kestrel. They would need his abilities to get the Crystal of Zaraboth, but Al had no desire to go anywhere near the dungeon. His memories of almost dying in the Velidred Castle dungeon still weighed heavily on his mind.

"I have my sword." Erik waved his sword overhead. "We should attack," he whispered.

"Isn't there some way we can reason with them?" Sherry asked. "Maybe Lily and I can go talk with them and see if they'll let us into the dungeon."

Lily shifted the terracotta pot that held the seven-petaled flower in her hands.

Al said, "They might let you talk with Kestrel, but they won't let him out of whatever evil cell they put him in. We need to disarm them and take the dungeon keys from them."

"He's right. That's the only way to get Kestrel out of the dungeon. Unless that Crown of Anticletus thing is working for you and you can manipulate them to your will," Erik said.

Sherry said, "No, it's been quiet in my brain these last couple of days inside the perimeter of the black obelisks. I suspect it won't work within its borders."

"Same with my magic." Al rubbed sweat off his forehead with his tunic sleeve.

Erik looked out the door at the guards. He returned and whispered, "They seem rather small, I think I can take them."

"You've never used a sword before and you think you can beat two trained guards," Sherry said, "Plus, we can't afford to have a noisy confrontation with them. That might cause an influx of larger, stronger guards. Can you think of any quiet ways to disarm these two?"

"If we could sneak behind them, then Erik could knock them out with his sword handle." Al imitated hitting someone on the head with the sword.

"That's it," Lily said. "Sherry and I will go talk to them and get them facing the other way. Then you," she pointed at Erik, "can sneak up behind them and hit them over the head. Don't hurt them, though."

"I'm pretty sure hitting them on the head will hurt them." Erik shrugged.

Lily said, "Well. You know."

They came up with a plan and timing. Al's stomach did flip-flops and tightened into a squeezed ball even though his only task required him to watch Erik's back to make sure no one came up behind them while they disarmed the guards.

Lily went first, followed closely by Sherry. Lily still wore her white initiate outfit and the makeshift scarf over her forehead. Sherry was back in the clothes she wore when she arrived at the castle.

Al stuck his head out the door and watched Lily walk to the guards and engage in a conversation with them. From the two candles that burned at the guard desk, Al could make out they were each wearing a sword, had a small shield, and each had a couple of knives sheathed at their breasts.

He pushed Erik back into the room. "We have a problem. The guards are women."

Erik asked, "Are you sure?"

"Yes."

"I can't hit a woman," Erik said.

"It's our only option to rescue Kestrel."

Erik said, "Maybe we can overpower them and just tie them up."

"Have you ever seen me fight? I can't overpower a sixth grader, and I have no plans to beat up on a woman."

"You can't expect me to hit a woman over the head with this." Erik lifted the Sword of Freedom into the air. "We'll rush at them, grab their arms, and tie them up."

Al said, "I didn't bring any rope, did you?"

"No." Erik's shoulders sagged.

"You must hit them over the head. Just like we planned with the girls."

Erik shook his head, but said, "Okay."

Al peeked out the door again. Sherry and Lily had moved to the other side of the desk and the guards' attention was now fixed on the girls. "Let's go." Al hurried forward as quietly as possible hoping Erik followed. He reached one of the guards first and grabbed her arms.

Erik held his sword over his head and brought the sword handle down hard on the other guard. A crack of bone sounded in the hallway and the woman slumped to the floor.

Lily's face showed surprise at the violence.

The guard Al held struggled with him and managed to get loose. She drew her sword.

Erik attacked her with the butt of his sword, but she pulled up a small shield to block his attack.

She jabbed her sword at his stomach, but he pulled back far enough for her to not make contact.

Al jumped out of the way.

The guard attacked Erik again with her sword, and he blocked with his sword diagonally across his chest. A clang of battle rose in the hall.

Lily gasped. "Don't hurt her."

Erik parried with the guard, as the clash of swords rang in the castle. "I'm hoping she doesn't hurt me."

The guard jabbed at Erik, "You will die, you flatlander beetle eater."

"Help me!" Erik pleaded.

Lily jumped on the guard's back and brought the flower pot down on top of the woman's head. A dull *thwap* sounded in the dimly lit hallway. The blow forced the woman to drop her shield. Dirt from the flower pot splashed around the guard, and the flower crashed to the floor in a mess of terracotta and dirt. Broken pieces of terracotta bounced off the floor in a high-pitched screech of tile against stone.

Erik still tried to get through the woman's defenses, but she managed to stay ahead of Erik's parries while struggling with Lily. The woman used her left hand to pull down on Lily's head, and she lowered her shoulder, flinging Lily to the floor. Lily landed on her back. The guard quickly took the point of her sword and touched Lily's neck with it. "Stop now, or the girl dies."

Erik stopped his sword fighting.

Sherry moved toward Lily but halted when the guard pushed on the sword, the point drawing blood.

Al held up his hands. "Okay, we've stopped. Let her go."

The guard adjusted the pressure on Lily's throat moving the sword slightly from her neck. She pointed to Sherry. "There is a bell on the desk. Ring the bell, so I can get some help for my friend here. If you kill her, you will all die."

"Sherry, don't ring the bell," Erik said.

The guard moved the sword to point at Lily's chest, a move that would penetrate Lily's heart and kill her instantly. "Ring the bell."

Al looked on helplessly. The three of them stood equidistant around the woman. If he lunged at her maybe he could disarm the guard. A failed attempt might kill both him and Lily. How had this rescue attempt gotten so out of hand?

Sherry moved toward the desk. "Isn't there anything we can offer you? Money? Freedom? We just want to help our friend who is scheduled to die in the morning."

"That isn't my concern. You can bring it up with the High Priestess. For now, you all are going into the dungeon."

Al's chest tightened, and adrenaline rushed through his body. They would all die unless he took action, but he couldn't get his body to move; he stayed frozen to the spot.

Sherry reached the desk but didn't ring the bell.

The guard looked over at Sherry and threatened again with the blade.

With her attention on Sherry, Al jumped against the woman, and the blade flew from her hand. It skittered across the floor clanging as it bounced.

Sherry said, "If that doesn't notify the other guards, then nothing will."

The woman tried to scream, but Erik had jumped on her and put his hand over her mouth. Al covered her mouth with his hand and used a strip of cloth from Erik's tunic to gag her.

Then Erik tied up her hands with additional cloth ripped from his tunic.

They dragged the women to the desk and tried to hide them in the corner. Erik said, "The one I hit on the head is still alive. There's a lot of blood. Let me heal the guard I hit over the head while you all go find Kestrel. I'll let you know if anyone approaches."

Sherry searched the women, found a set of keys, and opened the dungeon door. "Let's find Kestrel."

A shudder raced down Al's spine as they reached the floor where the jail cells were kept. There were ten openings that looked like they had been carved out of the castle's rock foundation. Metal bars had been mounted through the rock, preventing prisoners from escaping their captivity. Kestrel lay asleep on a straw littered floor behind the third cave cell.

Lily whispered, "Kestrel."

He moved a little but didn't awaken.

Sherry jangled the keys looking for the one that would open the jail door.

Al whispered, "Be quiet."

Kestrel woke and rubbed sleep out of his eyes. When he saw his friends, he jumped to his feet.

Sherry tried another key on the ring. It didn't work. She hurried to the next key.

"Any day now. We don't have much time." Al watched for a troop of guards racing down the stairs at any minute.

"I'm hurrying."

Lily approached the bars and locked her hands with Kestrel's. "Are you okay?"

Kestrel said, "My arm's broken, and something's wrong with one of my wings. I'm glad to see you." He reached out his good hand toward Lily.

Sherry snatched another key and tried it in the lock. The lock sprang, and she opened the door. "Let's go."

They hurried up the stairs.

Al peeked out the door. "All's clear."

They reached the hallway and turned toward the castle entrance. Erik had healed the unconscious woman and bound and gagged her, and left the two women together.

Lily lagged behind and took the time to scoop up the dirt and flower as they all waited in the hallway.

Sherry asked, "Will the flower survive?"

"We don't have time to get another one."

Al nervously watched for movement in the hallway afraid more guards might arrive.

"What if this is the only sacred flower?" Lily asked. "We have to keep it alive."

"You can't just hold it like that for the next few days." Al felt their time running out, but he realized the importance of the flower. "I don't know how long it'll take to get to the Red Castle, but we have to get a pot for the flower."

"Keep holding the plant for now." Kestrel said. "We'll make it work."

They ran to the castle foyer where the entrance had been left unguarded.

Erik and Al pushed open the heavy doors, and they rushed down the ramp. They found their horses, which they had already saddled in anticipation of a quick escape. Sherry got behind Lily on her horse, and they directed the animals toward the obelisk guardians.

A bell sounded in the castle tower.

It felt to Al as if his heart had lodged in his throat. He worried their farm mounts wouldn't be fast enough to help them escape the castle guards.

"Ride fast." Al said, "We have to get past the towers guarding against magic if we want to escape."

CHAPTER 43

Taka and his crew had captured Zita within a day of her being kicked out of the Castle of the Sacred Flowers. She planned to destroy the castle and all its inhabitants after she acquired the crystal.

No one in that castle would survive her wrath. For the last three days, Zita had ridden a horse through the desert. Taka had blocked her magic, and her hands were tied in front of her. She thought about racing from her captives with her horse to see if she could escape, but the landscape appeared rugged and brutal, and she lacked any hope of succeeding in the attempt.

They rode through a desert. Three days of riding in the hot, dusty landscape, and her throat seemed closed permanently with the fine dust that blew in the arid heat. Taka limited the amount of water anyone in the party could drink, but the heat seemed to suck the water from her body with every move. She didn't know why the horse didn't just die of heat exhaustion.

After they had left the Castle of the Sacred Flowers, they had stopped at a small desert village, and Taka had recruited others to join his group.

Toward evening, Taka raised his hand, and the twelve people that consisted of his entourage stopped their horses. "We will camp here for the night."

The sun neared the horizon and Zita both welcomed the time off of her horse and wished for an opportunity to keep riding at night so she could get out of the blasted heat. A couple of men from the desert village that traveled with Taka helped her off her horse. She brushed the dust from her tunic.

"Here, drink up." Lenny offered her a bota bag, a skin fashioned into a container to hold water.

Zita held up the bag and let the cool water slide past her dry, cracked lips. She wanted to splash it over her head, but she still bore bruises from the beating the men gave her for wasting water the previous day. She readjusted the handkerchief that she wore around her forehead to escape the harsh temperatures.

She surveyed the land. Peaks of red rock dotted the landscape. Off to her right, in the distance, stood an arch made entirely of rock. She wished she had time to go visit that structure. It looked interesting.

The party traveled alongside a deep canyon all day, keeping the natural formation on their left side. A river ran through the canyon, but Taka said it would be impossible for them to obtain water by descending into the canyon. They wouldn't be able to climb out.

Zita strained to hear the water, but only the sound of the wind blowing past her head reached her ears.

The men prepared the campsite, putting up a tent and taking the tackle off the horses.

Zita looked at the hard desert ground and thought about another night of sleeping in the severe environment. She walked a little way from the area being set up for the campsite. They wouldn't let her wander far, but she wanted to get a feeling for the landscape around her.

The second watch of the night would fall on Sims, and he always fell asleep during his time to watch. The others would be asleep and Zita could possibly escape into the night.

The moon goddess had assured her that she would be safe if she tried to escape tonight. Three rock structures in the distance looked like castle towers. She knew they weren't part of any man-made castles, but she thought one of them could help her hide from Taka and his crew. She studied the landscape, planning her route. She didn't think the moons would give her much light this night, despite the clear skies. Velidred would set before midnight and Anticletus wouldn't rise until just before dawn.

Dakarai yelled over to her. "Come and eat."

She took one last look toward the distant goal and went for the evening meal. The previous food had been bland, but tonight's meal smelled like the cook had added spices.

Dakarai asked, "What were you looking at?"

Zita said, "I've never seen the desert. It's fascinating to me. Did you see the arch in the distance? We should go over there and look more closely at it."

"Nope. We will follow the canyon tomorrow, just like we did today," Taka said.

Zita pouted, "You don't want to make this part of a scenic tour?" She tried hard to keep her emotions in check. Taka had given her the information she wanted. He planned to travel along the river, which meant she could safely escape toward the arch.

Taka's fingers held a piece of snake they had caught earlier in the day. The cook had fried it over the fire and that's what they were eating. He gestured with the snake piece at Zita. "We don't have time to take any scenic tours. I want us to get to the Red Castle and acquire the crystal before your troublesome friends show up."

She still hadn't told Taka how important Sherry would be to capturing the crystal. When Taka reached the Red Castle, he'd have to wait for Sherry and Al to show up. She knew he'd be livid when he found out, another reason to not be around. She would hide in the desert, not far from this trail, until Al and Sherry arrived. She needed to convince them she wanted to help them get the crystal.

They finished the meal as the sun set. The desert striations lit up with many reddish hues. Then the stars came out, the wind died down, and the desert got quiet. A couple hours later the Velidred moon set over the western horizon.

Zita lay in the dark, admiring a majestic array of stars that twinkled overhead in the clear desert sky. She sat up quietly, studying and identifying the different shapes scattered around the campfire. Many of the men snored and one turned over in the dark, but they all slept.

Her time to escape had arrived. They always tied her hands behind her back at night, which made sleeping difficult and made it impossible to steal a horse. It didn't matter, she didn't need a horse.

The wind had strengthened, and smoke from the campfire filled her nostrils.

She took a deep breath and struggled to her feet. With another glance at Sims, she felt assured that he slept. She couldn't allow Sims to catch her escaping.

With careful steps, Zita reached one of the full botas. It was a difficult task with her hands tied behind her back, but she managed to wriggle it onto her shoulder. Water would be a necessity to keep her alive until Al and Sherry arrived.

She crept toward the outer ring of the campsite.

Zita had to walk close to where the horses were hobbled, but they always made noises at night and she didn't think they would be a problem. A glance behind her as she walked past the horses assured her no one followed.

They had camped on a high flat area, and she had to thread her way between some rocks to reach the next clear path. As she reached the trail, she heard a soft rustling behind her. She froze. Sims must have heard her. She steadied her racing heart and turned toward the noise. No one followed; it must have been the horses finding a new sleeping position.

With a cresting surge of relief, Zita hastened out of the area into the desert darkness. The unlevel path had rocks and cracks strewn across its surface, and she stumbled in the dark but didn't go to her knees.

Adrenaline raced through her blood and she wanted to run as fast as possible, but in the dark that behavior would only lead to injury and possibly death. Slow and steady walking would allow her the best hope of escaping.

She stopped a couple of times to rest and wanted to get a drink of water, but with her hands tied behind her back, she couldn't come up with a way to hold the bag to her lips. Without knowing how many days she had to wait for the others she couldn't afford to waste a single drop.

It felt like hours as she hiked through the night. She passed bushes in the night and the smell of sagebrush drifted on the breeze. The stars had followed their paths in the night sky, the same as they had forever.

When her fatigue had reached a point where she couldn't continue, she found a place to sit in the dirt. She moved the bota from her shoulder onto a rock to her left, and she watched the pinks of the morning sun come over the horizon.

She needed a drink of water, and now she felt confident she could remove her bindings. With a little searching she found a rock with a sharp edge. It took her thirty minutes and her wrists were raw and scratched when she accomplished the task, but she cut the rope and removed her restraints.

Zita rubbed her wrists as she returned to the water skin. The water would taste wonderful to go with her freedom from captivity. She looked in the distance for signs they were following her, but she saw nothing but reds and grays in the early dawn. When she went to retrieve her water, something moved next to it.

A snake had wound its body around the bota bag and when she approached, it rattled its tail.

Zita backed away from the rock, closed her eyes, and shook her head. She didn't have time for these types of issues. She looked around her for a stick but found nothing. What else could she do to force the snake away?

Zita found a rock and threw it at the snake. It went over the snake's head, and it didn't move. She tried again and the rock flew closer to the snake but still missed. On the third try, the rock grazed the snake's body and bounced to the dirt.

Rather than moving off the rock, the snake took offense at the water skin and bit into the bag. "Don't." Zita screamed.

Her voice echoed off the rock structures, and she wondered if Taka and his crew heard her screams. She approached the snake and waved her hands at it.

It rattled its tail and struck at her.

She jumped back barely escaping its bite. Zita backed away and found another rock. She threw the rock and landed a good hit on the snake.

The snake slithered away from the bota bag and into a crack in the desert floor.

Zita grabbed the water skin and watched as water seeped out of the two holes created by the snake's bite. No, this couldn't be happening to her. She needed enough water for at least three days and maybe longer. As the water dripped onto the dry desert floor it quickly dried into a thick dusty paste.

Zita opened the skin and took a deep drink. She needed to have some of the precious water in her body before it all dissipated into the desert landscape. It tasted a little funny and she wondered if the snake had inserted its venom into the skin when it attacked.

After having some of the water, Zita turned the bag so the snake bite holes were to the top to staunch the flow of water out of it. Then she looked for a path away from Taka and his crew. She had her water, and now she needed to get far away and hide. She wondered how long Taka would spend looking for her. He didn't really need her, especially since he kept blocking her magic every time.

Of course, she could have used magic to remove the snake. *It's all Taka's fault I'm having so many problems; he's got me not even thinking about magic to solve my problems.*

She traveled for an hour, watching her back as she headed toward the arched rock. It looked to be miles from the canyon and Taka seemed to think going out of his way would be too much work.

An hour later her stomach felt weird and then suddenly she felt nauseous. She vomited the contents of her stomach on the dry red ground. With deep breaths she settled her stomach. If she got some of the snake venom in her, certainly vomiting like that had removed it from her system.

Zita didn't feel well, and she wobbled across the desert landscape. Her throat felt constricted and it became more difficult to breathe. She wanted to scream as panic began to set in. Her body couldn't give up on her. She had to find the crystal so she could reclaim Velidred Castle as her own.

Her muscles tensed and she looked out at the desert landscape where images of men flickered in the hot desert sun. Panic set into her core. Taka's men were coming for her. She couldn't allow them to capture her once again.

Zita ran away from her pursuers for half a mile before dizziness settled into her brain.

"It must be the heat," she thought. A large boulder stood in the sun and Zita noticed a shady area behind the rock. *I must sit and relax, maybe sleep. Give my body time to process the venom. I could use a nap. I'm safe for now.* Then she passed out.

CHAPTER 44

Zita woke tired and dizzy in the desert. She had trouble focusing her eyes, and it felt like someone was shaking her. Her mother wanted her to get out of bed and go to school but as a princess, she didn't have to go to school. Not today. Her mind wasn't working and she had cracked, dry lips. Her throat felt like she had been eating sand. Why did her mother keep shaking her?

Zita struggled to focus her eyes on the person shaking her. She swatted the arm away. "Get away. I need to sleep."

A male voice said, "You must wake. It is dangerous to sleep when you have been poisoned."

"I told you; I don't want to go to school today. I don't feel well. Go away."

"It's the poison. You can't sleep. You must stand and drink good water. Get up." The man helped Zita to her feet.

She wobbled on unsteady legs. The man put one of her arms over his shoulders. "You must walk to cleanse your body of the venom."

Zita tried to slither back to the ground. *I need to sleep. Why is this castle servant keeping me from sleeping? Wait until I tell Dad.*

The man held her tight with rough coarse hands and made Zita walk. They walked a few feet, and then he forced her to drink some water.

The cool water felt so good to her parched lips.

"That's enough for now. More walking. It's the only way to recover from snake venom."

Snake venom? We don't have snakes in the castle. Did some crazed wizard get past Dad's magic perimeter? Why would they let the snake attack a young princess?

Zita tried to sit on the ground.

The man held her tight. "Wake up, Lady. You must walk to flush the venom out of your system or you will die."

"Let me die. Living is too hard."

"No. I won't let you die. Sergei, bring me the water bag." He held the bag over Zita's mouth. Drink more water."

The water splashed around Zita's mouth and she sucked in air and water at the same time causing her to cough. "Stop torturing me. I won't talk."

"Help me get her to walk more, Sergei."

Sergei took Zita's other side and the two walked Zita back and forth in the shade of the boulder.

Time passed and the two people gave Zita water and walked with her.

Her mind cleared a little, and her eyes focused more clearly. *Who were these two people forcing her to march back and forth in this imagined desert? This is definitely not the castle servants.*

Zita pushed the young boy away from her and struggled to escape from the man. "Let me go."

He backed away. "Ah good. The venom is discharging from your body. There is hope for you."

Zita stepped back. "Who poisoned me?" Her head pounded in pain as she took in the two people and studied the desert landscape. A man and boy stood arm's length from her.

They wore leather leggings and thin cotton shirts that hung loosely below their belt line. Each wore a broad-brimmed hat that shaded their faces and necks.

The man held up Zita's water skin. "It looks like a rattlesnake kissed your water skin. When they do this, they deliver poison into the water. You drank the infected water."

"How long have I been out here in the desert?"

"We don't know. No more than a day. Most people die from the poison in two days."

Her escape from Taka came rushing back to her. Yes. She had escaped from her captives. The rattlesnake had taken a bite of her waterskin. Zita surveyed the desert landscape looking for Taka's crew. She saw no movement on the horizon. He had moved on, more interested in capturing the crystal than chasing after Zita. She had gained her freedom.

Zita examined the two people that had rescued her. One was a dark man whose weathered skin looked like the desert had baked all the water from his body. He wasn't much taller than Zita. The boy next to him looked to be ten years old.

"Thank you for rescuing me. Do you have food?"

"Not much, my lady." He rummaged in a cloth bag that hung over one shoulder and retrieved a stick of jerky. "This is all I have at the moment, but we are close to my village. Come. You are steady on your feet now, and we can walk to the village. Sergei get the rabbits."

Sergei picked up a staff from which hung five rabbits.

Zita accepted the jerky and thought of her good fortune. *I'm free of Taka and I can now use my magic again.* She shot a little magic air at a pebble on the desert floor and the pebble moved three feet. She felt excitement about her freedom, and hope of sharing in their roasted rabbit made her mouth water.

The moving pebble surprised the boy and he turned to his father. The man waggled his finger and shook his head.

Zita wondered what that meant. She followed the two people along a slightly worn path. Every hundred yards or so a small pile of rocks had been stacked on the left side of the path. She figured this is how they were able to know which way to go.

"What are you two doing out in the desert so far from your village?" Zita asked.

"I'm teaching young Sergei here how to survive in the desert, a lesson you need to learn if you plan to wander far from the villages."

The path they took led them in the direction of the rocky arch she had seen from the campsite the night before, or was it two nights before? She didn't know how long she had been away from Taka, but joy ran through her body, knowing she had escaped. He had said the arch lay too far from the canyon to visit, so heading that way assured Zita of her freedom.

Her rescuer asked, "What village are you from?"

Oh no. Zita thought. *I can't let them know that I'm escaping from Taka. Hopefully, these guys don't know Taka.* She struggled to fashion a lie that the man might believe. "Evil men attacked our village and kidnapped me. I managed to escape from them." Would the man believe this lie?

The man nodded but said no more.

A mile later smoke rose from a village that sat beneath the giant arch. The rocky structure curved fifty feet into the air and the native village sat on a giant flat rock a hundred yards in front of the natural arch. Zita stared in wonder at the scene in front of her. Children ran through the village having fun and screaming in joy. Men sat beside clay huts wrapping desert vines into baskets. Women walked through the village with clay pots on their shoulders which Zita assumed contained water for their households.

She smelled charcoal and the savory aroma of meat being prepared for a meal. A huge knot of tension released from her shoulders. She could stay in this village and wait for Al and Sherry. Maybe the villagers would send out scouts to notify her when they saw her friends.

"Sergei take this woman to our hut," The man said. "Get her out of the sun."

Zita welcomed the relief from the desert sun as she stooped through the open doorway and into the shade of the hut. It wasn't large, only a circular structure made of mud with a fireplace in the center and blankets placed on the ground around the fire.

"Please sit on the blankets." Sergei pushed Zita lightly on the back. "You can rest here. You look like you are sunburned." He went to a section of the hut and dug out a small jar from a basket. "Place this cream on your face and arms. It will help relieve the pain from the sun."

Zita accepted the cream and applied it to her face. It helped immediately and she rubbed it on her ears and arms. She had survived the desert and had escaped from Taka. Now she would plan how she could help Al and Sherry capture the crystal. She didn't have the scroll because she left it with Taka, but she felt confident she remembered enough of it to help them achieve their goal.

Sergei's father walked through the doorway with two other men. "She's in here, my friends."

CHAPTER 45

Al squeezed his horse's torso with his legs, wishing for it to hurry away from the Castle of the Sacred Flowers. He didn't have high expectations for his mount since it had been a farm animal from one of the Triponca farms near Paxton's house. The animal hadn't shown any true ability to be a war horse or even a race horse, and despite the danger from the castle, Al couldn't inspire the animal to move faster.

The tower bell tolled as the five friends raced from the castle, their goal to get beyond the black obelisks in the distance. Al knew once past the obelisks they would be able to use magic to protect themselves from the soldiers. The big moons, Anticletus and Velidred, weren't in the sky at this time, and the darkness made it difficult to push his animal through the castle village.

Al stayed behind Sherry and Lily while Kestrel rode next to Erik in front. Al held his staff in his hand ready to create a shield or throw a fireball, if necessary, at any enemy pursuit, but if they were caught before the obelisks, then they had no way to defend against capture. Erik's sword proved to be the best defense in their arsenal, but his skill came in at average at best. He hadn't shown the ability to defend against more than one attacker at a time.

Al kicked his heels into the animal's flank, but the animal didn't respond with more speed. The horses' hooves thudded across the draw-bridge as they cleared the castle village.

Al first heard it as it whistled past his head and then felt the wind of an arrow flash by his shoulder and crack into the wood of the bridge as they crossed.

He shouted, "They're shooting arrows! Hurry!"

He calculated they had at least a mile to go to reach the obelisks. The archers in the castle ramparts couldn't shoot arrows that far. Maybe they could outrun the arrows in another thirty seconds or so.

With a harder kick into the animal's side, his horse moved faster as arrows thwacked into the ground nearby.

Sherry and Lily rode together on one horse and Al could sense their horse beginning to tire. Even in the dark, the animal's labored breathing surpassed the thumping of the horses racing across the grassy field. Al slowed his own horse so they wouldn't be at the back by themselves. The land before them had been cleared long ago to prevent predatory armies from sneaking up and attacking, so Al knew they had nowhere to hide.

The bells continued to clang in the crisp night air. Suddenly Al heard another noise—the hoofbeats of many horses crossing the bridge behind them. The rhythmic clip-clop across the wood sounded loud in the dark of night. Al couldn't see the obelisks in the darkness and had no way to know how close they were to their goal.

Al shouted, "Hey guys, we're being followed."

"Hurry!" Kestrel yelled.

"My horse won't go any faster." Al knew adrenaline coursed through his body, but he didn't know how to impart that to his steed. His heart raced with fear as he snuck a peek behind him but saw nothing in the darkness.

Steel sliding out of sheaths rang behind him.

"How close are we?" Al asked.

"Not close enough," Kestrel said. "We might have to turn and fight."

Sherry yelled, "Fight with what?"

"I don't know."

A shudder ran through Al's body as he realized they weren't going to make it to the obelisks in time. He glanced behind, and their pursuers had cut the distance in half. He checked his ability for magic but felt nothing behind the confines of the black monoliths.

"Faster!" Al yelled.

Erik shouted from the front, "I see the obelisks."

"We can make it." Sherry yelled.

Al looked back and gasped as he discovered that soldiers had reached him. Two of the women brandished their swords as they came alongside. The teens' attempt at escape almost certainly would end in failure. Their horses weren't built and trained for this type of riding.

Al waved his staff at the soldiers in hopes of slowing them down and giving his friends a better chance to reach their goal. He rode side to side poking his staff at the soldiers, trying to knock them out of the saddle.

A soldier whacked at his staff with her sword.

One soldier grabbed Al's staff and pulled.

Al wobbled on his horse and yanked the staff back. Then he swung it in a wide arc to the other side and hit the soldier, knocking her back on her horse. With a mighty swing Al caught the soldier's neck and took her off the horse.

He readjusted the staff and tried the same maneuver on the other soldier, but the woman expected it and smacked the staff with her sword, chipping the wood.

Callahan the Curious, one of the voices on the staff, yelled at Al, "Are you trying to kill us? They're going to whack us into toothpicks."

Al withdrew his staff to his side. "Yeah, I didn't think about that." He swerved his horse side to side trying to avoid the sharp edge of the sword. Al looked ahead and saw the monoliths getting closer, a football field away. Hope bloomed in his chest.

A second soldier replaced the one on Al's right and lunged at him. She grabbed at Al's tunic, but Al leaned away, almost falling out of the saddle as the horse galloped forward.

The soldier swiped her sword at Al, but he smacked the soldier's hand with his staff, forcing the woman to lose her sword. She slowed to retrieve her weapon.

Al felt pretty good about himself, defending his friends with his staff, all while riding on a horse. He looked at Sherry, wondering if she had seen any of his heroics. She had her head down as her horse galloped to the obelisks.

Erik's horse ran fastest, and Al thought the horse had a good chance to make it without being captured. Then he exclaimed in disappointment when the horse tripped in the darkness and tumbled to the ground. Al and all his friends slowed their horses and circled around Erik.

Lily asked, "Are you okay?"

Erik struggled to stand and then withdrew his sword. "I'm fine. Come on. Let's circle up and fight."

The others dismounted their horses as the soldiers encircled them, brandishing their swords ready to engage in battle. Just like in the castle, all the soldiers were women.

Erik lifted his sword but didn't engage.

Kestrel placed his hand on Erik's arm. "Stand down. We'll all die."

"We were so close." Lily moaned. "Maybe we can make a run for it."

A soldier wearing a sleeveless tunic over her armor and a white plume on her helmet approached the five friends. "I would order my soldiers to kill you now, but it has been brought to my attention that you provided healing to our comrade. Still, I must take you all into custody and let the High Priestess determine your destiny.

Ten soldiers dismounted and approached the teens.

A light gleamed off of one obelisk and reflected onto Lily's forehead.

"Lily what are you doing?" Sherry asked.

Lily said, "We can't let these guys capture and kill us. We must do something."

"What exactly?" Sherry stepped back.

Lily, still holding the seven-petaled flower in her hand said, "Take the scarf off my forehead."

The commanding officer waved her right hand in a circle over her head. "Secure them and bring them to the castle."

When Sherry removed the scarf, the symbol on Lily's forehead glowed an otherworldly golden-white.

The soldiers halted upon seeing the glow gleaming from Lily's forehead.

Lily raised the flower to her forehead. Then she shouted,

"Oh' sacred flower divine,

I call you to be mine.

Come to my aid in my time of distress;

Dispatch my enemies, release the creature noblesse."

The soldiers stopped rounding up the teens, and stepped back toward their horses. The horses stamped their feet, whinnying and snorting.

The commanding officer chided them, "I command you to round up the prisoners. This woman's magic won't work within the confines of the obelisk. Move or prepare to suffer punishment for the next thirty days."

The soldiers moved back toward the teens but hesitated in placing their hands on them.

The flower's petals in Lily's hands changed colors, each becoming a different color—green, yellow, blue, red, purple, lime, and orange. The petals grew, wriggling into serpentine shapes, becoming seven different heads, each snarling and hissing like angry dragons. The light shining from the obelisk shone on the creature like a spotlight highlighting a circus performer in the center ring.

Lily placed the un-potted plant on the ground.

The soldiers hesitated for a moment as the creature continued to grow and growl, each head becoming more distinct like the head of a dragon.

One soldier grabbed Al to secure him. The lime dragon, with dark emerald eyes, its shimmering scales reflecting the light shining from the obelisk, struck like lightning, and bit the soldier's head off.

The soldiers drew their weapons and moved into a battle formation to fight the creature.

Al stared at the potted plant turned monster in disbelief, his mouth open in wonder at what he saw.

The others moved to the protection of the flower. Sherry pulled Al back with the others.

The soldiers swung their swords and moved and parried with the multi-headed creature. Soldiers who moved closest to engage with the beast were surprised by its speed as they fell in combat to its magic.

The creature's ability to flick and strike surprised Al, as it avoided contact with the blades. The soldiers moved back out of the creature's range. A couple of soldiers' swords made contact with the creature's scales, but their blades drew no blood. The many heads moved and swayed in perfect harmony as the soldiers tried to avoid death.

The yellow-headed dragon had a long heavily muscled neck. A red glow appeared near the base of the plant. Without warning, the yellow dragon spit out fire, lighting the dark night sky and forcing the soldiers back.

The blue headed dragon's neck curled and attacked with agile strikes. The dragon's scales reflected the blues of a shimmering ocean.

The creature had a powerful jaw, lined with razor-sharp teeth that gleamed in the spotlight. Two light blue curved horns extended from its forehead. It growled and snapped at nearby soldiers.

Each head maneuvered with perfect precision as one by one the soldiers fell. At last, the commander shouted retreat. Only five of the castle guards rode back toward the castle with their commander.

The creature roared in victory.

"Where did that come from?" Al asked.

"I don't know." Lily said, "Once the obelisk lit up, I just knew what the flower could do and what words to say."

The heads looked hungrily at Al. He backed up in fear.

"Uh, Lily, can you turn it off?" Erik asked.

"No, not really."

CHAPTER 46

Zita sat in the native desert hut. The two men that came into the hut were Taka and Dakarai. Her magic had been blocked by Taka. He had placed three native men outside the hut to guard her if she attempted to escape. Her hands were tied behind her back, and they had tied her to a metal stake inserted in the ground. She wriggled on the ground and tried to pull the stake up, but no amount of effort lifted it even a fraction of an inch.

He had truly captured her this time, and she suspected for the rest of the trip her captives wouldn't let her out of their sight. Zita had nothing to do in the hut so she tried to make contact with the moon goddess, but Velidred hadn't risen, yet.

Taka entered the hut. "Sergei tells me you recovered from the snake venom?"

"What's it to you?" Zita sneered.

"I have the scroll. You have no magic. I don't have to take you with me."

Zita tried to control her facial expressions. She should try to act sad that he wouldn't take her with him, because in reality, that's what she wanted. The others would come by eventually and she could reunite with Erik and help them capture the crystal.

Zita said, "I need that crystal."

"The crystal will never be yours."

"You don't have everything you need to get past the guardians. How do you expect to retrieve it?"

Taka smiled at her, a smirk at the corners of his lips. "I'm not worried about the guardians. I have Dakarai and the wand." He whipped the wand out of his tunic. "I'm confident in my ability to defeat any obstacle in my path."

"That's what Alpherge the Great thought, and look what happened to him."

"He didn't have the wand."

"And you don't have the Crown of Anticletus," Zita said.

Taka snorted in derision, "I don't need that. I acquired the missing ingredient today."

"Did you steal a magical item from this village?"

"No, I traded for a vessel."

A moment of concern coursed through Zita. Had Taka traded her to the desert people for this new vessel? "I thought we already had a vessel. I brought one from Paxton's place."

"Ha. That isn't *the* vessel." He lowered himself to Zita's eye level by squatting on his haunches.

Zita said, "The scroll showed a bowl, a vessel. What else could be needed?"

He whipped out the scroll and unrolled it in front of Zita. He pointed to the image that depicted the vessel. "See."

Zita examined the image. Water flowed from the crystal into a bowl being held by a woman. "Yes, like I said, 'we brought a bowl with us for the crystal.'"

Taka laughed. "It isn't the bowl."

"Did I bring the wrong color bowl? Is it not the right material?" Zita didn't like this little game they were playing. Why couldn't he just tell her what the vessel needed to be.

"Look again."

Zita re-examined the image. The water flowed from the crystal into a bowl, but the woman was drinking the contents of the bowl. "The woman?"

"Now, you got it."

Zita and her friends would never have been able to capture the crystal. It isn't the bowl. "Is there anything special about the woman?"

Taka said, "I spoke with the tribal Khan, and with his wisdom and knowledge he shared with me the reflections from his ancestral historical references."

"You are going to place your life in the hands of some tribal scriptures?"

"Listen to these words of their prophet from fifteen hundred years ago." He pulled the scroll around and stood to read it.

"You can't be serious. You expect a prophecy from ages past to help you acquire the crystal."

Taka read the script written on the scroll.

"In days of yore and ages past

A woman of nature and purpose steadfast,

Became a vessel beyond compare,

The spiritual crystal, a treasure rare.

She strove for peace and a bond with the land

To channel its power as nature planned.

Interwoven with the spiritual realm

She accepted the yoke of the magical helm.

To guide with mercy and forceful connection,
A woman strong but no magic direction,
She must have purpose to guide the essential
And a strong discipline to harness her potential

With all this power her spirit true
Sacrifice for all, a new world view.
For the good of all, the vessel untainted.
The crystal's use will lead the woman painted.

Listen to my words that shine.
The prophet speaks the words divine,
And know that the chosen of the land
Will wield the crystal in her pure hand."

Taka finished reading the prophecy.

Zita laughed, "And now you have made yourself the 'chosen of the land.'"

Taka stared into Zita's eyes. "Hear me. I am the chosen one. That's what drove me to join the Council of Nine at the age of twenty-five. I will have the power of the crystal, and no one will be able to defeat me. I've made arrangements that will secure the treasure."

Zita said, "What have you done?"

"I found a woman from the tribe to join us."

"Who else will be part of our caravan?"

"I'm taking ten guards and three wizards from the tribe with us," Taka said.

"Three wizards. That's more than you have. They could overpower you and Dakarai." She shrugged. "Their vessel, their wizards."

Taka held up the wand and the scroll. "I have the wand and the ability to cut off their magic. I'm not worried at all."

He might not be worried, but Zita saw this whole quest falling apart. Three more wizards. "We'll fill the vessel and then they will say, it's our vessel."

"I have the wand."

"Do you realize the wand might not be enough? Dad apparently had the wand for a number of years. He knew Alpherge planned to acquire the crystal, and yet he never grabbed the wand and tried by himself."

"Yes, because he didn't have the knowledge and power that I have."

Zita snorted, "You're nothing compared to Dad."

"We'll see about that." He walked toward the door, but when he reached the entrance, he turned. "You'll be traveling with us. In a box."

Zita stared at the red clay walls of the hut and screamed at Taka. "You can't do this to me." She saw that he had never planned to let her stay here. Of course, he needed another wizard on his side to acquire the crystal.

Taka directed the guards outside the door, "Load her in the box. And tie her securely to the braces. She's not escaping. We leave in thirty minutes."

CHAPTER 47

Zita wanted to kick someone or throw something, but the box Taka had placed her in didn't leave much room to even move. The sturdy, tightly-stitched bamboo would prevent her from escaping. The cylindrical shape made it difficult to stretch and the lid had been securely fastened to the rest of the container. They still had her hands tied behind her back. A tribal woman had been nice enough to place a blanket on the floor of the box for Zita.

She couldn't believe her bad luck at being rescued by the tribe only to find Taka already there waiting for her. The hot desert sun made her sweat, and the bamboo container didn't allow any breeze to enter. Zita fantasized about the violence she would pummel Taka with when she had a chance.

For now, she wished the caravan would stop and she could get relief from the heat and constricted confinement.

Near sunset the caravan stopped and two men unstrapped the restraints holding the lid in place and hauled Zita out of the container. They tossed her to the ground like a ragdoll. Zita studied her surroundings. The caravan had cleared the desert and now entered a plain with grass and scattered trees. A dormant volcano dominated the horizon. Thick snow glistened on its peak.

The smell of roasted chicken tickled her senses. Yes. She needed food. Zita struggled to stand, but riding restricted in the box all day made her unsteady and cramped. She rolled to her stomach and then worked her body to her knees. Once on her knees, one guard helped her to her feet.

Zita approached Taka. "How much further is it?"

Taka pointed in the distance toward the sun which seemed to sit on the volcano's slope. "Look at where the sun is. There is a lake in that general area of the mountain. The Red Castle sits on the lake."

"Will we get there by tomorrow?"

He grunted, but didn't answer the question.

She moved closer to him and whispered, "Listen, I won't try to escape anymore. I'll be useless if I'm locked in that box when you need me."

Taka turned to her, an angry scowl on his face. "We won't need you until we get to the lake. Have some supper and then back in the box."

"At least release my hands so I can eat."

Taka snorted but clicked his fingers twice. Two of the desert people that had been added to the group ran over to Taka. "Each of you bind her to one of your legs. Then she can eat. After she eats, put her back in the box."

The desert landscape had changed to grass from the unforgiving desert sand. They escorted Zita to a flat area and helped her sit. Then each tied a leg to one of hers before releasing the bindings on her arms.

Zita rolled her shoulders and rubbed her raw wrists where the rope had cut into her skin. She looked at her escorts. Tall, strong men, obviously added to the caravan for their ability to fight. She knew they would be useless against the crystal guardians. The guardians could only be defeated by magic. Why did Taka let the desert tribe convince him to bring all these strong warriors? They couldn't all be here just to guard her. Lenny and Sims wouldn't stand a chance against this many people even if Taka thought his team could beat them.

A woman brought a bowl of food to Zita. She had a striking figure, and her persona suggested a commanding presence. The woman stood tall and slim with high cheekbones. She wore loose-fitting clothing of a thin material, designed for life in the desert. A necklace dropped near her bosom, a simple pale blue stone with a touch of gold in its center. The woman had an aura of confidence and independence. She had a bearing as if a descendant of royalty. A daughter of the tribal Khan perchance.

Zita accepted the bowl of chicken, rice and beans, wondering if this woman represented the vessel the prophecy foretold. As she hungrily consumed her food, she watched the woman move. If she hoped to control the Crystal of Zaraboth, she needed more information about the vessel.

After a few moments, the woman retrieved a bowl of dinner and sat opposite Zita.

Zita introduced herself.

The woman nodded. "My name is Princess Ekaterina."

Zita bowed. "It is a pleasure to meet you."

"Taka tells me that you were once a princess."

Zita bit her lip in anger. *I will again become the master of Velidred as soon as I secure the crystal. But first I must know more about this woman so I can control this power.* "Yes, after my father's defeat, I lost the home I grew up in, Velidred Castle."

"I have heard wonderful things about Velidred. I look forward to seeing it someday."

Zita wondered if Taka had told Ekaterina about where he planned to keep her. *Does she know Taka has hopes of becoming the Velidred king?* "It was nice to be a princess at the castle. We had many servants who took care of me. But as a princess, didn't others serve you?"

"My father, the Khan, did not allow the servants to dote on me. I grew up serving others and spending most days with my spiritual director. As the oldest princess of the tribe, my role is to grow into the spiritual leader."

Zita stared into the woman's brown eyes. They seemed to call her to a peaceful existence. "That seems a worthy occupation. What brings you here with Taka and his men?"

"My father seems to think I might be the perfect vessel for the Crystal of Zaraboth."

Zita pursed her lips. *So, they have told her.* "I have heard of the legendary crystal, but I didn't realize that it took the form of a woman. That seems to be a massive commitment to your tribe. How do you feel about this responsibility?"

"My father instructed me it would fulfill my role as spiritual leader. My education and training make me the perfect vessel."

"Will you be able to live a normal life after taking on this capacity? Will it require you to give up certain aspects of your life? A boyfriend perhaps."

Princess Ekaterina seemed to process memories and glanced at one of the warriors traveling with the group. "I am a princess, and my duties are to the tribe. I am honored to have been chosen." Tears formed in the corners of her eyes, but no drops spilled.

It was obvious no one knew the full breadth of responsibility and capability of the Crystal of Zaraboth. As far as Zita knew, the magical object resided in a castle, and if you defeated the guardians and the magic that surrounded the object you could take it. But if the legendary object wasn't an object at all, but a human, then how do its owners use it?

"You are very brave to accept your responsibility as a spiritualist . . . so completely."

Ekaterina looked pensive but nodded.

Zita asked, "After you take on the role of the crystal, what are the plans for your future? Will you be going back to Velidred with Taka?"

Ekaterina did a quick scan of the people around her. Taka stood not far away talking with Sims and Dakarai. Were they listening to Zita and Ekaterina?

With a heavy sigh, Ekaterina said, "Yes, I will go back to Velidred Castle and take on my role there in service to Velidred and my tribe."

Zita noticed her captor's smiled a little as Ekaterina said this. Taka had better have a solid plan when they breached the crystal's defenses because the tribal Khan had no intention of giving up the crystal. It also meant that her plans to acquire it were at risk.

They talked for an hour about Ekaterina's spiritual training, about boys and the responsibilities of a princess. Zita came away with the feeling that the woman had similar dreams and goals as her own.

CHAPTER 48

Before long, the stars dotted the sky and then the whole firmament blazed in tiny points of light. The men re-tied Zita's hands behind her back and as they dropped her back in the basket, she noticed the crescent Velidred moon cast a faint redness.

Zita tried to relax on the blanket within the box. She found it easiest to sleep curled up in a ball like a dog next to a fire. *Yes, that is how Taka sees me, a dog to do his hunting for him. I must find a way to take back control of my situation.* She didn't know what she expected from the vessel but to find it to be, not an object, but a woman her own age surprised Zita. She wondered what it would take to control or turn the woman to work for her instead of Taka.

The sounds of the camp had turned to whispers and snores and Zita tired of plotting revenge against Taka and devising ways to make sure she ended up with the crystal. She hoped they reached the Red Castle tomorrow, and get out of this box for good.

As she drifted toward sleep a voice, shouted in her ear, "Why have you allowed your faith in me to dwindle and become useless? We have spent hours honing my gifts within you the last few days, and you have turned your back on me."

Luna Rosso's voice brought Zita awake. Being trapped in this box wasn't enough punishment, now she had to deal with the Velidred moon goddess. She tried to sit upright in the tight space.

Zita said, "I haven't turned my back on you. I don't have any magic. What am I supposed to do?"

Like a millipede crawling up her legs, the moon goddess sent pain that started at her feet. The pain crescendoed as it ascended toward her head and exploded in her brain like a thousand shards of glass.

Zita cried out in pain.

The noise she made must have awoken the entire camp as she heard guards grabbing weapons and running through the camp yelling at each other.

A man shouted, "We're under attack. Raise the fire and grab your weapons."

Men shouted and woke those who still slept.

Zita saw nothing, stuck in the box as she was. She only heard the sound of the camp in distress. She said in her mind, "I haven't rejected you. Taka has taken my magic."

"Your magic? You rely too much on your magic," Luna Rosso said. "I'm teaching you to have faith in the skills I teach, and yet you revert back to your simplistic magic. You must trust and have faith in me. Being my servant is where your true strength lies."

Zita understood what the moon goddess said, but still didn't feel like she had the ability to control humans. "You expect me to perfect the abilities you teach me, but it's only been a few days. I've known magic almost my entire life."

"You're weak and undisciplined. You expect all things to be simple."

She pouted. "I've worked hard to learn the advanced skills you teach."

Zita felt the pain start again in her feet. Her heart beat pounded in her ears as she hunched her shoulders hoping to throttle the pain. Her breaths were quick and raspy as the pain reached her core and increased in intensity. She would not scream this time. When the pain exploded in her brain, she thought her eyes would bulge out of her head, but she didn't even whimper as sweat streamed down her forehead.

Luna Rosso said, "You haven't worked hard enough. Trust in yourself and the abilities I impart to you. Believe in your intuition and have faith I'll be there for you."

"That's the problem, you haven't been there. How can I make the proper decisions when you don't answer when I call, or you're asleep at my time of need? I'm in this box because you allowed me to drink snake's venom. Where were you then?"

"Do you dare argue with me?"

Zita's current situation didn't inspire her to adore the moon goddess. She had traveled and slept in a tiny container not fit for an animal. Sweat ran into her eyes, and with her hands tied behind her back, she couldn't wipe her face. The feeling of being lightheaded weighed heavily on her mind. *Has the moon goddess rejected me?*

"I haven't rejected you, sniveling servant. You need to acquire the crystal for me."

"The odds are not in our favor. Taka wants it and he's being outsmarted by the desert Khan," Zita said.

"Then we will outsmart them both," The moon goddess said. "You should become adept at the skills I teach, to master your enemies and your friends."

Zita tried to rub her forehead against her shoulder for relief from the stinging sweat in her eyes. Despite many attempts, she didn't have the flexibility to reach her eyes and provide the comfort she needed.

A male voice said, "Well, whatever wild animal made that scream, we chased it away."

"I want guards to stay awake," Taka said. "Two guards in two-hour shifts until the sun rises."

The men groaned.

"I can master animals, but your techniques don't work on humans," Zita said.

Luna Rosso said, "I've shaped the course of human history for hundreds of centuries on this planet. Don't tell me what my techniques cannot do."

"What am I doing wrong?" Zita was tired of arguing with Luna Rosso. *If the moon goddess had any power on this planet, she would free me from this confining box.*

"Have faith in me, and let me experience human life through your eyes."

She clenched her hands into fists behind her back and muttered curses.

"Let us take this opportunity to practice."

"We can't practice. I can't use my eyes inside this box."

"Yes, you aren't yet able to manipulate people without seeing them, but now is a perfect time to test your abilities at this more advanced skill."

Zita rolled her eyes. She wanted to sleep, get out of this prison, and gain her freedom from Taka and the Velidred moon goddess.

"Good, let's work on freeing you from the box first. To begin, count backwards from ninety-nine."

Zita followed the moon goddess's instructions. The techniques reminded her of the ones Gadiel had used to teach her to shapeshift into other creatures. First, she needed to relax and quiet her mind. Those steps came back to her. As she relaxed, some of the anger she felt against Luna Rosso eased. The relaxation technique helped resolve some of the cramping she felt from not being able to stretch her legs.

When Zita had reached the point where she had alleviated most of the cramping signals her body sent to her brain, she said, "I am relaxed."

"Think about the men outside your prison. Of the ones you have spoken to, think of the person who is weakest in mental fortitude."

Zita rolled her eyes. "What does that even mean?"

"It means, dear child, that someone near you tonight will be easy to persuade to help you reach our goals. We will evaluate their mental state and convince them to help you."

Zita thought about the desert guards that traveled with Princess Ekaterina. They hadn't said much, so she didn't have a feel for their mental toughness. Taka's mental toughness knocked him out as a candidate, he seemed to have too much power to be influenced easily. Dakarai seemed to be a reasonable person and he might be swayed, but he still seemed to be a closed box to her.

Zita blinked her eyes thinking about the others in their caravan. That left Sims and Lenny. She laughed a moment thinking about manipulating Sims to pummel himself, but even though he didn't make good decisions, she thought he'd be tough to force to her will. Lenny might work. He wasn't the smart one in the group. He seemed to just follow along with whatever Dakarai and Sims told him to do.

"Okay, I have a candidate."

Zita sensed that the moon goddess smiled.

She asked, "Now what?"

"I will be your eyes. Lenny is twenty feet from you. He appears to be sleeping. Sweep your mind over the landscape that you remember. Picture it in your mind."

Zita closed her eyes and tried to remember what she had seen when she ate and talked with Ekaterina. Grassy land spread around them. A couple of rocks about the size of a cat lay twenty feet from her. They had dropped her box forty feet from the firepit. Probably a strategy by Taka to make her more uncomfortable in the cold night air. She lost concentration for a moment as she felt strong emotions of hate toward Taka. She pictured Lenny ten feet from the fire pit. Zita didn't think he had a strong constitution for pain and discomfort. The old man probably shouldn't even be traveling with them.

"Picture a door opening near the subject," Luna Rosso said. "You will go through the door and then Lenny will be sitting across from you."

Zita thought back to the times she had trained with Gadiel and he punished her when she failed a training exercise. One of the exercises involved a campfire in the woods. She pictured in her mind that same campsite deep within the night-time forest. It reminded her of Erik for a moment, and she longed to reunite with her friend, but she feared retribution if she didn't follow Luna Rosso's instructions.

Maybe Zita didn't have to open a door and go to Lenny, maybe she could get him to come to this mental manifestation of a place. In her mind, she sat on a log near the fire that had burned to mostly red coals. The fire crackled and popped as it burned down. The muted fire allowed her eyes to stay sharp in the darkness.

The moon goddess said, "Yes, that will work for our purposes. You must find Lenny and convince his mind to come to you. It will be easy since he's asleep. You have chosen a perfect candidate."

Zita focused on reaching out to Lenny. She stared into the dark forest of her mind, and saw many eyes peering at her through the trees. She drew back from the darkness.

"No, child, those are the minds of the people around you. Find Lenny among those presences."

Zita didn't want to alert the other minds to her own presence. What if she invited the wrong person to her campsite? Taka would do something to prevent her from manipulating his people. She saw the eyes and only needed to find Lenny's eyes. Though his eyes were probably blue as a young man, now they seemed gray and cloudy. She wondered if he could even see from them.

Zita probed the forest again and saw the many eyes staring from the foliage at her. She stood and glided to the forest edge. This imaginary world didn't require her to walk like a normal human. She peered at the eyes surrounding her. A set of young brown eyes appeared nearby that she was sure belonged to Ekaterina. She feared practicing this technique on the desert spiritualist.

She moved around her campsite examining the eyes and decided to look at the height each set of eyes represented. That helped her eliminate some of the blue eyes she found. Then she found Lenny's watery, gray, cloudy eyes.

She stared at the man and his eyes stared back at her. "Okay, I found him."

"You will invite him into your campsite. Be careful. Approach as someone young and humble. It's like trapping a rabbit. Small movements. Reach out with your mind."

Zita felt nothing for a long time. Static buzzed around her head like bees around a flower. Then the motion of a faint presence appeared. Lenny? She whispered, "Lenny."

The presence faded.

"Don't spook your subject."

Zita tried to re-focus on Lenny and made contact again. She concentrated on removing the buzzing bees to get clarity and amplify the connection.

A face took shape behind the blue, cloudy eyes. Lenny came into focus. Not his whole body, just his head and part of his shoulders.

"No. You must open the door to the whole being."

Zita concentrated once more. At first, she probed in hopes that his whole body would appear, but that proved futile. She needed to open the door to his consciousness. She stared at the floating head across from her. Lenny stared back, a blank expression on his face.

Zita asked, "Is he still asleep?"

"Yes."

Zita narrowed her eyes in annoyance. *What technique am I missing?*

Lenny's shoulders began to disappear like mist.

"Intensify your focus," She commanded.

"If I could do that, then I wouldn't need you looking over my shoulder." Zita had been instructed to stay relaxed, yet she felt tension in her shoulders and neck every time Luna Rosso corrected her. With a roll of her shoulders, she tried to unwound the increasing tenseness.

Lenny's face had faded, and only a little showed, as if he hid behind a thin veil. His eyes still reflected the little light from the fire pit behind her.

Zita inhaled deeply and pictured reaching out her hand to Lenny. She thought, "Take my hand, and sit by my fire."

A surge of energy poured through her hand and his whole body took shape. She gently pulled on Lenny's hand and led him to her imaginary fire. His calloused hand shook slightly, and with a slight touch on his left shoulder, she guided him to sit on the log next to the fire.

She settled next to him and again took his hand in hers. It seemed his thoughts streamed through the physical connection into her own mind. The barrier that stood between them vanished and Zita could communicate with the man.

Zita asked Luna Rosso, "Now, what should I do?"

"What would you like for him to do for you?"

Her first thought was to have Lenny kill Taka, but she realized that would only kill Lenny. Zita thought it would be nice to sleep outside the box, nearer the fire. The night had grown cold and she had no good way to manipulate the blanket inside the box.

The moon goddess agreed, "Yes. Have him release you from the box."

"Then I can escape again."

"No!" The moon goddess screamed at Zita and she almost lost her connection with Lenny. "You must go to the Red Castle with Taka and his crew. I will guide you in retrieving the crystal. Your skills are showing great promise tonight."

Zita almost laughed. She never expected Luna Rosso to praise her. She directed her thoughts at Lenny. "Wake up and open my box." She probed his mind with this command.

There still seemed to be some wall between them that limited her ability to force him to her will. She pushed deeper in hopes of opening the barrier. After a few moments of converging her mind with Lenny's, she opened the door to Lenny's brain.

A feeling of giddiness rushed over her. She had done it. She imagined the opportunities this might unlock for her in the future. She pictured retrieving the crystal for herself with this newfound power.

Zita re-thought the command, "Wake up and open the box that holds Zita."

Lenny sat next to her on the log; there was no movement or even acknowledgement that she had made contact with him. Had she failed? Had she done something wrong, why wasn't he moving?

Zita heard movement in the grass outside the box. *Something has gone wrong, and now Taka will do even worse things to me.*

A hand above the box manipulated the locks that kept the lid secured.

Zita asked, "Do I stay at the campsite of my mind or come back to reality?"

The moon goddess said, "Always stay with your subject until they complete the task you set for them."

Zita questioned if she could be in two places at one time. She concentrated on Lenny, while simultaneously fearing that it wasn't him opening the lid. She sat perfectly still, holding her breath waiting for the lid to open.

CHAPTER 49

Al and his small group had traveled in the desert for three days. They now sat camped in the shade of two large boulders. He had expected to see piles of sand and no clear path. Instead, they found themselves in a terrain of red rocks, cactus, and small sagebrush. Their horses had followed a well-traveled trail over worn rocks and between the desert brush. They hadn't brought enough water for their needs, and Sherry had taken to rationing the little they had left. The mid-day sun had left them parched and sun-burned.

They hadn't planned for how much water the horses would need each day, and they had no idea how much further they needed to go.

Al drank the little water that Sherry gave him. He wanted to complain, but when he opened his mouth, Sherry gave him a look and he didn't say what was on his mind. After drinking his portion, he licked his tongue across his raw cracked lips. His body didn't even sweat because of the dry heat, the sweat just instantly dried on his arms and chest and left salt trails on his clothes. He wished he had brought a hat of some kind as it felt like the top of his head had been sunburned. The smell of his clothes reminded him of the locker room at high school.

Sherry said, "Don't worry, we'll find water after the heat of the day passes. Just sit in the shade with cool thoughts."

Al rolled his eyes at her. "I'm dying of thirst and you expect cool thoughts to lessen my desire for fresh water."

"We're all in need of water. It doesn't help any of us if you continue to bring up how thirsty you are every ten minutes." She shook the skin of water in her hands. "Do you hear that?" "That's all the water we have left. I'm doing everything I can to conserve it to help us survive."

Warmth crept up his neck in embarrassment as he realized how childish he sounded. He examined the others. Erik hadn't said a single word all morning, and he usually talked a lot. Kestrel stayed close to Lily and they whispered to each other but hadn't said anything to the rest of them. They were all feeling the effects of the dry desert heat.

Lily still held onto the seven-petaled flower. She had figured out how to get the dragons to transform back into their plant form. Its dirt had grown dry and brittle. She turned to Al and Sherry, "We have to find water and a pot for this plant or we risk losing it completely. We suffered a lot to retrieve it, we can't let it die."

Sherry walked over with the water skin and dripped a few drops of water onto the flower's scorched soil.

Al watched in frustration as the drops of water irrigated the flower. He pinched his lips together in hopes that water would rush out of the rocks that shaded their positions from the sun. "Stop wasting our water on that stupid plant. It's not going to live in this environment. We should be saving the water for our own needs."

Lily said, "We have to keep it alive; it might be the only thing that allows us to reach the crystal."

"We've kept it alive as long as we could. We've failed to find the water that Kestrel claimed he could find for us in this blasted desert."

Kestrel's nostrils flared and he raised his head in a jerky movement. "Those flying people at the Sacred Castle broke my arm and damaged my wings. I can't fly at the moment."

"That's because you're afraid to let Erik heal you." Al berated Kestrel.

Kestrel's face reddened. "Erik said himself that he doesn't know how to heal my wings."

"Both of you just stop." Erik sat in the shade, with his head in his hands. "We can't afford to argue, it requires too much energy." He stood, stepped over to Al, and put a hand on his shoulder. "Just relax. I'm sure we'll find water when it cools off near nightfall and we can travel again."

"There's no way you can know that. Look around us. There's nothing that would make you believe there's water within a hundred miles of us. We don't have enough to go another twenty miles. What are we going to do?"

Erik said, "You're the great wizard. Touch that boulder over there with your staff and make water spring from it."

"Oh, you're a funny man. That's not how magic works." Al pulled away from Erik.

"Then sit down and relax."

Al was too worked up to relax. He wanted water and he thought about using his magic to levitate the water skin over to him, but decided against it. He stalked away from Erik to a different section of the shady area.

A large granite rock face eighty yards away towered above them and reflected the sun's heat out over the desert. As he stared at the rock, he noticed shadows in certain areas. He wondered if those were caves that might have water flowing through them.

Al pointed at the mighty rock. "Hey guys, I'm going to that rock face over there and look for water."

Kestrel looked where Al had pointed. "Don't waste your time. Whatever you think you see is nothing more than a trick of the sun. Just stay here and rest."

Al scrunched up his face and stared at Kestrel. "You're not my boss. I'm going to check it out."

Sherry rushed to Al and tugged on his arm. "Stay here."

"No. I see something, and I'm going to find out what it is. I'm doing it for the good of the group."

Sherry stared at the rock formation. "Please. Don't go."

"Come if you want, but I'm going."

Sherry looked at the others. Erik nodded his head.

"Okay, I'm coming with you," Sherry said.

Al stood triumphantly, happy that Sherry wanted to go with him. "Anybody else want to come with me and find some easy water?"

Kestrel signaled to Al with a wave of his hand that he could go by himself.

Erik hesitated. "No, I'm staying where it's cool."

As Al headed out of the shade, Erik yelled, "You should stay here too. There's no water over there."

Al indicated with a flip of his arm that he didn't care what Erik and the others thought. He grabbed tight to his staff and headed out of the shade toward the mighty rock and its shadowed crevices. He planned to find water, and they would thank him for it after he located it.

Walking out of the shadows forced him to reconsider his decision right away as the sun beat down on him, and the hot wind sucked the moisture out of him that he had consumed moments before.

Sherry trailed behind, but didn't bother to say anything.

Al would have been happy to go by himself, but he slowed so Sherry could catch up. But she never did. She just made sure to walk a few steps behind him. He leaned a moment on his staff as he rested.

The silent treatment again. He had experienced that a few times from her since coming to Aloheno. Al figured her thoughts leaned toward Paxton and how Paxton would make a better mate for her than Al. Well, he'd show her. When they came back with a full skin of water and even more for the horses, they'd be heroes.

He trudged across uneven rocks and cracked ground. Red dust kicked up around his shoes. They passed a couple of desert shrubs, and the smell of creosote tickled his nose.

Al had mis-judged how far away the rock face was, and he got tired of the uneven footing as he planned out his steps to keep from twisting an ankle in the rocky landscape. For the first time he thought about how embarrassed he'd be if they didn't find anything. He stopped and looked back at Sherry.

She stopped and looked at the ground.

"You can go back to the others," Al said, "I can do this myself."

"No." Sherry sounded tired. "We shouldn't be off in the desert by ourselves, we should always have a buddy with us."

"I'll be less than a football field away from you guys. If I get hurt, you can come and get me when it cools off."

"Stop it Al. I'm coming with you because we shouldn't be wandering off by ourselves."

Al felt properly chastised and realized he was ready to return to the others and stop this silly plan, but his pride prevented him from apologizing and turning back. He picked up the pace to his destination. Nothing moved in the hot desert sun. No lizards sunned themselves and no mammals scurried across the desert floor.

As he neared the rock face, the shadowy areas came into better focus. Kestrel was right. The angle of the sun on places where the rock jutted from the massive rock face threw deep, dark shadows against itself which looked like inviting caves, but were only illusions cast by shadows.

He walked parallel to the natural feature trying to find something to make him look less like a fool than he already did. He continued inspections around the large rock.

"There's nothing here," Sherry said. "We should return to the others."

"Let me look some more."

"I don't want to get lost," Sherry said.

"We aren't lost. Let me check just a couple of more shadows up ahead and then we can return."

They had reached the rock-face end and the desert landscape shimmered in waves of heat.

"Al?"

Al needed to accept defeat and turn around. This wild goose chase had made him thirstier, and now he yearned for another drink of water. He stopped and looked at Sherry.

She reached for his hand. "It's time to go back."

Al nodded, but glanced once more at the shadows on the red rock wall. He thought he saw movement on one of the shadows. "Hey, did you see that?"

Sherry said, "I didn't see anything."

"I saw movement against the wall. Behind those two large boulders. I think there might be a cave back there." He hurried toward the wall.

"Al, give it up. I'm going back." She turned toward the others' position.

Al continued towards the rock. "It'll only take a second." He walked on. A handful of tall boulders stood between him and the rock wall. He found a crack between two that allowed a person his size to squeeze through and behind.

When he reached the other side, he found a large, natural archway. He noticed movement deeper in. He thought, at the very least, maybe he could provide the group some fresh meat, like a small mammal or bird.

After walking under the arched entrance, he reached a natural alcove in the rocks. He stepped through the four-foot-thick arch expecting it to end in a cave, but the ceiling had weathered away and a hole to the sky opened above him. Looking down, Al gasped as he located a small pool of water, which lay under a small overhang. "Aha! I found water. Woohoo." He did a little dance near the pond.

Al ran to the small pool of water, knelt down next to it and sniffed. He put his hand into the water and drew some to his mouth. It seemed okay, and he drank a few handfuls to quench his thirst.

He felt his pulse increase and he pumped his fist into the air. Finding the pool of water excited him. *I've done it. I've been proven right again. Alpherge the Mighty has provided for the people he protects.* They could bring the horses in here to rest, and the others could refill their waterskins. He had been right, and he relished the opportunity to tell his friends.

He examined the cave. The tall rocks around the opening kept the area cool compared to the outside temperature. Someone had brought logs into the room-like space and a fire had been made at one time. Petroglyphs had been scraped into the red walls, and pictographs drawn using black paint. He studied the drawn stick figures and four legged animals. A hundred-foot box canyon sloped up the rock.

Continuing his examination of the room. he noticed the bones of animals and humans in one corner of the room and heard a faint hissing.

CHAPTER 50

Al scanned the fifteen by twenty-foot space for what might be making the hissing sound. He looked for danger within the box canyon, but saw nothing. If the hissing came from a snake, maybe it had a small hole in the alcove's walls. He searched for movement or holes along the wall, but could not locate the source of the noise.

Al had expected Sherry to follow him into the opening, but he didn't see her at all. Surely, she stood just outside the rocks. His excitement bubbled up again; he was more eager than ever to reveal his discovery to Sherry.

He turned to exit the alcove when the hissing returned, louder than before. Al scanned the rugged terrain of the box canyon. The rocky landscape seemed undisturbed, devoid of any immediate threats.

Just as he turned to rejoin Sherry, the hissing intensified, filling the small space with a deafening cacophony. The sound grew louder and more menacing than before, causing an unsettling shiver to run down Al's spine. He froze in place, his heart pounding in his chest, as he became aware that the source of the hissing was now much closer.

Carefully, he scanned the alcove once more, desperately searching for any. But the shadowy recesses of the alcove betrayed no secrets.

With a deep breath to steady himself, Al walked backwards toward the alcove's entrance in an effort to face the danger that lurked within, its presence now undeniable.

Drawing upon his wizardly powers and summoning his courage, he readied himself for a possible confrontation.

Al held his staff at the ready watching the alcove's sandy red floor for a snake undulating toward him. A shadow formed on the wall of the box canyon, but Al couldn't see what caused the shadow as it moved down the natural ramp.

He stepped back, not sure whether to run or challenge the approaching danger.

Then the snake's head breached the alcove and Al felt his stomach drop. He stood motionless as the menace wriggled off the box canyon floor. The giant snake's scales glimmered in the alcove's mottled light as it slithered to the sandy floor. The snake's foot-tall head with nine-inch fangs bobbed left and right in anticipation of its next meal. A long tongue flicked in and out of its mouth as it moved.

Al was paralyzed by the peril about to befall him. His breath came in short, shallow gasps as the long body slithered completely off the ledge.

The snake's scales rippled as it moved, its sinewy body gracefully curving and flexing as it approached in a seamless, undisturbed flow. The motion of its body appeared fluid and in complete harmony with its desert environment, dancing with a soft whisper of sand against its scales.

Al stood mesmerized, watching the snake's progression, powerful and elegant, a graceful blend of strength and beauty.

The snake hissed softly and flicked its tongue at Al, as if tasting him before killing and consuming him. It stopped five feet from Al and raised its head and body so they stood facing each other at eye level. The giant snake leaned in closer.

Sherry tapped Al's shoulder. "What's taking so long?"

Al jumped and reacted without thinking. He created a shield to protect himself and Sherry.

In a blur of motion, the snake struck at Al's head, but the magic shield prevented the creature from reaching him.

Sherry screamed as Al poked his staff at the attacking desert snake.

Sherry said, "Why are you hitting the snake with your staff? Don't you have magic?"

Al felt like an idiot. He had done this so many times since reaching Aloheno and finding he had the ability for magic within him on this planet. Yet, he always started any conflict with physical defense.

The snake drew back and then quickly encircled Sherry and Al's position. It couldn't break through the shield, but it would keep them from exiting the alcove in its current form. It seemed to know how to block them.

Al chanted, "Flash of safety," and his shield flashed with electricity and power and all the places the snake made contact with the shield its body twitched, but it didn't change its position. Instead, it squeezed the shield tighter.

"Will the shield hold?" Sherry asked.

"Of course, it'll hold. What can an average snake do to a magic shield?"

"I think this snake has encountered magic shields before and knows how to beat them."

An empty feeling in the pit of Al's stomach grew as he watched the shield bend in toward them as the snake squeezed. "Is it possible it's a magic snake?"

Sherry's pupils increased their size, and her voice took on a high-pitched nervousness. "It appears to be abnormally large, even on this strange planet. What other magic can you toss at it?"

A snap sounded at the base of the shield like a glass cracking. A large fissure formed in the shield running from the floor to the Al's shoulder level.

Sherry bit her lower lip, "Tell me you have another idea."

Al recognized Sherry's biting her lower lip as a sign of her nervousness.

He closed his eyes and took a calming breath, the hand holding his staff began to shake slightly. His heart hammered in his chest as he thought of ways to save the woman he loved. "I can do this," he whispered.

Another crack formed in the shield and the snake's body grew closer.

Al chanted, "Choque ola," a shockwave spell he used to throw when he played D&D back on Earth with his friends.

The shockwave spell, crackling with arcane energy, struck the giant snake with immense force. Upon impact, a powerful concussive wave radiated outward, rippling through the serpent's scaled body. The assault momentarily stunned the snake, and it recoiled from the magical onslaught.

The spell dislodged dust and loose debris, swirling in chaotic eddies as the shockwave echoed through the enclosed space producing a symphony of sound, a thunderous roar reverberating through the alcove. The mighty walls, solid and unyielding for centuries, trembled under the assault. Cracks spiderwebbed across the rugged surface, fragments of stone dislodged and tumbled to the ground below.

As the shockwave subsided, a hushed stillness settled over the alcove. The giant snake, recovering from the initial impact, resumed its sinuous movements, albeit with a hint of wariness. Cracks marred the alcove's once smooth surface like scars, and a cloud of dust hung in the air.

Dust settled on Al's magic shield, revealing the many cracks in the barrier.

"Did you kill it?"

Al looked at the snake as it nosed along its body as if checking for injuries. The snake head snapped at the shield in three rapid strikes, and the shield cracked once again. The creature squeezed its body tighter against the shield and the sound of cracking again penetrated the once secure dome.

"Do that shockwave spell again!" Sherry screamed and pounded on Al's shoulder.

"I can't. It's too dangerous. We'll have the whole rock wall down on us. We still have to get out by way of the arch."

The shield protecting the two friends exploded in a million pieces, leaving Al and Sherry exposed to the giant coiled creature.

In blazing fast speed, the snake wrapped its large green tail around Sherry.

Sherry pounded on the snake's shimmery scales as it squeezed her body.

"Al, do something!"

"I don't know what to do. It must be magical and somehow knows how to counter my every move."

"Use your staff."

Al poked his staff at the snake's mouth as it hissed back.

"Use magic."

Al feared hyperventilation as his breaths were rough and ragged. He managed raspy chopped words, "I can't think . . . of any . . . magic . . . with this snake . . . eyeing me for its next meal."

The snake moved with extreme grace and speed as it struck at Al.

Al managed to pivot away from the long teeth filled with venom and certain death.

Sherry gasped, "I don't have much longer."

Al felt weak in the legs as he glanced at Sherry.

The snake struck at Al again; its bite landed solidly on Al's shoulder.

He screamed in pain, as the snake's teeth penetrated his skin and venom flowed into his body. Agony ripped through him with a pain that radiated from the wound. Time seemed to slow as he felt the teeth reach his bone; the searing pain intensified with each passing second.

Sherry's scream echoed through the air, a mix of horror and despair. "Al!" she cried; her voice laden with anguish.

He mustered the strength to steal a glance at Sherry; their eyes locked in shared terror.

A guttural scream erupted from Al; his voice filled with raw torment. The world around him blurred as he grappled with the excruciating pain and the realization that deadly venom was unleashing its lethal effects.

The sound of his heartbeat pounded in Al's head. He couldn't think of anything but impending death. He crumpled to the alcove floor in disbelief. Just like his grandfather, he would die in his search for the Crystal of Zaraboth, but he wouldn't have the joy of seeing the object before he died.

Al reached out his hand to Sherry, but the beast's tail encircled her body, not allowing her limbs to move. Her breathing came shallow and fast and her eyes appeared to bulge from their sockets.

Al couldn't let Sherry die. His stupidity had forced her on this adventure. He had ruined her life by bringing Zita to her school many days ago. Now, he had lured her into this death zone, and he had no answers to save her.

Her face seemed to beg Al to do something. What could he do? He had only moments to live himself, but at least the creature had turned its attention from him and focused on Sherry. Al was given a few seconds to think of something to defeat this beast.

The snake's face seemed to dance around Sherry's head as she tried to scream, but no sounds came from her mouth. The creature must have squeezed all the air from her lungs.

Al picked up his staff which had fallen from his hand. He focused any remaining energy and tapped into the depths of his magical knowledge. He gripped his staff, raised it over his head, and uttered the command, "Nina rawraq espada."

In an instant, a brilliant burst of flames erupted from the staff, engulfing it in a searing blaze. The staff transformed before Al's eyes, reshaping itself into a fiery sword that crackled and danced with ethereal flames. The air around him shimmered with heat as the weapon blazed with an otherworldly intensity of red, blue and orange.

With newfound resolve, Al struggled to his feet and stepped forward. He wielded the flaming sword with a shaking hand. The staff-turned-to-sword radiated power, its fiery edge ready to cleave through any obstacle in its path.

With a mighty swing and an intensity that matched the blaze enveloping it, Al sliced through the serpent's scaled hide. Once, twice and a final third time.

As the flaming sword made contact with the serpent's flesh, the intense heat seared through its defenses, leaving smoldering wounds in its wake. The combined forces of fire and steel wrought havoc upon the giant snake, causing it to writhe in pain and fury.

The snake lost its focus on Sherry and advanced toward Al, a green liquid oozing from its wounds. Smells of iron and copper drifted into the air. The creature rose to strike, and Al swung again with purpose and resolve, opening a wound near the serpent's mouth.

It rebounded away from Al and hissed at him, snapping its jaws in ineffectual attempts to strike.

Undeterred by the creature's thrashing and snapping jaws, Al pressed his advantage. The flaming sword cleaved the air with an awesome display of power, cutting deep into the snake's body.

The snake bobbed and weaved.

Al continued his attack, unafraid of anything the snake might do to him now that his death drew near. He glanced at Sherry, and the snake had relaxed its tail, which banged futilely against the desert sand.

He shouted, "Run!"

The giant snake turned its eyes once more on Al and leaned toward the young wizard, but its muscles were cut too deeply to strike with speed and purpose.

Al fell to his knees.

The beast seemed to realize its opponent weakening, and it moved warily toward him.

Al tried to stand, but wobbled to the ground.

The snake slithered closer.

He had to finish the beast. Al didn't know if Sherry had left the chamber or not; all his attention was focused on his attacker. If only he could strike it one more time, it might be enough to win the battle. He rose on wobbly legs and stood defiantly with the sword raised high on weakened arms.

The snake coiled and shook the rattles on its tail. It raised its head. The beast struck with force.

Al managed once more to bring his flaming sword into contact, cutting a wide swath in the beast's neck. He stared into the snake's eyes, as they both drew closer to death.

But the snake wasn't done. It reared up once more to attack on its weakened frame.

Al saw the kill strike coming, but he couldn't move, as venom had pumped through his blood with his exertion. The snake's head slithered toward him, Al's body betrayed him, and he crumpled to the red sandy desert soil.

The serpent let out a piercing hiss and also collapsed. With a resounding thud, the snake's massive form smashed on top of Al. The formidable beast lay motionless. Al cheered at saving Sherry. Then he fell into darkness.

CHAPTER 51

The night time temperature had dropped and Zita felt a chill on her extremities as she cowered in the bamboo basket. She couldn't tell if friend or foe manipulated the locks that secured the lid. Lenny? If so, then Luna Rosso's techniques had worked, but if Taka or Sims had realized her intent to manipulate Lenny, then she could be in danger. What if the other guards observed Lenny opening the container? They would tell Taka, and he would punish her.

She heard the lock disengage. The sound of the chains slipping through the shackles disturbed the silence of the night. She suspected every guard in the camp must be awake and watching. The lid moved a little as if the person had trouble guiding the lid from around its base. Suddenly, the lid lifted, and Lenny stuck his hands into the box.

It took every bit of concentration she could muster to maintain contact with Lenny in the dreamlike forest. She feared his reaction if he woke from her manipulation at this critical time.

Lenny helped Zita out of the basket and walked her closer to the fire. He pulled a blanket off one of the soldiers and laid it a couple of feet from his own bed in the grass near the fire. He removed Zita's restraints and helped her to the blanket.

Zita's heart raced in surprise. Luna Rosso's techniques worked. She feared breathing for fear she would make a noise that might awaken any of the others. Even the guards that were supposed to be awake hadn't seen Lenny help her out of the container. She relished her freedom and looked at the Velidred moon to say a prayer of thanksgiving.

She lay on the blanket and concentrated on her mental connection with Lenny. In her imagined forest campsite, she told him to return to his bed, his task completed for the night.

He seemed surprised that she didn't need him anymore, but she released his hand and he walked back into the forest and joined the eyes staring through the trees. His physical body returned to his bed near the fire.

Zita stayed awake for a couple of hours after Lenny released her from the box. This close to the fire she was warm, and she talked with the moon goddess, discussing strategy. The moon goddess wanted her to get to know Princess Ekaterina better, so they could manipulate her once she became the crystal.

When Zita finally fell asleep, she slept poorly despite being able to move. She dreamed of evil red eyes in the forest and of those who wanted to place her in the box and eat her body. She woke to the sound of the cook cutting up the morning breakfast. Zita lay on the blanket trying to get her bearings. Her first thought came as dread of Taka and his reaction to her lying next to the fire. She feared his wrath since she had no means to protect herself from him.

The smell of cooking anouora, the frog delicacy that she loved, wafted in the still morning mist. Zita rose to a sitting position and tried to locate the volcano peak, but a heavy fog shrouded the horizon.

Lenny lay a few feet from Zita, snoring heavily. He wouldn't be happy when Taka found out he released Zita in the night.

Zita pushed to her feet and walked to the meal preparation area. The cook glanced up at Zita but didn't say anything to her or yell at the guards to come get her. She grabbed a slice of anouora and shoved the hot greasy strip into her mouth, enjoying the flavor. The cook gave her a warning glance when she leaned in for another strip. She knew that her luck would run out when Taka found her, so she didn't pursue making the cook angry at her, too.

Some guards who must have been awakened by the smells of breakfast came and stood by the fire.

"What are you doing out of the box?"

Zita said, "Waiting for breakfast."

"Does Taka know about this?"

"Don't know, don't care."

The guard nodded at his buddy, and the second guard moved to the other side of Zita.

"Taka won't be happy," The guard said.

Taka walked toward their group and said, "Won't be happy about what?"

The guard pointed at Zita.

Taka took one look at Zita and frowned. He moved his hands and said an incantation that bound Zita's hands and feet. He said, "Who let you out of the box?"

Zita's shoulder muscles tensed, and she gritted her teeth in fear of what might happen next.

He looked at the guards next to Zita. "Was it you?"

They both shook their head in denial.

She felt Taka checking his shield that prevented her from reaching her magic. Zita made no movements or attempts to struggle. "I got cold last night, so I released the lid and came close to the fire." She had made a plan during the night with the moon goddess and now she needed to convince Taka that she could be useful to him.

"Well, you're going back into the box."

"There's no need for that. I have no plans to escape," Zita said. "My last attempt failed, and now I'm interested in seeing the Red Castle."

Taka said, "I have every intention to throw you in the lake when we reach the castle. You'll never make it to the island."

"Can we talk?" Now came the opportunity for the implementation of Luna Rosso's plan.

"I'm listening."

"No, not here. I'm worried." She looked at the waking people at the camp site.

Taka walked toward her. "You're lucky to be alive, and yet you think you can command me?"

Zita whispered, "I can help you."

"I don't need your help."

"Let's get some space away from these guys." She nodded in the direction of the desert guards that seemed very interested in this conversation.

"What do you want, Zita?"

Zita leaned in close to Taka and whispered, "While resting in the box, I heard a couple of the desert wizards discussing plans they have for the Red Castle."

Taka seemed to take Zita seriously. He released her foot bindings and grabbed her elbow. "Okay, let's go for a walk. You better not try anything foolish."

They walked to the edge of camp, away from the horses and other travelers.

Zita examined the area and felt she could talk. "The two wizards were talking about dropping you and Dakarai when they reached the island."

Taka shook his head. "Nope, I have an agreement with the Khan about the wizards' role on this trip. You heard wrong."

Zita's body heated up as she realized that Taka wouldn't take the bait. Did he know that she was lying to him, or did he just not trust her? "Who's going to have your back when you reach the island? Dakarai? Against three desert wizards? Don't the desert wizards have the ability to block magic?"

"I have the wand and a strong defense system. If this is all you're worried about, then it's time to go back in the box."

Despite her tied hands, at least they were tied in front of her, she reached out and grabbed Taka's shoulder. "Don't put me back in the box. There's no need for that. We're close to reaching the crystal. I might be able to give you a warning or help you plan a strategy, but I can't do that in the box."

"The only strategy you're planning is how to escape again. I can't have you doing that."

"I had all night to make a run for it, but I didn't." She placed her hands in one of his hands. His hands were soft and pliable, not a laborer's hands. "You will need me today. If I'm in the box, I won't be able to react in time. Trust me."

Taka took time to remove her hands from his. "I don't trust you and I'll never trust you."

He wasn't buying any of her lies. She needed a different strategy. She had hoped for more time to talk with Princess Ekaterina. She thought if she got to know the girl better, she might be able to control her at the proper time. Maybe Taka had no idea how to control the girl.

"I can help you with the vessel," Zita said.

Taka snorted.

"Listen. The desert wizards are going to take her from you as soon as she transforms into the crystal. I've seen Dad work scams like this. Pretend you're with the other group as support, but once they have what you want, you take it from them. That strategy made him a rich king."

Taka took out the Imperium Wand and waved it around Zita's head. "I can use this wand right now and turn your brain into a bowl of mush. You're going back into the box right this minute."

"Wait," Zita begged. "What do you know about the vessel? I can get to know her better, and then you'll be able to more easily control her. You must think about control. This spiritualist will have the power to control you and the world once she has the crystal. How will you harness her power? Imagine if Forest River Blossom wielded that power, you'd never be able to control it."

Taka said, "Princess Ekaterina is a young woman. She doesn't have the years of experience that Forest River Blossom has. I'll be able to control her and the power that comes with the crystal."

"Are you sure?"

Taka fiddled with the wand, avoiding eye contact with Zita. He pressed his lips together and his brows drew closer.

Zita told herself not to smile, as she recognized the hesitation and doubt creeping into Taka's mind. She wanted to sell her idea a little more, but hesitated, realizing Taka's indecision as a vote in her favor. If he agreed to her plan, then she just needed to find out how to control the vessel.

CHAPTER 52

After breakfast, Zita hopped into the saddle of a brown and white horse as the caravan packed and began the final journey to the Red Castle. It felt freeing to get back on a horse after being locked in the prison of the box. By taking this horse, one of the desert guards was forced to walk with the other guards. She didn't care about that because she had bought her freedom. Zita practiced with the reins, leading the horse left and the right till she felt comfortable with the animal. She had convinced Taka they needed to work as a team and he allowed her to ride without restraints.

Today she needed to find out as much information about the vessel as she could. Taka would punish her if she didn't find a clue or two on how to control the desert princess. She wasn't sure how to get the information she needed or even what that information was, but being free of the box made her optimistic she would discover something useful.

The caravan moved slowly because the clouds lay low on the volcano flank. The thick fog slowed down the trackers that ran a few hundred yards ahead scouting for dangers. It turned out Taka didn't know what to expect as they neared their destination. The scroll mentioned the four guardians, but whoever wrote it didn't indicate when they would encounter the guardians. Were they only on the island or could they be expected as they approached the lake?

Zita sidled her painted horse next to Princess Ekaterina's black mare. The woman's horse looked strong and powerful, and Zita wondered how they could keep such magnificent horses in the desert.

Zita said, "Good morning."

"Oh, it's good to see you out of the box today. What a crude punishment for such a pretty girl."

Zita smiled at the compliment. "I'm working on being a more pliant princess."

"Yes. My father and mother taught me to be strong and independent, but then I would be punished when my independence didn't agree with their desires for my life."

Zita knew how that felt, as her father had controlled her every move. "I can relate, the last three years, as I matured into an adult, my father seemed to waver back and forth on how much freedom he wanted me to have."

"Exactly."

"That's a pretty horse you're riding."

Ekaterina patted her horse's neck. "Beleza has been mine for five years. She is a strong war horse."

"Beleza is an interesting name."

"Beleza means beauty in our tribe's dialect. Your horse is named Tawny. I wanted my father to give me Tawny when I was fourteen, but he wanted me to have an animal that could help keep me out of danger. Beleza has proven her worth."

"Have you been in battles?"

Ekaterina looked over at Zita. "I am the Khan's oldest and most valuable daughter. In the desert, other tribes find brides and power by kidnapping them from enemy tribes. They have no fear and are even willing to try to capture the Khan's number one daughter. They are swine. Twice, Beleza has kicked a would-be kidnapper or outrun a tribe of bandits. She is special."

"Does your spirituality help you see the bandits before they have a chance to put their hands on you?" Zita thought the answer to this question might help her determine Ekaterina's mental powers.

Ekaterina didn't answer right away, but instead stared off into the distance as if maybe looking into the future.

Finally, she said, "I can see into the near future. Less than three seconds. This ability allows me to recognize danger and foresee possible ways to escape before the enemy knows I've seen their scheme."

Zita's face dropped. This woman will know what the future holds three seconds ahead of any attempt to control her. The moon goddess and Taka won't be happy to hear about this capability.

"Is that why the Khan wants you to be the crystal? Your ability to see the future of any situation on top of the power of the crystal will make whoever controls you invincible."

Ekaterina stared into Zita's eyes and Zita wondered if the woman could read her thoughts, too.

"The Khan doesn't understand the crystal's strength. Taka doesn't understand it either. They will be surprised when I take control and wield its power."

Zita sat on her horse, flabbergasted at this new revelation. Here was another person looking to control the crystal and preventing her from using its power for herself.

"How do you know these things?" Zita asked. "I have a scroll acquired from my father that tells me very little about what the object can actually do. Other than the scroll, all I know comes from legends and myths."

"My spiritual advisor is Kartaban. A man believed to be a thousand years old. He has told me of the crystal. He personally knows five people who have owned the crystal during his years on Aloheno."

Tawny stopped for a second and tried to eat at a shrub as they passed. Zita edged the horse forward.

"Kartaban has trained me for the last ten years. He predicted my role as crystal. When I first came to him, I could see in the future just a fraction of a second. He took a personal interest in me and has trained me to enhance my capabilities."

Tawny wanted to stop again and Zita had to work the horse over from Ekaterina's right to her left side. The horse had too many temptations on the right side of the path while the path's left side opened to a mountain meadow and a few rocks. No shrubs to tempt the horse.

Zita had to be bold now. She must look strong to Taka and have some clues if she wanted to acquire this woman as crystal. "Can you share your expectations for the crystal?"

Again, Ekaterina peered off into the distance.

This woman was mysterious and strong. Her spirituality could prove difficult to crack even if Zita could master her. Is this why Zita's dad had problems with Forest River Blossom?

Ekaterina answered, "I'm advised to not share these revelations with others at this time."

Zita decided to change the questioning to less threatening subjects. "Have you traveled a lot?"

Ekaterina said, "I've never been out of the desert. The green of this land is quite interesting."

They rode together for the next two hours discussing the different castles and travels Zita had taken. The sun came up and burned off the clouds around the volcano top. The path had taken them to a ridge and as they crossed over it the Red Castle came into view.

The castle stood on an island surrounded by a red lake. Steam rose from the lake in the mountain coolness. As they neared the lake, the landscape changed from the green meadows to dry, scorched earth, with black sand covering the ground. The air stank of sulfur, and the lake's red water bubbled and steamed from underground volcanic hot spots.

The water glowed red, splotched with browns and blacks a blight of fungus and mold as vegetation died in the harsh environment. Off in the distance, some distance from the lake's shoreline, sat the island. A small, rocky pile of cliffs and jagged peaks jutted from the red-hot lake.

Zita stared in wonder at the alien environment they must cross to reach the castle.

They rode their horses through the sparse plants and trees. Their trunks and roots twisted, scrubby and burnt by the relentless seething steam from the lake. Lizards and other exotic reptiles basked in the sun, and rose-colored birds cawed and cheeped, their feathers reflecting the sun.

The whole party stopped a quarter-mile from their destination and Taka brought the caravan together.

"We have arrived," Taka said. "Be prepared for danger at every turn."

Two of the scouts rode back from their patrol.

"The boat dock is two miles in that direction." The scout pointed toward a jagged rock in the near distance. "Twenty soldiers at the dock, all armed with bows, arrows, and spears."

"Are they guarding the dock or preparing to go to the island to acquire the crystal?"

The scout said, "There are no boats at the dock."

Taka pondered this new information for a moment. "We can't reach the island without a trained boatman. Did you see a boat on the lake?"

"No."

"Will the soldiers be a problem?" Taka asked.

The two scouts looked at each other before their spokesman said, "We couldn't tell. They seemed angry."

"Was anybody else at the dock?"

"Yes. A dockmaster. But as angry as the soldiers appeared, he doesn't have long to live. They were stringing up a rope over one of the scraggly trees near the lake."

CHAPTER 53

Taka's warriors and wizards charged toward the dock. Zita rode hard on her horse, its hooves pounding the ground, the wind blowing her hair behind her as they approached the lake. Bubbles of heat lifted from the lake's red waters. She searched for signs of the insurrection at the dock and the soldiers that threatened the dockmaster.

When they came within a hundred yards of the dock, Taka's group of desert warriors drew their weapons and prepared for battle.

Taka shouted, "Save the dockmaster at all cost. We can't afford to let him die if we want to cross to the Red Castle.

Zita wondered at this information. Could they not cross the lake if the dockmaster died?

The soldiers were in the process of hanging the dockmaster when they noticed the incoming warriors and dropped the dockmaster to the wooden dock. Five archers quickly nocked their arrows and released a barrage at Taka's approaching warriors.

Taka grabbed Zita by the shoulders. "I'm allowing you access to your magic, don't make me regret it. Make sure to protect the dockmaster and keep him alive."

A desert wizard conjured a shield of magical energy around the group, protecting them from the arrows and spears being launched by the soldiers.

Zita felt almost giddy at the realization of having magic at her disposal during the attack. She feared being at the mercy of the other wizards during the attack. With shining eyes, she watched as the shimmering magic shield deflected the impending assault, and the soldier's arrows bounced harmlessly to the ground.

Zita prepared a spell, raised her hands, and sent forth a fierce gust of wind. It blasted toward the dock and knocked three soldiers into the hot water below.

The men screamed in agony as their bodies cooked in the hot volcanic water.

Taka's warriors took advantage of the chaos and charged toward the soldiers, their weapons glinting in the sunlight.

The soldiers regrouped and formed a defensive line, preparing to fend off the incoming attack.

One soldier who wielded a longsword broke free from the group, and engaged with the desert warriors. He attacked with practiced precision.

The desert warrior drew his own sword and braced for the incoming attack. The soldier launched a fierce strike, but the warrior deftly parried the blow and countered with a quick jab with a smaller sword, narrowly missing the soldier's face.

The soldier grunted in frustration and attacked again, but the warrior blocked the blow and returned a swift slice of his sword that left a deep gash on the soldier's leg.

Enraged, the soldier pressed his position, swinging his sword with reckless abandon. But the desert warrior remained calm and focused, his sword diverting each impact.

The two combatants circled, exchanging blows and testing each other's skill. The soldier's attacks became more frenzied. With lightning-fast reflexes, the desert warrior feinted left and then launched a powerful strike to the soldier's right side, catching him off guard, and sending him stumbling to the hot black sand.

The soldier, now on his back, couldn't raise his heavy sword in time as the warrior lunged forward with a decisive strike that pierced the soldier's chest.

The dockmaster, now free from the soldiers, picked up a nearby paddle and whacked the backs of any of the soldiers within reach of the paddle.

Zita saw the dockmaster's brave attempt, but she worried that he'd end up getting himself killed. They needed him to arrange transportation to the island. She left the safety of the desert wizard's shield to get a better angle on the dockmaster. She calculated ways to save him without getting too close to the fighting.

As the dockmaster engaged with one soldier, another soldier maneuvered behind him and raised his sword.

Zita saw the danger and launched a fireball at the soldier. The fireball struck the soldier before he could deliver a killing blow to the dockmaster. The soldier fell to the dock writhing in pain as he tried to smother his flaming clothing.

The dockmaster continued to harass the soldiers with his paddle and engaged with a soldier handling a large sword. As they battled, the soldier struck a winning blow cleaving the dockmaster's wooden paddle, which left the dockmaster with a knob of wood for protection.

"Why can't this man just walk away from this battle," Zita thought? *"Does he have a death wish?"*

She pushed closer to the combat and yelled, "Nokaut," and sent a spell to stun the attacker.

The soldier dropped his sword and tumbled to the dock.

Zita reached the dockmaster as the man tried to pummel the soldier lying at his feet. She pulled him back just as another soldier jabbed a knife at him which barely missed.

Zita encapsulated the dockmaster in a magic shield and two angry soldiers battered the barrier.

The battle grew intense and chaotic, with swords clashing against shields and spells blasting through the air. Taka's group proved more skilled than the soldiers, and with their magic abilities, gained the upper hand.

The desert warriors rounded up and secured any soldiers that still lived.

When the battle had ended, Zita dropped the shield and confronted the dockmaster. Finally getting a good look at him, the grandfatherly man appeared not a day under eighty years old. His skin sagged and he had gray, thinning hair, with age lines edged deeply into his face.

He stared back at Zita with intense blue eyes, he had the look of someone who had seen many adventures and survived to tell the story. *How had this crazy man survived as long as he had?* She glanced at the noose swaying from the gate above the dock.

Zita asked "Is your life's goal to get yourself killed?"

The dockmaster stood stoically. "I've been in more battles than years you've been alive. I had this battle under control. I know what I'm doing and don't need your help."

"You were a dead man if I hadn't saved you."

"I've lived this long without you, girl, don't try telling me how to fight off a couple of ruffians."

"A couple of ruffians? There were at least twenty," Zita said. "You're lucky to be alive, you stupid old man."

"I had it under control. Do you want to see what my fury looks like?" He lifted the paddle handle and aimed it at Zita.

Taka grabbed Zita and pulled her back.

"I'm sorry about my young protégé. She thinks she is all knowing and powerful."

The dockmaster spit tobacco juice into the red lake where three soldier's bodies had turned gray and lifeless. Bones from previous battles lay bleached in the shallow water.

The smell of burned flesh hung in the air.

Taka offered the man water and led him to the bench next to the hut.

After the man had drunk the water and stopped breathing so hard, Taka asked, "I don't see a boat."

The dockmaster harrumphed. "You mighty adventurers who come to claim the crystal for yourselves know nothing about the quest. The boat doesn't just sit here waiting for any demented youngster looking to make a name for themselves. You must bring a vessel. With no vessel there is no journey."

Taka nodded. "We have indeed brought a vessel, your lord. May we pass?"

The man looked at Zita. "If this little girl is your vessel, then no. I deny your passage."

Taka laughed. "No, this impertinent girl is not the vessel." He signaled for Ekaterina to come to him.

Zita crossed her arms and scowled at Taka.

Ekaterina approached and the dockmaster appraised her. He said, "May I see your hands?"

She offered her hands as if to receive a gift.

The dockmaster took her hands into his own. He closed his eyes and chanted.

Crystal born of flames and forged of heat,

Is this the relic of legends you seek?

Balefire crystal, from ancient tales and myth,

This paragon of purity, can she uplift?

Her life imbued with power, potential untold,
To rule this realm with love and blessings bold.
Crystal formed of fire, from ages past,
This gem of perfection, forever to last.

With magic and wonder, this crystal so bright
Shall guide the way with its radiant light.
A symbol of hope, a beacon of peace,
This crystal of fire, may her reign never cease.

A wind picked up across the lake, blowing hot air toward the people on the dock. The gust increased in ferocity and sound. The wind seemed to disappear for a moment and then engulfed Ekaterina, fanning itself into a flame that burned blue in the wind, but didn't touch the girl. The flame encircled the desert princess, and she stood unmoving in its presence. And just as fast as it appeared it disappeared.

Ekaterina didn't appear changed by the event, and had survived the encounter. But her normally neatly brushed hair was now blown and untidy.

Zita looked at Ekaterina, then Taka, "Is that it?"

Taka scowled at Zita and whispered, "Be quiet."

She scowled. *I just wanted to know if she passed.*

Taka turned his attention back to the dockmaster.

The dockmaster said, "The castle is a place of danger and mystery, a quest where only the resolute and most reckless venture. I suggest you go home."

Taka appeared undeterred by the gatekeeper's warning, and said with conviction in his voice, "We seek to prove our worth and will not be dissuaded. I listen to the whispers of the castle and heed its call."

The dockmaster stayed silent for a few moments. The honk-honk of birds searching for food and a splash in the water as they fished, carried over the water. A slight breeze full of acrid sulfur blew from the island. A blue and yellow lizard bobbed up and down on the black sand near Zita's feet.

"The boat is coming, pick your eight." The dockmaster nodded toward the boat coming toward the dock.

CHAPTER 54

Lily sat in the shade of the rocks as the dry desert air sucked the moisture from her body. She looked at the seven-petaled flower in her leather pouch, the dirt dry and crumbling. If they didn't find water soon, the plant would die and they might fail to defeat the Red Castle guardians and capture the treasured crystal.

She tried to form spit in her mouth, working her lips and cheeks to produce a little water. She spit onto the flower. Twice more she screwed up her mouth and spit onto the plant.

Kestrel said, "You can't keep spitting on the plant. You must preserve your own water stores."

"If we don't take care of the plant, it won't be able to help us." She looked down at the dying plant. "We don't know when we'll need it."

"Don't worry. We're smart. We can find other ways to defeat the guardians," Kestrel said.

"You don't know that."

"I know if you die, I'll never be able to live with myself because of my grief."

"It's been a while since we heard from Sherry and Al. Do you think they are okay?" Erik asked.

"I don't care." Kestrel said "He's going to come back without finding water, and then demand more water. Going off like that will hurt all of us. We don't have water to spare."

Erik stood and picked up his sword. "I agree, but they should have returned by now. I'm going to search for them."

"Don't waste your time," Kestrel sneered. "He'll come back when he's ready. I'm not wasting my rest time to step into the hot sun for some crazy impossible mission."

Lily had a prickling feeling across her scalp. With a shaky voice, she said, "I think you're right Erik. I'm worried about Sherry. She wouldn't have stayed in the hot sun this long."

Breathless and wild-eyed, Sherry raced into the shaded area. She charged toward Erik, desperation etched across her freckled face.

Sherry tried to say something, her mouth opened and closed, but she said nothing.

Erik grabbed her shoulders. "What? Where's Al?"

Sherry bent over in exhaustion and between heaves of air, she pointed outside the shade. "Al—"

Lily came to Sherry. "What about Al. Is he all right?"

Sherry shook her head and stuttered, "S—something terrible happened!" She struggled to catch her breath. "There's . . . there's a giant snake! It . . . it killed Al! We have to go back; we have to help!"

Her words hung heavy in the air. As Lily exchanged worried glances with Kestrel and Erik, their expressions shifted from confusion to concern. Sherry's distress appeared real, and the urgency in her voice left no room for doubt. Without hesitation, the group sprang into action.

Lily pushed Sherry from the comfort of the shade. "Lead the way," she barked, her voice firm and resolute. "We're with you. Let's save Al."

Sherry rushed out with Kestrel, Erik and Lily close behind. She led her friends to the red wall.

A mixture of grief, anger, and an unyielding resolve to help Al filled Lily's heart.

With cautious steps and heavy hearts, the group reached the desert alcove. Lily's eyes fell upon the lifeless body of her friend, partially concealed beneath the immense weight of the slain serpent. Uncertainty gnawed at her mind as they all stood in a solemn circle, unsure if Al had perished or if a glimmer of life remained.

"We can't waste any time," Lily shouted, her voice filled with determination. "If there's a chance, we have to act."

Nodding in agreement, Erik stepped forward, his grip tightening around the hilt of the Sword of Freedom. Its shimmering aura pulsed with restorative energy, promising aid in their time of need.

"Let's move the snake first," Kestrel suggested, his voice laced with caution. "We don't want to cause Al more harm."

Together, they strategized and devised a plan to disentangle the snake's massive body from Al's limp form. With synchronized efforts, they pushed, pulled, and lifted, gradually easing the oppressive weight from their friend's motionless form.

The feel of the serpent's body surprised Lily. She expected it to be rough and slimy, yet it actually felt cool, smooth and non-sticky.

As they moved the snake, hope flickered within Lily's heart, mingled with the fear that their efforts might be in vain. With the reptile's body finally removed, she stared at Al's gray and ashen face. His body lay unmoving in the dust, green snake blood polluting his body.

Lily felt lightheaded, seeing Al in this condition. "It can't be true. He can't be dead." She turned to Sherry.

Sherry's eyes were wide, her chest sunken as she rubbed absently at her arms.

Lily pulled Sherry into a hug.

Erik knelt close to the body, seeking any sign of life despite the stillness. "There's a pulse," he exclaimed, his voice a mixture of relief and urgency. "Al is alive, but time is running out. Let's hope it's not too late for the sword's magic to do its work."

Drawing upon the power within the sword, Erik invoked its healing properties, channeling its energies toward their injured friend. Time passed in slow, dreadful minutes as they waited for Erik's healing powers to do their work.

A warm glow enveloped Al's injured body, revitalizing and mending, as the life force within him stirred and strengthened. Slowly, Al's eyelids fluttered open. With a gasp for breath, and a cough, a spark of life rekindled within him.

"He's alive!" Sherry cried, tears of relief streaming down her face. "You did it! You saved him!" She dropped to her knees next to Al and showered his face with kisses.

Al moved his arms against the onslaught, pushing against Sherry and trying to pull back.

Erik touched Sherry's shoulder. "You might want him to sit up. I think he still believes the snake is attacking him."

Sherry sat back laughing as her voice choked with tears.

They propped Al against a wall in the alcove and gave him water from the waterskin as he recounted the battle against the giant snake. After the story of his mighty victory, Al said, "I found water."

Lily looked excitedly at Al. "Where?"

"Over in the corner." Al pointed at the little pool of water.

"Is it safe?" Kestrel asked.

"As long as a snake doesn't attack you." Al smiled.

They all laughed at the comment.

Kestrel refilled the water skins before he and Erik went to bring the horses to the water. The animals were skittish when they first entered the alcove, the stink of the dead snake overpowering the space. They calmed when he led them to the pool and drank.

Erik chopped up the snake for a meal, while Sherry and Lily went into the blazing sun to look for brush limbs and the woody remains of saguaro cactus. They returned with the fuel needed for a fire.

The five enjoyed a meal of roasted snake and drank their fill of water. Lily thought the snake tasted earthy or gamey and even a little rubbery, but it felt so refreshing to have something to eat.

Lily gave the flower water and tended the loose soil around its roots. She knew nothing about taking care of flowers or plants. Growing up on Earth, she had concentrated on cheerleading and singing in the school's choir. Gardening didn't show up on her high school resume. She hoped that what she did would save the plant, or the creature.

After the meal, they sat and discussed their next steps.

"Once the sun nears the horizon, we can head back out," Kestrel said. "This blasted heat is slowing us down. We must get to the Red Castle before Taka and Zita acquire the crystal and are long gone. The worst thing we can allow is for them to gain control over that much natural power."

"I don't think this sacred flower will live much longer without some better care," Lily said. "We need to find a pot of some kind to put it in."

"We might still run into a small village where we can purchase or trade for a container for the plant," Kestrel said.

Erik snorted, "Good luck finding any villages in this furnace environment."

"There must be a village somewhere along our route. It seems to be a well-used road we've traveled. How much longer do you think we still have to reach the Red Castle?" Sherry took a sip of water.

Kestrel stood and pulled a map from the horse's saddle bag. He unfurled it on the dusty floor and pointed to where he thought they were. He moved his fingers in a practiced motion along the map. "I estimate we'll reach the lake in three days."

Lily pointed to the map, "What does this dot mean?"

Kestrel looked closer at the dot. "It looks like a village, but it's out of our path. It would take four hours to reach the village and then another four or more back to our route."

"We have to do everything we can to save the seven-petaled flower. I plan on returning it to the Sacred Castle after we get the crystal," Lily said.

"You can't be serious. Did you not see the magic power the plant possesses? We could use that on some magical adventures," Al said.

"We stole it from them. Maybe if they had willingly given it to us, or we had traded for it in some way, but we out-and-out stole it from them. We have to return it." She looked at her fellow travelers as she felt the heat rise to her face. Her mom had been adamant about not stealing from others, and she felt guilty that she had taken this plant from the high priestess. She hoped they wouldn't punish her too badly when she brought it back to them.

"I agree we should take the time to get a pot for the flower. It's an awesome flower that turns into a seven-headed dragon, an epic-fantasy magical object. We can't afford to lose it to this desert heat," Al said.

"If we get to the Red Castle too late, Zita might be dead." Erik reached out to the map and turned it so he could read it better. "I'm sure Taka will kill her after he gets the crystal. He didn't seem like a compassionate man based on the stories you told me about him. I say we try to keep the plant well hydrated and continue on the journey. It's only three days. We have enough water to keep it alive for three more days."

Sherry shook her head. "We should go to the village and purchase a pot for the plant."

Erik argued, "What if one of our horses gets bitten by a snake? The journey has already been rough on the horses."

"I agree with Erik," Kestrel said. "We can't risk going to the village."

Lily felt her heart rate pick up, she hated to argue, but she felt it important they go to the village. She leaned in toward her friends and lowered her voice, "We need to go to the village. Everything in my being tells me it's the right thing to do for our journey."

The others looked at her and then each other.

Sherry said, "I agree with Lily."

"I'm with Sherry and Lily," Al said.

Erik examined the red dust, and rubbed his finger in the dirt. He looked at his friends. "Okay, let's find the village."

Kestrel shook his head. He cleared his throat, "I disagree with going to the village. I don't think we have time, but if you think it's the right thing to do, then let's go."

CHAPTER 55

Late in the afternoon, the adventurers walked their horses out of the cool alcove and mounted. Al hoped their decision to find a pot for the magic flower proved the right thing to do. He didn't know what kind of reception they would receive at the village.

Kestrel led the group along the trail they found on the map. As they traveled, Al suspected it was used by locals. Every quarter mile or so, someone had stacked a pile of rocks along the path which seemed to help guide the group along a designated trail.

Al still felt a little out of sorts after the snake-bite incident, but Erik had healed his shoulder and all that remained were scars identifying the entry points of the giant snake's fangs.

They traveled for two hours until the sun slipped below the horizon. Then they were forced to stop and wait for the Anticletus moon to rise, with hopes that there would be enough light to still travel.

Once the Anticletus moon had climbed over the mountain range in the east, Kestrel took the lead and they continued their journey.

Thirty minutes later they noticed the smokes of fires burning not far away, and they felt hopeful they would find what they needed.

A youth greeted them as they reached the village.

"Hello, I'm Sergei."

The five teens introduced themselves.

Lily held out her hands and showed the boy the flower. "We need a pot for this flower."

"Yes! Yes! I can help you. Dismount and follow me."

They all dismounted and walked their horses into the village. Al studied the tall mud huts. They had a single doorway and they were built at least as high as five people standing on each other's shoulders. He wondered if they were built like this to allow the heat to flow out of the building.

When they reached Sergei's family hut, he stopped them. "Wait. I'll get my parents. They'll be happy to help."

He went inside the building and came back with a man and woman. The man seemed happy to see them.

"These are my parents."

"Hello. Welcome to our village." The man invited them into the hut. "Come inside. Let us get you something to eat."

He pointed at Sergei. "Take their horses and place them behind the fences."

"No. That won't be necessary. We aren't planning on staying long," Kestrel said. "We're just looking for a vessel for a plant we found in the desert."

The man looked at the plant, and his eyes widened. Al wondered if he recognized it for what it was, but how would a simple desert villager know about the sacred flower?

Sergei's mother took Sherry's hand and led her into the simply furnished hut.

Al glanced at his friends. "Should we be doing this? Aren't we in a hurry?"

Sergei's dad said, "Nonsense. We don't allow visitors to leave without sharing a meal and water with them. That would be very rude here in the desert."

Kestrel tried to reason with the man. "No, we don't have time. We must be somewhere."

"This is the desert; there is always time."

Lily stared at Kestrel with an apologetic look.

Sergei began taking the horses two at a time and leading them away.

Lily and Kestrel walked into the hut, leaving Erik and Al waiting for Sergei to return for their horses.

Al looked out at the night-cooled desert. He didn't want to stop here for the entire night. They were running out of time. If they missed helping Zita by just a few minutes, it might make a huge difference.

Sergei came back for the last two horses, and Erik and Al entered the hut.

A small fire burned in a pit in the center of the hut. Smoke exited at the very top of the structure through a hole which allowed the smoke to safely leave the building.

The large space had been partitioned into separate living spaces. Blankets were laid out in one area, another had a table a foot off the floor with rugs prepared so visitors could sit and eat, and the last area had been set aside for food preparation and storage.

Sherry and Lily were seated at the table. Lily had wrapped her scarf around her forehead.

Sergei's father seemed very interested in the flower. "What is so important about this flower that you have traveled so far with it in this condition?"

Lily stumbled on the words, "I . . . just find the . . . uh . . . colors . . . of the flower interesting." A rush of red colored her pale face.

"I've never seen a plant like this in the desert. Where did you find it?"

"We were wandering around and just happened to see it," Kestrel said. "I couldn't tell you where we found it. Saw it maybe a day ago."

"May I touch it?"

Lily pulled it back toward her body. "No, I'm afraid it might die. If we could purchase a clay pot from you to help hold it in . . . .."

"Oh. We'll be happy to give you a pot for the pretty flower," Sergei's mother said. "Sergei, go next door and ask if they have a small pot for us."

Sergei's father said, "No. Sergei, go get the Khan and the gardener. We must learn more about this amazing flower."

Al thought the conversation was taking a turn for the worse. He didn't know what the desert gardener might think of the plant. Could these villagers know about the sacred seven-petaled flower? He thought bringing someone known as the Khan into the room would only prolong the time until they could leave. He imagined the Khan saying, "We must have a big welcome celebration for the adventurers." It might take them three days to leave.

Kestrel asked, "Why are you so interested in this weary, almost dead flower?"

"We farm and are always searching for interesting crops and new desert shrubs."

"Do you think this might be edible?" Sherry asked as her eyebrows lifted up on her forehead.

Al smiled to himself as he pictured plants that could eat the people that wanted to eat it.

Sergei's mom offered them each a bowl filled with a warm tantalizing smelling stew.

Sherry asked, "What is this?"

Al brought a spoonful to his lips.

Sergei's mom said, "Tartutle snake stew."

Al just about did a spit take. He swallowed the stew, which was flavored better than what they had done with the giant snake. The spices were delicious and he quickly consumed the contents of the bowl.

Sergei returned with the gardener and another man who was introduced as the Khan. The leader of this tribe wore a fancy headdress made of thousands of beads that rose six inches above his head.

The Khan welcomed them to the village. Then he demanded, "Show us the flower."

Lily extended her hand with the flower.

The Khan reached for it, but she pulled it back. "Be careful, it's fragile. Just look."

The Khan narrowed his eyes and grimaced. He didn't look too happy about the way Lily treated him. He seemed to think he could have whatever he wanted.

The gardener and the Khan studied the plant. The gardener said, "It's not of the desert."

The Khan turned his attention to Kestrel. "Where did you really get the flower? Do not lie to us."

Kestrel darted a gaze at Lily, who barely shook her head. He licked his lips and fixed his eyes on the Khan. "We found it in the desert."

The gardener shouted, "Impossible."

Sergei's dad touched the Khan's shoulder, and led him outside the hut.

Al struggled to hear the conversation but only picked up pieces and fragments of their discussion.

Sergei's dad said, "These are the foreigners Taka told us watch for and detain."

"They must be thieves," The Khan said.

A warning went off in his head. These people knew Taka, and he had warned them about their group. The conversation went on, but the other members at the table were talking and Al couldn't pick up the rest of the whispered discussion. Al looked out the door and saw Sergei's father watching him. He suspected they were planning to attack them. He leaned over to Erik who sat next to him.

Al whispered, "Tell Kestrel to prepare a shield."

Erik looked at Al in disbelief. "Why? Things are going great. The boy is getting us a pot for the flower. They are feeding us this great stew. Just relax."

Al nudged Erik and nodded his head toward the door. "Look at those two. They're planning something."

Erik glanced at the men by the door and smiled at Al. "Don't be so paranoid. The guy is the village leader. They might be talking about the weather."

Al darted glances at his friends at the table. Sherry and Lily were discussing the spices used in the tartutle soup with Sergei's mom. He thought with Kestrel's help they could stave off an attack of some kind. Neither were at full force with their magic at the moment because of their recent injuries. "No. They're not talking about the weather."

Erik touched Al's arm, "Sure, buddy."

Erik leaned toward Kestrel and whispered.

Kestrel flashed a sideways glimpse at the door, then gazed at Al for a moment.

Al sensed that Kestrel recognized the same danger he felt. With a wink at Kestrel, they both created their magic shields to include themselves and their friends.

The Khan walked into the hut and announced, "You won't be needing those."

A sharp coldness struck Al's core and his magic shield disintegrated. He jerked back from the table, reaching for his staff, but his connection to magic disappeared. "Come staff!"

The staff lay motionless on the floor.

Kestrel stood and stepped back from the table, his mouth flying open in surprise.

"What is it?" Sherry asked.

"We are done with your lies. You are nothing more than thieves," The Khan said.

A number of village men entered the abode and surrounded the table.

"Take the sword, staff, and flower." The Khan pointed at the flower. "Put the flower in a pot until we have a chance to study its properties."

Erik stood and grabbed for his sword, but not in time. Two men seized his arms and secured them.

Sherry tried to reason with the Khan. "But sir, we have done nothing wrong. We are just travelers passing through your village, looking for a vessel for our dying flower."

"The flower is not of the desert. For you to say it is means you are lying. And if you're lying about this, then your lies extend to other comments you make. I demand the truth."

A man snatched the flower from Lily.

Lily gasped in surprise and she stared incredulously at Sergei's mom.

Sergei's mom was just as surprised as the teens.

Two men confiscated Erik's sword and Al's staff.

Al shouted, "You can't have my staff."

"You're in my village. I'm the Khan. I take what I want."

Al reached for his staff, but his hands were forced behind his back.

"I won't be deceived by your lies." The Khan said, "Take them to the compound."

CHAPTER 56

Zita stood on the dock staring at the Red Castle towering over the little island mountain in the middle of the lake's heated volcano water. The dockmaster had stated that Taka needed to pick eight members of his party to travel on the boat to the island. She waited to hear who he planned to take with him.

She had mixed emotions on whether she wanted Taka to choose her to go with him or not. If he left her on the dock, then she could wait for Erik and his friends. Hopefully, they could find a way to defeat Taka and take control of the crystal, but did her friends have a vessel? She suspected they thought the same as she did and had brought a soup bowl.

She waited as Taka chose his eight. He pointed at Dakarai and nodded. Dakarai stepped gingerly into the boat, which rocked in the hot water. He moved to the front and gingerly sat on the bench as the boat rocked side to side.

It was a large wooden rowboat, twenty feet in length with a sleek hull. Four benches provided seating for two individuals per bench. At the rear stood the paddle master, a thin person wearing a hooded cape. Zita couldn't make out his face which was hidden within the hood.

Taka motioned, "Ekaterina, if you please."

Dakarai stood and held a hand for her to step down into the watercraft.

Taka seemed to be weighing his options of who to bring with him to attack the castle. Zita didn't know what arrangements he had made with the desert Khan. Was he required to choose a number of desert wizards and warriors?

He pointed at two desert wizards of the three they had brought with them. *Interesting,* thought Zita. *Will Taka come back and choose the other wizard later?* She couldn't see any reason for Taka to bring Sims or Lenny. What advantages would they offer? They had no magic and were too old to be in combat against magical creatures. He only had three places left, assuming Taka himself planned to be one of the eight.

"Lenny, stay here and wait for us to return. If you see any of Zita's friends show up, then light a signal on the beach here," Taka said. "Then take the warriors and keep them from reaching the castle."

Lenny nodded to his master.

Taka pointed at a warrior and Sims. "Hop in the boat."

What was the man doing? thought Zita. *A warrior is the worst choice he could make. They were all going to die, and it would be all Taka's fault.*

Taka stood on the dock staring at Zita and the remaining desert wizard.

Zita worried he would choose the other wizard, and she would end up losing her only opportunity to go to the castle and capture the crystal for herself. She felt her stomach quiver at the thought of missing this opportunity. She balled her fists and opened them, over and over, her warm, sweaty hands belying her nervousness at Taka's decision.

Taka pointed at Zita and said, "Can I trust you not to go off on your own and do something stupid that will ruin our chances at taking the crystal?"

"What can I do? You have blocked my magic, locked me in a box for two nights, and treated me like a prisoner. I can't help you if you need me."

He put a finger to his lips in deliberation.

This isn't a big decision. You're going to choose me, because I have the connection to the vessel. Just point at me, and let's get to the castle before it gets dark. It was late afternoon and Zita didn't relish taking the rowboat across the lake water in the dark. She glanced again at the gray skin of the men who had fallen in the water. *Was the lake magical? Could these men become alive and attack the boat?*

Taka swiveled his head toward the desert wizard, stared a moment at the man, then pointed at Zita. "Okay, hop in."

Zita tried to tamp down the excitement she felt at been chosen as one of the eight. She couldn't allow Taka to see how much this meant to her. She stepped down into the rowboat and sat at the back bench near the paddle master. A chill ran down her back as she sneaked a peek inside the paddle master's cowl. She swore she saw nothing.

Lenny helped the desert warriors stow boxes of food and supplies in the bottom of the boat.

Taka gave additional instructions to Lenny and the others, and then he joined them in the boat.

The paddle master placed his hands on the long oar at the stern. With expert control he moved the boat away from the dock and into the lake. The long arms of the paddle master's cloak prevented Zita from seeing the man's actual hands.

The paddle master slipped into a steady rhythm of push and pull on the long-handled oar that propelled the craft.

Sweat poured from Zita's forehead as they traversed the hot lake. How could the paddle master wear that cloak over his head and arms and not pass out from heat exhaustion? Zita looked for something that might save her if the boat sank, but there were no safety devices. She guessed it didn't matter as they would all die if they entered the water.

The only sounds were the splashing of the paddle in the hot water, and the birds overhead as they swooped behind the oar finding food churned up by the large paddle. She stared at the eddies created from the front of the boat. The paddle master suddenly stopped rowing and the boat's forward motion rapidly slowed and stopped.

Bubbles appeared, and then the lake burped; a large quantity of gas escaped as a big bubble which burst in front of them. The smell of rotten eggs overwhelmed the boat, and Sims bent over the starboard side and emptied his stomach.

Studying the rest of the lake, Zita saw similar gas bubbles exploding at the surface. Pink birds flew overhead, making loud calls, and when a gas bubble appeared, a bird would dive toward the water and retrieve a flapping fish in its beak which had been catapulted from the water. The birds' feathers seemed thin with translucent skin-like appearance.

She studied the island and the castle. Pink rock dominated the island shoreline. The rocks turned gray and dirty the higher up the mountain slope she looked. Very little vegetation grew near the water, only scraggly bushes.

As the mountain rose above the water, she saw green bushes scattered between the rocks, and near the mountain top, great trees obscured the lower sections of the castle. It shone with a pinkish glow in the late afternoon sun.

It took over an hour to reach the island shore. The paddle master pulled the boat up against a wooden dock that jutted into the lake. Zita and the others were soaked in sweat when they reached the island.

As soon as Zita stepped onto the dock, she began to search for dangers. They expected four guardians. Did they guard only at the castle, or could they expect to encounter the creatures on the path to the castle? She didn't know, but without access to her magic, she had to be prepared.

Taka instructed Sims and the desert warrior to unload the boat, but Sims got off the boat with only a small bag and headed down the dock to the pink sand beach where he waited for the others.

The desert wizards helped their comrade with the boxes and they set up a temporary camp on the beach. They prepared a meal and ate it as Taka studied Zita's scroll. She wanted to rip it out of his hands. He had never discussed what he found and she worried he might lead them into danger.

They emptied the boxes' contents into bags. And when they had completed the task, everyone but Taka slung a bag over their backs.

Taka spoke, "The first danger we will encounter might attack before we reach the castle. Be prepared for an attack."

"What is this first guardian?" Dakarai asked.

Taka studied the scroll. "As best as I can figure it's something called Ragadozo, part human and part beast."

"Should I vanquish it with magic?" Dakarai asked standing tall in the late afternoon sun.

Taka waved his hand in dismissal. "I don't think that will be necessary. It seems it has an affinity for gambling. We'll place a wager with it, defeat it by winning, and it'll be here for any that follow us." He glanced at Zita as he projected a superior look at her.

"Any suggestions for the wager?" Dakarai asked.

"Let's meet this creature before we choose a challenge. We want to assure we can win." Taka led them up the mountain trail toward the castle.

CHAPTER 57

The island mountain's peak stood half a mile above the water with the castle perched at its summit. They began hiking the mountain path that led to the castle, but it didn't go straight up but curved around and zig-zagged up. The eight pressed on, walking along a rugged trail of jagged volcanic rock, jutting boulders that appeared ready to topple upon the path at any moment, and a rock trail that undulated up and down in six-to-twelve-foot arcs.

The hiking exhausted Zita as the path zigged and zagged, sometimes upwards toward the castle and other times downward toward the lake. They encountered the scraggly bushes that seemed to grow in the middle of the path and made it difficult to push between the dangerous rocks.

After an hour of hiking, Taka, showing signs of fatigue himself, called a halt.

Zita originally thought she could take the crystal, run down to the beach, find the boat, and escape with the treasure. That dream seemed unreasonable now. She saw that getting the crystal and leaving the island with it would be difficult and come at a price.

She drank from her waterskin, enjoying the cool water flowing across her parched lips. The sun shone above the horizon, still about an hour from sunset. She hoped they found Ragadozo before dark. She didn't want to encounter a half human-half creature in the dark of night.

Almost on cue her eyes were drawn to a figure lurking behind a rock further up the trail.

Zita pointed toward the black boulder. "Do you see that?"

A creature peeked over the boulder, a human head with bushy untamed hair, and large eyes the size of saucers. Curved horns protruded from its forehead, curling back like a mountain ram's horns, which ended in sharp points.

The desert warrior grabbed his spear.

Sims said, "You won't be needing that." He sat and pulled a jerky from his sack.

Another desert wizard stood as if he intended to engage it in battle.

"No. Sit," Taka said, "Dakarai will handle this."

The creature left the safety of its rock and stood before the adventurers. It wore weathered leather armor, etched with battle scars and embellished with tribal markings, from the waist up. The creature's fingers, human looking and the size of large sausages, clutched a mace crafted from the femur of a stegox, stained with evidence of countless battles. Its eyes glowed a fiery hue, reflecting the reds of the lake and sky.

It possessed two sinewy, muscular legs with clawed feet that gripped the volcanic rock with expert precision.

As Zita watched the creature move, she examined its eyes, which seemed to reveal a level of cunning and intelligence, as if it possessed an analytical and discriminating view of the world. It stopped twenty feet from Taka's party, and a sly grin played upon its lips, revealing rows of sharp, predatory teeth.

Dakarai yelled, "May we approach in peace?"

The creature grunted approval.

They all followed Dakarai, but Zita held back, still unsure of her ability to defeat the creature without her magic.

As he advanced, Dakarai said, "I would like to place a wager with you. If we win, we can pass, if we lose, you may have one of us."

"I am Ragadozo, king of the island."

"I am Dakarai, a great adventurer and servant to the all-powerful wizard, Taka."

Zita rolled her eyes at Taka's introduction.

Ragadozo swung his stegox femur in a low arc near his feet and lifted it onto his left shoulder. "The wager isn't for one of you."

"What?" Dakarai asked.

"If I win, I will eat *all* of you."

Zita twisted her hair in her fingers and pulled back a short distance from the giant creature. Maybe he'd eat the others, but he wasn't going to eat her. If the creature ate Taka, would she get her magic back? She'd like the creature to eat Taka, that would give her great pleasure. But if Ragadozo grabbed Zita with his huge hands, it could crush her in a moment.

Dakarai stepped back to where Taka stood. "What do you think?" he whispered.

Taka stood, his hand holding his chin, thinking for a moment, then said, "A riddle. Let the creature give us a riddle, if we answer it, then we are free to continue our journey to the castle."

A riddle, Zita thought. *Couldn't these two wise guys come up with something they could use magic to manipulate and guarantee victory?* She had no idea what this creature might consider a difficult riddle for humans. She looked at her fellow adventurers. They all had looks of unease. Sims tugged on his clothing, as if trying to make it look good. The desert warrior fingered his spear, probably to throw at the creature if they lost the wager. The others seemed fairly confident. Zita looked back at the path from the beach and wondered if she could outrun the beast.

Dakarai walked back to Ragadozo. "You can ask us a riddle. If we answer correctly, we pass."

The beast laughed a low dangerous laugh, "And if you lose, you are this evening's meal. I accept."

Zita bit her bottom lip in fear and trepidation. She didn't think Taka and Dakari were exceptionally smart, and the others in the group were even less so. They were going to die without seeing the crystal.

Ragadozo boomed, "Are you ready?"

Dakarai glanced at Taka.

Taka nodded.

"Yes." Dakarai rubbed his hands together belying his nervousness at the wager.

"Listen carefully." The beast smiled. "The person who makes it sells it. The person who buys it never uses it. The person who uses it never knows they're using it. What is it?"

Zita felt dumbfounded. That didn't even make any sense. *Who buys something, but never uses it? How stupid is that?*

Taka and Dakarai stuck their heads together and whispered to each other.

Dakarai said something that Zita didn't hear.

Taka raised his hands over his head and shouted, "No, that's not it."

Dakarai yelled, "Well, what do you think it is?"

Taka stayed silent.

Zita felt a chill run up her spine. These two brain dead wizards were going to put them all in a pot of stew for this beast's next meal. She had to think of something. She reviewed the question. *The person who uses it, never knows they're using it.*

Sims walked over to Taka and offered an answer, but Taka quickly dismissed it. *Of course, Sims' intellect could best be compared to a rock or a fish.*

Zita thought some more. *The person who buys it, never uses it.* Does that mean the person is buying it as a gift for someone else? But why give the gift to someone who will not know they're using it?

The desert wizard pushed into the small group gathering around Taka. They engaged in a deep discussion, but then Taka shook his head.

Ekaterina stood next to Zita with her eyes closed. She seemed oblivious to the danger they all were in, trusting their destiny to Taka and Dakarai.

Dakarai offered a suggestion that Taka immediately shot down shaking his head vigorously.

Zita fingered the necklace her mother had given her those many years ago. Her mom loved riddles. She would have Cugbert ask her riddles and spend hours thinking out the solutions. If her mom was here, they would be saved.

Dakarai shouted at Taka, "Well, you come up with the answer." He walked to a large boulder to Zita's left and kicked the boulder.

Zita continued her mind journey remembering her mother. She hoped the gods of the dead would let her see her mom in the afterlife. She longed to smell her mother's sweet perfume and feel her warm embrace.

The desert warrior with the spear yelled out, "I know what it is."

Ragadozo asked, "Will this be your answer?"

Dakarai, Sims and Taka all shouted, "No!"

Ragadozo looked sad. And hungry.

Taka went to the desert warrior and they discussed the warrior's answer. Taka smiled a moment but then began a long diatribe about why the answer wasn't right.

Zita felt at peace. Her journey of life almost complete. She felt sad that she wouldn't be buried with the pomp and glory of a princess' burial in her fanciest gown, laid into a cedar burial box, and placed next to her mother's coffin in the family crypt. Would anybody even know that she had died?

Zita studied the bones that littered the pathway. Whose bones were they? Nobody knew. Nobody cared. She would die a nobody, her bones scattered with the others.

Dakarai had returned to Taka and they discussed more possible answers.

Who would buy my coffin? She'd never see Erik again. *Would he be able to recognize my bones from the others?*

Taka and Dakarai had grown silent.

Zita repeated the phrase, *"Who would buy my coffin?"* She thought back over the riddle. *The person who makes it, sells it.* The undertaker makes the coffins and sells them to the families who want to bury their loved ones.

The person who buys it, never uses it. If Erik bought my coffin, he wouldn't use it for himself, he'd place me in the coffin for my burial.

The person who uses it, never knows they're using it. I would be dead, I wouldn't know I'm using a coffin, unless I come back as a ghost.

Zita shouted, "I have it."

Taka and Dakarai came out of their self-induced silence and looked at her.

She hurried over to Taka and whispered.

He looked at her and shook his head. Then he stopped for a moment and suddenly nodded.

Dakarai joined in the group and they asked a few questions and all agreed on Zita's answer.

Dakarai walked to Ragadozo and stared confidently up at the beast. "The answer is a coffin."

A brief silence filled the air. Ragadozo had a grave expression on his face. He hesitated before answering. He lifted the stegox femur off his shoulder, placed it on the ground, and leaned on it.

Ragadozo's deep voice rumbled with discontent. "You have answered the riddle correctly, but we never agreed that you would discuss the answer with your friends. Therefore, you failed, and I eat you."

The creature swung the femur at Dakarai. He ducked, and the weapon swooshed over the wizard's head. Ragadozo's teeth looked blood red in light from the sinking sun.

Taka and the others were caught off guard by the beast's reaction and scattered behind the rocks.

Zita shouted, "Give me magic, so I can protect myself."

"Use your wits."

Zita climbed a rock to see the action unfold below her. She planned to kill Taka at the first opportunity. He could at least place a shield around her.

The monster stepped and tumbled among the rocks, almost making contact with the desert warrior, as he swung the femur in fast, wide arcs, but the humans moved faster.

Taka shouted, "Honor your wager."

Ragadozo said, "You have spoiled the bet. You cheat."

The desert warrior shoved his spear at the beast, and it found its path to the creature's leg.

Ragadozo stepped back and screamed. He recovered and chased the warrior around the rock, never quite able to catch the small man.

Zita suddenly felt the presence of the Velidred moon goddess. She called Zita. "What is this?"

Zita responded within her mind, and told Luna Rosso what had transpired.

"You must confront the beast."

Zita laughed. "Me? It'll kill me."

"Have you been practicing your skills?"

"Yes." Zita rolled her eyes.

"Let me see a demonstration."

The moon goddess couldn't be serious. Did she want to kill Zita as much as Taka wanted her dead? Zita felt the pain begin in her foot, and she quickly stood from behind her hiding place.

"Okay, I'm going. Stop it." Zita walked toward Ragadozo muttering to herself. *I'm going to die.*

CHAPTER 58

In a faint eerie glow of the Anticletus moon, a pale light washed over the desolate desert village, the tall mud huts stood like sentries in the light. The guards had forced the five teens into a walled, open-air compound. The brick walls stood fifteen-feet high and enclosed a space twenty feet by twenty feet. It had the smell of a holding pen for animals.

Sherry stood in the compound with her four friends. The desert air had cooled after the sun set and she felt goosebumps rise on her arms. They were stuck in this village with their magical objects stolen, Al and Kestrel's magic was blocked, and they were losing time in their attempt to save Zita and capture the crystal. What could they do?

Her normal Anticletus headache had returned with the stress of being captured, and she felt a tightening of her chest.

Her friends didn't seem to be taking the news any better than she was. Al paced back and forth across the enclosure. Lily's hands were tightened into fists, and her face held a tension-filled expression.

Kestrel seemed to be trying to resolve an inner conflict as he moved about, first scowling and then relaxing his facial muscles. She couldn't tell what his facial exercises meant. He would drop his shoulders and then hunch his back only to look up at the sky and heavily sigh.

Finally, he stopped pacing and said, "I can't."

"What?" Lily asked.

"I can't get my wings to work. Whatever their trick is to block magic, it also blocks my wings from deploying. I thought I could fly about the village and silently attack them, but I can't fly."

Erik had been evaluating the walls, but he turned to the group. "I don't see a way out. The walls are too high."

"We can't let them have the flower," Lily said.

"If they are Taka's friends, they might be planning to transport it to the Red Castle and give it to him. Sherry, do you think Taka acquired a seven-petaled flower?" Al asked.

Sherry shook her head no. "I got the impression the high priestess banished Zita, and unless Taka had another woman in his group, they had no way to enter the castle. I'm sure they don't have one."

"I'm not leaving without my staff, and we have to get the flower before they have a chance to leave the village with it."

Erik rubbed the back of his head, sighed, shrugged his shoulders, and returned to rubbing the back of his head.

Sherry had seen this play out in many classrooms on Earth as they grew up going to school together. The more frustrated Erik got, the more he rubbed the back of his head.

"Are they guarding the door?"

Lily went to the door and glanced around the slim openings. "Yes, there are two guards."

"Come over here." Erik whispered.

They hurried to the other side of the compound to huddle and strategize.

"What are you thinking?" Sherry asked.

Erik said, "If you three can lift me and Kestrel over the walls, then we can disable the guards and open the gates."

"That might work." Al smiled.

"After we get out of the compound, how will we find our stuff?" Lily asked. "Plus, you two don't have magic, so we can't use that on them."

"Well what plans do you have?" Erik put his hands on his hips in frustration.

"I don't know," Lily responded in a tight high-pitched voice, the strain of the desert and capture affecting her the same as the others.

Sherry stepped in between them. "Relax. We'll think of something. Lily, does your mark of the Pantaleon moon provide you with powers?"

Lily unwrapped her head scarf and appeared to delve within herself. A minute later she opened her eyes. "There is power there, I have access, I just don't know what to do."

Sherry asked, "Can you sense the seven-petaled flower from this distance?"

"No, I can't sense anything beyond the fence."

They stood silently staring at the ground with slumped shoulders and blank features.

Sherry didn't know what they were going to do. Her friends were normally good at coming up with ideas, and she wondered if the long travel or the surprise of being captured was too much for them. She felt resignation at their fate.

Lily sat in the dirt and asked, "What do you think the Khan will do with us?"

"I've heard of tribes like this in the desert that have been known to decapitate people for lying," Kestrel said.

Lily gasped.

"Do we really need to hear that right now?" Erik asked. "It's not like we could tell them what the flower's real purpose is and where we got it. He's right—we are thieves."

"We're not thieves." Lily stuck her nose in the air. "I plan to return it to the high priestess."

"Yeah, we've heard that a thousand times." Al looked at the fence.

Lily harrumphed at Al. "Well. It's true."

"Quiet." Sherry saw the group getting angry at each other. What ideas could she offer to give them hope? She looked at the walls, studied her friend's faces, and stared up at the beautiful night sky filled with stars. Nothing came to her.

Kestrel said, "Remember I thought it was a bad idea to come to the village. *'We'll just go to the village and get a container for the flower.'*" He mimicked Lily's statement.

Lily turned her back on Kestrel.

Slowly, one by one, the teens sat in the dirt.

Erik had a look of emptiness and failure on his face. Sherry hoped he would come up with a good idea to rescue them, but she saw his drooping posture as a sign that he had given up. She thought back to the times on this adventure to Aloheno when his ideas resulted in her rescue. Even when she didn't like his ideas at the time, they usually worked.

Sherry's head ached from the effects of the pull of the Anticletus moon, a consequence of her ability as the Crown of Anticletus. The moon's pull always caused her headaches, and even though she had worked for months with the spiritualist, Forest River Blossom, they had never found a cure or even relief from the pain.

She worried the headaches would shorten her life. Forest River Blossom feared that if they didn't control those periods when the moon hurt her the most, Sherry's life on Aloheno would be short-lived. Though the spiritualist had never specified if her life would last weeks, months, or years.

Tonight, in the clear skies of the desert, she needed to rescue her friends. They needed to find Zita and help her with her illness. Tonight, she needed to take on the crown.

Sherry sat in the dirt and imagined what she wanted to accomplish. The group needed to be released from this prison, their magical items and their horses returned so they could leave the village.

She felt her pulse quicken and a lightness in her chest. She smiled as the blue translucent glow of the Crown of Anticletus formed around her body.

Sherry poked Lily in the side. Her friend looked with sparkling, happy eyes at Sherry. They both stood and rose from the dirt, brushing off their outfits as they stood.

Lily said, "Come on boys. We have to save Zita."

They all looked at Sherry and quickly rose from the dirt.

Kestrel looked confused. "What is the magic within the crown that is different from my own ability to fly? Why doesn't the village effect on magic not block your powers."

Sherry shrugged. She walked to the compound entrance. "Guards. I need to talk with you."

A guard responded, "There's nothing to talk about. You'll meet with the Khan in the morning, he will proclaim your sentence, and we'll watch you liars die."

Sherry said forcefully, "I must speak with the Khan now." She sensed the crown's power working on the guard's weak mind and hoped it would influence the Khan just as easily.

"Stay and watch them" One guard motioned to the others. "Don't let them escape. I'll get the Khan."

"Just tell the guard to let us go," Erik said.

"No, it's better we go through the Khan. Otherwise, he might kill these two guards. They are just doing their jobs," Sherry said.

The five teens waited anxiously at the gate for the guard to return. It took ten minutes, and the guard returned with a large group of men.

The guard spoke to newcomers he had recruited, "The Khan says they are using magic to manipulate me. Use your wizardry to stop them."

"They have no plans to take us to the Khan. They're using their wizards to block our magic," Kestrel said.

"Don't worry. Sherry can do this." Lily smiled.

Sherry sent out a telepathic signal to the guards and the wizards trying to contain them. She didn't know if the desert wizard's ability to block magic might prove a deterrent to her abilities, but she had to try something.

Sherry delved into the mind of one guard. She manipulated his thoughts, planting seeds of doubt and empathy. "We have come in peace and mean no harm to this village. You must release us."

"We shouldn't be holding these people captive. We should let them go." He approached the gate.

A desert wizard stopped him. "They are very powerful. We must prevent further manipulation and learn how to control this mighty force."

"I am not yours to control. You must bend to my request. It is an easy thing for you to do. Release my friends and me, and return our belongings and horses."

The wizard seemed to fight back against her telepathic capabilities. He had a strong mind, seemingly resistant to her mental manipulation.

"All who come to our village must follow our laws. You have no ground here to be released."

Sherry realized that her abilities would prove more valuable and work better if she could see the people she tried to manipulate. She concentrated on the guard. "It is imperative we see the Khan. The desert wizards are causing you to fail in your duties. The Khan will kill you if we don't see him in time."

The guard rushed the door with his keys jangling in his shaking hands.

Two wizards wrestled with him to stop him from releasing the prisoners.

Sherry glanced at the Anticletus moon. It had hurried across the sky, and it wouldn't be above the horizon much longer. She had to move quickly.

She didn't know what she did, but she concentrated intensely. As her power strengthened, the visual effects intensified. She radiated a strong, ethereal glow, highlighting her presence amidst the darkness. Wisps of energy started to weave through the air around her, intertwining with her movements like vibrant threads of light. She sent the threads through the cracks in the gate toward the two wizards holding the guard with the keys.

Sherry verbalized the command, "Let him go. Help him open the gate. It is the Khan's command." Sparkling arcs of energy crackled and surged around her, forming intricate patterns reminiscent of hieroglyphics and ancient images.

Her friends stepped back from her as electric forces flew from her fingers.

She commanded again, "Release him. It is the command of the Crown of Anticletus."

The keys jangled once more at the gate.

The head wizard shouted, "Stop him."

Another wizard said, "We can't, they have shielded him from our magic."

The door opened and Sherry's eyes had become radiant, glowing with an otherworldly light. All the wizards stared at her as she walked through the opening. The wizards seemed mesmerized at her transformation as much as the warriors.

She commanded, "Take me to the Khan. She grabbed a guard's arm. Take my friends to their horses and help prepare them for the road."

The guard led Erik, Lily and Kestrel to the horses.

Al fell in next to Sherry. "I'm coming with you."

"You don't have to." She smiled up at him, but he followed after her.

The head wizard took Sherry and Al to the Khan. When they reached the Khan's hut, the man stood with them just outside the door.

The Khan stared at Sherry. Her figure exuded an aura of authority. With a resonating voice of profound power she commanded, "Release us and return our possessions."

The Khan shouted at the head wizard, "What is this? I commanded you to keep them prisoners, and you openly deny my commands."

Sherry repeated the command and felt the sense of awe and reverence within the Khan. The strings of blue dynamic energy she had seen before now wriggled toward the Khan as a formidable force of nature, produced by a force whose might commanded the respect of all.

The Khan didn't respond, he seemed to be attempting to drive a block between Sherry's commands and his own brain.

Sherry gazed quickly at the moon. It hung half in the air and half below the horizon. She had only moments to gain control and manipulate their release. If she didn't dominate this conversation now, and the moon set, then the Khan would kill her before the moon rose again the next night.

As the Khan's block closed on Sherry's powers like an elevator door closing, Sherry renewed her efforts at control. Her stomach clenched tight in answer to the forces happening within her body. She couldn't believe the man could block the Crown of Anticletus. She couldn't allow herself to fail.

The Khan's alert gaze and firm jaw belied the energy he was using to stop Sherry's manipulation.

Al shouted, "Come staff!"

The Khan's attention on Sherry wavered for a moment as his awareness of Al standing next to Sherry broke his concentration. He moved back into the hut's entranceway trying to block the staff from flying to Al.

The Khan yelled at the head wizard. "Stop him."

Sherry commanded the head wizard, "Release your magic block on the boy."

The staff flew between the Khan's outstretched arms into Al's hand.

Al threw up a shield between him and the Khan.

The Khan didn't waver and delivered a powerful blow against the shield which destroyed it in an instant. He fired a bolt of lightning at Al, knocking him to the ground.

Sherry recognized the Khan as a powerful wizard chieftain. She couldn't allow him to kill her friend. Using the emotions of her love for Al that swirled within her soul, she concentrated on the thin strip of the moon to pull even more of its wonder and potential. The force came from her inner being, a force she didn't know she contained, released in a meditative strike of mindful fury at the Khan.

The block the Khan had placed between them sealed. He smiled in triumph.

But it didn't hold. Sherry's crown blasted the Khan's block, and her command forced him to his knees. She couldn't trust the man, knowing she had only moments to free her friends and leave the village with their belongings before the Anticletus moon set. With a twist of energy, she emptied the Khan's mind.

CHAPTER 59

Zita stalked toward the creature named Ragadozo. Luna Rosso had forced Zita to use her powers of persuasion on the creature. She had no choice but to attempt to sway the creature from eating them all.

"Hey cheater, come over here and look at me."

Ragadozo stopped chasing the warrior and looked at Zita. "Do you plan to fight me?" He swung his weapon and Zita felt the wind of it blow past her hair.

Zita had no intention of fighting anyone. The red scorpion began its journey from the corner of her eye and Zita inched toward the beast.

Ragadozo raised the stegox femur over his head, as if readying a quick downward blow at Zita.

"Look at me, you big hairy beast." Zita motioned the creature closer.

Ragadozo stopped and stared at Zita's eyes.

His eyes were so big, the blue of a lake on a cloudless day. She lost concentration, but only for a moment. Then she commanded him. "At no point did you tell us that we couldn't collaborate on our answer. Is that true?"

He dropped to his knees and looked more closely at Zita's eye. "Yes."

She commanded him. "We won the bet."

He nodded multiple times, his horns almost hitting Zita's forehead when he nodded.

"Can we pass unmolested?" She sent a command for the creature to agree to her command. She found Ragadozo as docile as the rabbits she had practiced on.

Ragadozo bowed his head as if he had been criticized for doing something wrong. He said in an apologetic tone, "Yes."

Zita looked back in triumph at Taka and Dakarai. "You heard the man. Stop hiding and let's move."

Taka stepped to her and grabbed her chin. "What did you do to him?"

She stood stoically not answering his direct question. "How do you block my magic."

He squeezed her chin to the point she thought he might break her jaw, and then released her with a twist of his wrist.

They tramped past Ragadozo and continued the journey up the island's winding mountain path. The sun had set over the horizon, and they had entered a forested area. The sultry night air hung heavy, devoid of even the faintest whisper of a breeze. As they navigated the rocks, bushes and occasional tree, the heat intensified, wrapping itself around everything and everyone. The atmosphere was drenched in heavy humidity, leaving a lingering film of perspiration on every exposed surface of Zita's body.

Insects had awakened after the sun set and began to find the enticing, sweaty bodies of the adventurers.

Sims whacked his arm and screamed, "Get away from me, you nasty bugs."

Zita kept wiping her face, arms and legs with her hands to keep from being bitten constantly. She felt on edge wondering when they would encounter the second guardian, a creature known only as Risastór Skordýr. She hoped it didn't ask them riddles because she felt lucky they had passed the first test.

Despite the buzzing and biting of the insects, the night was still as if frozen in time. Nature held the island captive, a false sense of serenity impending an explosion.

Taka led the group along the tortuous, never-ending serpentine trail, everyone holding torches to light the way.

Zita saw the tension in every face as they all searched the boulders and trees, waiting for an upcoming onslaught by a terrible beast. She heard a buzzing as they climbed and moments later a cloud of insects attacked the group. They spluttered and spit the flying insects out of their mouths.

Sims cried out, "The second guardian must be these blasted biting gnats."

Taka raised his hand to stop the adventurers and whispered, "Quiet."

Zita wondered what he heard. She couldn't hear anything with the tiny insects buzzing within her ears.

Taka gave the signal to continue and Zita hoped they would move higher and get out of this cloud of attacking insects. They kept dive-bombing her eyes, causing them to tear up. She rubbed her fingers in the corner of her eyes, trying to dig the little gnats out.

Zita couldn't see anything as she walked and missed Taka's signal to stop. She plowed into Ekaterina's back. "Sorry. I can't see a thing."

"Yeah, it's horrible, isn't it?" Ekaterina asked. "We have sand flies in the desert, but never this bad."

"Do you think this is the second guardian?"

Taka whispered, "Quiet. It's tracking us."

Ekaterina touched Zita's shoulder and whispered. "Drop to the ground. Now!"

Zita didn't hesitate. She threw herself face down on the volcanic rock and covered her face. She heard a giant buzzing hover over her before it zoomed past.

Zita waited a couple of seconds and rose to her feet. "What was that? Did you see it?"

Taka said, "Risastór Skordýr. It's huge. I expected something smaller. Let's move." He trotted faster up the trail.

Zita helped Ekaterina to her feet. "Thank you. That was close. I think you saved my life."

They pushed up the hill, all the travelers staying close to each other. Safety in numbers, Zita thought. She stayed close to Ekaterina. The vessel's ability to see into the future might be the only thing to save her.

A sudden rustle in the shadows caught Zita's attention. The second guardian emerged onto the path. It towered over Taka's motley crew on six slender yet powerful legs. The monster had a wide body, yet it was held aloft by small, fast-moving transparent wings. It floated in the air just off the ground in the middle of the path.

The giant insect's exoskeleton gleamed with an iridescent sheen. A complex pattern of intricate markings on its body played off the light and shadows cast by the torches waved by the adventurers.

Zita stood transfixed as she gazed into its multitude of eyes. She guessed the number of eyes at twenty arranged in four symmetrical rows, glistening with a glowing yellow luminescence. What worried her most, though, were the creature's massive jutting mandibles edged with dozens of sharp teeth.

The creature reminded her of a bumble bee as it hovered in the air. The beating of its wings made a horrible noise which she hoped would drive off the gnats, but they worked in unison with the beast.

One desert wizard shouted, "I will defeat the beast." The man jumped in front of Taka and confronted the creature. The wizard used magic, trying to make a quick kill of the creature. A blast of fire came from the wizard's hand and struck the creature on its left side behind its bank of eyes.

The fireball bounced off the insect's exoskeleton and landed harmlessly on a boulder. Risastór Skordýr buzzed around the path; its six legs not touching the ground but seemed to help it navigate the terrain with ease. Its wing's beat louder as it circled the adventurers in low-flying attacks.

Zita found a niche of safety between two boulders that leaned against each other. She thought back to the scroll and remembered this as the creature they were supposed to use the seven-petaled flower on. And now they were forced to take it on without the flower's power.

The desert wizard tried a second attack, blasting air at the creature. Risastór Skordýr seemed to enjoy the air and just hovered in place while the onslaught occurred. The wizard couldn't hold the spell and when he dropped his arms, Risastór Skordýr charged, taking the offensive.

Taka and the others moved back into safe nooks and crannies in the landscape.

The desert wizard withstood the siege, striking out at the creature with a knife.

They stood in battle, the wizard sliced with his knife, while Risastór Skordýr buzzed and weaved, trying to strike the wizard with its saw-like mandibles. Neither were getting the upper hand.

Zita watched with rapt attention, though she wondered why the wizard didn't set a magic shield to protect him from the creature.

Ekaterina shouted at the wizard, "Drop down."

He didn't listen and kept jabbing his knife at the insect.

Risastór Skordýr faked right.

The wizard over-extended his hand in that direction, only to find Risastór Skordýr rotated the back of its body and jammed its stinger into the wizard's side. Everything moved in slow motion. The wizard tried to find purchase with his knife, but the creature continued to out-maneuver the human.

Whatever venom the insect's stinger held took effect quickly, and the desert wizard dropped dead in the path. Risastór Skordýr retracted its stinger and rose into the air. It swooped over the adventurers and disappeared up the path.

Zita didn't move. Nobody ventured back onto the now empty path.

Finally, Taka crept from his hiding place. "Let's move."

Zita didn't want to go forward. She huddled in place within her tiny niche, a place she considered safe and secure. Risastór Skordýr wouldn't be able to hurt her if she stayed in her current location.

Ekaterina stepped over to Zita and held out her hand. "I will keep you safe."

Zita listened for the low rumble that identified Risastór Skordýr's presence. Her pulse raced, and the world seemed to spin. She couldn't continue this journey. It wasn't safe. She should have waited for Erik. With a deep and unsatisfying sigh, and shaking arms, she took Ekaterina's hand. They had to defeat the monster to win the crystal.

The group hurried up the trail. How much longer would they have to navigate the sinuous rocky route before they reached the castle? Zita looked back three times, wondering if they would see Risastór Skordýr again. With luck, the creature had gone back to eat the fallen wizard, and they just needed to reach the castle gates for safety.

Risastór Skordýr buzzed into the vicinity, bringing all the gnats with it.

Taka had them all huddle together. He asked, "Who wants to battle the creature?"

Nobody volunteered.

Taka pointed at Zita. "You fight it."

Zita stepped back. The man couldn't be serious. Her nostrils flared. "I'm not going against that creature. I don't even have magic."

"I'll give you back your magic. Only for this battle. I can't have you stabbing me in the back."

Zita pointed a shaking finger at Taka's face. The heat of rage empowered her. Her lips pulled back, baring her teeth. "You have my father's great wand. You attack the creature."

Taka grabbed the front of her tunic and pulled her close. He stared into her eyes.

Zita smelled the spicy remains of their last meal on his breath. She tried to pull back, but he held tight to her tunic.

He said, "I'll give you your magic and you will defeat Risastór Skordýr, or I'll kill you now."

"I can't defeat the creature."

"Then one less mouth for me to feed. I need the others, but I don't need you."

Zita's vision clouded, and the blood hammered in her head. Fatigue, hunger and thirst racked her body, and she wanted to scream.

Ekaterina's soft hands touched Zita's shoulder.

Zita flinched.

Ekaterina said, "I'll help you, my friend."

Zita didn't want to do it at all. She was numb. She pushed Taka's chest.

He held tight.

She pushed again. "Let go. I'll do it." She didn't know what she'd do, but she didn't have a choice.

Taka released his grip on her tunic.

Zita smoothed out the fabric. "My magic."

Taka took out his wand. "I'm warning you. Try anything funny and I will make you wish you were never born."

Zita remembered her father saying those words to many political friends. He followed through on those threats enough times that few tried to disobey him. She believed Taka would be just as brutal.

She raised her hands. "Magic. Please."

Taka waved the wand at Zita. He nodded at Dakarai, who also manipulated his hands and said a small chant.

Interesting, thought Zita. The *two wizards together held the shield over her magic.*

As the first tendrils of magic coursed through her veins, a profound sense of elation washed over her, like meeting a long-lost friend returning after a prolonged absence. A rush of energy surged through her body, revitalizing her spirit and awakening a dormant power within.

Risastór Skordýr's low rumble approached the adventurers from nearby.

Zita's senses sharpened. She perceived the subtle shifts in the world around her with newfound clarity. She felt powerful, a profound connection to the planet and to the Velidred moon. Could the moon's power help her defeat this flying irritating creature?

Zita threw up a shield to cover her and Ekaterina.

The others found hiding places in the rocks and alcoves.

The insect buzzed and hovered, weaving closer and then further from Zita. She thought of ways to kill the insect. Her favorite spells included a fireball and air, but when the desert wizard tried those spells, they proved ineffective.

The creature moved closer, its wings sending gusts of wind at the shield Zita used to protect herself and Ekaterina.

Zita watched and studied its movements, trying to see a pattern that she could use against it. At the very least, Risastór Skordýr as an insect probably did the things normal insects did. She needed to come up with some way to kill an insect, the same solutions the maids used to keep the castle mostly bug free.

She racked her brain trying to remember the mixture the maids used.

Risastór Skordýr hovered closer, and the beating of its wings seemed to be having an effect on Zita's shield. The shield seemed to wave in the wind, more like a bubble than hard, sturdy structure.

Ekaterina yelled, "Get down."

Zita didn't hesitate, she dropped to her knees as the giant insect's stinger whizzed past her face.

A sudden coldness stabbed at Zita's core. The desert wizard didn't shield because he couldn't shield. The creature's wings could disable magic systems. Ekaterina's ability to see into the future had saved her, again.

Zita and Ekaterina danced around the path, trying to stay one step ahead of the insect as Zita tried to remember the substance used by the castle maids. It had something to do with earth and algae, a substance safe to humans, but dangerous to insects.

She conjured a magic question that she sent forth to the water surrounding the island. This magic was similar to the magic that she used when searching doors for traps.

Where can I find algae on the island?

A shadow of herself raced down the island mountain, searching for algae.

The request came back with a couple of different locations she could choose from. There were places on the island that didn't have beaches, just rocks stabbing out of the water. Where the water splashed up on the rocks, she found the algae. The hot water and shadowed rocks that only received sun light for brief moments each day made a perfect place to produce it.

Using magic, she created a chant that allowed the shadow to scrape the rock and gather a large quantity. She called for it to come to her. It landed in the sandy soil where she stood and deposited the algae. There wasn't as much of it as she thought, but she hoped it would be enough. She gathered it into her hands.

Zita asked, "What attracts insects?"

Ekaterina answered, "Lights? In the desert the insects are attracted to light."

"Yes, that's perfect."

"And sweet scent from a flower."

Zita said, "Splendid." A plan hatched in her mind. She called forth the spell to create a cloud of fog and threw up her shield again. She worried the fog might prevent her from seeing an impending attack from Risastór Skordýr, but she thought if she played it right, she might succeed.

As the fog rolled in from the mountain top, all the adventurers turned quiet. Zita thought the others might be as scared as she felt.

The buzzing started up again and she felt the creature's wings battering the shield.

Zita extinguished all the torches the humans had carried up the mountain.

Sims cursed.

Taka whispered, "Quiet."

Zita floated a torch away from her body. It hit a boulder and she re-positioned it. She couldn't send it too far away if she wanted her scheme to work.

Risastór Skordýr continued to batter the shield, and Ekaterina screamed to move. Zita dropped to her knees and crawled in the opposite direction as the torch. She immediately lit the torch and directed a scent of a flowering crabapple at it.

She heard the creature move away. The buzzing retreated from her position but not toward the torch.

Zita increased the scent. She could barely make out the light of the torch in the dark and fog. The scent of crabapple almost overpowered her.

Ekaterina pulled Zita into a protected alcove.

Risastór Skordýr buzzed by them and then hovered over Zita just inches above her head. The insect hadn't taken the bait of the sweet scent and light from the torch. She didn't know what other techniques to use to make the creature move toward her trap. They were doomed.

CHAPTER 60

Ekaterina tapped Zita's shoulder and she backed up closer to the desert princess. The woman's ability to see just moments into the future had been the only difference between life and death for Zita.

The cloying heavy scent of crabapple flower overwhelmed her, making her sick to her stomach. Despite her discomfort, she increased the scent and brightened the light from the torch.

The combination of light and fragrance finally worked and the insect hovered toward the brightly burning torch.

Zita collected the algae mixed with dirt picked up from the trail, formed it into a powder and launched it using the sand spell to splatter it against the insect.

She didn't move.

They waited. Zita didn't know how she would know if her plan worked or not. She held her breath, worried that the solution had failed.

Time slowed and the gnats moved away. The buzzing stopped and silence descended on the adventurers.

Had the solution worked, or had the insect decided to come at her a different way? She sent up a breeze to blow the fog and scent away.

The giant insect lay in the path. It wheezed and struggled as the natural sand and algae dug into the insect's exoskeleton, dehydrating the beast and slowly killing it. She suspected it would take hours for Risastór Skordýr to die completely, but they appeared free to continue to the castle or the next guardian, whichever came first.

Zita glanced at Taka. Victory against the insect seemed to have sapped her strength. She didn't even feel like gloating, as fatigued wracked her body.

Then Taka blocked her magic and she struggled even to stand. It was only the power of her magic that was keeping her upright.

Zita wondered if they had circled the island ten times as they tracked through the dark night forest. Velidred and Pantaleon had taken their stations in the night sky, but the forest canopy prevented any of the moonlight from reaching the forest trail. Taka led the group. Fatigue had overtaken the adventurers and they shuffled wearily toward the castle.

Taka raised his hand in a signal for everyone to stop.

Zita stopped and stood next to Ekaterina. They had become close friends during the journey from the desert. Zita wanted the woman to succeed as the vessel for the crystal, but she didn't want to have to hurt her if it became necessary to obtain the crystal for herself.

The forested area had turned into a jungle, vines encircled the trees, and the air smelled of sweat, dirt and decay. Zita wished for a breeze to bring them relief. If she had her magic, she would cast a spell to provide them with a cool gust of air.

Snakes slithered through the undergrowth, and the roar of a predator sounded in the distance.

Taka said, "That's the third guardian. Xalawad Furioso. Also known as the Rampager. It's a creature of desert myths. Any desert chieftain would tell you it doesn't exist."

"Do you know how to defeat it?" Zita asked.

Taka stared at her with an expression of incredulity. "If I thought it didn't exist, then would I know how to defeat it?"

Zita raised her hands and backed away. She hoped Taka planned to have someone else fight the creature instead of her. She didn't have the strength to beat the next guardian on her own. Whatever it was, the creatures were dangerous and she didn't want anything to do with yet another one.

"The Khan thought the creature might secrete an acidic poison through its pores and also be able to spit it," Taka said. "The acid will destroy metal shields and weapons."

"How about magic shields." Zita felt hope for reaching the castle slipping away.

The remaining desert wizard said, "Some believe that the magic shields will hold."

After her experience with Risastór Skordýr, Zita didn't think the magic shields would last long against an acid attack. She suspected the acid had a magical component to it with the capability to burn through most anything.

The roar sounded, closer now.

Taka shouted, "Move forward. Look for an area that'll give us an advantage if it attacks us. "

They tramped on, the desert warrior whacking at low hanging trees and bushes that grew along the trail with his long knife. The man looked exhausted, but he probably feared Taka, so instead of resting, he continued to make a path for them. The desert warrior slashed at a limb and as it fell to the ground, the castle came into view. When they emerged from the dense jungle, they stepped into a small clearing where they stopped to admire the castle.

Zita's eyes widened in awe at the castle laid out before her. It towered into the night sky, so high she couldn't see the ramparts in the dark.

The castle's weathered stone walls stood as a testament to the passage of centuries, adorned with intricate carvings that hinted at a storied past. Vines and ivy wound gracefully up the sides, their fast-growing tendrils lending a touch of nature's embrace to the ancient structure. Moss clung to the stones, imbuing the castle with an aura of mystique.

The castle entrance beckoned to them a hundred yards away. A wrought iron gate shut out the jungle dangers that threatened to overtake it.

The creature roared from their right.

Taka yelled, "Run to the gates. We can outrun it."

Everyone sprinted toward the castle.

Something rumbled behind them, and the ground seemed to bounce and shake.

Zita glanced back. A giant creature with an enormous mouth and sharp teeth chased after them. It ran on two gargantuan legs, its body weight causing the earth to quake.

Zita didn't know where her strength came from, her body shook with fatigue, but an intensity she didn't know existed brought increased strength and stamina. She ran past the desert warrior who had spent the night slashing at the undergrowth and past Ekaterina. If she beat them to the castle, maybe she had a chance to stay alive.

The animal roared, and she felt the wind from its powerful lungs. Could its spittle reach them from here? Zita pressed her hands over her ears to stop the terrible sound. A quick glance and she noticed the creature had almost reached the exhausted desert warrior who had fallen behind the others.

She raced on, her breaths coming in raspy gasps. Despite the pain in her legs, she sprinted to the castle gates.

Zita reached the gates. Taka had opened them and let her through. Everyone but the desert warrior and Ekaterina stood behind the gates. She leaned forward with her hands on her knees as she sucked in life-giving oxygen. A quick glance at the others in the group and Zita gasped. "Where's Ekaterina?"

Taka pointed toward the monster.

The desert warrior had stopped and turned toward the gigantic monster that chased him. Ekaterina stood next to the warrior ready to do battle with it.

Zita watched the battle unfolding in the clearing. She didn't know why Ekaterina had chosen to stay with the warrior. "Ekaterina, come to the castle! Let the warrior fight the beast."

The desert spiritualist, vessel for the crystal, stayed with the warrior.

The warrior drew his sword and lunged toward the beast, but the creature swung its tail. The huge tail moved in a flash, knocking the man to the ground.

Zita asked, "Why didn't Ekaterina warn the warrior about the impending doom?"

"The Khan suspected that her powers might not be available when we breached the castle walls," The desert wizard said.

"She's not even behind the castle walls." Zita wailed. "Why won't she come to the castle?"

"Do we know the power of the castle?" he asked.

"We can't let her die. Taka, do something."

He nonchalantly responded, "If you want to help her, then you may try."

"Does she know about this limitation?" Zita looked incredulously at the men around her.

The desert wizard shrugged.

Zita rolled her eyes. "Taka, give me my magic, I have to save Ekaterina."

Dakarai narrowed his brow, "You can't trust her this close to the crystal. If she wants to save Ekaterina, let her do it without magic."

"If you let her die, then you won't have a vessel."

Taka seemed to take that information to heart. "Release her magic. We won't let her back into the castle without blocking her again."

The magic almost burned into her body as if the castle added power to Zita's natural magic. She felt invincible and charged into the clearing to save Ekaterina.

Zita yelled at her new-found friend, "You aren't safe. Go to the safety of the castle walls."

But Ekaterina stood next to her tribesman, talking to him in a calm voice, directing his attack.

As Zita rushed toward the battle, she took a closer look at the creature. What did Taka say it was? Xalawad Furioso, the Rampager. She expected the beast before her to have a scaly hide, but instead, feathers arrayed its arms and they added nobility and grandeur. She would have likened it to an angry chicken, but its size, larger than her father's manor house, wouldn't let her make the comparison.

The warrior swung a mighty blow at the creature's vulnerable neck. The blade made contact and sliced through the feathers.

Xalawad Furioso stepped back and roared.

Zita quickly threw a magic shield over all three of them hoping to buy them time.

Spittle from the monster's mouth dribbled onto the magic shield, opening pock marks and holes where the acid ate through the shield.

"Watch out for the acid!" She yelled.

The animal's feet were enhanced with razor-sharp claws. The arms appeared short, tipped with a single claw, and ended only a few feet from its body, but feathers extended ten feet past the creature's claws.

A crown of feathers extended from the beast's formidable head, framing a pair of piercing dark red glowing eyes that seemed to gaze upon the world with a mix of intelligence and primal instinct. Its sharp curved teeth spoke of its predatory nature, while the intricate patterns of feathers that adorned its snout, accentuated its regal countenance.

Despite the sizable feathers, Zita didn't believe the animal could fly. She wondered where the creature originated? Were there others on the island? She guessed the hot volcanic water prevented the animals from leaving the island.

She shouted, "Let's walk back to the gate, Taka doesn't think the creature will follow us behind the castle walls."

The warrior didn't seem to care. He glanced back at Ekaterina before rushing at Xalawad Furioso.

She grabbed at Ekaterina, but the woman shook off Zita's hands. She continued to help the warrior.

Zita wondered if the others were wrong. Maybe Ekaterina still had the ability to see the future. But maybe it wasn't three seconds anymore as the instructions she gave the warrior seemed to be barely faster than the animal's attacks.

A movement of Xalawad Furioso's feathered arms sent ripples through the plumes adorning the creature's back. Its muscular build seemed a perfect design for relentless pursuit and swift strikes. The combination of feather and scales created an intriguing juxtaposition, as if the creature embodied both the gentleness of flight and the primal force of the ancient world.

The warrior seemed to tighten his grip on his sword and charged at the beast once more. He unleashed a flurry of calculated strikes, aiming for vulnerable spots on the creature's frame. Twice he struck the creature, slashing his sword across its body.

Xalawad Furioso screamed but retaliated with strikes of its own. Three times the creature's talons struck home and the warrior lost his left arm.

Finally, Zita thought. *The warrior will now realize he's not invincible and we can return to the castle's safety.*

The warrior didn't give up his attack, and he ignored the fact he had just lost an arm. He jabbed his sword into the creature's gut, a mighty blow. He drove the sword deep and twisted as he pulled it out.

The animal screamed in pain, its spittle splattering the shield with acid.

Zita watched the acid eat through her shield.

Xalawad Furioso ignored its injuries, raised a foot, and grabbed at the warrior, finding its mark.

Ekaterina howled as Xalawad Furioso delivered a fatal blow to her fellow tribesman.

Ekaterina had given no notice to the warrior. Had she lost the ability to see the future?

Zita shrieked as a gaping hole opened in her shield. She clenched her jaw so tight it hurt. Her legs felt weak, and she didn't think she could make it back to the castle.

Spittle dripped all around them as the creature moved towards them.

Zita could tell the warrior's attacks had harmed the creature, but it wasn't surrendering. She needed to strike at the animal fast before it could dance away.

The warrior's sword slipped from his grasp, clattering to the ground, as he collapsed.

Ekaterina picked up the sword.

What is wrong with this woman? We need to escape, not keep attacking.

The creature circled the two women.

Zita tried the mind tricks the moon goddess had given her in an attempt to control the creature's mind, but fatigue racked her body and she couldn't find the tranquility necessary to manipulate it.

Ekaterina slashed at Xalawad Furioso, but missed.

The beast continued to circle. It roared, forcing spittle from its mouth that splattered into the air.

Zita sent out a magical chant, "Ataque de víbora." It struck as if a hundred vipers attacked the creature at once. Each bite landed home on the animal's body and delivered a large amount of venom. She knew the chant came from the moon goddess, enhanced by the castle's magic. Zita had never used that chant before, and she couldn't have sent as many at one time without the Velidred moon goddess' help.

Zita quickly raised another shield.

Xalawad Furioso stumbled and weaved, unsteady on its enormous legs.

Zita grabbed Ekaterina and yanked her toward the gate's safety. She needed to get her to the castle.

The men at the gate cheered them on.

The beast stumbled, but roared. It chased the women, but Zita's attack had left the creature unsteady and off-balance.

As Zita pulled Ekaterina along after her, it seemed the woman began to have trouble walking.

"Stay strong, if we can get you to the castle, you'll be okay." She didn't notice any bites the animal had inflicted on Ekaterina and assumed the woman's problems were just fatigue and grief at losing a friend.

The beast slowed and fell to the ground in a great rumble. Dust jettisoned into the air as it collapsed.

Ekaterina slowed even more.

Zita pushed her on.

Ekaterina stumbled.

Zita held her elbow, trying to support her.

Deep lines of agony tracked across Ekaterina's pale, almost ghostly face. Splotches of red dotted her face and arms, and she looked as if her life force had drained from her body. Her skin was clammy and damp, as if covered in sweat.

Zita didn't think the sweaty skin meant anything. After all the hard work to get up to the castle and the dangers they encountered, Ekaterina had reached a point of weariness. They all were, but something wasn't right.

Ekaterina's breathing became labored, erratic, and shallow, punctuated by occasional gasps for air. She seemed to struggle with each breath, like her lungs were burdened with an unseen weight. The rise and fall of her chest were accompanied by raspy, wheezing sounds that hinted at the distress within.

Zita asked, "Why didn't you run to the castle with us?"

Ekaterina mouthed the words, more than spoke them. "He . . . was . . .," She coughed and spit blood. "My . . .

betrothed." Her limbs twitched with spasms, the poison's relentless assault on her nervous system continuing to breakdown her body's natural defenses against the attack. She fell to the ground as the essence of life seeped out of her.

Zita went to her knees and wailed. She held Ekaterina's head to her breast and rocked back and forth at the woman's senseless death.

CHAPTER 61

Al rode his horse over the small hill, and beheld the red lake and the island in the middle of the lake. The Red Castle stood at the top of the island, the morning sun enhancing the castle's ruddy façade. The lake seemed angry, as a strong wind blew across the landscape, creating pink white caps on the water.

He stopped, and the rest of their group joined him to inspect the scene.

Erik said, "Do you think this is it?"

"Yes. All the literature, legends, myths I've heard over the years describes it like this." Kestrel took a drink of water from his waterskin.

Sherry asked, "How long has the crystal been stored in this castle?"

"Hundreds, maybe thousands of years," Kestrel said.

"After we capture the crystal, how are we to protect it?" Lily asked. "Do we have to find our own island and castle, or do we just use its energy and keep it in its current location?"

Al looked at the others. No one had a clue. This was definitely something they hadn't considered. How do you hide a magical object as powerful as the Crystal of Zaraboth? He hoped it wasn't large. Perhaps, it would fit in his pocket.

Kestrel pointed to the lake. "There's the dock. Maybe we can find a boat."

Al studied the water which seemed to bubble in the early morning light. He wasn't sure he wanted to cross the lake.

"Let's go." Erik nudged his horse ahead.

They rode toward the dock. As they got closer, Al said, "I don't see any boats."

"There's a hut next to the dock." Erik nodded in its general direction. "Maybe we have to wait for the next boat that comes along."

Al considered the fact that other adventurers might be trying to capture the crystal at the same time. "Is it possible Taka took the only boat available and we're out of luck?"

"Let's hope not," Sherry said, "for Zita's sake."

A shout sounded from their left. Twelve men rode toward them screaming, "Attack!" They wore the colors of the desert warriors they had met when they were captured by the Khan.

Al raised his staff in surprise at the shouts from the warriors. "Don't these guys ever give up? Why would they follow us?"

"I think these are Taka's guys," Erik said. "They were already here. I recognize his thug Lenny there in the back."

Al noticed the air around them seemed charged with magical energy, and the sound of the charge echoed off the island mountain. He threw up a shield.

Erik said, "Prepare for battle."

A wizard from Lenny's group conjured a fireball and launched it at the five teenagers. The projectile streaked through the sky, leaving trails of smoke and embers.

The fireball bounced off Al's shield in a swirl of reds and oranges as it diminished across the field.

Kestrel responded with a fireball of his own. It seared toward the attackers only to be diverted by a gust of wind summoned by the desert wizard. The fireball crashed against a boulder standing in the field.

The desert warriors charged with raised swords. They made an ululating cry with their tongues, showing strength and power in their attack.

A chill went down Al's back. They couldn't afford to lose this battle, yet they had no weapons, only magic and Erik's Sword of Freedom. It didn't look good.

Amidst the chaos, the desert wizard continued to cast spells. He unleashed torrents of fire and lightning upon the group. Fiery explosions and electrified shockwaves erupted around them, shaking the ground beneath their feet and casting mesmerizing hues across the red morning sky.

Erik shouted, "Al, can you throw up a wall of dirt before their advance?"

Al responded by lobbing a magical bolt of lightning at the ground twenty feet in front of the attacking warriors.

The warrior wizard didn't expect a move of that kind and had no time to block it.

The lightning bolt struck in a fury of power and the ground exploded, throwing warriors off their horses and slowing their advance.

Kestrel moved his horse forward and raised his hands above his head. He circled his arms in a wide arc, and shouted into the violent rain of stones and dirt, "Casúr chaos."

Twenty large hammers flew through the air, in a wide arc, a militant show of force. They encircled the warriors and began their assault honed like guided missiles. The desert wizard didn't seem to know how to stop all the hammers. His warriors were spread too far apart to shield them all at once.

The hammers struck home, and three warriors fell to the ground after the attack.

Seven warriors maintained their positions on their mounts and resumed the charge at the teens.

Erik drew his sword and forced his mount to gallop at the approaching warriors.

Sherry shouted, "Erik, what are you doing? Stay with us."

He ignored Sherry and kept advancing.

"What is he doing?" Al asked. "Doesn't he know we can't protect him unless he stays near us?"

"Follow him. Protect him." Sherry screamed. "We'll be useless to Zita without him."

Al booted his horse and raced after Erik. As he rode, he thought of ways to defeat the opposing wizard. As long as the man could protect the warriors, then Al and his friends couldn't win this skirmish. He wished he had Taka's ability to block magic. Then it hit him. What if this desert wizard could block magic? Here he was riding straight at dangerous warriors and if he lost his magic, he'd be dead in a heartbeat.

Erik reached the warriors and engaged with one of them. The skilled desert warrior easily forced Erik off his horse.

Al moved closer to the action but feared participating in hand-to-hand combat. He activated a shield that could protect Erik and himself.

Al cast a spell, "I Hehe Lapalapa." He raised his hands, releasing a surge of mystical energy through his fingertips which gathered into a concentrated ball of fire. The air crackled as he unleashed his spell. Flames curled from his fingers, twirling upon itself until it formed a sphere. The spell pulsated with a life of its own, eagerly awaiting Al's command. This was no ordinary fireball.

With a deft motion of his hands, Al set the flaming sphere into motion. It started small as it first hit the ground and then gained in height as it rolled toward the desert warriors, its flames leaving a scorching trail behind. As it gained momentum, the sphere moved with remarkable agility, gliding across the terrain, a fiery spirit in pursuit of its enemy.

By the time the sphere reached the warriors, it had grown to a ball of fire six-feet in diameter, a mighty force to be reckoned with. The sphere swiftly closed in on the warriors, its searing heat and intense brightness mesmerizing. The ground quivered beneath the horses' hooves as they stopped their forward charge.

The sphere collided with the first warrior an explosive impact which engulfed the rider and horse in a brilliant blaze. The inferno instantly consumed the unfortunate pair, their screams drowned out by the crackling flames.

The flaming sphere rolled onward, leaving nothing but charred bones in its wake. It engulfed the second warrior; the scorching flames licked at his leather armor and melted his resolve. The horse reared up, bucked and whinnied in panic before it succumbed to the blaze.

A third and fourth warrior fell victim to the relentless spell, as the sphere engulfed them with unforgiving fire. The scene became a chaotic symphony of heat, smoke, and the terrified screams of the doomed riders. The horses veered wildly; their fear-stricken eyes reflecting the inferno that surrounded them.

Yet, as quickly as the spell had manifested, its power dwindled. The flames within the sphere grew dimmer and lost their intensity. With a final burst of light, the sphere fizzled out, leaving behind scorched earth and burnt bodies.

The remaining three warriors who managed to avoid the spell's wrath cast fearful glances at Al, contemplating their next move with trepidation.

Erik brandished his sword above his head, but the flaming sphere had spooked the warriors and they retreated to the safety of their wizard. Erik chased the warriors on foot.

Al shouted, "Stop!"

Erik didn't listen. Al sent a spell that tripped Erik, who fell face first into the scorched grass.

Al rode his horse up to Erik.

Erik stood, brushing soot and grass from his tunic. "Why did you do that?"

"Look at your arm, he sliced you at least twice. I can't protect you if you don't stay close to me."

"I had him on the run." Erik pointed at the warriors retreating from the skirmish.

Al laughed. "*You* had him on the run? I'm the one that sent the flaming sphere."

Erik examined the ground. "Was I in danger?"

"No, I controlled it." Al sat on his horse.

"Let's go after them."

"I'm worried about getting too close," Al said. "The desert wizard might be able to block my magic. They have that skill. I don't know how to break the block. Let's stand back." He convinced Erik to stop his assault and the other teens rode their horses up to them.

Lenny and the warriors had stopped fifty yards away looking unsure of their next move.

"Is the battle over?" Lily asked.

Kestrel said, "I'm not sure."

"I have us covered with a shield for the moment." Al raised his staff over the group to show the shield's coverage.

An argument broke out between Lenny and a warrior.

"Does Lenny want them to continue?" Al asked.

"I have a spell that will make him stop their attack." Kestrel raised a hand. "Infect Eagla." He pushed his cupped fingers toward Lenny.

An eagle burst forth from his fingers and swooped low over the warriors, wizard, and Lenny, its sharp talons raking near their heads.

The warriors dismounted their horses and dropped to the ground, covering their heads with their hands.

Lenny yelled at the warriors to rise, but even he assumed the same position.

The desert wizard seemed unaffected by the spell.

"What was that?" Al asked.

"A spell to make them fear me."

Al pointed. "It didn't work on the desert wizard."

"He might be shielded, or he has a way to block the spell," Kestrel said.

Lenny pulled out a white cloth and waved it in the air while dodging the diving eagle.

"Is he surrendering?" Sherry asked.

"Knowing Lenny is a henchman for Taka, I would be very cautious." Al turned to Kestrel and asked, "Do you think the wizard can block our magic?" *All this damage and killing will be for nothing if the wizard blocks Kestrel and me.*

Kestrel shrugged.

Al spoke to his staff, carved with three wizards, Isabel the Insidious, Callahan the Curious, and Alpherge the Mighty, his grandfather's spirit. The carvings held the essence of the living wizards. "Staff, is there a spell that breaks through an incantation that blocks a wizard's magic?"

Isabel said, "There is, but you're not skilled enough to wield the enchantment."

"The boy has considerable skill," Callahan said. "Didn't you see that flaming sphere. Brilliant move."

Alpherge the Great said, "It requires three wizards bonded using the uklonite zakone magije spell."

"What's that?" Al asked.

"Dispel the laws of magic chant. You must join hands, think of the color blue, and each chant the spell at the same time. Then it disrupts the magic block and allows you to continue to cast."

Al cleared his throat. "Hmm. We might be in trouble, since there's only the two of us."

"It's a chance we have to take. Let's take them up on their surrender. We're running out of time to find Zita," Erik said.

Al looked up at the castle. He wondered what might be happening there.

Kestrel called back the eagle of fear and the warriors rose cautiously from the ground as the horses whinnied nervously. They gathered in a circle around Lenny and then followed him toward the teens.

The warriors walked in guarded movements across the smoldering grass, checking on fallen comrades and horses.

As they got closer, Erik yelled, "Drop your weapons."

They stopped. Lenny talked with them for a few moments and then he walked alone to the teens.

When he reached them, Lenny said, "We surrender, but we have terms."

"What terms?" Erik's forehead wrinkled.

"I see there are only five of you. When you go to the castle, you have to take three of us."

"Why would we agree to that?" Al asked. "We can kill you right here."

Lenny raised his hands. "It's my understanding there are guardians on the island, protecting the castle and the crystal. You might need our help. Wouldn't an extra wizard prove useful, a warrior to haul water up the mountain for us? An extra sword handler?"

Erik and Al exchanged glances. Al raised his hand at Lenny. "Stay there for a second." He got the group to huddle up away from Lenny.

Sherry leaned forward and whispered, "Lenny is a thug. We can't trust a thing he says. You saw what they did to Paxton's place. It would take only a second for him to turn on us and stab us in the back."

"Lenny didn't seem to be as destructive as Sims," Al said, "but it could be dangerous to bring him with us. Whose side will he take when we meet Taka?"

Kestrel wagged his head from side to side with indecision. "An extra wizard could prove useful as we encounter the guardians. Maybe we could sacrifice Lenny to a guardian and they will let us pass."

Al let out a loud guffaw. "That would be perfect." He began to see where an extra pair of hands might be necessary and another wizard might be handy to have with them, since they really didn't know what they might be up against.

"What do you think Lily?"

"I'm afraid to even go to the island." She looked into Kestrel's eyes. "But if Kestrel thinks it's a good idea, I'm okay with the plan."

"It's down to you Erik. What say you about the additions?" Al pounded his staff into the ground.

"I don't know. They might come in handy."

Al disengaged from the huddle walked back to Lenny. "Okay. The wizard, a warrior and you."

Lenny smiled.

Despite the turmoil roiling within Al's gut, he reminded himself that they had defeated Lenny, the desert wizard, and the desert warriors, thanks to their need to rescue their friend, Zita. He promised himself to stay vigilant and watch for signs of treachery from their new companions.

Erik said, "If their wizard tries to block our wizard's magic, or the warrior fights us, I will kill you first."

Lenny raised his hands. "That is acceptable." He whistled to the desert tribesmen, who slowly approached the teens.

Al's mind raced. They had just agreed to work with Taka's henchman and a desert wizard who could potentially block Al's magic at a critical juncture in their attempt to capture the crystal. Trepidation pulsed through Al as he considered whether they had made a grave mistake in trusting their enemy. Had they just sacrificed their whole quest with this alliance?

CHAPTER 62

When they reached the dock, they found the dockmaster sitting on a bench next to the hut. Lily hadn't seen the man when they first arrived, so the noise of the battle must have brought him from the hut. Heat that poured off the lake warmed the cool air as they approached the dockmaster.

Lily grasped her flower pot and checked on the flower. It still looked healthy. She adjusted the scarf on her head that hid the symbol of the Sacred Castle.

The dockmaster asked, "What do you kids want?"

Al said, "We would like a boat to the island. When does the next boat arrive?"

"Aren't you a little young for a journey like this?"

Lily was tired of everyone on this planet saying the same thing to them every time they had tried to change things. With a commanding voice she said, "We've traveled a long time and distance to get here. We've fought beast, man, and nature to arrive in one piece. What time does the next boat arrive?"

Erik mumbled, "Wow, didn't see that coming."

"Do you have a vessel?"

Sherry reached into her horse's rucksack and pulled out a clay pot with a painted green edge at the top. She handed it to the dockmaster.

"What am I supposed to do with this?" The dockmaster asked while a grin parted his lips.

Lily said, "That's our vessel."

The dockmaster laughed so hard he bent to his knees trying to catch his breath.

"Isn't this the right vessel?" Lily asked Kestrel.

"I thought so. That's what the desert village gave us."

Lenny looked at them with a crooked smile. "The vessel is a human being."

Lily's eyes widened as she took in a small intake of breath. "A human being? Are you kidding me?"

"Does that mean we can't travel to the castle and capture the crystal?" Al asked.

The dockmaster got his breathing under control. "I can't let you go to the castle without a vessel. You would only die."

"Where are we supposed to get a vessel?" Lily asked. "What person would agree to something so bizarre? Can one of these warriors be the vessel?"

"No, the vessel has to be an unmarried woman."

Lily looked over at Kestrel in disbelief and shook her head. "So, it's either Sherry or me."

"With all the trauma you experienced at the sacred castle, you can't agree to this," Kestrel said. "Think of . . .," he rubbed his own forehead, "you know."

Lily grimaced. The symbol on her forehead. Right now, it seemed pretty useless. Its only power seemed to be its ability to control the seven-petaled flower. She didn't even know if she could become the vessel and still control the flower.

"What's involved with being the vessel? Is there some kind of test, to see if we qualify, or do I just say 'I'm the vessel' and hop in the boat?" Lily asked.

The dockmaster said, "There's a test. I don't know much about it other than you tell me you're the vessel, the test is given, and you die if you fail, or I allow you to cross the lake if you succeed."

All the teens looked at each other. Lily's pulse quickened as she pressed her lips tight. She should sit down and think about this. Kestrel might be right.

She looked at her best friend, Sherry. Her face expressed all that Lily felt within herself; fear, concern, and maybe doubt. Her friend had experienced so many hardships on this planet all because Lily had followed Kestrel through the portal. The time had come for her to step up and do something brave and support the group.

Lily and Sherry both said at the same moment, "I'll do it."

They smiled at each other and embraced.

Lily disengaged and asked, "The vessel is for the crystal? If we capture the crystal, does the crystal then reside in us?"

The dockmaster said, "You become the crystal."

"As the crystal, does that mean I am locked into this location as a resident of the castle for the rest of my life, until someone comes along and takes the crystal from me?"

The aged dockmaster's weathered face bore the history of countless trials; his eyes glimmered with a wisdom forged from many decades of guarding the precious magical object.

His voice resonated with authority, "The magical object, borne of forgotten realms and cloaked in potent enchantments, need not remain confined within the sacred walls of the castle." He pointed a bony finger at the castle. "Yet, know this: the castle, a bastion of strength and sentinel of secrets, has valiantly safeguarded this relic for a thousand years and more."

His words carried the weight of ancient legends and whispered prophecies, an echo of countless battles fought and victories won. The dockmaster's gaze pierced Lily's soul, her heart stirred by the gravity of his words.

He continued, "Many are the greedy who seek the power of its charms, but all who seek its power perish in the end."

Lily let out a little shriek.

Sherry held out her hand to her friend and they grasped each other tightly.

Al said hesitantly, "Are you sure we want to do this?"

"It's my fault. If I had gotten out of the mountains and to Paxton's place sooner, maybe we could have changed Zita's mind," Erik said.

"There's nothing you could have done. Taka would have taken her no matter what," Sherry said. "I've seen his power and ruthlessness. We can't let him take the crystal."

"So, do we still want to go?" Al asked.

"Let's wait here and see if Zita returns," Erik said, "if she doesn't return, then it means she wasn't able to capture the crystal. I'll return to Cugbert and continue to work on the next stage of my Pankratios service."

"No, we have to try and help," Lily said. "There must be something we can do."

"You heard the guy." Kestrel took her hand and lowered his voice, almost pleading, "If the magic says you aren't vessel material, then you die."

Al said to Sherry, "The same goes for you. What will we do if you both die?"

Lily gave the pot of the seven-petaled flower to Sherry, "Zita's my cousin and I want to help her." She kissed Kestrel, and then stepped close to the dockmaster. "I will try first."

Quest for the Crystal

Kestrel tried to stop her, "Don't do it, Lily. We don't know how it will affect you."

"It is my duty and my responsibility." Lily's fingers felt cold and a tingling sensation stabbed at her chest.

The dockmaster appraised her. "Allow me to examine your hands to see if you will qualify."

Lily offered her trembling hands.

The dockmaster took her hands into his own. His hands felt like history had been stored in every crack etched into his leathery palms. He closed his eyes and chanted.

> *Crystal born of flames and forged of heat,*
>
> *Is this the relic of legends you seek?*
>
> *Balefire crystal, from ancient tales and myth,*
>
> *This paragon of purity, can she uplift?*
>
> *Her life imbued with power, potential untold,*
>
> *To rule this realm with love and blessings bold.*
>
> *Crystal formed of fire, from ages past,*
>
> *This gem of perfection, forever to last.*
>
> *With magic and wonder, this crystal so bright,*
>
> *Shall guide the way with its radiant light.*
>
> *A symbol of hope, a beacon of peace,*
>
> *This crystal of fire, may her reign never cease.*

A wind picked up across the lake, blowing hot air from the castle. The gust grew in wildness and fury. The wind seemed to hesitate, and then it engulfed Lily, encircling her like a dust devil in a Montana farm field. It whipped itself into a blue flame that burned in the wind but didn't touch her. The flame surrounded Lily but she continued to stand motionless in its presence.

As she stood within the flaming tornado of fire, images of ancient battles danced in her mind, conjuring visions of warriors clad in gleaming armor, their swords clashing with righteous fury. The many guardians of the castle's secrets protected the magical artifact in this real-life vision.

Despite the fire not hurting her physically, the intense environment evoked fear within her. Lily hoped her friends knew she still lived within the tornado's fury. She hoped she survived this test.

A woman's voice spoke to her from within the flames that surrounded her, "What are you willing to give up to become the crystal?"

Lily thought through the question. If she became the crystal, it sounded like she might be hunted by others to use the powers gained from the object. The last person to capture the crystal found it necessary to create this magical area to protect their treasure. Was she willing to live a life like this for literally thousands of years as the crystal?

She might have to give up her relationship with Kestrel. They had gotten so close over the last few weeks; it would hurt to let him go. Yet, if she said yes, she'd be making a commitment to her home planet. She hoped her mother would be proud that she chose to help save her cousin instead of only thinking of herself. If she said 'yes,' they could take the next step to rescue Zita.

Lily said, "Yes. I am willing to give up anything necessary to save my cousin. Whether it's my own comfort, safety, or even my own life, I would not hesitate to make any sacrifice required. My friend's well-being is paramount, and I would do whatever it takes to ensure her rescue."

The fire roared, blocking out all sound and sight. The images of the fire seemed to burn within her retinas.

The voice spoke once more, "In the face of adversity, how do you maintain your determination and focus?"

"I remind myself of the purpose of my life on this planet. I draw strength from the love and bond I share with my friends. I visualize their faces, their smiles, and keep reminding myself that their lives are in jeopardy. This fuels my resolve to push forward, no matter how daunting the situation may be."

The tornado of fire resolved to reds and yellows, and Lily wondered if the tests were finished and if she had passed. Then it roared once more as if driven by more fuel being added from above.

The voice said, "This is the last question."

Oh good, Lily thought, *I'm almost finished.* Thinking that only made her anxious about what might occur next.

"Why is your friendship with these people worth risking your life for?"

Lily thought back to her brief time on this planet. She had been kidnapped and her life had been in danger. Erik, Sherry and Al didn't hesitate to come after her. They put their lives at risk to save her from peril at the hands of Zita's dad. Al survived the dangers of the dungeon to save her. Erik had talked Zita into helping to rescue her when she had to do things that put her own father at risk. And Sherry had turned into the Crown of Anticletus and helped keep Lily from a prison that would have killed her.

Lily answered, "My friendship with these people is worth risking my life for because they have been there for me through terrible dangers and risks. They have supported me, encouraged me, and stood by my side when I needed them most. We share a deep connection and understanding that transcends words. The thought of losing them is unbearable, and I believe that true friendship demands unwavering loyalty and sacrifice."

The fury of the tornado increased, producing a horrible noise. Lily held her hands over her ears until the sound dissipated. She felt the skin on her forearm grow hot. Something pressed upon her arm. Then a mark appeared. It started as a faint, shimmering yellow glow and gradually grew brighter and more defined as a tattoo formed on her wrist. A warm, tingling sensation spread across her body, as an infusion of magical energy bolted through her body.

"We have sealed the deal. You are now a worthy vessel for the Crystal of Zaraboth."

Lily looked down at two symbols tattooed on her arm. The first showed a penciled line of a tornado and the second an image of multiple rings intertwined in different ways with space between the rings.

As quickly as it had appeared the phenomenon disappeared in a bright flash of flame.

Lily shook her head and then ran her hands through her wind-blown blond hair, trying to tidy it.

She turned her attention to the dockmaster who said, "The castle is a place of danger and mystery, a quest where only the resolute and reckless venture. I suggest you go home."

Lily reeled from her experience with the crazy flaming tornado, as she thought through the deal and commitment she had agreed upon. Her heart pounded as she wondered what she had just agreed to. She had started this trip with her friends from Montana and boyfriend, Kestrel, but at this moment things had all changed. After the next few hours, she might never see them ever again.

Kestrel whispered, "You must say something to the dockmaster. Respond to his comment."

Lily snapped back to the situation at hand. She didn't know what to say and stood there with her mouth open.

Al stepped in front of Lily. "We seek to prove our worth and will not be dissuaded. I listen to the whispers of the castle and heed its siren call."

The dockmaster stayed silent for a few moments. Birds screeched in the distance, searching for food.

Lily stared at the dockmaster. The man didn't move or say anything. He acted like someone spoke to him through an ear piece or something. Had Al said the wrong thing?

The dockmaster intoned in a deep voice, "The boat is coming, pick your eight."

CHAPTER 63

A long rowboat docked at the platform next to the hut. Lenny and the desert wizard jumped in first. Al worried that the remaining warriors would try to get in, leaving him and his friends left standing on the dock. His stomach felt queasy, and the smell of rotten eggs seemed to burn into his sinuses.

Al didn't feel so good about this trip. The boat didn't look that sturdy or have very high sides. When he looked into the water and saw human remains cooking in the hot volcanic water, he almost threw up. They were all going to die.

Sherry and Lily got in behind the first two, followed by Erik and Kestrel. Al stepped into the last row and sank onto the bench. The desert warrior chosen by Lenny joined Al on the bench. Al felt like he should move closer to the side to give him room to defend himself in an attack from the warrior, but he feared the water more and returned to a position closer to the center.

The paddle master's face was shrouded within his hooded cape. Al couldn't even see eyes peering from beneath the cowl, and he decided to just sit and stare straight. He thought back to the days in high school and reading about Greek mythology where Charon transported people along the river Styx to the land of the dead.

The lake burped, emitting a noxious plume of sulfur. Al's nostrils quivered in revulsion as he attempted to block the putrid stench that snaked its way into his very core.

The rower valiantly plied his oar against the hot volcanic waters, battling not only the relentless winds but also the waves that surged with an otherworldly force. The boat swayed once or twice, forcing Al to hold tightly to the bench.

When they reached the island dock, Al hurried out of the boat and got as far from the lake as possible. He felt fortunate the wind blew away from the island at this point.

They had no supplies other than the water skins.

Erik said, "Be on the lookout for the first guardian. Who is it again?"

"A creature by the name of Ragadozo," Al said. "If I remember what I read, the creature likes to gamble."

Erik's eyes widened in disbelief. "Are our very fates determined by the whims of luck?"

Suddenly, a thunderous voice boomed, resonating through the air, as a creature made its presence known to the adventurers. "Cease your steps, mortals, for I am none other than Ragadozo," it proclaimed, its words dripping with ominous warning. "Proceed no further, lest you wish to become a delectable feast for my insatiable hunger."

Al jumped at Ragadozo's command. The creature had a human head with bushy untamed hair. Its large eyes were the size of saucers. Curved horns protruded from its forehead.

Erik said, "Let us pass, our group of adventurers have important business at the castle."

"I decide who has business at the castle, and I have decided you do not."

Al didn't believe he was about to say these words, but that's what he remembered from his time reading the scroll. "I bet you're wrong."

"I accept that bet. If you win, I'll let you pass. Lose and I enjoy a wonderful meal."

Al gasped as he noticed bones on the ground. Some looked like animal bones, but most of them appeared to be human. He hoped they were right that they could win this bet. He wasn't feeling very confident. He would be a little more relaxed if he could just zap the creature with a fireball.

Al glanced back at the others and they all nodded at him to continue. He handed his staff to Erik.

Ragadozo placed a large animal femur, streaked red with blood, on the ground and dug into the pocket of his leather shorts. He pulled out a handful of five flat stones. "We'll toss these stones. It's a simple game. Each stone two colors." He flipped a couple of stones showing the different colors. The colors he showed were either red, blue, yellow or green.

"I toss the stones into the air, when they land, we'll evaluate their colors. It's simple."

Al felt his pulse increase.

Ragadozo said, "When the stones land, we look at the colors that face the sky. A red stone beats a blue, which beats a yellow, which beats a green. Got it?"

Al didn't have it. His nerves were on high alert and he had hoped for a game of strategy instead of the simple luck of a throw of stones into the air.

"Best two out of three tosses, wins." Ragadozo tossed the stones in the air and Al moved back to make sure they didn't land on him.

They landed in the dirt all within about three feet of each other. Ragadozo regarded the toss and moaned. "Not a good throw for Ragadozo."

Al examined the stones. A yellow showed, along with a green, a blue, another green, and the last one a blue. It looked like they might have some luck.

Al picked up the stones and studied one of them. Then shook them in his hands as if he were playing D&D back home with multi-sided dice.

With a mighty heave, he tossed them into the sky. They bounced against each other a little, making a clacking noise, and then he read off his throw, "Yellow, blue, yellow." He moaned. "Two yellows."

"Yes, two yellows." Ragadozo cheered.

The last two stones landed. "Red and blue."

Ragadozo read off the score. "My yellow cancels one of your yellows. We each have two blues and they cancel each other. Your yellow beats my green and your red beats my green. You win the first hand." Ragadozo looked sad.

Al looked at his friends, smiled, and gave a thumbs up.

"You always did get lucky when we played fantasy games," Erik said.

"This time you go first."

Al picked up the stones and rubbed some of the dust off. He took a deep breath.

"You can't use magic." Ragadozo pointed a fat finger at Al. "If you cheat you lose."

"I'm not using magic," Al said. "I'm just cleaning the dust off the stones." He loosened the nervousness in his shoulders and tossed the stones into the air.

When they landed Al evaluated his score. "I have a yellow, blue, yellow, yellow, and red." He didn't feel too confident about his throw.

Sherry said, "Don't worry Al, you have this."

"My little friend, I think I will eat the red head first."

Ragadozo picked up the stones, with good dexterity in his large stubby sausage fingers. He shook them like Al did and tossed them.

They landed and Al read off the colors, "Yellow, red, blue, blue, and yellow." He had to think about what he saw.

Ragadozo called out the results. "My two yellows cancel two of your yellows. Our reds cancel each other and one of my blues cancels your one blue. That leaves my blue beating your remaining yellow. Ragadozo wins." He smiled, but his large teeth made it look like he wanted to eat something. Al turned his gaze away from the big hairy beast.

"My turn." He manipulated the stones into his hands and shook them. He dumped them with a little toss into the dirt at Al's feet.

A yellow, green, red, blue and yellow.

Ragadozo frowned. "Two yellows aren't good, but I can still win. I'm hungry tonight."

Al picked up the stones for his last throw. He blew into his hands.

Ragadozo stopped him. "No magic."

"It's not magic, just something we used to do on Earth to bring us luck." Al laughed. "I promise I didn't do magic."

Al didn't know why he laughed. His stomach felt like someone had tied it in knots and pulled them tight. He looked at his friends. Would they blame him for making the throw that killed them all?

He took a deep breath and launched the stones into the air.

The first landed as a yellow, which canceled Ragadozo's first throw. The second stone landed in the dirt showing a red. "A red, guys, I threw a red." He knew the stones contained only one red stone and it matched the red that Ragadozo threw. They still lived.

The next stone bounced off a boulder with a chiming sound, and it landed showing a blue. He needed another blue to beat Ragadozo. He groaned as the next one came down as a green. After four stones they were even. The last stone had a green on one side and a blue on the other. A blue would beat Ragadozo's yellow, but if the green side landed the teens would become the monster's next meal.

Al glanced back at the island dock and the boat had left. They weren't getting off the island alive if they lost.

The stone seemed to float abnormally long in the air, spinning fast, showing green, then blue, green, blue and then at last it landed.

CHAPTER 64

Al watched with anticipation as the stone flipped through the air, hoping the stone landed with the blue side up. It hit one of the other stones already on the ground with a solid thud, and then flipped once more and landed. The stone showed blue.

"We win!" Al raised his arms high above his head and moved his feet in a little dance.

Ragadozo bellowed, "You cheated. Ragadozo saw you blow magic on the stones."

Al held up his hands. "No. No magic. I cannot manipulate stones as they flip through the air." Erik handed Al his staff.

Ragadozo looked hungrily at the adventurers. "Ragadozo will eat you anyway."

Al swung his staff back and forth in the air and looked sternly at Ragadozo. "You will let us pass, or I will blast my way through you."

Ragadozo seemed to consider Al's words. He moved his mouth as if he were chewing his thoughts. He scratched his neck and then pulled on his left ear. Ragadozo's gaze appeared to evaluate the power of the small humans at his feet. "No! Ragadozo eats people who cheat."

"We didn't cheat." Al had to convince the monster that he wasn't going to bully them so he cast a fireball at a bush and it burst into flames. "Will you let us pass, or do I have to hurt you?" Al didn't want to hurt the giant; it seemed like a generally likeable monster as monsters go.

Ragadozo watched the bush burn for a few seconds. "Even though you cheated, you may pass."

"We didn't cheat." Al didn't wait, he hurried past the large, part human, part monster, before it changed its mind.

The others quickly followed him up the path.

Al checked behind him to verify that Ragadozo wasn't sneaking up on them. Everything looked okay.

They traveled up the twisting path for two hours. Little gnats attacked them in the hot, muggy heat, which forced Al to smack his arms and face repeatedly to reduce the feasting on his skin.

Erik asked, "Do you know where we're going?"

"I'm just taking the path in front of us," Al said. "I haven't seen any other path."

"Wouldn't it be faster if we just headed straight up the mountain?" Lenny asked.

"It might be faster, but I'm guessing not, otherwise the trail would go that way." Al pointed with his staff. "Onward."

Lenny said, "I'm thinking they purposely make us take this path to weaken our resolve when we reach the castle."

"Well, it's working," Al said.

"Shouldn't you guys be watching for the next guardian?" Sherry asked.

"Maybe the rest of the guardians are at the castle," Lenny said. "That way we can get help from Taka."

Kestrel said, "I wouldn't assume that."

"The next creature is called Risastór Skordýr. The scroll just showed a hand drawing of a bumblebee," Al said.

"A bumblebee?" Erik asked. "That doesn't sound so scary. We can beat a bumblebee. Can't we?"

"If it's a swarm of them like these dratted gnats, then we could be in trouble." Kestrel swatted his arm and moaned.

Something next to the path caught Al's attention. He pointed his staff at it. "Hey, look at this."

A large insect carcass the size of a bus lay on its side next to a boulder. Al poked it with his staff and a thousand flies and gnats swarmed over its body.

"Looks like Taka's group already killed it for us."

"Sweet," Erik said.

"Magic guardians can sometimes be killed, but regenerate." Kestrel stood back at a distance from the swarming insects. "If it is a bumblebee, then there might be a whole nest of these creatures."

Al examined the trees above them, searching for a beehive large enough to hold a bumblebee this size.

"Do you think Taka made it past this creature then?" Kestrel asked.

"We'd see some indication that they had died here if it was recent," Erik said. "I say, they made it past this guardian, and Zita is still alive."

A low buzzing sound caught Al's attention. "Do you guys hear that?"

Erik said, "It sounds like a couple of small airplane engines diving at us."

# # # #

Lily swiped at the gnats chewing on her arm. She felt relieved that Zita still lived, but her mind tumbled in a whirlwind of apprehension and unease. Each step brought her closer to the crystal they sought, but it also amplified her concerns of being seen as a pawn in this perilous game.

Her friends were the smartest of the smart at their Montana high school. Now, she had this crazy pattern permanently marking her face and the two tattoos that emblazoned her arm. The dockmaster had called her the vessel. What did it really mean? She suspected her dream of marrying Kestrel and living in his family's castle while raising their own family was dwindling. She had made the decision to be a pawn in a deadly game and she already regretted her decision to be the vessel for the crystal.

The limbs of the trees up ahead seemed to shake and flutter as if some animal flew between the trees grabbing the limbs for support. A cloud of insects flew into their path, forcing Lily to close her eyes at the onslaught. The buzzing grew deafening.

Al shouted, "Everyone get down."

Lily couldn't see anything, so not knowing what to do she dropped to the ground.

A creature buzzed above her, its wings flapped furiously, which forced the little insects to the sides of the path.

Lily glanced above her, where she saw three giant bumble-bees hover above the group. The giant insects circled the group of eight.

Erik said, "How are we supposed to defeat so many of these creatures?"

"I believe the scroll says this is where Lily is supposed to use the seven-petaled flower," Al said.

Lily's heart sank. They were expecting her to actually fight these creatures with her seven-petaled flower. She looked at the pot in her hands. The soil looked a little dry in the volcanic heat.

The flowers looked a little worse than they did when they defeated the Sacred Castle's guards. She searched her mind for some indication on how to encourage the flowers to mutate into the killer dragons. Lily shouted, "I don't know how to activate it."

Kestrel crawled over to her. "Do you put it up against the mark on your forehead?"

Lily had trouble hearing him with the loud buzzing of the insects. "I don't know."

"What did you do at the Sacred Castle?"

"I didn't do anything. It just transformed into the dragon heads once the light interacted with it from the obelisk."

One giant insect hovered closer and closer to the desert warrior who panicked, jumped up and raced back toward the island beach.

The insect followed the screaming man. A stinger suddenly appeared and stabbed the man. He ran ten feet before crumpling to the ground.

Lily felt dizzy, and black spots formed in her eyes. Her hands trembled shaking the plant.

"Relax Lily. It'll be okay." Kestrel reached to her forehead and pulled her scarf off.

"I don't know what I'm supposed to do. I want to help, but how?"

"Do you know an incantation?" Kestrel stroked her hair.

She shook her head.

"Can you drive mental energy into the flower?"

Lily shrugged, but tried. She willed the flower to grow into the seven-headed dragon, but it just sat in its pot looking slightly wilted.

The giant insect moved closer to Kestrel; its stinger pointed downward.

She couldn't let the creature kill Kestrel. As fear gripped her heart, Lily hesitated for only a moment, her trembling hand reached up to touch the symbol on her forehead. Her touch against the sacred mark sent a surge of tingling energy through her. She knew deep within that she had to overcome the block of magic and unlock the potential of the seven-petaled flower to save her friends and herself.

Summoning her resolve, she delved into her inner well of strength, seeking the knowledge and courage to activate the dragons. She closed her eyes and focused, trying to minimize the worry that the plant only worked within the energy of the obelisks at the Sacred Castle.

In her mind's eye, she envisioned the unseen forces converging around her, their power surging through her the jungle air. She raised the potted plant to touch the symbol marking her forehead, and felt her a force merge with the flower's latent magic.

With a surge of raw energy, Lily channeled her will and spoke ancient incantations, giving voice to her intentions with words she had never used before, in a language she didn't know. The flower trembled in response, its potential awakened by the ancient words.

Lily looked at Kestrel, who had created a shield to protect them, but the shield seemed to crumble under the vibrations of the bees' wings. She looked at her friends; each had a giant insect hovering closer.

She sang a song from Earth that she liked. A song of mystery and magic. It had moved her on Earth and she had remembered it here on Aloheno. The song echoed through her mind and the dragons stretched from their flower positions within the pot.

She didn't have to direct them; they seemed to know what to do. They seemed to sense a natural force that directed them to protect her and her friends.

The flower's petals changed colors, each different, green, yellow, blue, red, purple, lime, and orange. The petals grew, wriggling into sinuous shapes that became seven different heads. When each had reached full size, they began to snarl and growl.

Lily placed the pot on the ground and snuck into a small space between two boulders. Kestrel knelt in front of her, tossing electrical shocks at the insects.

The dragons of the plant reached their full height and began their assault on the insects. They roared in the battle while the buzzing of the giant insects forced Lily to hold her hands over her ears.

The orange dragon danced around one giant insect, as each tried to find a way to get past the other's defense. The sunlight glimmered off the dragon in an array of kaleidoscopic colors. The dragon's head moved lightning-fast, but the giant insect seemed to move even faster.

Lily's friends had all found time to move into small alcoves along the path for protection.

With a swift and merciless strike, the colossal insect's stinger pierced the majestic orange dragon's scales, plunging deep into its vulnerable flesh. The dragon screamed in agony. The wounded dragon's neck thrashed about wildly.

The orange dragon's strength waned; its life force ebbed away with each moment. Its vibrant, iridescent scales dulled, losing their luster, as if it surrendered to the grim fate that awaited. A mournful roar erupted from its mighty jaws.

Lily rushed out from her hiding place to attend to the orange dragon.

Kestrel tried to stop her, but he wasn't fast enough. "Don't go out there. It's not safe."

Lily stepped to the plant. It was difficult getting close as the remaining dragon heads fought the foe on all sides.

The lifeless body of the orange dragon settled upon the earth, its presence loomed large, even in death, its once vibrant red eyes now glazed over.

Lily dashed to its side and stroked its scales as its body trembled in the dirt. She gently rubbed the rough exterior of the beast; it generated a slight electrical discharge as she stroked its neck. She mourned the loss of the creature.

The blue dragon's teeth tore through a giant insect's exoskeleton and greenish blue liquid sprayed from the wound over rocks and bushes.

The insect tried to fly away, but its muscular connections to its wings were severed after the bite and it flew in a circle and smashed into a boulder.

The yellow dragon moved quicker than its enemy and managed to bite off the insect's wing, followed by an attack to the creature's back.

The insect attempted to strike with its stinger, but the dragon moved too quickly, bobbing and weaving away at critical moments. Without its wing, the insect couldn't stay in the air. It dropped to its small, but sturdy legs, and tried to run away from the battle.

The yellow dragon snapped at the fleeing insect and crippled its legs with a mighty bite.

The dragons worked in coordination and took down the remaining giant insects.

Lily heard the others whooping and hollering as she stroked the scales of the dead orange dragon. Tears welled up in her eyes, reflecting the anguish that gripped her soul. The weight of loss pressed upon her chest, making it difficult to draw a steady breath.

The other dragon heads swooped to their fallen comrade's body and began licking its scales. As they licked the orange dragon, it shrank, but once it returned to its flower shape in the pot, it dropped, spent, to the dirt.

As she wiped away her tears, Lily's gaze lifted, fixing upon her companions, united by grief and a shared purpose. With a deep breath, Lily steadied herself next to Kestrel.

Al shouted, "Let's go. We don't know if they retreated in fear or plan to return with a bigger army."

CHAPTER 65

Zita sat on the castle floor in the great room. The remaining members of Taka's party had camped out in the room for three days, waiting for Al and his group to arrive with a new vessel since Ekaterina was truly dead. Zita had tired of waiting and wanted to continue the quest for the crystal. She stood and looked out the castle window. The dead, feathered creature lay rotting where it had fallen. Nothing she did could make her feel comfortable.

"Let's take the stairs to the next floor and see what's there. We can identify a guardian and come back here to strategize on the best way to kill it."

Taka said, "I know what's there. A wild mage named Geirhild Hlifsteed. She carries the staff of Thorspikeson, a powerful staff made of ebony and mahogany with one end covered in gold and the other covered in bronze. She is a mage of great power and a legend at commanding the forces of nature."

"Then let's attack her and defeat her and grab the crystal."

"We lost our vessel. Without her, there is no reason to attempt to capture the magical object."

"So, your plan is to wait a hundred years until another group arrives with a vessel? I have no plans to stay here that long waiting for another group of adventurers."

"I have great faith that your friends are on their way to save you," Taka said, "if they found a vessel, then they are probably on the island right now advancing toward us."

Zita snorted, "They thought the vessel was a soup bowl. They aren't coming." Despite her words, she felt warmth radiating through her body at the thought that even Taka thought Erik and her friends were coming, but where would they find a vessel?

"Wait, I thought you left Lenny with a couple of wizards to keep them from crossing the lake."

"Lenny wouldn't be able to stop them, but I thought he might delay them, in case we had what we needed to make a play for the crystal."

Zita thought, *we still need the Crown of Anticletus, so without Sherry we would fail anyway.* She just had to be patient. "Do you have a plan to defeat Geirhild Hlifsteed?"

Taka didn't say anything for a few moments. "I have the wand, which I believe will be enough to defeat her."

"By yourself, you'll defeat this great legend?" Zita smirked at the man's arrogance.

"You discount my abilities, little child."

Zita thought his magical abilities were overrated. She didn't think he could defeat the great mage by himself. She wondered what it would take to defeat a master in all the elemental forces.

She looked out the window once more and saw movement in the grass. Had another monster replaced the one she killed?

"Taka, I see something in the meadow. Does the monster live, and will it enter the castle?"

"There's only one monster, the last known member of its breed." He hurried to the window. "It's almost like you willed your friends to the island."

Zita finally saw what caused the movement. They walked in pairs, and then the man she waited for, Erik rounded the trees. Zita bolted out the door and raced across the lawn toward Erik.

As she approached, Erik must have recognized her, because he pushed past his friends toward Zita.

She jumped into his arms, peppering him with kisses. She was euphoric at being reunited with Erik.

The others joined Erik and Zita, all saying their hellos and asking about each other's welfare.

"Are you by yourself?" Erik asked.

Zita shook her head. "Taka's here."

"Has he blocked your magic?" Al asked.

She nodded in disappointment.

Al looked at Kestrel. "What should we do?"

"I have no defense against their spell. We have to accept the fact that we can't get past that block."

Taka and Dakarai strolled up to the teens. "Don't even try it. We already have your magic blocked."

"What happens if you need our help?" Al asked.

Taka smirked. "We have everything we need now that you have arrived with a vessel." He examined Lily and Sherry looking for signs of who had chosen to be the vessel.

Zita wondered which one had volunteered. She searched their eyes for an indication, but neither showed any signs on their faces that they were the vessel.

"Zita, you asked when we are going to defeat Geirhild Hlifsteed. In the hour," Taka said. "Come into the castle, my friends, and rest. We have a busy night ahead of us."

Zita talked with her friends as they sat and ate. She asked them how they defeated each guardian, and they asked her the same questions. They caught up on the news since she departed, but mostly she just stared into Erik's blue eyes.

An hour passed quickly, and Taka gave the signal to move. He positioned the two desert wizards and Dakarai ahead of him as their magic hadn't been blocked. The others he pushed behind him. "If you want to live, I suggest you stay behind my protective shield."

Zita shook her head at the arrogant man. Even though she knew the magical strength of everyone in the castle, she didn't think they could defeat the legendary mage.

They climbed three flights of stairs until they reached a long corridor. Within the magnificent castle, the corridor stood as a testament to its past grandeur. Its stone walls were adorned with exquisite tapestries depicting ancient battles. The air felt thick with a sense of anticipation.

The corridor stretched far into the distance, seemingly endless, with arches and alcoves lining the sides. Shimmering sconces illuminated the way, casting dancing shadows that played tricks on the eye.

The corridor's acoustics amplified even the softest of sounds, creating an eerie echo that whispered through the air. It felt as if the castle itself held its breath, waiting to witness the clash of primeval magical forces about to unfold within its ancient walls.

At regular intervals along the corridor, towering suits of armor stood sentinel, their metal forms reflecting the dim candlelight. Their presence added an intimidating aura, as if they were guardians of the castle's secrets, watching the adventurers' every move and preparing to attack at a moment's notice.

Zita could discern faint traces of enchantments, arcane symbols etched into the stone floor but worn from numerous footsteps through the centuries. These spiritual markings added a supernatural touch that hinted at the castle's past.

She felt a prickling on her scalp as unease crept up her spine. She sensed the air being charged with magical energy. Had Taka released his magical shield already? She didn't think this battle would go in Taka's favor, and she wished he would unblock her and her friends so they might help.

The long corridor offered both advantages and challenges. Its length allowed ample space for strategic maneuvering, providing opportunities for Taka's wizards to plan and execute their spells. However, its narrow confines limited escape routes and forced the combatants into close quarters.

Zita couldn't stand the tension. Where was Geirhild Hlifsteed? They could have already passed her in the hallway, and she might be behind them already. She looked behind her, though the corridor remained empty.

"I don't have a good feeling here. Give us our magic so we can help you."

Taka laughed, "Everything's under control."

Exquisite stained-glass windows adorned some of the alcoves where light from an unknown source filtered through, casting a kaleidoscope of hues upon the stone floor. These stained-glass scenes depicted ancient legends and mythical creatures, which enhanced the imminent clash of magic.

Zita looked at her friends. Al's face had turned ashen white. Lily kept blinking her eyes. Erik would look forward a moment and then glance behind as if in anticipation of someone coming up from behind. Sherry had a firm grip on Al's arm. They were as scared as she felt. She wanted to go hide in one of the alcoves, though even those scared her with their armored sentinels.

A wave of energy crashed through Taka's magic shield and blasted the leading desert wizard. He flopped like a dying fish as a ball of electricity pulsated off his spasming body, which eventually lay limp on the floor. Geirhild Hlifsteed had attacked first. Zita didn't even see the mage.

Taka returned to his feet and waved his wand. He chanted a spell that Zita didn't recognize. The whole corridor flickered with a swirling vortex of enchanted wind that blasted in the direction of the attack from Geirhild Hlifsteed.

When the magic hit the mage, she materialized at the far end of the corridor. She stood holding the staff of Thorspikeson, its gold end pointed toward the ceiling. The mage accepted the blast from Taka and didn't even flinch.

Zita assumed Taka's attack wasn't to injure his adversary but to make her visible. It's difficult to battle someone you can't see.

The mage pointed her staff at the adventurers and delivered a powerful tide of blue luminescence down the corridor. The spell journeyed into each alcove and touched each armored sentinel.

Zita watched in horror as the sentinels came to life in a symphony of creaking metal.

"Taka, I want my magic. Don't leave us hanging without a way to protect ourselves."

Taka shouted, "Don't worry, I have this." He pointed his wand at Dakarai. "Cast forth the spell of ancients, it's time for us to take our advantage!"

The sentinels formed together in the corridor and marched toward the adventurers.

Zita and her friends had bunched up into a tight group. With a glance behind, Zita saw additional sentinels forming a battle line. She yelled, "We have soldiers behind us."

Dakarai raised his hands in a magical connection as Taka waved his wand at the mage.

Zita had never seen any magic like this before. Taka forced a swirl of maroon and white down the hallway and it smacked into the line of advancing armored soldiers. The first two lines of empty armor flew into the air, bouncing off the ceilings and scattering their lifeless armor across the floor.

The magic did nothing for the attackers behind Zita.

Al tapped his staff on the floor and shouted, "Taka give me my magic, I can't help you without it."

Erik drew the Sword of Freedom from its sheath and prepared for battle.

Zita didn't like the way the battle was shaping up. Taka could handle some of the mage's power and magic, but he didn't seem to be fully in control. He had gotten himself entangled in a situation far beyond his capabilities.

Zita cried out again, "Taka, let us help you."

He replied, "I got this."

Erik battled the sentinels that had approached from their rear. Zita watched his awkward swordplay. The sentinels' swords raked his arms and legs, drawing blood, but thankfully not enough to kill him. The battle with the enchanted armor drew closer to the adventurers.

Sherry pulled Al into one of the corridor's vacated alcoves and held him tight.

Al protested, "Wait, I can help."

"Not without your magic."

Kestrel pushed Lily in with them. Erik continued to block the sentinels' swords, backing toward the alcove with the others as they continued to battle.

Zita saw that in a few moments they'd be trapped, and their only hope to stay alive depended on Erik's ability with the Sword of Freedom.

CHAPTER 66

Zita worried about Erik and her own life as the mage's armored sentinels continued to advance toward the rear of Taka's team. The corridor space became crowded as the sentinels advanced and surrounded the adventurers.

Zita yelled at Taka, "They're coming at us back here. Give us our magic so we can help you. Can you afford to lose your only vessel?" She looked into Lily's eyes, trying to discern which of the two women had become the vessel.

An explosion rocked the corridor, and the sentinels between the mage and the adventurers erupted against the walls and ceiling. Many of the metal soldiers shattered into piles of metal, as the force of the blast created a great soundwave that rocked the passage forcing Al, Sherry and Lily to fall to the floor.

Erik swayed as the blast wave buckled the corridor floor, but he managed to stay on his feet as he continued to parry with the armored sentinels.

Geirhild Hlifsteed forced a spell through the corridor causing plants to grow instantly in the enclosed space. The rapidly growing vines searched out the adventurers.

Zita bit her lip at this new attack from the mage. The mage's magic filled the air with an ominous aura. Her thoughts raced as the impending danger closed in. Taka was out of control. His obstinance, and the failure of his efforts to defeat the mage would be the death of the rest of the group.

Geirhild was indeed a mighty mage, one that could simultaneously manipulate the sentinels, block Taka's attacks, and use the power of nature.

Zita stepped on the growing vines, trying to prevent them from twining themselves around her.

Al walloped the vines with his staff to no avail; they continued to grow and advance.

Taka sent forth the immense darkness spell. Its ancient shadow pulsed through the hallway toward Geirhild. If it landed, it would force the mage into a transitory state between light and darkness, disabling her magic and power.

The mage raised her staff, and a radiant shield of light formed around her. The darkness was deflected and dissipated harmlessly around her.

Zita had to talk sense into Taka, and she didn't have much time. A vine had found her and wrapped its dangerous creepers around her leg. She refused to die like this, at the hands of a crazed wizard who was too power-hungry to accept help. Taka could not defeat the mage, even with the Imperium wand.

Zita cried out to Erik, "Help me get this vine off." She tugged on the out-of-control plant.

"I'm a little busy back here." He whacked at his attackers with a wild swing that missed.

"Please?"

Erik turned, and brought the sword down hard on the advancing plant that had encircled Zita's leg. He split the plant from its root and Zita managed to unwrap the vine from her leg.

A jungle had grown between Taka and Geirhild.

Zita ran to Taka and grabbed his arm. "Let us help you. Remove the block."

"Get away from me, I almost have her beat." He shook off her arm and forced a ray of fire from his wand directed at the growing plants.

The forest went up in flames.

Zita went ballistic. "Are you crazy? You'll kill us all."

Black smoke darkened the corridor ceiling as the fire burned out of control, advancing toward Zita and the others.

Taka sent out another blast at Geirhild, but Zita didn't think she had stayed in the same location once the fire started.

Zita looked around her for any signs of the mage.

The smoke grew thicker.

Dakarai ran to Taka. "I'm going to release the block on the others."

"Don't do it. I can defeat the mage myself."

Dakarai grabbed Taka's shoulder. "Let them take the blunt force from the mage. That will leave our magic intact to grab the crystal. Let them die."

That seemed to make Taka happy. He smiled and nodded at Dakarai.

As the smoke billowed into the corridor, it hindered visibility and filled the air with acrid fumes. Zita felt a surge of adrenaline which heightened her faculties. An alarm raced through her body; her instincts screamed for them to escape the encroaching peril. The noxious smoke stung her eyes and made it difficult to see and breathe. Her lungs ached for clean air, and a primal fear rose within her as she sensed the imminent threat of the fire's wrath.

In spite of this danger, Zita felt the return of her magic. She reacted swiftly and conjured a gust of wind to push back the smoke. Her mind raced as she searched for the most effective spells to combat the flames and protect her friends.

Al beat her to it as he cast an incantation at the fire that summoned water which gushed from the ceiling cascading on Zita and her comrades.

Kestrel chanted a spell that Zita remembered from her childhood. Castle wizards used the spell to keep the castle square free of weeds and high grass. The enchantment made the vines whither, and they died and turned brown beneath their feet.

Erik continued to battle the sentinels with his sword. His arms were sliced and bloody from the many nicks of his opponent's swords.

Zita had to help Erik. She couldn't afford to see him sliced into pieces. As the group's healer, they needed him alive.

She raised her hands to the sky and commanded, "Braeda burt bladey."

The sentinels continued their attack on Erik.

Zita wondered if she had said the wrong words. Her father had taught her the spell years ago when they were having fun one night. The spell should melt the sentinel's blades, but nothing happened. Had the mage made the spell ineffective or had she said the wrong words?

She tried again switching the last word from bla-day to bla-dee. "Braeda burt bladee."

The sentinels lunged at Erik, their swords aimed for him, but upon contact with Erik's blade, a remarkable sight unfolded. Instead of Erik's weapon suffering the same fate as the others, the sentinels' blades began to melt. In a surprising turn of events, their swords became molten metal, causing a chain reaction of chaos.

The once-formidable sentinels, their ability to slice stripped away, found themselves in a twisted ballet of metallic collision. Their molten weapons intertwined, and the sentinels clashed and clanged as they crashed into each other.

As the echoes of metal clanging upon metal died away, Zita searched for Geirhild. The mighty mage stood tall, her staff pulsating with raw power, while the other wizards—Al, Kestrel, Taka, Dakarai and the desert wizard—exchanged determined glances.

Zita realized that direct attacks might not be enough to defeat their adversary. She began weaving intricate spells, casting illusions of multiple wizards, creating a dazzling display of mirrored images. The mage's eyes darted around, looking for a target.

Al raised his staff and pointed it at the mage, sending a powerful force wave hurtling towards the mage. The wave crashed into the mage's shield, causing it to flicker.

With a gesture, Kestrel cast a powerful binding spell in an attempt to restrain the mage's movements. But the mage, channeling her immense power, shattered the bindings with a twist of her staff. The spell also caused an eruption of energy that pulsated through the corridor and knocked the adventurers to the floor.

Zita's illusions disappeared into nothingness.

Al said, "I don't think we can defeat her."

Taka commanded, "Keep attacking, she can't defeat us if we keep attacking."

Zita rolled her eyes. Did Taka never engage in a battle with someone more powerful? She couldn't believe the man's arrogance. Sometimes you're outmatched, but Zita knew they had to keep trying to defeat the mage. She wanted the crystal in order to win back the crown of Velidred.

Zita looked at her friends, and they seemed to liquefy before her. Their images turned into an unsolid jelly-like substance; they wobbled back and forth. She reached out to Erik. "Are you okay?"

"I'm okay. You look like your very substance has been altered into a fluid."

Zita touched Erik's arm, surprised when he felt solid. The mage had used a reality distortion spell on them. They weren't injured in any way, but the distortion of their bodies disoriented her. She had trouble standing, turned, and vomited on the floor.

Two others in the group experienced the same problem.

Al raised his hand to his mouth and tried to swallow, before belting out, "Any of you know how to beat this spell?"

Taka raised his wand and pointed it at the mage. With a flip of his wrist, he chanted the words, "Återställande av jämvikt." A Restoration of Equilibrium spell sped from the powerful Imperium Wand.

Zita waited for the spell to work. She had seen the spell work in the past, when a wizard had sickened the castle because she hadn't gotten her way. Her dad had used the spell to restore the castle to normal.

Nothing changed.

Zita wanted to say something, but her stomach lurched and she went back to her knees. There had to be a solution to this spell.

Al stood, but to Zita he appeared to wobble. She had to close her eyes because looking at him made her feel worse.

"Klarhet I sinnet!" Al commanded as he spun his staff over his head in great sweeping circles.

"What was that?" Erik asked.

Al said, "Clarity of Mind. It's supposed to create a protective aura around us, shield our minds from external influences and restore mental clarity."

Zita felt vulnerable, groveling on her hands and knees as she tried to balance. *What else can the mage be planning? We're all in trouble.*

She took a chance and opened her eyes. The room spun around her and she closed them again.

"It's not working." Erik dropped to all fours.

Zita tried to concentrate her mind on defeating the mage's spell. The group of adventurers was in a state of disarray and confusion. Her own mind seemed to pulsate. Here they were trying to send fireballs at the mage, and she used a simple chant to disorient her enemy, which left them incapacitated.

Still on all fours, she slowed her breathing and focused on a spot on the floor five feet away. Her mind had shifted from unease to desperation in solving this problem. Her arms shook and trembled as she rocked in place. She refused to die at the hands of the mage, and resolved to find an answer to the bewitchment that had left her immobilized.

She strove to quiet her racing thoughts, searching for the mental clarity she needed to beat the mage's powerful spell. After many moments reviewing her repertoire of sorcery, she remembered one that she had never used, but had seen in a scroll, years earlier.

A flicker of relief washed over her face as the idea of using the temporal anchoring chant emerged from her inner thoughts. Zita felt a glimmer of hope that this spell might withstand the mage's onslaught. She hoped it wasn't too late.

Zita focused on the spot on the floor, anchoring her in the present. Only intense concentration could help her to speak the incantation correctly. She narrowed her thoughts to the present moment and poured every ounce of energy she possessed into the incantation. She thought of her friends and visualized the results she hoped to achieve with the magic.

Tentatively, she lifted one hand to cast the spell. Remaining poised to return to a stable four-point stance, she concentrated on saying the words, "Temporalis Anchora." Her thoughts and desires intertwined within her mind, and she knew that she must focus on the necklace around her neck as the spell left her fingers.

CHAPTER 67

The Temporal Anchoring incantation formed as a bubble around Zita, and grew into a gentle surge of energy. She forced the bubble to expand and it enveloped her friends and the other wizards. The disorienting effects of the distortion spell seemed to drain from her mind. Her thoughts cleared, and her senses sharpened.

Zita's senses seemed to harmonize with her body, and the nausea sensation subsided. In a couple of moments, Zita felt strong enough to stand. Erik helped her to her feet.

"Did any of you see where the mage went?" Taka eyes were bright and his pupils tight. The stress of this test of his magic against the mage's power was taking its toll on him.

"I thought Zita's spell vanquished our enemy the mage," Al said.

"The mage still lives, and we are certainly outclassed," Dakarai said.

"Why didn't she kill us when we were incapacitated?" Al asked. "That would have been easy for her."

No one answered the question.

"How are we supposed to defeat her?" Lily asked.

Zita walked over to Taka. "We defeat her by working together." She pounded her finger in his chest. "Haven't you ever joined forces with other wizards?" She needed to break down his wall of I'm-better-than-everyone-else if they hoped to defeat this powerful mage.

Taka slapped her hand away. "If you ever touch me again, I'll to block your magic and you'll never have access to it."

Zita stood face to face with him. "You would be dead now if not for me."

Taka pushed her away. "Let's find the mage." He walked away from Zita.

Zita rushed after him ready to re-engage, but Erik grabbed her shoulder and held her back.

"Let's find the mage before we irritate Taka any more. We need your brains and magic to defeat the mage."

Zita said, "We need more than just me. That's what I've been trying to tell this brain-dead know nothing wizard."

"He'll get there. Have patience," Erik said.

Zita's jaw hurt as she attempted to loosen the frustration steaming through her body. In a strained voice she said, "Have patience? We almost died back there. We don't have time for patience. Geirhild is playing with us. When she decides to kill us, it'll be too late to work together."

Erik gently guided Zita away from another confrontation.

They walked through the corridor, tension exuding from the adventurers as they inspected each alcove for signs of the mage or tell-tale traces of magic that might lead to her.

"Have you ever worked in a bonded group?" Al asked.

"I've seen it done by my father." Zita wiped sweat from her brow. "I've never actually done it myself."

"What's involved?"

"The wizards join hands and this physical contact creates a conduit for their magic to flow harmoniously, fostering a collective bond. Similar to the magic block that Taka employs, our magic is not our own to use. We are locked into the lead wizard's focal point. That wizard's power is then enhanced by the others."

Al whistled. "That sounds interesting. Is that something we have to practice?"

Zita nodded. "It takes years to get it right."

"Then why should we bother? I've never done it. Kestrel, have you practiced this magical bonding?"

He shook his head.

"Won't it be more dangerous if we are bonded and aren't able to utilize our own skill sets?" Al scratched the back of his neck. "We would have died back there if we all hadn't tried to reverse the spell. It's only when you used your spell that we counteracted it enough to break it."

"Yes, there is a risk involved, but we can't beat her as individuals." Zita rubbed her hands across her face as frustration built within her.

When the adventurers reached the end of the corridor, they hadn't found Geirhild. A set of stairs led upward.

"Follow me and be ready for combat." Taka commanded.

Zita looked back at the corridor. The sentinels lay in heaps on the floor, and the ceiling was blackened with soot from the fire. The odor of fire still smoldering filled the corridor. The magic-induced plants smelled of late fall decay.

She pointed up the stairway. "Lead the way."

With an explosive force surging from their rear, a powerful gust of wind blasted them towards the wall.

Zita hit her head and bounced off the wall, landing in a heap on the floor. Her world went dark.

CHAPTER 68

Al hit the wall with his shoulder and he lost his grip on his staff which fell to the floor. He reached to retrieve the staff, but it flew from the floor down the corridor into Geirhild's open hand.

As she scrutinized the staff with intense curiosity, a sense of amusement overtook her, and she erupted into a maniacal laughter that echoed through the air. "Alpherge the Mighty still lives in the magic of the staff. I thought I had defeated you many years ago, and yet you live."

Al cried out, "Give it back. That's my staff."

Geirhild threw a fireball at Al, and he dropped to the floor as it exploded against the back wall.

He suddenly seemed to burn with fever, and he tightened his hands into fists of rage. He had worked so hard for the staff and now it lay in the hands of a crazed mage too powerful to defeat.

He shouted, "Come staff!"

Geirhild laughed.

Al checked on the others. Erik tended to Zita, who lay motionless on the floor. Taka wasn't in sight. Had he already escaped up the stairs? Dakarai looked dazed. Kestrel wobbled on unsteady legs; a gash had opened on his forehead, and blood dripped into his eyes. Lily dabbed at Kestrel's wound with a cloth.

Al's eye widened in disbelief. *I can't defeat the mage by myself!* He looked at the others. They were in big trouble.

Geirhild's presence seemed to shimmer as a radiant aura enveloped her.

Al threw up a shield. Whatever she planned to throw at them, he would do everything possible to save his friends.

Geirhild touched the gold end of her staff to the top of Al's staff. White-blue energy flickered between them. As she pulled the staffs apart, electricity sparked, creating a crackling sound, a sharp, repetitive popping noise. The pungent smell of ozone permeated the corridor.

The sizzling continued for a few seconds, then it turned into a low hum that crescendoed into a buzzing that reminded Al of being near transformers on Earth.

The mage looked up at Al and grinned.

Al's blood pulsed in his head, the sound thrashing in his ears, as he waited for the mage's next incantation. He held his trembling hands in front of his face, trying to hold the concentration needed to maintain the shield. His shields normally held pretty well, but he didn't trust this one against the mage's knowledge and power.

The mage let loose her fury.

The sorcerer's conjuration bolted down the corridor, but it seemed that time slowed. The mage had added a trick that forced time to stall.

Al thought his heart would stop beating as the lightning took seconds to reach him instead of an instantaneous strike. The mage continued her desire to toy with her weaker opponents. He held his shield firm against the expected onslaught but worried it wouldn't hold.

The bolt drew closer.

Kestrel's hand touched his right shoulder.

A second hand touched his left shoulder. Dakarai stood next to him.

A surge of magical energy flowed into the shield.

The bolt struck the shield, causing it to blow inward, closer and closer to Al's face, but then the shield rebounded away from him.

Geirhild did not relent. Another bolt struck the shield and came even closer to Al's face.

He felt the bonded magic from the other two wizards, and the shield held.

A third electrical strike flared from the staffs in Geirhild's hands as she sent more power into the incantation.

Dakarai said something behind Al.

He didn't know if he heard Dakarai or only sensed what was about to happen, but he dropped to the floor along with the others.

The bolt struck the shield, which bubbled inward and finally broke. The bolt struck the back wall, shattering bricks which crumbled to the floor.

The desert wizard came up to the others.

Al looked at Erik, who still attended to Zita. She lay prone on the floor as Erik protected her with his body from flying debris.

"Should we run like Taka?" Al felt his heart beat rapidly at fear of his imminent death.

Dakarai said, "No, we have to bond and synchronize our magical focus. Our only hope is to work in harmony."

"It could take years." Kestrel maintained his firm grip on Al's shoulder.

Dakarai held out his hand to Al. "We have only moments. Grab my hand."

Al placed his hand in Dakarai's. Kestrel and the desert wizard joined with the others.

"Are you leading this, Dakarai?" Al asked.

"No, you're stronger."

Fear gripped his chest. "I don't know what I'm doing." He wondered if Dakarai had put him in this position so if they failed, Al would die instead of him.

The mage started marching toward the four wizards. She used magic to clear the floor of the sentinel debris, sending it banging and crashing against the walls and into the alcoves.

A funny thought entered Al's mind, *who is responsible for cleaning up this mess?*

Geirhild looked angry, and Al tried to anticipate what spell she might throw. But they couldn't just play defense, that strategy would eventually kill them. They needed an offensive plan. Al wished he had his grandfather and the other wizards on the staff to talk to and give him guidance.

The mage stopped twenty feet away. The air crackled with an electrifying tension as the mage raised her hands, gripping the two staffs tightly. In a swift, precise motion, she brought the two staffs together with a resounding smack that echoed through the corridor.

The collision of the staffs reverberated with a startling intensity, producing a thunderous sound that pierced the air. The sheer force of the impact sent shockwaves rippling through the castle, causing the very corridor floor to tremble beneath the wizards' feet. The clash of the staffs had unleashed a seismic disturbance, momentarily distorting reality itself.

As the sound reverberated through the corridor, an enigmatic aroma wafted through the air. The scent combined a complex blend of arcane energy, ancient tomes, and a hint of something elusive and forbidden.

Al and the others shook and swayed as the shockwave rippled under their feet.

Al felt the sound waves wash over them, a tangible force that resonated within his being, stirring a mix of awe, trepidation, and determination. The aroma enveloped him, infusing the air he breathed with an aura of anticipation.

The four wizards held their clasped hands and rode out the wave as it rebounded back toward the confident mage.

Al thought of the power of his staff. Maybe the staff wouldn't come when he called, but could he influence it in any way while Geirhild controlled it?

Al raised his hands despite the thunderous sound reverberating around him. He dragged Kestrel's and Dakarai's hands into the air with his.

The flame sword Al had created days before when he fought the snake came to his mind as a weapon against the powerful Geirhild. He needed to turn the staff and make it attack Geirhild. He concentrated on the plan and forced his trembling frame to calm.

He shouted the command, "Nina rawraq espada."

In an instant, a brilliant burst of flames erupted from the staff, engulfing it in a searing blaze. The staff transformed once more into a fiery sword that crackled and danced with ethereal flames. Al moved his arms awkwardly while holding onto the other wizards. He forced the staff to move in the air and attack Geirhild.

She wasn't expecting the attack, and the burning metal slashed at her stomach and drew blood.

Geirhild screamed.

Erik yelled out, "Yes!"

Al kept up the attack, forcing the mage to retreat. She lost her grip on Al's staff. As the wizards channeled their magic into Al, an intricate interplay of energy manifested between them. Ethereal arcs of light pulsated between them, harmonizing the synchronization of their magical powers. This energy connection amplified their collective strength.

Al struck her calves with the flaming sword and she fell to the floor.

Geirhild turned her head to look at the flaming blade above her. She held out her hands in defense.

Kestrel whispered, "Finish her."

Al never felt comfortable on this planet doing the things to humans that this ancient and backward society required, but he felt Dakarai's presence through the magic bond they had created and it forced him to attack. Al closed his eyes as he plunged the sword into the mage's chest.

As Al gazed upon the lifeless body of the once-mighty mage, conflicting emotions surged within him—intertwining happiness and sadness, mingling regret with a sense of accomplishment. He grappled with the weight of his actions, knowing that he had no other choice but to resort to such a drastic measure.

Kestrel slapped Al's shoulder. "You did it."

Al looked at the ceiling. "Yes. Not just me. All of us." Deep within his consciousness, a bittersweet realization took hold—they had succeeded in vanquishing the mage.

Sherry came to him and held his hand. "Are you okay?"

He nodded slightly and pulled her in for a tight hug.

They all gathered around Erik who tended to Zita. He had pulled the Sword of Freedom from its sheath and pointed its sharp end to her head.

Sherry asked, "Will she be okay?"

Erik shrugged, "She's still breathing. I need to delve a little into her brain. She hit the wall hard with her head."

Al said. "She's pretty hardheaded, I wouldn't have expected the wall to have that big of an impact on her."

Sherry poked him in the ribs. "Don't be mean."

They stood staring while they waited for Erik to finish healing Zita. After five minutes, she opened her eyes and looked at everyone.

Erik held her hands and then helped her to stand.

Zita glanced down the hallway at the mage, and her eyes widened in surprise.

Dakarai said, "We followed your advice and bonded our magic, otherwise we'd all be dead."

Zita smiled.

Al shouted, "Come staff." His staff flew into his hands. "Let's go capture the Crystal of Zaraboth." He triumphantly headed toward the stairs.

Kestrel stalked to the mage and peeled the ebony and mahogany staff from her fingers. "You won't need this."

They climbed three sets of stairs. Al found himself huffing and puffing by the time they reached the towers.

Taka stood outside a doorway. He stared intensely into the room and what he saw within it.

Al came up beside him and his jaw dropped.

CHAPTER 69

Zita stood in awe; her eyes fixed upon what she saw in the castle's tower room. A burst of crackling energy greeted her, tingling her senses. In the center of the spacious chamber, bathed in a radiant glow, stood the very object of their desires—the legendary artifact, Crystal of Zaraboth, pulsated with an otherworldly light, casting intricate patterns on the stone walls, a tapestry of arcane symbols and mighty power.

Zita's heart beat faster, and she tried to get moisture into her dry mouth as excitement bubbled within her.

A woman stood on a dais in the center of the chamber, where twenty interconnected metal loops spun around her, reflecting an internal light streaming from the woman.

The flashing lights within the room made Zita want to close her eyes, yet the object seemed to create a desire within her to run to it.

Lily walked up next to Zita. When she peered into the room, she gasped.

Sherry stood next to Lily and draped an arm around her shoulder. "You don't have to do this."

Taka set his gaze on them, "Yes, she does. We didn't travel this far to turn back without the crystal."

Sherry glared at Taka, before leaning in close to Lily. "We will take this one step at a time."

As Zita gazed in wonder at the magical artifact, a voice drifted into her mind. It was the moon goddess of Velidred.

"Can you feel it? The crystal beckons us to control its power. Send out your consciousness and tickle its mind. I must have a look inside."

Zita locked eyes with the woman inside the rotating rings, peering deep into her radiance. The intense light seemed to penetrate Zita's very being, illuminating the recesses of her mind and kindling a flame of ancient knowledge within her. The artifact whispered to her of forgotten realms, beckoning her to unravel its secrets.

Time seemed to stand still as Zita became lost in a trance-like state, transfixed by the luminous spectacle before her. The symphony of light and energy enveloped her senses, heightening her awareness of the immense power contained within the crystal. She tried to create a connection, to forge a bond between mortal and magic.

A cloudy luminescence formed between Zita and the crystal, like the wisps of fog rising from the pre-dawn grass. It oscillated between, green and blue, in soft undulations like a whisper from a lover's lips.

Something collided with Zita which sent her sprawling to the floor; her connection with the crystal severed. When she looked around, Al lay on the floor beside her.

She smacked Al hard against the side of the head.

"Stop that. I just saved your life. That's the same thing that killed my grandfather."

"How would you know that?" Zita asked.

"The staff just told me. You would have disintegrated. One moment you're here, and the next you're a million, no, a billion pieces, blown into the air, like an aerosol spray."

She glared at Al as she watched the luminescence return to the woman embracing her figure, and casting a soft glow that accentuated every delicate contour of her form. Her stature exuded an otherworldly aura of grace and poise.

Zita thought the woman reminded her of Ekaterina, the desert spiritualist, now dead, that had been chosen as the new vessel. The woman carried the essence of ancient lands in her being. A golden undertone harmonized with her origins, a testament to the lineage that coursed through her veins.

The moon goddess sent rivulets of pain through Zita's body, the pain starting small and increasing with each second.

She tried to respond in an appropriate fashion, but the goddess didn't listen. "I command you to retrieve the crystal at once and make it mine."

Zita went to her knees as tears streamed down her face. "I cannot, it's too dangerous."

The moon goddess said, "I will help you."

Zita fell to the floor, hugging her knees in the fetal position, unable to withstand the pain coursing through her body by the moon goddess.

Erik came to her side and tried to help, but she pushed him away. "You can't help."

He looked pained that she pushed him away. "It's the Corruption of Evil, isn't it?"

She managed to nod despite the pain.

Erik pointed at the other wizards in the room. "We have the ability to drive it out. We can put it back in the sword."

She whispered, "It's too dangerous in the castle. There's too much magic in this place. We might all die." At that moment, she wanted to die. She began a furious conversation with Luna Rosso listing all the reasons that now wasn't the proper time.

After what seemed forever, the moon goddess released the pain. Zita managed to crawl and struggled to her feet.

"Let's bond our magic and acquire the crystal," Taka said. "I'll lead the bond."

"I bet you'd be happy to do that. You'd also kill us all," Zita said.

"I've had enough out of you. Dakarai, link with me so we can block her magic."

Before Dakarai could get close to Taka, Zita said, "Did you read the scroll? You're missing something."

Taka stopped Dakarai. "What am I missing?"

"Do you have the Crown of Anticletus? Without that, we'll all die, whether we bond or not."

Taka rolled out the scroll and he moved his finger down the page as he read through. Toward the end he poked the scroll with his finger and looked at Zita. "Okay, you're right. Do you have it?"

She opened her empty hands. "I do not."

Taka's nostrils flared. "Where is it?"

Zita smiled in victory. She knew something that Taka didn't for once. "It's not my job to tell you."

Taka's face reddened and he pulled out his wand and pointed it at Zita.

Sherry stepped in front of Zita, facing Taka, and held up her hands. "Relax. The crown won't work until the Anticletus moon rises in about two hours. Let's take a break and talk about our next steps."

Taka stared angrily at Zita, but withdrew his wand. He asked, "Who has the crown?"

Sherry said, "I have it."

"I want to see."

"You literally can't see it until the moon rises."

Taka gave an angry snort and bared his teeth. "You better not be playing me. I don't plan to let you out of my sight until the crystal is in my hands."

"For a mighty wizard, you didn't come here very prepared." Zita chided her adversary. "Why should we allow you to have the crystal? In the face of adversity, you ran away like a child."

Frustration began to show on Taka's face as the room filled with tension.

Dakarai took Taka by the shoulder and moved him into an adjoining room. "Let's wait it out. We should plan our strategy so we don't make a mistake."

All the remaining adventurers gathered in the small room. There were no chairs or tables, and Zita and the teens from Earth sat with their backs against a wall. Taka stalked back and forth, looking at the uncurled scroll in his hands and muttered to himself.

Sims, Lenny, Dakarai and the desert wizard all sat along the opposite wall whispering.

Zita talked with the moon goddess in her mind. She tried to convince her that they couldn't try anything without the crown. It took a while to convince Luna Rosso of that truth.

Then Zita wondered what Dakarai and the others were whispering about, so she asked the moon goddess for a way to listen to their conversation. She felt Luna Rosso enter her mind and felt a tiny thread of magic winding its way from her side of the room to Dakarai's side.

Dakarai said, "Yeah, it'll be a risky operation, but if we pull it off, we'll be in possession of the crystal."

Sims leered at the women on the other side.

"How do we keep them from taking it from us?" Lenny asked "They have three wizards and the redhead has the Crown of Anticletus."

"We can block their magic," Dakarai said. "They have no defense against our magic."

"What if the crown interrupts that block?"

Dakarai looked at the other side of the room, focusing his gaze on Sherry. "I'll let you and Sims distract the redhead and steal the crown. Then we can take the crystal and be on our way. We'll leave the teens here in the castle, and be back to Velidred before they can get off the island."

They all laughed.

Taka sat next to Dakarai and showed him the scroll. "It says here we need four wizards to bond before attempting to transfer the crystal."

"That means we have to use one of the teens."

Zita felt Taka's eyes on her. She looked down at the floor afraid he would know that she listened.

"I think I have the most control over Zita. I've been managing her for the last few days. The young Alpherge is dangerous with that staff. The kid defeated King Haskell."

"They won't just watch us take it," Dakarai said, "They'll be a pain."

Taka lifted the lid on his pouch and showed Dakarai the pouch's contents.

Dakarai nodded. "Right, put them to sleep. They won't notice us leaving."

Zita knew she needed the teens from Earth, and Kestrel to defeat Taka's group and keep the crystal for herself. She would tell them of this conversation and make sure Taka's plans didn't work.

Taka pointed at the scroll and discussed three things that must occur to disengage the crystal, dismount it, and transfer it to the new vessel.

Dakarai asked some follow-up questions.

"Remember the goal." Taka took the time to look at all three of his henchmen. "Once we possess the crystal, we shall wield unimaginable might. Be alert."

Taka handed the sleeping potion to Sims and told him to put it in the teen's waterskins.

Zita nudged Al who sat to his right. "Don't drink anything from your skin after we stand."

Al looked confused.

Zita whispered to her friends, "They plan to knock us out. Taka doesn't want you, Erik or Kestrel involved in the transfer. Be careful."

CHAPTER 70

Kestrel took Lily's hand and kissed it. She felt the blood rush to her face as her cheeks heated from her love for Kestrel. He had been there for her, and even though her friends from Earth had tried to separate them, Kestrel had stood strong.

Lily knew what had to happen to her as the vessel, but this renewed affection from Kestrel meant a great deal to her.

"Can we talk?" Kestrel's eyes looked dark and serious, a somberness she hadn't seen from him in a long time.

"Sure, what's on your mind?"

"Not here. Let's go out in the hallway."

He took Lily's hand and led her from the chamber into an out hallway.

Taka said, "Don't go far."

Kestrel waved him away.

After they reached the hallway, Kestrel dropped Lily's hand and paced back and forth.

Lily stopped him. "What is it?"

Kestrel hesitated before he spoke, "This offering is too great. We still have so much life ahead of us. There must be another way to achieve our goals without you making such a profound sacrifice."

Lily understood now what troubled Kestrel. She said softly, but determined, "I understand your worries and fears, and I cherish the life we've shared. My heart aches at the thought of leaving you, but this decision is not just about us. It's about a cause larger than ourselves."

Kestrel pleaded, "What about the life we had planned together? Is becoming the vessel worth losing all of that?"

A range of emotions shot through Lily. She had to bid farewell to the life she expected with Kestrel, living in the family castle, helping the local villagers, and starting a family. She didn't know if today would be the last time she could hug Kestrel.

Lily glanced at the woman pulsating in the tower chamber. The current vessel stood stoically waiting to be … what? Summoned, used, or coerced to complete a command? What lay ahead for her as the vessel?

Kestrel's voice cracked, and he turned his face away from Lily, his arms and shoulders stiff and tense. "I can't bear the thought of losing you. I don't want a world without you by my side. Can't we find another way, a safer way?"

"There's no one else to become the vessel."

"We can go back to the desert village and find a new vessel. Someone without as much to lose."

Lily took his hands. "You don't realize that every woman who might volunteer for this has something to lose. Loved ones, family, dreams, and maybe even a career. We do it for the others in our life."

Kestrel shook his head. "You've seen Taka. Can you really expect to serve him for a thousand years?"

Lily had thought the exact same thing before she made the decision. Taka definitely seemed the front runner for taking ownership of the crystal. She thought if Al or maybe even Zita could be the crystal's master, then it would be a better experience for her. The lack of knowledge about what might happen overwhelmed her. In fact, no one knew what could be expected in the transfer. She might not even survive.

Kestrel stared into her eyes and held her hands tight as if he wouldn't let her go.

"I wish there were an easier path, a safer alternative." Lily squeezed his hands to communicate her love for him.

Kestrel leaned in and kissed Lily. She savored the kiss and felt it might be the last kiss she would ever share with the man she loved. After a moment he jerked back, glared at Lily and stormed away.

Lily watched him go as thoughts of her own mortality and the fleeting nature of life wove through her mind. She contemplated what her life's next would mean. Would she be a mindless vessel to be commanded and manipulated, or would she have power of her own?

Sherry rushed toward Lily. "Are you okay? Kestrel looked angry."

Lily nodded and tried to loosen the knots she felt in her shoulders and stomach. "He wants me to say no to becoming the crystal."

Sherry looked at Lily with compassion. "We don't know for sure if any of this will work." She looked at Lily's forehead. "The symbol of Pantaleon on your forehead might cause problems."

Lily shook her head. "The high priestess made reference to a superior motive to my life. I think this is what she meant by that statement."

Sherry said, "Yet, she wanted to keep us in the castle until after our initiation process completed. She had to know that we were in pursuit of the crystal."

Lily gasped, "The seven-petaled flower. You'll return it to the sacred castle when we finish this quest, won't you?"

Sherry smiled and touched Lily's forearm. "I'll be happy to. You still care about getting that plant back to the High Priestess. You're crazy you know." Sherry gave Lily a hug.

"I know Al, Erik, Zita, you, and Kestrel will defeat Taka, and we can all change this planet. This quest is not just about me; it's about making a difference, protecting those we care about, and creating a better future for everyone."

A gleam formed in Sherry's eyes, and a knowing grin spread across her face. "I admire your selflessness and your unwavering dedication. Just remember that your well-being and happiness matter too. If, at any point, you have doubts or second thoughts, please know that I'm here for you."

Lily's stomach muscles tightened and she stood taller. "Thank you for being there for me. Your friendship gives me the courage to move forward."

They embraced and Lily held tight to her friend for what might be the last time. She stared into the tower chamber where the vessel still stood, unmoving, stoic and static."

CHAPTER 71

Lily held hands with Sherry as they stared out the tower window and watched the Anticletus Moon ascend behind the volcano. An unspoken communication seemed to flow between them as they waited for the moon to rise above the horizon. Lily's stomach cramped at the expectation of the transfer of the crystal.

At last Sherry said, "Anticletus has risen."

Taka smiled. "Let's go then, but before we go, we must toast to a successful quest."

Erik grimaced. "With what, the pungent and stale water in our waterskins?"

"That's all we have, and we don't know how long this process will take." Taka raised his waterskin. "It might be hours. We don't want to be dehydrated when we make the transfer and something goes awry."

They all grabbed their waterskins.

Taka waited for everyone to prepare their skins and then with a flourish raised his waterskin toward the ceiling. "To the convergence of magic and destiny! May our combined powers lead us on this perilous path, and may the mystic forces guide us towards the treasure we seek. Together, we shall overcome any obstacles that stand in our way and emerge victorious in our quest. Here's to the melding of our strengths and the triumph that awaits us!"

Zita mumbled under her breath, "Yeah, now you want us to work together."

They all lifted their skins and drank.

Taka looked at Sims.

Sims smiled, raised his eyebrows and nodded.

Taka said, "Here's the plan. Dakarai, Zita, my wizard friend from the desert, and I will go into the tower chamber and bond our magic. I'll lead."

He pointed at Lily. "You stand next to the crystal. As close as possible."

The tightness in Lily's core had transformed into a rolling, quivering, empty feeling in her stomach; leaving her on the verge of nausea. She took deep breaths as she attempted to regain control over her unsettled stomach.

Taka examined the scroll. "The Crown of Anticletus must stand between us and the vessel."

"When do I take on the crown?" Sherry asked.

Taka scrutinized the scroll once more. "It doesn't say." He looked at Sherry. "It might be risky to try to transform in the chamber with the crystal. I say mutate into before you leave this room."

Sherry nodded.

"What do you want us to do?" Al asked, waving his arm to include Erik and Kestrel.

Taka said, "We won't need you for this first part, so you can stay in here with Lenny and Sims."

Sims smirked.

"You don't want my—" Al fell to the floor and his staff bounced once and came to rest next to him.

"What did you—" Kestrel and Erik crumpled to the floor next to Al.

Sherry looked in disbelief as Al fell and she rushed over to her friends.

Lily gasped. "What did you do to them?"

Taka nodded at Sims. "Don't let them interrupt the proceedings as we transfer the crystal."

Lenny and Sims answered, "Yes, Boss."

Taka turned to Sherry. "Okay, time for us to see the Crown of Anticletus."

"Not until you tell me what you did to the boys?"

Taka strode over to Sherry and grabbed her by the back of her neck and walked her over to Lily. "I made sure they won't bother us. You're lucky I didn't kill them. You can have them back after I have the crystal. Now show me."

Sherry's face went red and her eyebrows narrowed. She hunched her shoulders as if Taka had squeezed her neck as he shoved her toward Lily.

Sherry scowled at Taka, looked at Lily once more, and then closed her eyes.

Lily felt the tension build in the room as they waited for Sherry to transform. Suddenly, a radiant light emanated from Sherry, bathing the room in a soft, ethereal blue glow. The glow intensified, growing brighter and more mesmerizing with each passing second.

As the light intensified, wisps of shimmering energy swirled and danced around Sherry, intertwining and weaving intricate patterns in the air. The room filled with an unearthly radiance, casting moving shadows upon the walls.

Sherry stood motionless despite the swirling light, as a majestic crown materialized, suspended in mid-air above her head. The crown sparkled with blue iridescent gemstones, their brilliance reflecting a spectrum of colors. Each gemstone seemed to hold its own story that whispered of ancient wisdom.

The Crown of Anticletus settled on Sherry's head.

Lily heard Sherry speak to her without saying anything out loud. "I am with you, be brave."

Lily gave Sherry a quick smile.

Taka led them into the tower chamber.

As Lily beheld the captivating woman on the dais, the feeling of awe and reverence troubled her. The vessel embodied both serenity and power, an enigmatic figure standing at the threshold of mortal existence and the realm of the divine.

Lily walked toward the crystal, close enough to touch, but she kept her hands by her sides as the luminescent light flickered in the darkness of the chamber. She thought, *this is it, then.* Memories of the people she cared for and the experiences she would miss tugged at her heart. A moment of sadness, longing to once more embrace her friends.

Taka commanded the wizards, "It's time for us to bond."

Zita bonded with the desert wizard first and the air crackled around them as the bond became firm. Then Dakarai took Zita's hand in his, and the atmosphere became charged with electric energy.

Small static discharges flew off the crystal and Lily stepped away from the dais.

Zita's green eyes glowed, an ethereal sign of the arcane magic that pulsed through the bond.

Taka pointed at Lily. "Stand closer to the dais. We won't be able to complete the transfer if you're too far away."

Then he took Dakarai's hand. A spark of electricity bounced off the ceiling and Lily felt her hair rise from her head as if she was standing in a field during a lightning storm. The ends of her hair snaked in multiple directions.

Taka controlled the bonding, and an aura surrounded the four wizards. It manifested as a shimmering veil of luminous bands of light that twirled and twisted around the bodies of the four wizards. The aura shimmered and swayed as if moved by an invisible breeze, its movements akin to the delicate choreography of a celestial ballet.

Taka tried to remove the Imperium Wand from his tunic, but his arm seemed to lock in an unusual position. He struggled with the force that prevented him from grabbing it, a look of anguish painted on his face.

Crackling and popping enveloped the room.

Zita shouted, "You'll kill us all if you try to use the wand. Try to make the transfer without it."

"I will use the wand." He overpowered the force that pulled at his arm. He retrieved the wand, and waved it at Zita.

Taka shouted, "Sherry, come into the room."

Lily watched in fascination as her friend walked into the room. Her soft, diffused glow bathed the chamber in a gentle glow. Lily didn't think the room could hold any more magical power but as Sherry neared them, it seemed as if the very atoms of the universe were electrified.

Taka took control. He waved his wand at Sherry, and Lily saw a thread extend from the wand toward Sherry. It snaked and wiggled in the charged atmosphere. When it reached Sherry, Taka extended the thread of magic towards Lily.

Lily took a deep breath as the magic crept closer. A brilliant explosion of color seemed to detonate within her brain when the thread touched her. She felt weak in her knees, but managed to stay on her feet.

"The first step is to disengage the crystal." Taka raised his hands and waved the wand over the chamber as he chanted in a voice that reverberated with power and authority,

"In realms of ancient lore, where magic thrives,

Unravel now the enchantments that bind,

With mystic words and gestures alive,

Let ancient powers flow through heart and mind.

Khulula izibopho, ritual of old,

Invoke the spirits, release what's confined,

As incantations weave stories untold,

Free the artifact, where magic's entwined."

Lily felt a breeze blow across her face, and she turned to look at the crystal. The silver rings that spun about the vessel slowed and came to a stop.

Faint whispers filled the air, carrying echoes of ancient spells and forgotten incantations. Ancient symbols and intricate patterns materialized in the air, glowing with a radiant, ethereal, yellow light.

Lily didn't know how, but she recognized the symbols. She could read them, and interpreted them as instructions on the use and care of the crystal. They moved fast across her field of vision seemingly across the thread of magic that stitched them together. She read and translated fast in hopes that she would remember them if she needed to.

Lily stared motionless at the silver rings that surrounded the woman on the dais. The rings had stopped their rotations, but the woman remained unmoved within its cage. She wondered why the rings had stopped spinning. Had the spell failed? She felt hope move in her soul for a future with Kestrel. A subtle, lingering scent of ozone filled the chamber, reminiscent of lightning or electrical energy.

Static electricity continued to affect Lily's hair, as it pulled away from her head in every direction. The energy pulsed in an uneven rhythm as if a crowd of people clapped, but some of the people weren't in sync with the others. She worried something wasn't right, the notes of the hidden melody were slightly off key.

Taka held his wand pointed toward Lily; his magic bonded to his co-wizards. Smoke, light, and dust swirled around Taka and the others. He chanted,

"Cage of enchantment, yield to my decree,

Unleash the treasures that lie within thee.

With words of power and authority profound,

Release the vessel, let freedom resound!

Spirits of old, with powers untold,

Heed my command, release the hold.

By magic's decree, unlock this cage,

Set free the vessel, unbound from its stage."

Lily faced the dais and watched as the silver rings seemed to unwind from their positions trapping the woman. Each ring separated and unclasped at a single point. At each end a portion of the ring disappeared an inch at a time, like a fuse that is lit at two ends, and burns toward the center point, until the fuse has burned itself out.

One by one, the rings vanished, their enchantment dissolving into the unseen. The woman remained motionless throughout the process her gaze fixed forward as if trapped in an enchanted trance. She seemed unaffected by the disappearance of the rings, maintaining her unwavering focus as though she existed in a different plane of consciousness.

A transparent barrier formed around the woman, crackling with mystical energy.

The tension building within Lily had almost reached a point of explosion. She looked back at Sherry. Would this be the last time she would knowingly be with her friend? She feared the future that awaited her in this magical castle. Lily had been a free woman before this moment with a future she had known or at least a fate she could guess, but her decision to say yes to become the vessel had changed that destiny to one of captivity.

Sherry seemed to hear her thoughts.

"Be strong my friend," Sherry said. "I will be with you and will always be your friend."

It gave Lily encouragement.

A movement at the chamber doorway caught Lily's attention. As she turned her gaze, she beheld a fantastical sight. Framed within the ancient archway stood three figures adorned with intricate patterns that glimmered with magical essence. A smile crept across her face.

CHAPTER 72

Al stared into the tower chamber where a storm of magical energy raged. He held his staff and Erik next to him, the Sword of Freedom lifted toward the frenzied storm. Kestrel stood on Al's other side holding the mage's dark, gold-tipped staff loosely by his side. A tingling sensation spread through the air, tickling the skin, and hinting at the immense power being harnessed in the chamber.

They had pretended to fall asleep from the drugs Sims had placed in their waterskins. They waited a few minutes after Taka left before disabling Sims and Lenny. They left them bound in the chamber.

They didn't know all the steps necessary to retrieve the crystal, so they bided their time until they knew Taka had released the crystal.

Al asked, "Are we ready to do this?"

"Let's bond, otherwise their power will be too much for us." Kestrel held out his hand.

"Will our magic be enough?" Al asked.

Kestrel didn't look very confident. "We won't know until we try. Taka can't have Lily." He raised the ebony and mahogany rod. "I feel great magic in the mage's staff."

"Go ahead and link with Erik and the sword. We've bonded in the past, so I know it's possible."

Al waited while they proceeded through the steps. Kestrel seemed to have a little problem, but then figured it out and Al saw the bond completed.

Lily had noticed them, and Al worried that her attention might draw Taka's wrath before they were ready. He wished they had bonded before looking in the room. At the moment, Taka seemed absorbed in the process to release the crystal.

Al grabbed Kestrel's hand and chanted,

"With a bond of magic, united as one,

Combine our strength, the spell begun.

Elemental forces, spirits untamed,

We call upon you, by names unrestrained.

Through fire, earth, wind, and sea,

We merge our powers, in harmony.

Sorcery deep, weave a mystical thread,

In this sacred union, let our magic spread.

Together we stand, bound by this decree,

Our bond as one, dauntless, courageous symphony."

Al felt the magic flow through him. Kestrel had been right about the mage's staff as it contained the legendary mystic power of the ancients. He filled himself with the magic until he almost burst.

"Now that we are bonded as three, see if you can prevent Taka from blocking our magic with your grandfather's spell." Kestrel commanded.

Al didn't know if the enchantment would still work since Erik wasn't really a wizard, but they had to try if they hoped to gain the crystal. "Think of the color blue and let's all chant the spell at the same time."

In unison their voices rang out, "Uklonite zakone magije." *Dispel the laws of magic.*

Taka still hadn't noticed the three of them as Al continued the process to capture the crystal.

As Taka completed the next step, the air settled, and a momentary stillness descended upon the scene, awaiting the commencement of the final step, transferring the crystal from one vessel to another.

A subtle undercurrent of anticipation tinged with a hint of trepidation ran through Al's veins. He knew that unlocking such a potent artifact carried great responsibility, and he feared their actions might cause the whole room to explode and fail to contain the crystal in a new vessel.

Taka's voice radiated with authority and wisdom as he addressed the woman on the dais now exposed with no protective silver rings. "Fair maiden, step down from the dais, and venture forth into the realm."

Taka's hand shook as he raised the Imperium Wand toward the woman.

Kestrel whispered, "Go now."

Al, Erik and Kestrel stepped into the chamber. Al pointed his staff, Erik his sword, and Kestrel the gold end of Geirhild's staff at the vessel. Al shouted, "Liberate the crystal, freedom from strife, accept the new vessel, transfer your life."

As soon as Al released the spell, sparks bounced off the walls and domed ceiling within the small chamber. As the magic from the seven wizards intertwined within the tower chamber, a palpable sense of imbalance filled the air. The room became a maelstrom of conflicting energies. The walls shimmered and rippled and the very foundation of the chamber quivered under the strain. Everyone reeled, trying to remain on their feet.

Taka yelled, "You fools, you'll ruin everything."

Kestrel shouted, "Al, command the vessel to your voice. You must take control before Taka."

Whispers of forgotten incantations echoed in the space, their words distorted and fragmented.

Al had doubts about his role in this process. Sherry seemed upset about his presence. Had she planned something and now he had ruined her plans? She should have told him. Taka seemed to route his magic through Sherry, and Al wondered if he could go directly to the vessel.

Kestrel kicked Al's shin. "Chant the words before it's too late. Take control."

With a commanding voice that cut through the chaotic currents of magic, Al raised his staff and uttered the incantation from his grandfather,

"O unruly forces, bend to my will,

By ancient power, I command you, be still!

From this storm of magic, chaos untamed,

Submit to my presence, let order be reclaimed!"

As he spoke, tendrils of magic extended outward and intertwined with the energies that swirled in the chamber. With a gesture of his hand, he channeled a focused thread of magic and directed the surging power toward a singular purpose, to take control of the crystal.

The currents of magic responded and formed a shield over Taka's magic thread, which allowed Al to take control. The chaotic tempest continued its untamed, feral magic. Streams of magic emitted from Taka's wand and flowed through Sherry, but they weren't aimed toward the vessel. Taka directed them toward Al and those he had bonded.

Al responded to the incoming magic directed at him, his enhanced power from Erik and Kestrel's magical artifacts giving him confidence. Their magic met Taka's at a point between Sherry and Al. Sparks flew in all directions as the two wizards strove for mastery of the other.

Sherry looked at Al and smiled. Then Taka's magic seemed to dissipate. Had she joined the fight on Al's side? He didn't realize she could manipulate magic like that using the Crown of Anticletus, but he remembered the help she gave when they defeated King Haskell on the volcano.

Taka's attack had stopped and he stood dumbfounded, anger brewing on his face.

Al redirected his attention to the vessel on the dais. She seemed to have awakened from her centuries-old trance and was watching the swirling patterns of light and magic flash about the chamber.

He knew he needed to take control before Taka could yet intervene before he burned his magic out.

In this moment, the tower chamber was a microcosm of raw magical forces, a testament to the volatile nature of uncontrolled power. The very fabric of reality strained under the weight of the wizards' collective magic, their combined energies clashed and surged in disharmony.

Al had to calm the chaos before he manipulated the vessel into Lily, the new vessel.

Taka moved his bonded wizards toward Al and his friends. "Block their magic. Hurry, before they transfer the crystal and take control. It's mine!"

Kestrel poked Al in the ribs. "Finish the transfer."

Al said, "I can't get control of the vessel. He has it locked down with a barrier I can't penetrate."

"If you don't get control, then Taka will kill us."

Al thought, *That's just great. As if things couldn't get worse. Taka would block their magic and probably kill them in the process.*

Taka stalked toward them, his nostrils flaring, and eyes cold, hard and flinty.

Dakarai shouted, "The block isn't working. What have they done?"

Erik shouted at Al through the maelstrom, "Send your magic through Sherry. She might already have an entry point through the barrier."

Al took a deep breath. He didn't know enough about this process to be randomly trying to send magic through his friend. He had no clue how any of this worked, and he could easily be transferring the vessel into Sherry.

Taka closed the distance between them.

Al guided his staff at Sherry. Tendrils of the magic originally pointed at the vessel obeyed Al's command and shifted to Sherry. She seemed to recognize Al's intention and she guided the thread of magic toward the vessel.

Erik was right. Al watched as the thread of magic penetrated the barrier and undulated toward the woman, the living vessel, on the dais.

Eyes narrowed in concentration; Al's hands glowed with an ethereal synthesis as they traced intricate sigils in the air. The magical lines shimmered and fused with the Crystal of Zaraboth, and established a connection. He commanded,

"In the realm of wizards, where spells take shape,

Some seek to tame the feral, their ambitions escape.

But in the heart of tameless magic's core,

It resists its control, no more."

The woman's face lit up and she stared at Al.

As Al's gaze met the figure's piercing eyes, he sensed the majesty of this encounter. It hinted at a deeper connection to a world that overflowed with magic where extraordinary beings and wondrous realms intertwined.

With an outstretched hand, Al invoked the age-old incantations, his voice resonated with the power of ancient tongues. As the words spilled forth, he melded his essence with the vessel, establishing a bond of command and control. "Exorior vos ad novum vas, in nomine potentiae!", he spoke which roughly translated to, "I raise you to a new vessel."

"You fool you're going to ruin everything." Taka touched Al's chest with his wand and blasted a spell at his adversary.

CHAPTER 73

Al's chest erupted with a blaze of searing pain as Taka's powerful blast struck him with brutal force. The sheer impact sent him hurtling backward, his body convulsing in agony. With gritted teeth and an unyielding spirit, he desperately clung to the remnants of his fading consciousness.

As his life force waned, he heard Sherry's anguished scream. In the maelstrom, he fought to maintain his connection to the mystical artifact, to seize command over the powers that lay within. His heart pounded, he worried that he had failed just like his grandfather.

He sensed Erik next to him, their bond still in harmony. At first a feeling of shock coursed through the bond, but then without words, Erik spoke of courage and not giving up.

With an iron resolve, Al focused his shattered thoughts on the crystal. He felt weak, yet with delicate manipulations, he fought to direct all the power of the bond to gaining control of the crystal and the forces at hand.

The energies of the universe shattered against his soul, demanding he release his link with the Crystal of Zaraboth.

As Al lay motionless, his breath shallow and his life force flickering like a dying ember, his loyal friend, Erik the healer, pointed the Sword of Freedom at the wizard. The sword pulsed with a gentle radiance, sending restorative energy as its sharp point touched Al's chest.

Al felt Taka's magic working its way toward Sherry. Taka wasn't going to let the teens take the crystal without a fight.

Al watched as Erik tried to hold the sword steady in his trembling hands. "Stay with me. I can heal you." Beads of perspiration glistened on his brow.

For the second time in just a few days, Al's life wavered at the mercy of Erik's healing powers. He tried to think back to when they were just two high school buddies and Erik wanted to get a date with Lily. Erik had proven himself a great friend, healing him and staying with him for these outrageous quests that led them to the edge of life and death.

Al stared into Erik's eyes which were focused on delivering the healing powers Al needed. Had this been too much for the amount of luck they had been given on this planet? It seemed that Erik's healing magic had reached its limit. Al coughed and looked down at his chest where he saw blood oozing from the wound.

He glanced at Sherry, for what he feared would be the last time he saw her. Al fought the numbness disabling his mind.

Sherry's mouth opened wide; shock registered on her face at watching him die.

His life couldn't end like this, he needed to talk with Sherry, tell her about the plans he wanted to implement in his life to spend more time with her.

Al coughed up blood. He mouthed the words "I love you." to Sherry.

With big eyes, Sherry stared back, pulling at the magic that held her bound to her spot in the chamber. Then she tilted her head to one side and pursed her lips in confusion. She snapped her head at Taka.

Taka had regained control of Sherry and was working to bring his power back to the crystal.

Al closed his eyes, but then a surge of healing energy poured into the wound; curative magic coursed through his veins, mending his injuries. And then, as if drawn back from the abyss, he opened his eyes with a renewed vitality.

In that transient state, where the boundary between magic and mortality blurred, Al became a conduit of immense power. The crystal responded; its dormant energy reawakened in response to his desperate call. He commanded the artifact to yield to his will. Al seized control of the arcane forces that swirled within the chamber.

Erik's unwavering loyalty and the healing power of friendship had saved Al once again.

Al knew they weren't finished, and he wondered why he had to transfer the crystal to Lily. Why couldn't they just keep the old vessel and use it?

Sherry said to him telepathically. "You are right, we can use the old vessel, but she will be joined to Lily instead of you. Lily is prepared for the junction."

With a deep breath, Al tapped into his inner reservoir of mystical knowledge, and delved into the depths of his mind. He needed to merge Lily's consciousness with the essence of the artifact, forming a symbiotic link that would grant Lily control over its enchantments.

He felt his grandfather's hands clasp over his own in this state of being between death and life. His grandfather guided his hands to move the staff in a perfected sequence to channel the union of the crystal with Lily. Al hoped it would work.

# # # #

Zita disengaged her bond between Dakarai and Taka. Her yearning for power had reached its zenith, and it came time for her to take control of the crystal. She watched Al get to his feet in the crystal's chamber, while watching his actions ruin everything.

A surge of anguish and rage consumed Zita as the realization dawned upon her – the crystal she had sought with relentless determination, pouring hers and the Velidred Moon Goddess' dark ambitions into its control, had been snatched away by the teens.

After breaking her bond with the other wizards, she searched for a way to claim control of the crystal. Al had said the words, but had he completed the incantation? Why had Taka hesitated when Al, Erik and Kestrel entered the room?

Betrayal gnawed at her heart, twisting her features into a mask of fury and bitter disappointment. The stolen artifact represented more than mere power to her; it symbolized the culmination of her grand design, her path to dominance over the Velidred kingdom. Its theft tore through the fabric of her carefully constructed ambitions.

Without the crystal, she would never be able to take back Velidred Castle from the usurpers like Prince Krunal and Taka. Luna Rosso had promised her the power to take control of the crystal. The moon goddess had disappeared when Zita needed her help.

With a glimmer of desperation, Zita mustered her remaining reserves of power, seeking recourse to her bond with Luna Rosso, determined to reclaim control of the artifact. She delved into the depths of the moon goddess' wisdom, seeking an incantation to shatter the bonds that held the crystal in Al's grip. Zita refused to allow Al this victory.

Drawing upon the moon's shadowy forces that had been her ally, Zita began a final incantation. She poured her remaining vitality into the spell, sacrificing even more of herself to the Moon Goddess in a desperate attempt to reclaim what she believed to be rightfully hers. The air crackled with tension, an invisible battlefield between opposing wills.

The smell of rotten eggs permeated the room as she pulled power from the volcano below her, magic it held deep within its molten core. She touched her mother's necklace to imbue even more power into her invocation.

Her incantation hit the shield that Al had set over his treasure, and her magic sparked where it touched. Lightning and thunder crescendoed in the chamber.

Zita felt the steady beat of blood pulsing through her brain. Her rage intensified as her dreams for her life and future were once again being yanked from her by the teens. She needed to pull the crystal back within her powers. She transferred power from Velidred Moon to the crystal.

When Zita's incantation reached its peak, a profound realization washed over her. The crystal, now infused with the essence of another, resonated with a power that defied her attempts to sever the connection. Its loyalty had shifted to a person in the room who had wrested it from her grasp.

A surge of searing pain coursed through Zita's body, a backlash of energy as her incantation collided with the impenetrable force that safeguarded the artifact. Her voice wavered, faltering under the strain of her futile exertion. The sheer resilience of the bond that had formed between the artifact and its new master proved insurmountable.

The Crystal of Zaraboth remained stubbornly beyond her reach. Weakened by the tremendous energy she had used to capture it, Zita collapsed to her knees, her spirit shattered.

The stolen artifact, the key to her return to power at Velidred, now slipped through her fingers like sand, leaving behind a void of unquenchable longing. She felt robbed of her prize, and a profound sense of inadequacy gnawed at her ambition for power.

CHAPTER 74

Lily stood next to the woman on the dais; her stomach churned with nervous anticipation and anxiety.

The old vessel had been released and now the time came for the crystal to transfer into Lily. In a moment her old life would end, her dreams shatter, and her body would become a magical artifact. She looked at Kestrel with longing and wondered if he felt the same way about her.

Her nerves felt tangled in a knot that tightened with every passing moment. Waves of queasiness washed over her. She took deep breaths, attempting to steady her racing heart and regain control.

The figure on the dais exuded an aura of otherworldly wisdom and power. Lily stared into the vessel's eyes and they seemed to open onto a vast darkness, where orbs floated in the air casting a mystical glow that illuminated the space.

As Lily's gaze met the figure's piercing eyes, she sensed that this encounter was no mere coincidence. It hinted at a deeper connection to a world brimming with magic, where wondrous realms intertwined with the spiritual.

A bolt of electricity shot from the vessel's body to the symbol from the Sacred Castle on Lily's forehead, the holy mark of the Pantaleon religion. A great boom of thunder sounded within the chamber, vibrating within her ribcage. She stumbled backwards from the impact, holding her arms out to the side for balance. Sherry caught her in her arms and embraced her.

Lily relaxed into Sherry's embrace and felt comforted in her arms. She didn't know what had caused the bolt of energy that knocked her back. The vessel still stood on the dais, staring at Lily. She remembered what she had seen in the woman's eyes, vast worlds and distant galaxies, but she couldn't fathom what it all meant.

She checked on Kestrel to make sure Taka hadn't injured him, and he smiled back at her which comforted her.

Taka moved toward Al and Kestrel; his wand raised as if readying another dangerous spell.

Lily shouted, "No. Don't touch them."

Taka released a spell at Lily, but she deflected it against the wall.

Lily thought back to the ancient symbols that had floated from the crystal when Taka unlocked the silver rings that bound the vessel to the dais. They were instructions on how to use the crystal. Somehow, she felt that she could utilize those instructions in her present state.

She felt Taka throw up a magic block over all the wizards in the room. Al's shield collapsed. Kestrel raised his hands as if to block any spells that Taka might send at him, but Lily knew Taka's power would overpower her friends. It fell to her to test the crystal's power.

Taka pointed the Imperium Wand at Kestrel. He shouted at Al, "Transfer the crystal to me or your friend is dead."

Al raised his hands above his head. "I can't."

Taka shook his head. "I tried to ask nicely."

"The crystal doesn't belong to me." Al hunched his shoulders in an "I'm sorry" gesture.

"What happened?" Taka asked. "Did you fail?"

"It didn't work," Al said. "I lost connection with it when you blasted me."

Taka looked at Zita. "Do you have it?"

Lily searched through her memory for the instructions for the crystal, looking for a command or spell that might disable Taka's magic and save her friends. She knew that she didn't have long to immobilize Taka. Lily had never had great dreams of magical grandeur and great adventures like Al and Erik. She wanted to dance, marry Kestrel, and raise a family. She had no clue what to do with the power transferred to her.

Zita looked at Taka with annoyance. She spit out, "You would be dead right now if I controlled it. My desires for the crystal have been stomped on since I first started working with you. I don't have it."

"Then you will die when I gain access to it."

"Are you sure Dakarai didn't steal it from you, or maybe your friend from the desert, has it?" Zita pointed at the desert wizard bonded with Taka.

Dakarai spoke fast, "We don't have it, Taka. Don't let her fool you. One of them has it."

Taka smiled triumphantly, "That leaves you, Kestrel. If you don't give it to me, you'll never be the Falcon Prince again. You will die, while I control the crystal."

"It doesn't work like that." Kestrel smiled back. "If you kill me then the crystal will transfer to Alpherge here because we had bonded in the same way you and Dakarai bonded."

"I'll kill you all then."

Lily found the symbols that she remembered and tried to make sense of what she knew. Taka's confusion about who wielded the crystal gave her some more time to research, but she knew that her moment to control this situation would end soon. She had never considered herself the smartest of her little group of friends. They had enjoyed each other's company in their small Montana high school, but the others were the educated ones. Why had they chosen to transfer the crystal to her?

The archaic symbols weren't written left to right the way she had been taught to read. The symbols were arranged top to bottom and were difficult to search and interpret. She needed a magical spell or tool to totally eliminate Taka. His ability to block magic made him difficult to control.

Lily had never played the D&D games that her friends had enjoyed on Earth, so some of the terminology that she read didn't make sense to her. What were portals, planes, and other dimensions? She kind of thought she knew since Kestrel had originally walked her through a portal between Earth and Aloheno. She considered the possibility of sending Taka through a portal to another dimension.

Taka turned his wand toward Lily. "Kestrel, I'll blast her into a million pieces if you don't relinquish your control of the crystal."

Lily knew that her shield stood strong, protecting her and Sherry from Taka's wrath.

Kestrel was looking at her, a question on his mind that she tried to determine based on his expression.

Was he asking her if she knew how to defeat Taka and save her friends?

Lily shook her head.

Kestrel's expression became crestfallen.

She needed to work faster.

Taka fired another bolt at Lily.

The bolt struck the shield, ricocheted and exploded against the chamber's wall, blasting a hole in the rock.

"How do you do that?" Taka glared at Sherry, "Do you have power that can't be blocked?"

Sherry smiled.

Lily shouted, "Got it!" She would send the evil wizard into a portal so far from Aloheno that he'd never return.

Taka looked at her, and Lily saw that he finally realized the truth. His mouth dropped in surprise.

Lily chanted,

> *"Through the nexus of realms, where fate's winds coincide,*
>
> *I summon forth a portal, where boundaries reside.*
>
> *From depths of shadow to realms aglow,*
>
> *Unveil the unseen, let this gateway show."*

The chant served as the key to unlock a portal and granted Lily access to worlds beyond the Aloheno reality. A surge of energy coursed through her veins, and power reverberated from her forehead which opened a portal before her. She didn't know if she managed the portal with the symbol on her head or the crystal. The whole experience unnerved her. The air shimmered, and a swirling vortex materialized, bridging the gap between realms.

A hole had opened, like a doorway, only unlike any doorway she had ever seen. Purples, blacks and grays spun counterclockwise between Aloheno and the other dimension. Amazing creatures glided through the dark sky, their bodies glowing like fireflies. The atmosphere carried a hint of familiar scents, and the echoes of distant whispers permeated the air. A horn sounded in the distance.

Al said, "Hurry, I don't like the sound of that horn.

Taka raised his hands and stepped back from Lily and the others. "I'm sorry, I'll give your friends their magic back."

"Drop the wand and we'll let you live." Zita moved toward Taka.

Taka pointed the wand at her. "No. It's mine."

"It's my dad's and belongs to me. Drop it."

"I should just kill you all."

"We'll let you live, or . . .." Zita pointed to the opened portal.

Sweat poured from Taka's forehead as he searched Zita's eyes in indecision.

Taka stared back at Zita. "Do you promise?"

Zita nodded.

In contrast to the warmth surrounding the crystal in the chamber, a refreshing, cool breeze from the opened portal brushed against Lily's skin. It provided a soothing sensation, offering relief from the intensity of the magical energies at play in the room.

Taka dropped the Imperium Wand.

Lily chanted once again,

> *"Through the currents of destiny, heed my call,*
>
> *From the grip of this world, you shall be enthralled.*
>
> *Step beyond the veil, where shadows dance and dreams take flight,*
>
> *In this dimension of wonders, you are banished from sight."*

As the incantation reached its crescendo, a surge of energy emanated from the portal. The force of the new dimension tugged at his very essence, drawing him closer, and with a final push, Lily released the binding that held Taka in place. A giant whoosh sounded in the chamber which allowed the dimensional rift to consume the evil wizard, and whisked him through the portal into the new world.

The portal lay open and the flying creatures seemed curious about the door.

Al squeaked, "Can you close the door?"

"How about Dakarai?" Erik asked.

Dakarai knelt before Erik. "I'm here to serve."

Lily nodded.

Zita grabbed the Imperium Wand, a smile on her lips.

Lily realized that Zita still had only her own aspirations in this quest, and they shouldn't trust her until they had time to remove the Corruption of Evil.

A couple of the flying creatures approached the portal, curious about the opened doorway.

Al begged, "Please close the portal door."

"I'm trying. Give me a second." Lily read through the document that scrolled through her mind. The process was frustrating and difficult with people demanding her to do it all so fast. She wondered if she had stayed as an initiate of the Sacred Castle if she could have learned to handle this power.

The horns sounded once again from the portal. Taka lay on the ground on the other side of the portal staring up at three of the large creatures who had taken an interest in him.

Lily took a deep breath. "Okay. I think this is it."

"Portal's dance complete,

Sever ties to distant realms,

Closure finds its peace."

CHAPTER 75

Lily watched the swirling portal vortex consume itself, closing the opened door. Right before the door closed, she heard Taka scream from the within the portal. Had she become a killer? That wasn't the kind of person she wanted to be. She wanted to be rid of this power for fear of what she might become as its guardian and wielder. The Crystal of Zaraboth stood on the dais, unmoving. Lily saw her friends standing nearby looking at her.

Erik said, "This moment feels surreal. We have faced monsters, overcome treacherous guardians, traps, and now we hold the very essence of magic in our hands." He slapped Al on the back.

With both hands Al thrust his staff above his head. "The legends will sing of our valor and determination! Our names will echo through the annals of history, forever immortalized as the ones who captured the Crystal of Zaraboth."

Together, they celebrated in the chamber, their laughter mingling with the echoes of the past. Their voices reverberated off the stone walls, carrying their shared emotions and memories of the perilous journey they had endured together.

Lily watched the others from her position near the vessel. This whole magical potential that had been thrust upon her had left her filled with trepidation and fear. Did her friends expect her to protect them? She wanted one of them to protect her. The last thing she wanted was to be the owner of the most powerful magical artifact in this world.

Kestrel looked at Lily. "Are you okay?"

Lily shook her head, her whole body trembled. Her heartbeat raced with fear and confusion. She couldn't speak.

Kestrel held out his hand. "It's all right. We're with you."

Lily stayed in the room and grabbed at Kestrel's hand and held tight.

Kestrel yelled at the others, "Hey guys, wait up." He looked into Lily's eyes. "What's wrong?"

Lily felt the tears well up in her eyes as her shoulders curled forward. Kestrel's warm fingers made her own feel like they had been dropped in an ice bucket. Her friends were all excited about capturing the crystal, but none had thought about what to do with it. They didn't really expect her to walk out of the castle with the vessel in tow, did they?

She fought back tears. "Have you . . .?"

Kestrel embraced her with a tight hug. "It's okay, I'm with you."

Lily glanced at the woman, the vessel, the Crystal of Zaraboth. She nodded in the woman's direction. "What are we supposed to do with her?"

Kestrel smiled. "Bring her with us."

"Is she supposed to follow me like a puppy dog?"

Kestrel's smile faded. "I guess we didn't think this all the way through, did we?"

The other adventurers entered the room.

Erik asked, "What's going on?"

Lily thought that her friends would make fun of her and she hesitated to say anything. She knew they didn't think she was as smart as they were, but this was important. "What do you do with the most valuable magical object in the world?"

They all took a stance as they finally asked themselves the question that she had asked before leaving the room.

Al's lips were pressed tightly, a clear sign he had entered thinking mode.

Erik smiled, but then the smile wavered.

She figured the concept had finally struck home.

Sherry opened and closed her mouth a couple of times, each time looking like she had prepared to say something, but then changed her mind.

Kestrel stood silent beside her.

"Maybe we should shield it or protect it." Al said.

"Yeah." Kestrel looked at the others. "But how?"

"We should leave it here." Dakarai offered. "We can create our own guardians to replace the others."

"No!" Zita shouted. "We need it back in Velidred where it can be used."

"That would be a good place to hold it until we open the portal to Earth," Al said.

"That might work." Erik moved next to Zita and put his arm around her shoulders.

Zita shook off Erik's embrace and moved a step.

"Do you think we can get it out of the castle and down to the boat?" Lily asked.

"Of course," Al said, "we have defeated all the guardians. The mage is dead, we just walk out of the castle and down to the boat."

"I'm thinking we should shield the crystal." Dakarai glanced at the others.

"We should make it disappear." Zita pursed her lips.

"What do you mean disappear?" Al asked.

"Send it to its own portal."

"That sounds too dangerous." Al shook his head. "Who would control the portal?"

"I can." Zita stepped toward Lily.

Erik stopped her. "Not until we heal you of the Corruption of Evil. Someone else would control the portal."

Dakarai said, "I can make a portal for you."

The others all said in unison, "No!"

The desert wizard said, "Those bands of silver rings that imprisoned her on the dais is an old desert trick. We could implement those over the vessel."

Lily glanced at the vessel. A regal woman, her olive skin glowed unnaturally. She couldn't bear to wrap the woman in those awful silver rings again. "No, we can't do that. She should be able to walk around without being imprisoned. She's alive, not just some inanimate magical object."

"Let me ask my grandfather his plan to contain the crystal if they captured it," Al said.

He asked the figure on his staff and the staff answered. "We planned to take the crystal with us. We planned to turn the vessel into a gaseous form and transport her in a waterskin back to the castle."

Erik said, "Really? A simple waterskin. How are we supposed to keep track of that? Anybody could grab it from us and then what happens?"

"When the crystal is in gaseous form, you won't be able to use its power. You'll have to rehydrate it before use. It doesn't have to be a waterskin. I actually wanted to use a chalice, but the Wizard Ishwa told me the more ornate the container, the more others would want to steal it."

"That sounds like trouble waiting to happen," Erik shrugged his shoulders.

"Do you like the idea of changing it to a gas?" Al seemed to ponder the idea himself.

Erik thought for a second and then answered, "That's not a bad idea. I'm assuming your grandfather knows the spell."

"Wait, before you boys decide what to do with this woman, let's ask Lily her thoughts," Sherry said. "Lily, what do you think of changing the vessel into gaseous form? Are you okay with that idea."

Lily felt a tightness in her chest. She thought of those old cliches from Earth of how trapping a genie in a bottle makes them a prisoner. She wanted the vessel to live a normal life as a woman, not just be trapped in a container. "I want her to live, to get married, to have children, and to grow old."

Dakarai laughed, "It will never work that way. You must shield it from others. Once others know you have the Crystal of Zaraboth, your life will never be the same. You'll become a target for every ne'er do well on the planet."

Lily wanted to scream. She thought this woman should have freedom, and she felt willing to swap lives with the woman to let her have a life. "Then transfer the crystal into me like we originally planned. It's not fair for her to be locked up like a prisoner for another thousand years."

"The woman will live less than an hour after we make the transfer." Dakarai answered.

Lily was crestfallen. Her knees buckled slightly, but she recovered and stood. *Wasn't there anything they could do to help the poor soul?* She rubbed her forehead and felt the Sacred Castle's symbol on her forehead. All these changes to her life scared her.

"I think my grandfather's plan is the best for now. We turn her into a gas and poke her in a waterskin."

Strained glances bounced between the people in the room.

"Whose waterskin?" Erik asked.

Sherry said, "Lily's."

"Wait, after we trap the poor woman in the waterskin, who will let her out?" Lily asked. "I don't have magic to turn people from gas back to humans. One of you will have to be by my side at all times. What if I'm attacked?"

"We can enchant the side of the waterskin to recognize your touch. If you're in danger, you can rub the waterskin, which will rehydrate the vessel back into human form. It's like a fingerprint lock on a cell phone." Al had a confident look on his face.

Her friends had turned into monsters. Their plan meant making this woman into some magic genie held in a leather skin against her will. Would her friends have been so callous to her, if they had transferred the crystal into her body? She looked at them and snorted. *Yeah*, she thought, *they would*.

She shook her head, but said, "Yes. Let's do it."

They all looked at each other.

"It's agreed then." Al turned to Lily.

Everyone in the room nodded.

The vessel stood on the dais, her form unchanged, and her eyes unblinking.

Lily opened the spout to her waterskin and poured the water onto the chamber floor. She felt sad for the woman, to be used without care or concern. She wondered about the woman's family, probably hundreds of years dead by now. A ghost to all who knew her.

Al raised his staff and repeated the chant his grandfather gave him.

"Spirits of the air, heed my decree,

Grant this human a change, let it be.

From solid to gas, I command the shift,

Invisible essence, into the leather swift.

Bind their essence within this skin,

Trapped and contained, while time spins.

With this spell, their form is sealed,

A captive spirit, forever concealed.

Until that moment when its power is needed,

Let its owner's touch be heeded,

At which time release and enhance,

This magical object's worldly dance."

Lily looked with sadness as the vessel of the Crystal of Zaraboth turned to gas and swirled on the dais, once, twice and a third time. It started as dark gray smoke, but on the second swirl it changed to light blue. The final loop the smoke changed to white and it swooped into the opened waterskin. The leather exterior of the waterskin bulged as if it had just filled with water.

"What now?"

"Put the top on it and take it with you like you normally would," Al said.

"This might be okay right now, as we travel home, but we'll need something different when we reach the castle."

"Don't worry," Al said, "we can find an alternative container when we get back to Velidred."

Lily looked at the others with hesitation. "I was planning to go back home with Kestrel."

Al, Erik and Zita all looked at each other.

"We need to open the portal to Earth," Al said.

Lily pouted. "I don't want to be at your beck and call every time you two want to go on an adventure or quest. That isn't my style." She could see the boys would try to pull her into every little idea they had about searching for magical items or treasures. Imprisoning the vessel in the waterskin and now having to follow the boys in their whims fueled her mounting frustration.

"Don't worry, we just want to open the portal," Erik said, "then you and Kestrel can get married and live the life that you want."

"Did you hear that, Sherry?" Lily asked. "After I open the portal, which I have no clue how, they will leave me alone."

Sherry took Lily's arm. "It'll be fine. I'll make sure they don't take advantage of you. Come on, let's head to the dock and get off this island."

They walked through the chamber door into the hall. Kestrel and Erik brought out Lenny and Sims from the other room and herded them down stairs.

Lily clutched the waterskin at her side like she would a purse in a dangerous city neighborhood. She felt thirsty and tired. The anxiety had been building within her for the past few hours and now she wanted to sit and rest. She needed time to come to grips with what she carried at her side. She imagined trouble would follow her the rest of her life as soon as the word got out that she had the Crystal of Zaraboth. Lily tucked the flower pot holding the seven-petaled flower underneath her other arm as they walked out of the tower.

CHAPTER 76

Al walked out of the Red Castle tower and down the stairs. He thought about ways to celebrate their magnificent triumph now that they had captured the crystal. He had proven his power and magic. Now, others could refer to him officially as Alpherge the Mighty. A full wizard, with another victory attributed to his name.

He reached the bottom of the stairs and entered the corridor where they first met the mage. Early morning sunrise shone through the stained-glass windows on the corridor walls and the colored light reflected off the sentinel's suits of armor that cluttered the floor. A wide path still lay down the middle which the mage had cleared. Al's breathing accelerated just a little as he reached the half-way point of the corridor. He felt tingling in his limbs.

Al tightened his grip on his staff and glanced back at his friends. Erik had unsheathed his sword, Kestrel's knuckles were white on the mage's staff, and Zita had withdrawn the Imperium Wand looking left and right as they walked.

With a quarter of the corridor to walk a slight buzzing sound arose, and Al stopped. The air grew thick with the eerie buzzing. He peered at the end of the corridor and saw a dark cloud forming above the stairs. It pulsed with an ominous energy. His stomach clenched and he his fingers grew cold.

Suddenly, the cloud erupted, unleashing a torrent of swarming locusts. They descended upon Al like a relentless storm, their wings beating with a deafening hum. Despite the panic that gripped him, he knew he had to act quickly.

He was late creating a shield and over a thousand of the locusts were enclosed with him. They darted and weaved through the air, finding every gap in his defenses. He could feel their tiny, sharp legs as they scratched against his skin.

Behind him the others had erupted in shouts and curses as the little insects continued their relentless attack. *Where had the insects come from?* Al had figured after beating the guardians on the way into the castle, they wouldn't have to fight them again especially not within the castle walls.

The locusts' bites stung, leaving red welts on his flesh. Their incessant buzzing and the sound of their tiny jaws echoed in his ears, threatening to overwhelm his senses. Al fought against the urge to panic, focusing on finding a way to counter this onslaught of insects.

Gathering his concentration, he channeled magic, and called upon the elements to aid him. Al summoned a gust of wind, hoping to disperse the locusts, but they clung to him, undeterred. The cloud of insects grew darker, as if they were fueled by the very magic that should have repelled them.

Al whacked at the insects that swarmed his arms and legs, his eyes overbright and feverish in his desperation. He couldn't withstand their onslaught for much longer. In a final act of defiance, he unleashed a powerful burst of fire, creating a ring of flames to encircle him. The intense heat and flames scorched the locusts, causing them to scatter and retreat.

"Where is all this coming from? We defeated all the guardians." Zita waved her arms at the onslaught of locusts.

"There is magic in the room." Al held tightly to his staff, searching the hallway for an answer.

"Can you locate its source?" Zita asked.

"No."

With a renewed determination, Al pressed forward, ready to face the invisible foe head-on. Their spell had tested his resolve, but he couldn't let it break him. He figured another adventurer had come for the crystal who didn't realize he and his friends had already secured the powerful treasure. They probably thought Al and the others were another set of guardians they had to defeat.

He didn't know why he couldn't see his opponent. Were other adventurers attacking the castle with an invisibility spell? That wasn't a bad idea. He needed to see his attackers.

Al chanted,

"Veil of shadows, release the obscure,

Reveal the hidden, our sight secure.

Invisibility's grasp shall be no more,

let truth be shown as I implore."

He cast the invisibility purge spell designed to make objects that were close to him visible. At first, he didn't see anything, and then he saw her. The mage wasn't dead.

The mage shouted, "I demand the return of my staff and the crystal."

Her injuries were severe and blood oozed down the front of her gray robe. How had she lived? They had verified her death, hadn't they?

"It is mine now." Kestrel blasted a fireball at her, but she blocked it with a wave of her hand.

A surge of raw magic erupted from the mage's outstretched hand, hurtling toward Al with unstoppable force. The air crackled with power, and his instincts screamed at him to move.

He moved too slowly. The spell, known as "Knock Asunder," slammed into him with an incredible impact. The ground beneath his feet quaked, and a shockwave rippled through his body like an invisible force had grabbed hold of him, and threatened to tear him apart from the inside.

His limbs flailed uncontrollably as the spell propelled him backward, the sheer force of the spell overpowering any attempts to steady his body. He fell back into Zita and Lily knocking them both to the stone floor. Lily dropped her waterskin holding the crystal within its leather surroundings.

Agony surged through Al as the impact rebounded against the floor, his bones protesting the brutal assault. He slumped to the ground, breathless and disoriented.

His mind raced, desperately searching for a way to counter this devastating attack. The domination of the spell hammered against a makeshift shield that wasn't strong enough to hold back the mage's immense power.

Sweat streamed down Al's face. In a final surge of willpower, he released a counterblast, a burst of energy to push back against the devastating spell.

A momentary reprieve opened as the opposing forces clashed, a discordant blend of raw power and determination. The air crackled with the interplay of magic, each force vying for dominance.

The mage blinked and Al saw her knees buckle. She still suffered from the injuries of the earlier battle. The magic assault ceased. The oppressive weight lifted from Al, and he lay on the ground, gasping for air. The spell's grip had loosened, its power broken.

Zita yelled at Al, "Form a bond. We have to be bonded to beat her. Hurry before she recovers."

Al jumped to his feet and bonded with Kestrel. Kestrel bonded with Dakarai, who quickly bonded to Zita. She would control the bond. Al hoped they lived through the battle.

CHAPTER 77

Zita felt the surge of power enter her body as she bonded with the other three. The truth became obvious—they would have to defeat the mage if they wanted to leave the island. The mage's power held strong, despite being weakened in the earlier battle and, even now, she battled them without her staff. Zita had taken control of the bond, and now that she held the Imperium Wand, she felt confident they had the power to defeat the mage.

Zita saw the desert wizard step in front of the bonded wizards. The desert wizard threw a spell at Geirhild Hlifsteed as she stood blocking their path in the corridor. The spell bounced off a weak shield the mage had created.

Geirhild responded with a chant, "Encase in Amber."

Zita used the bond to create a shield. She concentrated on covering the bonded wizards, and included Lily, Sims, and Lenny in the shield, but she hadn't had time to shield the desert wizard. *Why hadn't he bonded with the others?*

A surge of arcane power crackled through the air, weaving its way toward the unprotected wizard like tendrils. Zita could feel the spell's icy grip reaching out, threatening to trap him in a timeless prison. Panic flickered, but she refused to succumb to fear. She trusted her shield, but worried about the desert wizard taking the brunt of the sorcery.

The desert wizard dodged and weaved, narrowly avoiding the initial assault of the spell.

But the mage adjusted her aim and directed the enchantment to strike once again.

Glistening strands of golden energy surged forth, swirling through the corridor with malevolent grace. The desert wizard danced between them with fluid and precise movements. The relentless spell finally ensnared him within a solid amber prison, freezing him for eternity.

The ambient temperature dropped, and the air grew thick with an otherworldly glow. The very ground beneath Zita's feet seemed to quiver. She could almost taste the resinous scent of amber riding the breeze.

Gritting her teeth, Zita unleashed a surge of raw elemental power. Flames erupted from the Imperium Wand. Aided by the bonded power of four wizards, it created a blazing inferno that clashed against the encroaching amber strands.

Zita's breath came in ragged gasps as she poured their combined energy into the spell. In a blinding burst of light and heat, the fiery onslaught proved victorious. The amber liquid that flowed through the air melted, and fragments of translucent resin showered the castle floor. Zita stood, sweat-soaked and battle-weary, triumphant against the mage's desperate attempt to defeat the adventurers.

Geirhild screamed in blind fury, her back stiff and rigid, her neck muscles corded in frustration. "I will not be defeated. Return my staff."

"That's not happening, I like this staff." Kestrel lifted it."

The Velidred Moon Goddess suddenly filled Zita's mind. "Imprison the mage to defeat her."

Zita asked, "How do I do that?"

A fireball flashed off Zita's shield and bounced off the corridor ceiling in a fiery burst of colors. Shards of brick broke off and caromed off the magic shield showering the wizards and the others.

"I don't know how to do that; I have a better idea. I must weaken her first."

Luna Rosso said angrily, "Listen to me."

Zita ignored the moon goddess and chanted, "Borda do esquecimento," which she translated in her mind to "Edge of Oblivion." She waved her wand in a large circle at the mage. The force from the bond surprised her and she almost lost her balance as the power surged through the wand.

Zita calmed her mind as the magic bolted from the wand, and a steady stream of intertwining blues and gold raced toward her adversary. She smiled inwardly at the thought that she didn't really need the moon goddess, she had everything under control.

The moon goddess attacked Zita with a mighty shockwave that started at her feet and traveled up her spine. The vicious attack snaked through the magic bond and the four wizards dropped the bond and all four fell to the floor screaming in pain.

Zita's magic sent at the mage fell harmlessly to the floor.

Al asked, "What happened?"

Zita couldn't tell them that Luna Rosso, an ally, tried to kill her when she didn't obey her command. Why had she ever thought that she could control a force as powerful as the universe itself?

Lily asked, "Are we unshielded?"

Erik pulled out his sword, "I think I can help." He quickly scraped the sword point along the corridor floor encasing the adventurers within its circle. Then in a loud voice he chanted,

"With sword in hand and circle drawn,

Let the Sword shield be firmly spawned.

Barrier strong, impenetrable light,

Protect this space with sacred might."

The mage sent a fireball at the adventurers.

Erik's shield shone with a blue and orange luminescence. As Zita watched the fireball travel down the corridor, she wondered if the shield would hold. The Sword of Freedom was a tool of healing. She never imagined it might be used in battle to create a shield.

The fireball blasted against the shield, which held, but its light dissipated, just as the final remnants of the fireball scattered ineffectively around them.

Zita shook off the moon goddess' attack and helped the others to their feet. "Quick, we need to bond again."

"What happened to you?" Al asked.

"I'll tell you after we defeat the mage. Now hurry, we don't have time to waste."

They quickly bonded although Zita thought the bond felt weaker. She hoped it didn't matter.

The mage strode confidently toward the adventurers, her gaze fixed on Kestrel.

"Hey Kestrel, maybe you should give the staff back to her," Al said.

Kestrel raised the staff. "Never. It's a spoil of war."

Luna Rosso said to Zita, "Are you ready to listen to me? I want the crystal."

"Yes! What's the spell?" She couldn't afford another attack from the moon goddess. For a goddess, it seemed she liked to make her subjects cry out in pain way too much.

"You must imprison the mage's soul."

"Imprison it in what?"

"It's best in a piece of jewelry that you wear."

Zita touched her necklace. It already contained magic. What might happen if the mage ended up harming her as much as the moon goddess. *This couldn't be right, there had to be another way.*

Geirhild moved closer.

"Zita, what are you thinking right now?" Al asked. "If the mage reaches us, we're toast."

The necklace she wore around her neck meant so much to her. It was a strong and emotional connection with her mother. Her memories seemed to be all boxed up into this small object around her neck.

Zita took a deep breath, "Okay, okay. Point your staff and any magical items at the mage. We'll have one shot at this."

Zita chanted as Luna Rosso said the words to her,

"Through mystic incantation's weave,

From mortal form, their soul retrieves.

In realms unseen, let shackles bind,

Imprisoned essence, no freedom find.

With this spell's might, her fate assign,

into my necklace for all time."

The mage continued her charge at the adventurers, a spell forming on her lips and fingers as she neared the others.

Zita's spell discharged from her father's wand, from Kestrel's stolen staff, from Al's grandfather's staff, and from a leather bracelet around Dakarai's wrist. Zita had never seen anything like it. The spell spun the streams from the four magic items into a single stream of power that burned so bright she couldn't look directly at it.

As time slowed to a crawl, the weight of uncertainty bore down upon Zita. Seconds seemed stagnant, her mind racing while time lagged and she contemplated the gravity of the moment. This could be her last chance to make a difference, to alter the course of her own fate.

Thoughts and memories swirled in a tumultuous vortex. She replayed the choices that had brought her to this precipice, the battles fought and the sacrifices made. The agreement that brought the moon goddess into her life. Her decision to bring Taka into the equation. Her desire for the Crystal of Zaraboth. Doubt gnawed at her. She questioned her abilities, wondering if this spell would be enough to turn the tide. Her fingers trembled as she gripped her wand.

In the midst of her contemplation, her gaze fell upon her comrades. They had placed their trust in her, looking to her for guidance and salvation. She noticed the waterskin that Lily had dropped only a few paces from her current position.

As the last precious seconds ticked away, she found solace in knowing that she had lived a life driven by purpose. Whether she succeeded or failed, her actions had meaning.

With renewed vigor, she embraced the present moment. Zita savored the subtle details—the soft caress of a breeze blowing through the corridor, the flickering of candlelight— that might be her last experiences in this realm. She vowed to make every second count, to live this day. She would fight, she would resist, and she would make the most of these last few seconds, for she knew that even the briefest of moments could shape destinies.

CHAPTER 78

The forces of the mage struck the magic of the four bonded wizards. A swirling tempest of hurricane-strength winds battled against each other. Geirhild gained the upper hand, her wizardry beating Zita.

Has Luna Rosso failed me? Zita slumped to the floor, the Imperium Wand still sent out tendrils of magic, but its power struggled against the mage's superior strength. Their conjuring wasn't enough.

Two tendrils from the Imperium Wand broke through Geirhild's wall of energy like a tiny hole in a dam. The mage's wizardry continued unabated toward the adventurers.

Al stood rooted to the floor, his staff radiating a thousand blue tendrils of sorcery at Geirhild.

Kestrel's knees were bent as he battled hurricane force winds, his jaw tight as he held the mage's staff.

Dakarai appeared calm in the face of danger, but his furrowed brow betrayed his true feelings.

The mage's enchantment reached them and blew them back against the wall. Zita was tossed on top of Al. His staff lay ten feet away. Lily's hair caught on fire forcing Erik to use his hands to extinguish it.

Zita searched for the bond with the others, but they had lost their connection. Kestrel lay unconscious against the corner. Lenny, Sims and Dakarai were in a pile of bodies next to the stairs.

She felt her head spinning, her heart thudding dully in her chest. Geirhild was going to win. Zita's ragtag group of wizards weren't enough to handle the mage's expert skills.

Geirhild stood triumphant; a grin spread across her face as she marched across the hallway raising her hands in preparation of her final strike.

Two blue, almost imperceptible, tendrils of Zita's spell continued to advance toward the mage from the Imperium Wand now lying on the floor.

Zita's hands went limp as she realized they had lost. She had no more energy to attack Geirhild and a painful lump built in her throat. She stared at Lily's waterskin lying on the floor. Should they release the crystal before they died? She crawled to the waterskin and reached out for it.

One blue tendril reached Geirhild and touched the mage's arm. She tried to swoosh it off with a flick of her fingers. It didn't come off, but instead penetrated her skin. Her eyes narrowed as if a little confused.

Zita watched as the second blue tendril struck Geirhild in the left shoulder forcing the mage back.

Will that be enough? Zita wondered.

A hole blossomed in the mage's left shoulder and a golden light shot from the point toward Zita.

Geirhild's mouth slackened and her eyes widened. "No!" She exclaimed and swiped at the holes opening in her body.

Zita sat up in curiosity looking at the mage. A second light emitted from Geirhild's arm. The light traveled toward Zita and seemed to join with the other ray of light to coalesce into a single beam.

At first Zita wanted to shield herself from the advancing light, but Luna Rosso spoke to her.

Accept her into your jewelry. We will deal with its power at another time.

Zita pulled her necklace from beneath her tunic.

The light hit the necklace and seemed to be absorbed into the jewelry. It took ten long seconds for Geirhild to explode into many tiny points of light, but each point of light entered Zita's necklace. A final single speck of light landed and with a swoosh her pendant somehow sucked it inside.

The room remained silent for a moment as Zita sucked in slow, even breaths. She sat at the edge of fatigue, looking pensive. Her instincts told her not to let her guard down, while curiosity about what just happened ran through her body. What had Luna Rosso done to her, the necklace, and the mage? *Do I treat these points of light with respect or is it power for me to use?*

Sherry moaned and Al crawled over to attend to her. Lily, with her blond hair burned and ragged, sat next to Kestrel trying to revive him. Erik walked toward the stairs to retrieve his sword. Dakarai, Lenny, and Sims spent time untangling themselves from each other.

Zita's knees buckled as a feeling of relief surged into her core. A sudden lightness and giddiness welled up within her.

Luna Rosso asked, "Do you have it?"

Zita looked at her pendant and thought, Y*es. My pendant holds the mage.*

"Not the pendant, do you have the waterskin?"

Zita saw the waterskin holding the crystal abandoned and lying on the floor. She grabbed it and pulled it into her body. She glanced at the others who hadn't realized what had happened, and she jumped to her feet. Zita seized the Imperium Wand lying nearby, dashed through the hallway, and down the stairs.

She clutched the waterskin tightly in one hand and the wand with the other as she darted along the path and through the dense forest. Zita didn't know if anyone yet realized what she had done, and she checked behind her every few steps. Her legs were weak from the effort of using her magic, causing her to stumble and sway down the path. She hoped to reach the beach, before others appeared.

Soon she heard the footsteps of pursuers echoing through the woods. Her neck felt stiff and her muscles strained as she ran. Zita didn't know who had figured it out, but she was being chased. As she raced through the trees, her mind raced too. She knew that her magic alone might not be enough to outwit them. She needed a plan.

Her breaths came in large gasps of air as the last twenty-four hours had sapped her strength. For a moment she worried about the giant insects as she raced through a cloud of gnats that she sucked into her lungs. She stopped for a few seconds coughing and sputtering trying to clear her airways.

Halfway down the mountain the forest thinned and she saw the beach with the glimmering red water ahead. Her heart raced with hope. She knew whoever chased her was gaining ground, their heavy feet pounding out a rhythm behind her.

With a burst of inspiration, Zita veered from the path, plunging into a thicket of thorns, brambles and boulders. Her hands and tunic tore, and she almost lost the wand. She knew she had to create a diversion to confuse the people following her. Using magic and the power of her wand, she conjured an illusion of herself continuing along the trail while she hid behind a large boulder fifteen feet from the footpath.

Dakarai, Sims and Lenny rushed past her position and chased after the fake image, giving her a momentary advantage. She sent her double away from the boat dock and used this precious time to sprint towards the beach with all her might, her breathing ragged.

As she reached the sandy shore, she saw the row boat bobbing next to the dock, its strange paddle master waiting expectantly for them. Her heart raced with elation. She struggled, running through the sand windmilling her arms frantically to keep her balance.

Dakarai yelled in the distance. "She tricked us."

Zita summoned magic to create a shimmering shield of energy in hopes that Dakarai wouldn't block her magic. She ran across the dock to the waiting boat and paddle master.

She felt magical energy collide with her shield, but the shield held.

She jumped in the boat and shouted at the paddle master. "Go now!"

Dakarai shouted at the paddle master, "Wait. We want safe passage to shore."

The paddle master waited.

Zita wanted to fire a bolt of magical energy at the paddle master. She could kill the man and row the boat herself. Just then a bubble of sulfur burst at the surface near her and she realized how difficult it might be to navigate the boat through the bubbling inferno lake.

Dakarai reached the dock and Zita pointed the Imperium Wand at him. He shook in violent heaves with each breath. He held his hands above his head.

Between breaths he said, "I won't block your magic. Let us go ashore with you. We'll help you take back Velidred." He nodded at the waterskin. "You have it don't you?"

Her muscles tensed as she worried about what game Dakarai might play with her. With a strained voice, she said, "It's none of your business what I have or don't have. I don't want you to go to shore with me, and I definitely don't need your help taking Velidred Castle back."

"Let's be reasonable here." Dakarai pleaded. "My friends and I can be quite influential. Though you may not like our methods, we were a big help to your father when he desired the castle. Think about it."

Zita had thought about it, and she didn't like their methods. She figured Sims would put a knife in her back without hesitation if Dakarai told him to. Sure, they might help her take the castle for now, but how soon would she be fearing them. *Plus, Dakarai can still block my magic at any time he wants.*

That's it, I need to learn that skill and how to stop others from using it on me. She decided to strike a bargain. "I'll let you come with me, but you must teach me how to block the magic of others and prevent others from using it on me. And you promise not to use it on me until I know all the details."

Dakarai dropped his eye contact with Zita and looked toward the red lake. He then looked at Sims and Lenny and shrugged. "It's a deal."

"On your blood." Zita waved her wand at Dakarai.

"Agreed," he grunted.

The incantation sealed the deal in ancient blood magic and Zita could rest comfortably with the knowledge that Dakarai couldn't block her magic anymore. Velidred Castle would be hers again.

Zita thought about the necklace which now contained the mage's soul. How might that play out in the coming weeks? She suspected Luna Rosso had a plan that would make Zita's life crazy.

"Quick! In the boat." Zita commanded.

As the paddle master maneuvered the boat into the lake, Zita looked longingly at the Red Castle wishing for one more chance to see Erik. Was there a future for them at Velidred Castle? Would he be able to forgive her this betrayal?

# # # #

Al looked at his friends, battered and bruised. He shook his head, trying to disengage the unease tightening his chest.

Erik had managed to revive Kestrel, though the Falcon Prince's injuries were severe.

"Are you sure you can't find the waterskin?" Al asked. "Where could it have gone?"

Sherry comforted her friend. Lily had bruises on her face and arms and the smell of burnt hair drifted in the hallway.

"I don't see it anywhere. Is it possible Zita took the crystal?" Lily asked. "That might explain why she dashed out of the castle followed by those thugs."

"Did the wind blow it over by the stairs?" Al was fearful. If Zita held the crystal, the Imperium Wand, and the Corruption of Evil, they might never be able to heal her.

"I told you. We looked over there already." Sherry's lips were pinched. "The only thing that makes sense is that Zita dashed off with it."

"Maybe Dakarai—"

Sherry shouted, "Zita left first. She has it."

Al hung his head and sighed, "Well let's go to the dock and see if we can find her."

Lily went to the wall, scooped up the seven-petaled flower, and stuffed it back in its pot.

They couldn't hurry as they all were injured and in pain. Kestrel seemed to have taken the worst of Geirhild's attack.

The attack had weakened Erik to the point that his attempts at healing Kestrel were only enough to allow the Falcon Prince to stand and walk without help.

They trooped out of the castle and through the forest to the water's edge. No rowboat waited for them at the dock.

Al dropped his hands to his side. "Do you think Zita can use the crystal in its current form?"

Kestrel sat on the sand and sighed. "She might need Lily's help in removing it from the waterskin."

He took Lily's hand in his when she sat next to him. "I'm never going to help that woman ever again. We'll find a way to protect you, because if she needs you, she'll devise a plan to kidnap you like her father did." Kestrel squeezed her hand.

An ear-splitting, bone-rattling explosion shattered the peacefulness on the island. Across the water, an inferno of crimson flames rocketed into the sky casting an otherworldly glow. Water erupted from the lake as birds took flight.

Erik pointed across the lake, his hand shaking. "I don't think the boat is coming back to the island." Billowing plumes of smoke rose in the distance in the direction of the dock and dockmaster's hut.

Al moaned, a long, low sigh; the sour taste of defeat filling him with woe. "We've failed. We'll never open the portal and will never see our parents ever again."

Sherry walked to Al and put her arm around his waist. "It'll open someday."

Al pulled her close, hoping she was right. He wondered what pain and suffering they had released onto Aloheno.

The End

Thank you for reading my book. If you enjoyed it, won't you please take a moment to leave a review at your favorite retailer?

Thanks!

Kenneth Brown

MORE FROM THE SERIES

The Mountain King Series by Kenneth Brown

Haskell – Orphan to King – Prequel to the Mountain King Series

Eclipse of the Triple Moons

Zita's Revenge

Rescue of the Stone Warriors

Quest for the Crystal

Go to https://kenbrownauthor.com/ for more details.

KENNETH BROWN

This is Kenneth Brown's fourth book in the Mountain King Series. He has been writing professionally since the release of his first book in 2018.

He loves to hike, spend time with his family and sing in the church choir. Even though he started writing later in life, he loves to create worlds, creatures and characters to have exciting adventures in those fantastical worlds.

Check out https://kenbrownauthor.com/ for novel release dates and details about the author.

BONUS MATERIAL

Thank you for purchasing this book. We hope you enjoyed Quest for the Crystal. Please take the time to write a review of this book on your favorite book buying website.

To find out more about the author, Kenneth Brown, and get advance notification about future books, check out the website, Ken Brown Author, https://kenbrownauthor.com/. Join the Kenneth Brown Readers Group to receive these great benefits.

- Get the latest information on New Releases
- Insider Looks at Outlines, Plots, Characters, Deleted Scenes and Exclusive behind the Scenes Glimpses at Kenneth Brown's Writing
- Sneak Peeks of Upcoming Chapters
- Ask the Author Questions
- Exclusive Offers
- And MORE

Find out more about the exciting prequel to The Mountain King Series, Haskell – Orphan to King. Read the fantasy story of how Haskell lost his parents, and rose from orphan thief to become King Haskell, the Mountain King. An exciting tale of intrigue, fear and magic.